PRAISE FOR
ANNE GRACIE AND HER NOVELS

"[A] confection that brims with kindness and heartfelt sincerity. . . . You can't do much better than Anne Gracie who offers her share of daring escapes, stolen kisses and heartfelt romance in a tale that carries the effervescent charm of the best Disney fairy tales." —*Entertainment Weekly*

"I never miss an Anne Gracie book."
—*New York Times* bestselling author Julia Quinn

"For fabulous Regency flavor, witty and addictive, you can't go past Anne Gracie."
—*New York Times* bestselling author Stephanie Laurens

"With her signature superbly nuanced characters, subtle sense of wit and richly emotional writing, Gracie puts her distinctive stamp on a classic Regency plot."
—*Chicago Tribune*

"Will keep readers entranced. . . . A totally delightful read!" —RT Book Reviews

"The always terrific Anne Gracie outdoes herself with *Bride by Mistake*. . . . Gracie created two great characters, a high-tension relationship and a wonderfully satisfying ending. Not to be missed!"
—*New York Times* bestselling author Mary Jo Putney

"A fascinating twist on the girl-in-disguise plot. . . . With its wildly romantic last chapter, this novel is a great antidote to the end of summer."
—*New York Times* bestselling author Eloisa James

"Anne Gracie's writing dances that thin line between always familiar and fresh. . . . *The Accidental Wedding* is warm and sweet, tempered with bursts of piquancy and a dash or three of spice." —*New York Journal of Books*

"Threaded with charm and humor. . . . [An] action-rich, emotionally compelling story. . . . It is sure to entice readers." —*Library Journal* (starred review)

"Another [of] Ms. Gracie's character-rich, fiery tales filled with emotion and passion leavened by charm and wit." —*Romance Reviews Today*

"The main characters are vibrant and complex. . . . The author's skill as a storyteller makes this well worth reading." —*Kirkus Reviews*

"A well-plotted, richly emotional and delightful read, this Regency novel brims with wonderful characters and romance." —Shelf Awareness

"I've already read this book twice and I know it won't be long before I'm pulled back to these characters again . . . and again . . . and again." —*The Romance Dish*

Titles by Anne Gracie

Merridew Sisters

THE PERFECT RAKE
THE PERFECT WALTZ
THE PERFECT STRANGER
THE PERFECT KISS

Devil Riders

THE STOLEN PRINCESS
HIS CAPTIVE LADY
TO CATCH A BRIDE
THE ACCIDENTAL WEDDING
BRIDE BY MISTAKE

Chance Sisters

THE AUTUMN BRIDE
THE WINTER BRIDE
THE SPRING BRIDE
THE SUMMER BRIDE

Marriage of Convenience

MARRY IN HASTE
MARRY IN SCANDAL
MARRY IN SECRET
MARRY IN SCARLET

The Brides of Bellaire Gardens

THE SCOUNDREL'S DAUGHTER

The Scoundrel's Daughter

ANNE GRACIE

JOVE
New York

A JOVE BOOK
Published by Berkley
An imprint of Penguin Random House LLC
penguinrandomhouse.com

ISBN: 9780593200544

First Edition: August 2021

Printed in the United States of America
1 3 5 7 9 10 8 6 4 2

Book design by George Towne

To my longtime writing buddy,
Alison Reynolds, with thanks for the friendship,
the support and encouragement, the entertainment,
and the flowers

Prologue

He was making excellent time. Gerald Paton, Viscount Thornton, glanced behind him and grinned. No sign of his rival, Brexton. His team barely checked their pace as they passed between the narrow stone walls of the bridge and flew around the corner. They were beautiful steppers, well worth the sum he'd spent on them.

He pulled out his watch, flicked open the cover and checked the time. Three and a half hours. He was not only going to win the race, and two hundred guineas, he might even break the Prince Regent's rec— What the hell?

A large white goose stood in the middle of the road. Swearing, he hauled on the reins. His horses instantly slowed, but even so it looked as though the blasted bird might not see another dawn. He wouldn't particularly regret the loss of a goose, but his horses would find running over it horribly distressing.

A girl ran out into the road and scooped up the bird. And then stood there facing him.

"Out of the way!" he yelled.

She didn't move, just stood there holding the goose in her arms and looking defiant.

He tightened the reins and hauled back on the brake. The curricle swerved to the left. There was a swirl of dust, the goose flapped its wings and honked, and his horses plunged and snorted. The wheels of his curricle bumped and scraped against the wall of the nearest building. And came to a halt just inches from the wretched girl and her blasted goose.

"Get the devil off the road!" he snarled. "Don't you realize, you fool woman, that you could have been killed!"

"Yes, and whose fault would that have been?" she snapped back. "You weren't even planning to stop, were you?"

"Nonsense. I slowed right down. If the blasted bird had any sense, it would have moved—"

"Who do you think you are? This is our village. You have no right to bowl through it at such a breakneck speed. What if a child had run out into the street? What then? Would you have happily driven over a child as well?"

"Of course not! Isn't it obvious that I was slowing down—even for that stupid damned goose? Now move!"

"Don't swear at Ghislaine."

Ghislaine? Ridiculous name for a maidservant or farm girl or whatever she was.

"Dammit, Ghislaine, get out of my way. I'm in the middle of a race." Even now, he could hear the sound of horses approaching.

"A pox on your stupid race. And Ghislaine is the goose. She's a very special goose, aren't you, Ghislaine?" She stroked the goose's neck, murmuring soothing sounds.

"I don't care what sort of a goose either of you are," he roared. "Get off the damned road and let me pass!"

But it was too late. Brexton came racing up behind him and passed him at a smart clip with bare inches to spare, his wheels almost grazing Gerald's.

"Flirting with pretty village maidens, Thornton? More

fool you. See you in Brighton!" Brexton called as he passed. Laughter drifted back as he drove out of sight. It was as fine a piece of driving as Gerald had seen, and it put him in an even filthier temper.

"Now look what you've done!" he snapped at the girl.

She strolled off the road. "Oh pooh. All this fuss over a silly race? Men like you, you're—"

Gerald didn't wait to hear the rest of the sentence. He snapped the reins, and his curricle moved off.

Lucy Bamber walked back to the comtesse's house. She smiled to herself at the remembrance of the man's indignant expression. "We showed him, didn't we, Ghislaine?" She was fed up to the back teeth with men, especially the high and mighty lordly types who thought they ruled the world. She'd met enough of them at the comtesse's.

She turned the corner and came to an abrupt halt. A dusty traveling carriage stood outside the comtesse's house. Another one. Her first impulse was to hide until whoever it was had left, but a moment's reflection made her reconsider. The comtesse's visitors sometimes stayed for days. The comtesse would need her to be either '*ma charmante invitée*'—my charming guest—or her servant, whichever the old lady deemed appropriate at the time. Given Lucy's current appearance, in an old dress and an apron and with her hair blowing loose and wild across her face, it would most likely be the maidservant.

Which meant she would be fending off wandering hands for the duration of the visitor's stay. Not that playing the charming guest was much different, just that the wandering hands were more subtle. Fine gentlemen—she despised them all.

Lucy opened the gate and set down Ghislaine. She removed the apron, dusted down her dress, picked off a goose feather or two, gathered her hair back into a tidy knot—it had come loose in her pursuit of Ghislaine—and entered the house. The door to the sitting room stood ajar, and she paused to peek in. "*Est-ce toi*, Lucille?" the comtesse called. "*Entrez*." Oh dear. The old lady was in one of her moods.

Lucy reluctantly obeyed. A gentleman stood in front of the fire, his back to the door. The comtesse lay reclined on the chaise longue, a handkerchief soaked in eau de cologne—Lucy could smell it from the door—pressed to her forehead. It was not a good sign.

"Madame?" she said.

The gentleman turned and Lucy's jaw dropped. "Papa?" She hadn't seen or heard from him for more than a year.

He didn't say anything for a moment, just scanned her from head to toe, frowning as if displeased by her appearance. He pursed his lips and gave a brisk nod. "It's time you were married, Lucy. Pack your things. We're leaving."

Chapter One

London, 1818

Finally she had a use for the epergne.

Alice, Lady Charlton—the *dowager* Lady Charlton, though she had neither the years nor the advantages of most dowagers—gave a last satisfied rub to the large silver epergne, which was extremely ugly but quite valuable. She'd always hated it, not simply because it was hideous, but because her sister-in-law, Almeria, who'd resented Alice from the start, had bestowed it upon her as a wedding present. It was, Alice believed, the ugliest sufficiently expensive gift Almeria could find.

Now Alice was going to sell the horrid thing. An appropriate gesture to mark the end of her troubles.

Eighteen months since her husband, Thaddeus, had died, the flood of his outstanding debts had—finally!—slowed to a trickle. Alice had almost stripped the house bare to pay them, and now she was feeling hopeful, almost happy. What would it be like to live free of obligation? To choose whether or not to live up to people's expectations?

She'd been trying and failing at that for the past eighteen years. More. Her whole life, really.

She didn't really know what she wanted her life to be—well, she did, of course, but God had denied her that joy—and now she had to look to her future and decide how she wanted to live. At least she was secure and had a home to live in, thanks to Granny leaving her this house in London.

A presence in the doorway caught Alice's attention. "Yes, Tweed, what is it?"

The elderly butler's pained glance at her apron and stained old cotton gloves was a pointed reminder of his deep disapproval. "M'lady, m'lady, m'lady, you should *not* being doing menial tasks like that. Cleaning silver is a dirty job."

"It certainly is," Alice agreed cheerfully. They'd had this discussion before, but beggars couldn't be choosers. "And I'm glad to say I've just this minute finished it." She placed the epergne beside the rest of the silver she was selling and sat back. "Something you wanted, Tweed?"

"A *person* at the front door, m'lady. Insisting on speaking to you."

Alice frowned. "A *person*? Insisting?" Tweed had a fine-tuned vocabulary concerning callers, a combination of word and tone. A "person" was very low down on the Tweed Scale and the kind of caller he usually sent packing.

"You didn't deny me?"

Tweed looked vaguely apologetic. "It's the third time the fellow has called." He presented a card on a silver salver. "An Octavius Bamber, m'lady."

She picked up the card. Octavius Bamber? She'd never heard of him. "Not another debt collector, surely?" She'd hoped she'd seen the last of them. But no, Tweed knew to send them to her late husband's man of affairs.

"No—at least I don't believe so. But there is . . . something." Tweed hesitated, then said, "He's no gentleman, m'lady, but something he said just now made me a little uneasy. I think it might be wise for you to hear what he has to say."

Tweed's instincts were generally good. He'd been Granny's butler forever, and he'd known Alice since she was a baby. If he thought she should see this man—after denying him twice—she would take his advice.

"Very well. I'll speak to him in the front parlor." She stripped off her gloves and apron, smoothed her dress, tidied her hair and went downstairs.

She entered the parlor quietly and came to an astonished halt. Octavius Bamber, his back to the door, was examining the contents of the room like a . . . like a bailiff. Or a debt collector. Lifting up ornaments, scrutinizing them, replacing them and moving on, quite as if he had every right to paw through her possessions. He peered at the signature on one of her paintings and scratched the ornate gold frame, presumably to test the gold leaf.

She cleared her throat, and he turned. His gaze swept over her in much the same way as he'd examined her belongings, as if calculating her value. *One widowed countess, slightly used, not particularly pretty.* She stiffened.

"So, Lady Charlton, you've finally deigned to see me." Quite unembarrassed at being caught snooping, he replaced the jade figurine he'd been scrutinizing, crossed the floor and held out his hand. "About time, too. Octavius Bamber at your service."

Ignoring his hand, Alice gave him a cool nod. Ladies didn't shake hands, especially with unknown gentlemen, and this man had already annoyed her.

Who was he, and what could he possibly want? She'd never set eyes on him in her life. Of medium height, he was closer to fifty than forty and dressed expensively, if not particularly tastefully, in tight trousers, a florid waistcoat, a frilled shirt and a snugly fitted bottle green coat. A number of gaudy fobs dangled from his gold watch chain, and he wore several large, glittery rings. His thinning gray hair was elaborately tousled, and he reeked of pomade.

"Don't fancy shaking hands with the likes of me, eh?" He shrugged. "Doesn't bother me. I don't mind a touch of hoity-toity—when it comes from a true aristocrat, that is. And you're the genuine article, ain't you, m'lady? Widow of an earl, and the granddaughter of one."

Alice didn't respond. He obviously knew something of her background, but it was none of his business, and besides, it was irrelevant.

Without being invited to, he seated himself in the middle of the sofa, crossed his legs and sat back, his arms draped along the back of the sofa, perfectly at home. His gaze swept the room. "I see you haven't yet sold off all your pretty bits and pieces. How much longer do you reckon you have 'til the money runs out?"

Ignoring his impertinence, she said crisply, "The purpose of your visit, sir?"

To her surprise he chuckled. "Like to get right to the point, eh, m'lady? Well, I don't mind that. Don't mind you looking down your nose at me, either. That'll change shortly. You're going to be grateful I've come." He gave her a knowing smile, which slowly hardened. "I've business to discuss."

"If it's business, take it to my late husband's man of affairs."

"Oh, but it's not that sort of business, m'lady. This is more"—his smile widened—"personal."

"Then state it quickly and begone," she said, hoping her nervousness wasn't visible. After eighteen months she'd thought she was finished with the mess Thaddeus had left her after his death. Apparently not.

He produced a thick packet of folded letters tied with a puce ribbon, placed it on the low table between them and sat back with a smug look.

Alice frowned. "What are they?" They didn't look like bills.

"You know perfectly well what they are, my lady. Your husband's letters."

She shrugged, feigning indifference. "My husband wrote many letters."

"Ah, but these are love letters. To Mrs. Jennings."

Cold slithered down Alice's spine. "Who?" she managed.

But Bamber wasn't fooled. "Come, come, your ladyship, no point in pretending you don't recognize the name of your husband's mistress. Very loyal to her, he was. Twenty years and more these letters go back."

Twenty years. Longer than her marriage.

He continued, "And the most recent, written just days before he died." He gave her the kind of knowing look people gave when they knew just where and how—and in whose bed—her husband had died. Her brother-in-law, Edmund, the new earl, had tried to hush it up, but Alice could usually read it in their eyes when someone knew.

Bamber leaned forward, undid the ribbon, flipped through the letters familiarly, then pulled one out. "Here's one of the older ones. Take a look. It mentions you—many of them do, actually. See if it sparks some memories." He held it out to her.

Alice didn't want to touch the wretched thing, wanted to snatch it and the rest of the letters and hurl them unread into the fire. But the stupid, self-destructive impulse to *know*, to turn the knife, made her reach out and take the offered letter between nerveless fingers.

She slowly unfolded it. Thaddeus's writing, big and bold, sprawled across the page. Phrases jumped out at her . . . *my dreary virgin bride . . . cold as a fish and about as appealing . . .*

Bile rose in Alice's throat. Oh God, it was a description of her wedding night. In the worst kind of detail. Mocking her. Making fun of his bride's ignorance and inexperience—to his mistress.

She crumpled the letter between numb fingers. "Where did—"

Bamber placed another letter in front of her. And then another, and another and another, leaving just enough time for her to glimpse—and flinch at—the contents before placing another letter on the top of the growing pile.

Vile, clever, mocking phrases stabbed at her, stripping her composure bare, each letter adding to the excoriation. The most painful and humiliating moments of her life, laid out for all to see, in black and white, described in Thaddeus's distinctive, ruthless, incisive style. The pile grew until finally she could bear to look no more. Sickened, she shoved them away and sat back in her seat.

"Where did you get these?" The words came out hoarse.

"Bought them from the lady herself. Cost me a pretty penny, they did."

Alice said nothing. She was numb with shock and disgust.

"He had quite a way with words, your husband." Bamber's gaze slid over her speculatively. "The detail he goes into. Quite . . . specific. Juicy."

Alice swallowed. She could just imagine.

He patted the pile of letters and said brightly, "Nasty fellow, wasn't he?"

Sick to her stomach, Alice looked at the thick stack of letters resting under Bamber's pudgy hand. So many more letters as yet unread. Thaddeus's opinion of his wife had only worsened with time.

"What do you want?" It would be money, of course, but the question was how much. She would have to sell her home after all.

He smiled and nodded, as if pleased with her bluntness. "I want you to bring my daughter out."

It was so very far from what she'd been expecting that it

took a moment for Alice to make sense of what he'd said. "Out? Out where?"

"In high society, of course. You bring her out, take her to balls and whatnot, introduce her to all the toffs."

Alice stared at him blankly. "Why?"

"I want her to marry a lord," he said.

"Which lord?" she said faintly.

"I don't mind—as long as he *is* a lord. I have a fancy for my grandson to have a title. Lucy's no beauty, but she's well enough, and with your sponsorship . . ." He sat back, crossed his legs and regarded her complacently.

Alice shook her head, her mind numb, and yet at the same time whirling. He had no idea what he was asking. "I'm sorry, but—"

"I'm sure the *ton* would love to read these letters, Lady Charlton," he interrupted in a silky voice. "I could make a pretty penny by publishing them. Quite lubricious they are, and not just the bits where he's writing about Mrs. Jennings's many charms. He writes quite a lot about you, too. Not quite so juicy, but . . . fascinating all the same."

There was vomit in Alice's throat. She forced it down.

Bamber continued. "Your husband left his mistress quite well-off, didn't he?" He glanced meaningfully around the room. "She's not selling off her paintings and pretty bits and pieces. She didn't need the money and had no plan to sell the letters . . . until I mentioned the possibility of publishing them. Quite excited that thought made her." He paused to let it sink in. "She really has it in for you, don't she, your ladyship?"

It was true. Mrs. Jennings was a butcher's daughter and the widow of a stonemason. Thaddeus had wanted to marry his beautiful mistress, but his father, the old earl, was outraged at the notion and insisted he take a bride from the aristocracy—a pure young girl who would bear him an heir—or be cut off without a penny.

Thaddeus might have loved his beautiful mistress, but

he loved money more. For that, Mrs. Jennings had always hated Alice.

Your husband left his mistress quite well-off. And all this time, Thaddeus's legal wifc had been battling with his debts, the result of his carelessness and financial irresponsibility. Several times Alice had teetered on the brink of ruin, but she'd always handled things, made some arrangement, found something to sell. And finally she was almost debt-free.

Now, none of it would matter. This ghastly man and his packet of vile letters was going to plunge her into a different kind of ruin.

Crossing his legs, he leaned back and gave her a long, pensive look, before adding with casual relish, "Wouldn't your fine society friends enjoy reading all these letters. All those fascinating, intimate, explicit details."

Her stomach cramped. They would. They wouldn't be able to help themselves.

She would never be able to look anyone in the face again.

"But if you agree to sponsor my daughter into society and help her find a lord to marry, nobody need ever know."

Alice's breath caught in her throat. Could he possibly mean it? He'd just give her the letters. And not publish them? "What are you saying?"

"The day my daughter marries a lord, I'll give you these letters, free and clear. You can burn them or do what you like with them."

Her heart sank. She was desperate—more than desperate—to get those letters, but with the best will in the world, what he was asking was impossible. She opened her mouth to explain why, but his next words robbed her of breath.

"I know it's expensive to launch a young lady in society, and I'll cover all the costs." He pulled out a thick wad of banknotes from a pocket and laid it on the table. "That for her board and lodging." He laid another bundle of banknotes on top of it. "That to cover her dresses—from a proper high-class mantua-maker, mind. The special dress for the royal presentation—"

Royal presentation? Only girls of the highest birth were presented at court. "That's completely out of the quest—"

"This for shoes and fans and shawls and all the rest of the folderols that ladies require." He added to the pile of notes on the table before her. "And naturally I'll pay you a fee for your own expenses." With a dismissive glance at her dress, he set the last bundle of banknotes down with a flourish. "Can't have my daughter's sponsor looking shabby, can we?"

Alice stared. She'd never seen so much money in her life. But what he asked was preposterous. "I told you—"

"Of course, once she's married, as well as the letters, you'll get a bonus, depending—I want a proper lord, mind. A duke would be best, but there's not many of them around, so something a bit lower down will do. But I won't stand for nothing lower than a baronet. My grandson will have a title, or I'll want to know the reason why." He sat back and eyed her smugly. "That's opened your eyes, hasn't it, my lady?"

Alice couldn't deny it. He talked of shopping for a lord as if it were as simple as choosing cabbages from the market. "Mr. Bamber, even if I agreed to do what you asked, society doesn't operate like that."

He snorted. "Of course it does. Money talks to toffs the same as it does to everyone else."

Alice eyed the stack of notes wistfully. Ironic that after all the scrimping and saving she'd done since Thaddeus had died, here she was having to reject an offer of a huge sum of money. But money was no longer her priority. The letters were the only thing that mattered to her now, and she would do almost anything to get them.

But he didn't know what he was asking.

How could she make him understand? The ton was *exclusive*, meaning its members actively worked to *exclude* people. Entry to the highest levels of society was not simply granted to people with money—it was all about birth and blood and breeding. Connections. Belonging. The daughter of a poor vicar with an aristocratic lineage was welcomed, whereas a rich man's daughter of no particular background would be rigidly excluded. There were hundreds of unspoken rules designed especially to keep out people like this man and his daughter.

"I'm sorry," she began, "but it's just not possible."

His cozy tone turned cold. "I think you'll find it *is* possible, my lady. Even quite desirable. If you ever want to hold your head up in society again, that is." He retied the ribbon around the remaining letters, making a neat bow, and slipped them into his breast pocket. He nodded at the letter still clutched numbly in her fist. "You can keep that one as a little reminder of what's at stake."

Sick at heart, knowing she was spelling out her own ruin, she forced herself to explain. "In society—the society in which I move, that is—everyone knows everyone else, or knows *of* them. It is usually a mother or a grandmother, an aunt or some kind of relative who sponsors a young lady for her come-out. How would I explain the sudden appearance of your daughter?"

He shrugged. "Tell 'em she's some kind of cousin."

She considered it for half a minute, then shook her head. "No, it wouldn't work." He opened his mouth to argue, and she hurried on. "My own parents were poor, but my lineage on both sides can be traced back to the Conquest. As a result, I am related to half the ton, and my husband was related to the other half. People in society know my relatives, down to the last second or third cousin and beyond. If I claimed to be related to your daughter, a dozen elderly ladies would be busy tracking down the bloodlines to sort out exactly how we are related. They'd spot her as a fraud immediately." And both she and his daughter would be disgraced.

Though not as badly as if those letters got out.

Frowning, he rose and began to pace around the room. Alice watched him, biting her lip. She had to get those letters. She glanced at the poker hanging beside the fire, and a brief, mad thought passed through her mind. But she couldn't do it.

He paused, staring intensely at a china shepherdess, then turned, a look of triumph on his face. "Tell 'em she's your goddaughter then." He plumped himself back on the sofa.

Alice stared. "But she's not."

"The old biddies don't need to know that."

She thought about it for a moment, then regretfully shook her head. "That wouldn't work, either. I'm a terrible liar." It was the truth, too, and he seemed to read it in her expression.

He fell silent, his eyes narrowed as he pondered the problem. Suddenly his face lit up and he snapped his fingers. "Then we make it not a lie."

Alice blinked. "How?"

"We'll get her christened and you can be godmother."

"She's never been christened?"

He shrugged. "No idea. That side of things I left to her mother, God rest her soul. But even if she was, there's no evidence to say so." He picked up the pile of banknotes and flipped them like a pack of cards. "Now, my fine lady, do you agree? Or do I take my money away and let society drool and snigger over your husband's letters?"

His calm ruthlessness appalled her. Could this mad scheme possibly succeed? His words dripped like acid into her brain. *Let society drool and snigger.* Did she have any choice?

Hoping to buy some time to come to terms with the situation, she said, "I . . . I'd have to meet your daughter first."

"Easily done. I brought her with me." He rose, threw open the door and stuck his head out. "Hey, you, butler." He snapped his fingers impatiently.

Tweed glided to the door, oozing silent outrage. Ostentatiously ignoring Bamber, he looked at Alice. "Was there something you required, m'lady?"

Again, Bamber snapped his fingers, treating her butler like a waiter in a low tavern. "My carriage is sitting outside with my daughter in it. Fetch her in here."

Tweed gave no sign that he'd heard. He simply looked at Alice and waited. She nodded. "Yes, please ask the young lady to step in, Tweed."

"Very good, my lady." He stalked away.

"Insolent fellow," Bamber commented. "I wouldn't let him get away with that kind of behavior if I were you, my lady."

Alice tamped down on her irritation. "Tweed has served my family all my life."

He snorted. "And it shows. You need to treat your servants more strictly, my lady—show 'em who's boss. If that fellow was my butler—"

"But he's not," Alice said firmly.

They sat in silence until Tweed ushered in a young woman, eighteen or nineteen years old. A little on the plump side, she was dressed in an expensive-looking, frilly, fussy pink dress, which in Alice's view, did nothing for her. The girl's light brown hair was an elaborate mass of stiff, careful curls, and a rope of unlikely pearls was looped several times around her neck. Her complexion was good, and her eyes were a pretty hazel color framed by long dark lashes. As her father had said, she wasn't a beauty, but she was attractive—or she would be if she were better dressed.

The girl stood stiffly just inside the doorway. Her expression was wooden but somehow carried a hint of . . . was it mulishness?

She made no move to engage Alice, didn't even look at her, just stared across at the window, as if wishing she were elsewhere. For a girl supposedly determined to enter society and marry a lord, she wasn't trying very hard.

"My daughter, Miss Lucille Bamber, my lady." Bamber

snapped his fingers at his daughter. "Well, get on with it, girl. Make your curtsy to her ladyship."

Was that a flash in the girl's eyes? Alice couldn't be sure. The girl sank into a graceful curtsy and said in a low voice, "How do you do, Lady Charlton?"

Alice inclined her head in acknowledgement. Someone had schooled the girl in deportment, at least. And her accent was good, better than her father's.

"Prettily done. Now, don't stand there like a looby, girl, come and sit down." Bamber patted the space beside him.

Alice compressed her lips. The way he spoke to his daughter annoyed her, but there was more at stake here than bad manners.

Miss Bamber crossed the room and seated herself on a chair—not beside her father on the sofa. Interesting.

"I understand you wish to enter society, Miss Bamber," Alice said.

The girl gave an indifferent shrug. She didn't even look at Alice.

"Of course she does. She's very eager to mix with all the lords and ladies," Bamber said in a honeyed voice that failed to disguise his irritation. "Come, tell that to Lady Charlton, puss."

"I'm very eager to mix with all the lords and ladies," Miss Bamber repeated in a wooden voice.

"There, you see?" Bamber sat back.

Alice did see. The girl might have been taught to curtsy, but her manners were appalling. "Have you had much experience of parties and balls before, Miss Bamber?"

"No."

"But she can dance," her father said. "She's as light as a feather on her toes, and as you can see, she's been well trained in doing the pretty."

Doing the pretty? Hardly. But Alice persisted with the interview. It was all a farce anyway. Unless she could find some way out of this mess, she was going to have to launch this overdressed, sullen girl into the ton anyway. Thaddeus's horrid letters were an axe over her head. But success was looking more and more unlikely, for if the girl wasn't enthusiastic, what hope did Alice have?

"And you are looking for a husband?" Alice prompted her.

For the first time, the girl met Alice's gaze—a brief, flat, unreadable look—but she said nothing.

"Of course she is, it's her dearest wish," her father said. "Forgive my little puss, Lady Charlton. She's shy, a little overwhelmed at being in such refined company. But that will change, won't it, Lucy?" Beneath his coaxing tone was a hint of threat.

"If you say so, Papa."

"Good, now wait outside, my dear, while I have a word in private with Lady Charlton." Lucy left.

"Well? What do you say, Lady Charlton? Do we have a deal?" Bamber said.

Alice stared at him helplessly. She had no choice, she knew that—the thought of those letters being made public was too dreadful to contemplate—but introduce this stiff, churlish creature to society? Finding her anyone to marry would be hard enough, let alone a lord. She couldn't imagine how it could possibly be done.

She opened her mouth, but her throat was dry, and she couldn't bring herself to agree, couldn't even speak. It was all too soon, too sudden. Too impossible. Too ghastly.

There was a long silence. Then Bamber pursed his lips. "Perhaps you need time to think it over." He indicated Thaddeus's letter, still crumpled in her fist. "Read that again, Lady Charlton, and consider the consequences of refusing me. I'll call again tomorrow at ten. Be prepared for a christening." Without waiting for her response, he left.

As soon as she heard the front door close, Alice dropped weakly back onto her chair.

"Is everything all right, m'lady?" Tweed asked from the doorway. He looked worried. His glance fell to the letter she was still clutching. Repressing the impulse to throw it in the fire, she folded the letter and tucked it away.

"I wouldn't mind a cup of tea," she managed.

Tweed hesitated. "Did I do right by admitting him, m'lady?"

Lord, if he hadn't, who knew what Bamber might have done? What if he'd gone straight to a publisher . . . *Let society drool and snigger over your husband's letters.*

She repressed a shudder. "Yes, Tweed, your instincts were not at fault. You did the right thing."

A troubled furrow appeared between his brows. "Will we be seeing more of him, m'lady?"

"I'm afraid so. He will be calling again tomorrow morning." She hoped that would be all. With any luck, Octavius Bamber would fall into the Thames overnight and drown, taking the letters with him. But fate would not be so kind.

That night, Alice climbed into bed, took out Thaddeus's letter and read it for the dozenth time. The scorn, the mockery implicit in his words, in his description of the intimate act of her wedding night—her wedding night!—brought it all back to her. That night . . .

She'd been so young, so very nervous. She hardly knew him, after all—their entire courtship had lasted only a few weeks, and they'd never been alone together—but she'd thought she could fall in love with him, her new husband, so tall, not exactly handsome but very impressive. So worldly and knowledgeable compared with her country-girl naïveté.

She'd been just eighteen. Innocent, ignorant, hesitant, shy.

He'd been drunk. Rough. Crude. Hasty.

He'd ripped open her nightgown, the one she'd so carefully embroidered, anticipating the night she would finally become a woman, a wife. He'd stared down at her nakedness and made some disparaging comment about the size of her breasts, and then he'd shoved her legs apart and thrust roughly into her.

She'd had no idea of what to expect. She wasn't prepared for the pain, the rough squeezing of her breasts, the shock of his brutal invasion of her unprepared body.

She endured it as best she could, and he finally rolled off her and staggered out of the room—he hadn't even undressed, just unfastened his breeches. She lay for a long time, unmoving—in shock, she thought now, looking back—until finally the cold air chilled her bare skin enough to make her curl up and haul the bedcovers around her.

And then, finally, the tears came, slowly at first, then in great choking sobs.

Before the wedding, Mama had told her that it wouldn't be pleasant the first time, but she'd added vaguely that it would probably get better with time.

It never had.

Her wedding night became the pattern for the rest of Alice's married life. She never knew when Thaddeus would take it in his head to plant an heir in her—that's what he called it. She was grateful not to have to think of it as "making love."

He'd enter her bedchamber with no warning—sometimes in the middle of the night, often in the wee small hours, usually drunk—undo his breeches and pound into her. And leave as soon as he'd finished.

It got so that she would be wakeful half the night, waiting for him to come and get the business over with so that she could sleep. She'd doze off, but the slightest noise would startle her out of a sound sleep. It was exhausting.

The circles under her eyes were visible, but the few who ventured to comment on them did so as a sly joke, implying that her eager husband was keeping his pretty new bride awake far into the night. Alice never denied it. It was true after all. In a way.

One time, utterly exhausted and weary of waking

through the night in imagined fear, she'd locked her door to ensure she'd get some sleep. Enraged, he'd kicked the door down, and when he left, she was badly bruised and aching for days afterward.

But no matter how often—or how hard—he did it, he never managed to get her with child. "Useless, barren, cold fish," he'd called her.

She'd had nobody to confide in, to talk about how difficult—unbearable, actually—she'd found it. Just days after her wedding, her parents had departed for the Far East—her father's dream, to bring "enlightenment to the heathens." Then, not a month after their arrival, Mama became poorly and in a short time had sickened and died. Papa passed shortly afterward.

Grandmama, with her painful arthritis, had become a virtual recluse, and Alice hadn't wanted to distress her with things she could do nothing about. What was the point anyway? Marriage was "'til death us do part."

Besides, though she knew it wasn't logical, she'd felt too ashamed. She was a failure as a wife: she couldn't please her husband, and she couldn't conceive a child.

So having no other choice, she endured it. And having no desire to feature in society as a victim, she worked hard to give the impression that she was content in her marriage—not that anyone would believe her if she told them the truth: in public, Thaddeus could turn on the charm.

Eighteen years. Half her life trying to please a man who wouldn't be pleased.

Now Thaddeus was dead—and if the manner of his passing was another source of shame to be endured, at least her marriage was finally at an end. He'd left her nothing but debts—the entailed property went to his brother, and he'd made no provision for his widow, only his mistress and his illegitimate son. His heir, but for Alice.

And then Grandmama—God bless her—had died and left Alice this house. A home of her own. Security.

Alice glanced at the letter in her hand. The last shameful legacy from her loving husband.

She put the letter aside, blew out her candle and lay in the dark, thinking. She wasn't feeling sick and frightened now; she was feeling angry.

She hadn't endured eighteen years of marriage, hadn't maintained a public air of serenity—and Lord knew, there were times she almost couldn't manage it—for the truth about her marriage to come out now.

Bamber's demand was ludicrous, but that wasn't Alice's concern. At all costs she had to prevent the publication of those letters.

If only she'd had the presence of mind to snatch them from him and hurl them into the fire when he'd first brought them out. But she'd been in shock and hadn't thought quickly enough. There was nothing to do now but carry out his wishes, introduce his dreadful daughter to society and try to find her a lord to marry.

And *then* she would be free and her life could begin.

Chapter Two

Alice, having spent most of the night sleepless and trying in vain to think of a way out of the mess, had no appetite for breakfast.

"Oh, and Tweed," she said as the butler turned to leave, taking her cold, untouched breakfast with him. "The young lady who visited us yesterday will be coming to stay for an indefinite period. Please have a bedchamber prepared. The blue room, I think."

"Yes, m'lady." Tweed bowed, his expression conveying the kind of blank imperturbability that told her—skilled as she was in the many nuanced Shades of Tweed—that he was dying to know but would rather burst than ask her why on earth she would consider bringing the daughter of such a man into her household. Let alone installing her in the blue bedchamber!

Bamber called promptly at ten. In a tight voice, Alice agreed to sponsor Lucy Bamber into society.

To her surprise, Bamber had booked a church that very morning for his daughter's baptism. He'd obviously had no doubt that Alice would agree to his terms, because barely were the words out of her mouth than he was calling for his carriage and telling her to put on her coat and hat, that he'd booked a church for his daughter's baptism and that the vicar would be waiting.

At the last minute she remembered that as a godmother—even a spurious one—she ought to give Lucy something to commemorate the event, and casting around for something suitable, she thought of the Bible Thaddeus had given her when they'd first become betrothed.

It was a beautiful thing, bound in white kidskin with a mother-of-pearl cover and virtually untouched. At the time she'd been entranced, but of course, once she was married, the associations with Thaddeus had soured her on it. Now it seemed a perfect gift, releasing her from the unhappy memories it evoked and entering a new beginning with a new owner.

She wrapped it in a pretty shawl and gave it to Lucy in the carriage on the way to the church. The girl muttered a grudging thank-you—prompted by her father—and stuffed it unexamined in her reticule. And for the rest of the journey, which took almost an hour, she had ignored Alice and said not another word. Sulking.

Alice was quietly simmering. Miss Lucy Bamber needed a lesson in manners.

It was strange being part of the baptism of an adult. Of course Alice knew adults were baptized—her father had been a vicar, after all—but it was usually only when someone converted from another religion. She was more used to babies being baptized.

Now, standing at the font of the small village church, listening to the minister's words, she felt a little uncomfortable, but she could see no way around it. If she were to introduce the girl as her goddaughter, she had no option but to go through with the ceremony.

She'd been a godmother twice before, when holding the tiny warm bundle in her arms had made her ache with longing for a babe of her own. But it wasn't to be.

She stood by while the minister went through the ceremony in a brisk, almost businesslike manner. Miss Bamber bent awkwardly to allow the holy water to be poured over her head, and the minister and Alice each said their part. It was all over in minutes.

As they emerged from the dim hush of the church into the bright daylight, another carriage pulled up behind the one they'd come in. It was empty except for the coachman. "That's for me," Octavius Bamber said. "I have business elsewhere. You don't need my escort back to London." He handed his daughter into the carriage, saying, "Be good for her ladyship now, puss."

His daughter just looked at him. She hadn't said a word to him during the entire journey out from London and had simply stared out of the window. Now she gave him a flat look and turned away, no farewell or anything.

As a beginning, it was more than unpromising.

Bamber turned to Alice to help her up the steps, but she glanced at the girl in the carriage and stepped away out of earshot.

"There are things we need to discuss," she said.

"Nonsense, you know what you have to do and what will happen if you don't. Best you get on with it." He handed her a bundle of banknotes. "This will keep you going for the first little while. I'll make arrangements to send the rest later."

"But—"

"Off you go now. I'm a busy man." He started toward the second carriage.

"Mr. Bamber!" She had to make one thing clear to him.

He turned back. "What?"

"Do you intend to call on your daughter and me in London? Because if so, I have to say—"

"Call on you? Good God, no. Why on earth would I come calling on you? We've made our agreement, and that's the end of it. It's all up to you now."

It was exactly what she'd planned to tell him—that if he wanted his daughter to be accepted by the ton, it would be best if he stayed away—but all the same it shocked her that he could so easily hand his only daughter over to a complete stranger.

"But your daughter . . ."

He shrugged. "She's eighteen, a grown woman. I'll keep an eye on you, naturally, to make sure you're holding up your end of the bargain, but I'll do it from a distance. I'll attend the wedding, of course, give the bride away, but that's the extent of it. I want her off my hands and settled. Oh, and Lady Charlton, you have until the end of the season. If she's not married, or at least betrothed by then, I will have those letters published."

"The end of the season? But that's—"

"Plenty of time. Now, good day to you, your ladyship." He climbed into his carriage, rapped on the roof and drove off, leaving Alice staring after him with her mouth open.

He'd left Lucy without a backward glance, without even a proper farewell. Leaving his daughter in the care of a woman who had every reason to despise her.

What sort of a man did that? Foolish question. Bamber was a blackmailer. A scoundrel with delusions of grandeur. And apparently a heartless parent as well.

She stuffed the banknotes into her reticule and climbed into the carriage, feeling the first glimmer of sympathy for Lucy. But the girl scowled and turned her face away, hunching herself into the corner of the carriage and staring out the window. Dumb insolence or nerves? It was hard to tell.

They set off back to London. The miles passed in silence.

Alice considered her options. If she ever wanted peace again, she had to get this girl married off as quickly as possible, to a lord and by the end of the season, no less. But who would want her?

She had no desirable family connections. Her father was unspeakable, but he seemed to have plenty of money. Lucy wasn't bad-looking: if she could be brought to behave in a more amenable manner—and to dress better—there might be a chance.

But who? She sat staring blankly out the window, making a mental list of unmarried lords. No point pursuing those gentlemen who currently graced the ton's unwritten list of the catches of the season. That left the less desirable ones, the fortune hunters, the sworn bachelors, the widowers . . .

Alice knew plenty of widowers. Her sister-in-law, Almeria, was forever pushing them at her. She was determined to get Alice off the family's hands and ignored Alice's repeatedly expressed intention never to marry again.

But Lucy was very young. Alice was reluctant to match a young girl with a much older man. She might not like the girl, but she didn't want her to be miserable in her marriage.

Oh, why did it have to be a lord? There were plenty of perfectly nice, perfectly eligible gentlemen looking for a bride.

Her eyes ran over the frilled and flounced orange dress the girl was wearing. The first thing would be to get her some elegant new clothes. Alice would have to approach that tactfully. Taste was such a personal thing.

Several times on the trip back to London, Alice tried to make conversation, but the girl answered with either a shrug or a flat, insolent glance or with nothing at all.

Alice's mood went from seething with anger to despair and back again. How on earth was she going to get this overdressed, mannerless creature accepted into society? For two pins she'd send her back to her father. But the consequences of that would be appalling.

She was well and truly stuck with her.

Eventually the carriage pulled up in front of Alice's house. The coachman put the steps down and began to dump Lucy's luggage on the front steps. For a girl about to make her come-out, there wasn't much. Lucy picked up a battered old carpetbag and a bandbox. Tweed appeared at the door, and after ushering Alice and Lucy inside, he began collecting bags.

Mrs. Tweed, the cook-housekeeper, waited in the hallway. Alice greeted her with relief. "Mrs. Tweed, this is Miss Bamber, who is going to be staying with us for some time. Would you show her to her bedchamber, please?"

"Pleased to, m'lady. Welcome to Bellaire Gardens, miss. Tweed and me hope you'll be happy here." Mrs. Tweed gave the girl a motherly smile and took the bandbox from her. She would have taken the carpetbag, too, but Lucy clung to it.

Alice said briskly, "Yes, welcome, Lucy. Now off you go upstairs. Mrs. Tweed will answer any questions you have about the house. Freshen up and we'll take a spot of luncheon in half an hour. After that, my maid, Mary, will help you unpack. We'll have to share her, I'm afraid. My staff is rather . . . sparse at the moment."

Lucy frowned. "I'll unpack for myself."

"As you wish," Alice said indifferently. Less work for Mary. She'd inherited her grandmother's staff along with the house. None of them was particularly young, and Alice had known them all her life. Grandmama had also left her an allowance that covered the servants' wages and the household expenses. If she were frugal.

She just hoped that Octavius Bamber hadn't underestimated the cost of launching a young lady in her first season.

"Tweed generally sounds a gong ten minutes before mealtimes to let you know when to come downstairs. Mrs. Tweed will show you where we will eat."

Lucy went upstairs with the Tweeds, and Alice fought the urge to collapse into the nearest chair and pour herself a glass of something strong.

She regretted now that she'd had the blue room prepared

for Lucy. She'd given the instructions in a foolish moment of sympathy, a reaction to her own dislike of the father and his impossible ambition for his daughter. But now, having spent several hours in a carriage with her, exposed to her sullen, barely cooperative conversation—like drawing teeth, and she was *not* shy, whatever her father claimed!—Alice had decided any sympathy was wasted.

Lucy Bamber was reserved, difficult and prickly. And her dress sense was dreadful. It was not a promising start.

Somehow Alice had to find a titled gentleman willing to marry this rude, spoiled hedgehog of a girl.

Lucy followed the housekeeper up the stairs. Past the first floor—"Reception rooms," the old woman told her. Past the second floor—"That's where Lady Charlton's bedchamber and favorite sitting room are." She led Lucy up the narrower stairs to the third floor and down the corridor to a room right at the back of the house. Lucy's lip curled. That'd be right. In with the servants, no doubt.

Mrs. Tweed opened the door and gestured for Lucy to enter.

The ancient butler set down a valise and two bandboxes and trudged off to fetch the rest of her luggage from the hall, while his wife bustled about the room, twitching things into place and explaining things in a familiar, chatty manner. Lucy wasn't really listening.

Papa had stressed to her that she must learn to treat servants properly, to speak firmly to them when you wanted something and to ignore them for the most part, as if they weren't there. Because that's what the aristocracy did.

Most importantly, she was not to allow any cheek or personal references. He'd explained that Lady Charlton had no idea how to treat servants and had allowed hers to get into some very bad habits. He'd added that her butler was a very cheeky fellow in need of a severe set-down.

Lucy didn't think the butler was the slightest bit cheeky. She found his solemn air of dignity quite intimidating. And now the butler's wife was being all cozy and motherly. What was she supposed to do about that?

And they were both practically a hundred years old. Their faces were as wrinkled as the skin that formed on warm milk, the housekeeper's hair was silvery white, and the butler had almost no hair at all, just a thin fringe of white circling a shiny pink pate. She was plump; he was thin and stooped, and he wheezed slightly as he set the last of her baggage down in front of the wardrobe.

It made Lucy a little uncomfortable, letting an old man carry her things up all those stairs. She knew how the aristocracy treated servants. She'd learned it the hard way, and she didn't much like it.

"Now then, miss, you let us know if there's anything else you need," the old woman finished. "Tweed and me'll do what we can to help you settle in. Nice to have a young lady visiting," she added warmly and patted Lucy on the arm.

Lucy murmured her thanks and wondered whether she ought to have reprimanded her for that pat on the arm. She was certain Papa would have, saying it was encroaching and overfamiliar and she was not to allow a servant to treat her that way.

But it felt . . . nice. Friendly. Not encroaching at all.

Oh, she was never going to manage this. Marry a lord? She couldn't even handle servants. What had Papa been thinking?

The comtesse had treated Lucy as a kind of mix between a pupil and maidservant. She was prideful and arrogant and impossible to please, and would drill Lucy mercilessly for an hour or two each morning, rapping out orders in French about how to curtsy according to rank and instructing her in other obscure rituals of the *ancien régime*. Correcting her accent. Teaching her to behave as *ma charmante invitée*. Then she would send her off to dust the furniture, scrub the floor, fetch the eggs and chop onions in the kitchen, like a servant. Frau Steiner had been much the same, only with her, it was music, not manners. And all in German.

Would Lady Charlton be any better? She doubted it.

The minute the Tweeds had closed the door behind them, Lucy plumped down onto the bed. Her fists were knotted in frustration, and she wasn't sure whether she wanted to scream or cry—or both. But what was the point? Papa had done what he always did: appeared out of the blue, swept her away to God-knew-where, for who-knew-what reason, dumped her in a strange place with a strange woman and minimal explanation—and then left.

Lord knew when she'd see him again.

The comtesse had been most put out by the lack of notice, but Papa had ignored the old lady's ranting. His behavior had been a far cry from when he'd first brought her to the comtesse—then he'd been all over the old lady, as charming and obsequious as a honey-dipped snake. But he'd got what he wanted from her and was barely polite to the old lady now. He'd hustled Lucy away so quickly she had no time to say farewell to anyone. Not that she'd had any actual friends there.

They'd stopped for a few days at Epsom—for the races, of course—and afterward Papa had presented her with several new dresses, including the ugly pink one she'd worn yesterday and the orange thing she was wearing now. She detected the less-than-subtle taste of one of Papa's ladies—he liked them bold and a bit vulgar—and she'd said so, quite bluntly.

Papa said it didn't matter, that she was going to London to make her come-out and marry a lord, and that the lady who would sponsor her come-out would take her to the finest French mantua-maker and order her a whole new wardrobe. In the meantime Lucy would wear what he had provided and like it.

There was never any point arguing with Papa. He never listened. And since all her old clothes were faded and a bit tight—it was several years since she'd had anything new—she had no choice but to obey. Though not the bit about liking it.

She flung herself back on her new bed. She felt like drumming her heels on the counterpane, kicking some of her frustration away. But it was quite a nice counterpane, and she was still wearing her new high-heeled half boots, and it wouldn't be a good idea to have her first act in this house be an act of vandalism.

Besides, experience had taught her that giving way to temper only ever made things worse.

She took ten long, slow breaths, forcing herself to become calmer. There was no point in being upset—she was stuck here in this house with this woman who Papa said was going to get her married to a lord.

A *lord*! Really, Papa was the absolute limit. As if any lord would be interested in plain Lucy Bamber, of no particular beauty, no fortune, no background and no accomplishments. Another one of Papa's plans that was bound to end in humiliation—Lucy's humiliation.

She'd begged and pleaded with him to change his mind, but he'd turned a deaf ear to all her pleas and arguments, and as always, here she was, delivered like a parcel and abandoned.

For two pins she'd run away, only she didn't have two pins, or even tuppence—and in any case, where could she go? She had nowhere to run to and she wasn't naive enough to try. She'd tried once, and afterward Papa had made her walk by herself down a grimy, narrow street lined with scantily dressed girls and women, some her age and younger, selling their bodies, calling out their "wares." It was a terrifying lesson in the fate of unprotected girls, and she'd never forgotten it.

You needed money to run away, and Papa had seen to it

that she didn't have a penny of her own. She'd seen the thick wad of banknotes he'd given to Lady Charlton.

This mad scheme of his. Whatever did he imagine would come of it?

And though she wouldn't mind getting married, she really, really didn't want to marry a lord. She'd met enough of them at the comtesse's to know what they were like, and she'd known several girls from titled families at the various schools she'd attended—horrid, snobbish cows, for the most part.

Those girls had despised Lucy for her accent, her lack of family, her lack of "background"—and Lucy had despised them right back.

Lady Charlton would despise her, too, she knew, even though Lucy's accent was better now. And those lords of hers would take one look at her and turn up their aristocratic noses. Or slip their horrid, soft white fingers into her clothing, assuming she would be honored by their lordly attentions.

She'd given quite a few lordly types a nice shock when she'd reacted to that kind of attention. Though some of them got quite excited by a slap. Horrid beasts.

No, she really didn't want to be part of fashionable society, where everyone thought themselves superior to everyone else. She had to find some way out of this stupid plan of Papa's.

She rolled off the bed, made use of the necessary, then washed her hands and face. A marble-topped table held a large jug of water—still warm—a bowl for washing in and a small cake of soap. It was good-quality soap, too, and smelled faintly of roses.

Why was Lady Charlton doing this? Why would a grand lady like her agree to take in an unknown girl and try to find her an aristocratic husband. For money?

It was obvious that Lady Charlton was a trifle purse-pinched—Lucy had noticed the darker patches on the walls of the upper floors where paintings had once hung, and there was evidence that there had once been rugs on the floors. But despite its faded elegance, this house was impressive and right in the heart of fashionable London. It would be worth a mint.

Maybe she was a gambler and was in debt and had no choice. That was a possibility. She didn't think it was for love. Papa had a way with the ladies, but his taste ran more to vulgar widows—mutton dressed as lamb. Lady Charlton was quietly elegant, not his style at all. Though you never knew with Papa.

She dried her face and hands on a towel.

Had Papa somehow forced Lady Charlton to take her in? It wasn't as if he hadn't done that kind of thing before. And whenever Papa coerced people into taking Lucy, they invariably took it out on her.

But this room . . . Lucy looked around the room with a new eye. It was a very nice room altogether, by far the nicest bedchamber she'd ever had. It wasn't large, but it was spotless. Papered in a pretty pale blue, the room had a large window on one wall that let in plenty of light. As well as the bed—which was large and surprisingly comfortable—there was a tall chest of drawers, a spacious wardrobe, a dressing table with a looking glass attached and, beside it, a full-length cheval mirror.

It wasn't opulent, but nor was it shabby. It was clean, attractive and comfortable. She hadn't expected that.

The clock in the hall chimed the quarter hour. Lucy glanced at her reflection in the cheval glass and pulled a face. Oh, how she hated this dress. The sooner Lady Charlton took her to that fancy French dressmaker, the better. If she listened to what Lucy wanted, that is. Not that anyone ever did.

Beneath the window sat a small chaise longue and beside it a narrow shelf of books. Lucy loved to read, and had a weakness for the kind of books that Papa called "rubbishy novels." Curious, she went to investigate the titles—and then stopped dead. Her room was at the back of the house, and she had expected to look out onto brick walls or a dingy laneway. She stared out, entranced.

Her window looked out into trees. A hundred shades of green in the heart of gray old London. She pressed her face against the glass, looked down and felt some of the tightness in her chest slowly loosen. Between a gently fluttering veil of tender spring leaves, she could make out a smooth swathe of velvety green lawn.

There were neatly edged garden beds, bursting with bright spring colors: golden daffodils, tulips in red and yellow, and something blue—hyacinths or maybe the last of the bluebells. Beneath the taller flowers, a rich floral tapestry in soft jewel tones that she thought might be primulas. Mama would have known; she loved flowers.

It was hard to be sure, to see exactly which flowers were out. Narrow pathways wound between the lavish, exuberant flower beds and disappeared behind a bank of shrubs, leading who knew where.

In the middle of the garden sat an odd, intriguing little building made mostly of glass. She dodged, trying to look through the screen of leaves, but the breeze was making them dance and shift, so it was difficult to see. Was it a temple? A folly? Oh, and was that an arch of wisteria? Who owned this wonderful garden so full of delights?

A heavy *bong* reverberated from below, startling her and reminding her that she was supposed to go down for luncheon. She hadn't been able to eat a thing this morning, she'd been so full of dread. And frustration. And anger. Now she was ravenous.

She dragged herself away from the enticing view, tidied her hair and hurried down the stairs. The last house she'd lived in that had a proper garden with flowers had been one she'd lived in with Mama, but that was small, just a few flowers in front and mostly vegetables behind. Now she only had to look out her window to gaze into a magical garden. And in London, of all places. It was an unexpected gift.

She passed a number of doors on her way downstairs. Spare bedchambers, Mrs. Tweed had told her as they'd passed earlier. Any one of them could have been hers. She doubted any of them had a view: they faced the side of the building, so would probably look out onto a brick wall of the house next door.

But Lady Charlton had given her unwanted guest a light, pretty room with a magical view. Why? Lucy couldn't understand it. If Papa had forced Lady Charlton to take Lucy in and present her to society, Lady Charlton would surely resent her.

If their positions were reversed, Lucy would probably want to stick her uninvited guest in a stuffy closet or some dark little hole. Or a chilly attic room, like the one the comtesse had given her. Or squeezed her into a dusty room filled with old furniture and boxes, as Frau Steiner had. And in the various schools she'd attended, Lucy had always been given the most uncomfortable bed or the dark corner nobody else wanted.

She'd never in her life had such a pretty, comfortable bedchamber, let alone one with such a lovely view. It was quite a puzzle.

Chapter Three

Alice had made a poor start with Lucy, she realized as she washed her hands before luncheon. She'd let her resentment and anger toward Bamber spill over onto the daughter, which was hardly fair. The girl had made no effort to cooperate or even be polite, but then, if Alice had been put into a similar situation, she might feel like being rude and resentful, too.

She wouldn't have shown it, though. Alice had spent a lifetime being a good, obedient girl. And then a good, obedient wife.

And what had that achieved? Certainly not happiness. Perhaps if she'd rebelled earlier . . . No. Pointless to repine over the past. She just had to get this girl married off, and then she would be free to become the kind of woman she wanted to be.

Whatever that was.

Lucy was just eighteen, and Alice's memory of that age was that it was full of emotional ups and downs. At eighteen, in a matter of weeks, Alice herself had been betrothed, married and pitchforked into London society. Alone, because shortly after her wedding, Mama and Papa had sailed for the Far East.

It wasn't all that different from Lucy's situation now. Left alone to sink or swim.

As the elder, Alice needed to take the lead, because if this scheme were to work, she needed to establish a relationship with Lucy that was, at the very least, civil and cooperative.

Luncheon was a simple meal of clear soup, bread and butter, sliced ham and a green salad. After grace, they drank the soup in silence. Then as they were buttering bread and serving themselves ham and salad, Alice spoke. "Are you happy with your room, Lucy?"

Lucy nodded and continued buttering her bread.

"My maid, Mary, will come after lunch and to unpack for y—"

"I said, I don't need her. I'll unpack my own things."

Alice blinked at the abrupt declaration, but all she said was, "Very well."

For the next few minutes they addressed themselves to the meal.

"You're not his usual type."

The comment out of the blue startled Alice. "I beg your pardon?"

"I wouldn't have picked you as one of Papa's fancy women."

One of his fancy women? Alice stiffened. "Are you implying that there is something—*something personal*—between your father and me? Because if so, you are quite, quite wrong."

Lucy quirked a cynical brow. "Really?"

"Yes, really! I met him for the first time yesterday."

The girl narrowed her eyes. "You never met him before that?"

"Never. I hadn't even heard of him."

"Then why . . ?"

"Why did I agree to take you into my home and sponsor your come-out?" It was a fair question and not unexpected.

Lucy nodded. "And go through that—that stupid god-mother rigmarole. Mama had me baptized when I was a baby."

A trickle of relief ran down Alice's spine. So the girl didn't know the sordid details of the arrangement her father had made with Alice. "It's business."

"So you're doing it for money." It wasn't a question.

Alice nodded, hoping she looked convincing. Money played no part in why she'd agreed to this mad scheme, but she *was* accepting money from Bamber to cover the costs. But the less Lucy knew about the arrangement, the better.

At least the girl was talking now.

She tried for some more pleasant conversation. "Where do you come from, Lucy?" The more she knew about her background, the easier it would be to introduce her.

Lucy poked at her salad. "Nowhere."

"What do you mean 'nowhere'?" Everyone came from somewhere.

Apparently uninterested, the girl lifted a shoulder.

Alice persisted. "Well, where were you living before your father brought you to me?"

"With another woman, a Frenchwoman in Sussex." Her tone was world-weary.

"And this woman was your father's . . ." Alice paused delicately.

"No. She wasn't one of his mistresses. She was old." She glanced at Alice. "Much older than you."

Alice was slightly shocked at the casual way this girl spoke of her father's mistresses. At Lucy's age, Alice had had no idea that men even kept mistresses. She'd been so innocent back then.

Bamber had implied that Lucy's mother was dead. Perhaps that's why Lucy was so knowledgeable about the ways of men, because she'd been brought up by her father.

"How long did you live with this Frenchwoman?"

"The comtesse? Just over a year."

"Comtesse?"

Lucy nodded. "She escaped France during the Terror. Her husband was killed and her castle was burned to the ground, so she never went back. She had plenty of visitors, though."

"I see. Well, where did you live before you went to stay with the comtesse?"

"With Frau Steiner."

"Let me guess—she was German."

"Austrian. And before you ask, I was with her almost a year."

Alice raised a brow. "And before that?"

"School. Miss Fitcher's Seminary."

"And before that?"

"School. Miss Mitchell's establishment."

"Before that then?" Alice was getting a little annoyed at the girl's deliberate evasiveness.

"School. And before that, another school. And before that, another," Lucy finished, throwing Alice a faintly challenging look.

The conversation paused while Tweed bought in stewed apples and a baked-rice custard.

"Are you saying you were expelled from all those schools?" Alice said after Tweed had left. Good God, what had she got herself into?

Lucy lifted an indifferent shoulder, as if she had no idea, and cared even less. Alice frowned. Lucy had been asked to leave at least five schools, and there must have been a good reason for that.

But she could tell from Lucy's mulish expression that she wasn't going to explain, and Alice didn't want to push the issue, not this early in their acquaintance.

"Did you never go home in between these schools?"

"No. I told you—nowhere to go to."

There was a certain bleakness to that. Alice hesitated, then said gently, "I was sorry to hear you lost your mother, Lucy. How old were you when she died?"

Lucy helped herself to apples and rice custard. "Eleven, and before you ask, we moved around when Mama was alive, too. And the day after her funeral, Papa put me in school."

"I see." Alice didn't, not at all, but she was beginning to see a pattern. The way Bamber had dumped his daughter on Alice and left gave her an inkling of what kind of life the girl might have had.

The details of Lucy's history, scant as they were, gave her much to think on, although it was mostly speculation. She and Lucy needed to become friendly enough for an exchange of more personal information, rather than this cautious fencing. Then she would understand better. But clearly, it would take time.

After luncheon, Alice headed out to make some morning calls, leaving Lucy to entertain herself and unpack. Once Lucy was properly dressed, she would accompany Alice on the calls, but not yet.

If she had to bring this wretched girl out, she needed to reconnect with the social scene. She'd been out of circulation for the last eighteen months, first because of her year of mourning, and later because she didn't really feel like facing all those curious looks. And ugly suggestions. The rumors about Thaddeus's manner and place of death were still circulating.

Now they served as a reminder of how much worse it would be if those letters ever got out. The knowledge stiffened her backbone.

She called on her sister-in-law, Almeria, first. Almeria was far from her favorite person, but now that she'd become the Countess of Charlton, it was incumbent on Alice to pay her respects before she started making other calls. To do otherwise was to court insult, and Almeria was very prone to seeing insult where none was intended.

It was strange, arriving at her former home as a guest. She'd never liked the house: the furnishings and decoration were heavy and too ornate for her taste, and she'd always found it cold. It had always felt like Thaddeus's home, not hers, even though she'd lived there for eighteen years and spent much more time there than he did.

Almeria, dressed in her signature puce, with silver piping, was receiving, and several other ladies were also making calls. The butler, Dawes, who had been Alice's butler until eighteen months ago, announced her arrival. "The Dowager Countess of Charlton."

After the introductions—the other guests were two society matrons and their young daughters, just out this season—Almeria turned to Alice with an opening salvo. "You're looking sadly pinched and drawn, Alice dear. Dying of boredom, I expect. You really should get out more. You widows mustn't let yourselves get any drearier, you know."

Alice inclined her head politely and said nothing. The other guests exchanged glances.

Almeria continued, "I, on the other hand, have been a positive whirlwind of activity, bringing this house up to scratch." She laid a hand across her chest, indicating utter exhaustion. "How on earth did you bear it, my dear? Everything so outdated and shabby." She smiled sweetly and turned to the other ladies. "Of course, coming from an obscure country vicarage, dear Alice would have no notion of how an earl's town house ought to appear. But I have it in hand now."

Alice said nothing. Thaddeus had refused to let her change a thing, but she had no intention of justifying herself to Almeria. The house hadn't been to her taste, but it had never been shabby or outdated.

As a new bride, she'd been taken aback by Almeria's constant saccharine-coated hostility, but eventually someone had informed her that Almeria had set her cap at Thaddeus and was thought to be first in the running to be his bride, but as the years had passed and no proposal was forthcoming, she'd given in and married Thaddeus's younger brother instead.

And then, ten years later, Thaddeus swept back from a rural visit, betrothed to a young lady nobody had ever heard of—neither a great beauty nor a great heiress, though her bloodline was distinguished. A simple vicar's daughter.

Almeria had never forgiven Alice for succeeding where she'd failed, and now that Almeria was the countess and Alice the dowager—*and* she'd produced a son, while Alice had proved to be barren—Almeria couldn't pass up any opportunity to crow over their change in status.

If only Almeria had married Thaddeus. What might Alice's life have been then?

"So what have you been doing with yourself, Alice dear?"

It was said in such a world-weary, patronizing voice that Alice found herself saying, "I have a guest staying with me. A young lady."

"A guest? You mean a lodger, I suppose? Dear me, how the mighty have fallen," Almeria said with a titter and a meaningful glance at her other guests.

"No, not a lodger," Alice said, with an edge to her voice. "I am preparing to sponsor the young lady's come-out."

Almeria's eyes narrowed. "Young lady? Which young lady?"

Alice instantly regretted mentioning it. "My goddaughter, Miss Lucy Bamber."

"A goddaughter?" The finely plucked brows twitched. "I know both your goddaughters. Why have I never heard of this one before now?"

"I have no idea who you might or might not have heard

of, Almeria." She was pleased to hear she sounded quite cool. "I have known Lucy Bamber since before she was baptized." Which wasn't a lie, not really.

"Bamber?" Almeria pursed her lips. "I don't know any Bambers. Who are her people? Where does she come from?"

Alice went blank. Oh heavens. What to say? She should have thought this thing through before making her announcement. Her own fault for letting Almeria goad her into speaking unprepared.

"Aunt Alice?" came a voice from the doorway. Almeria's son, Gerald, Lord Thornton, entered the room.

"Gerald, my dear boy, safe home at last!" Almeria turned to her guests and explained, "My son was in a curricle race, all the way to Brighton. So dashing! And so dangerous. Tell me, dearest boy, did you break the Prince Regent's record?"

"No, Mother, I did not." He turned to Alice and bowed over her hand. "Aunt Alice, how lovely to see you. You're looking very well, I must say."

Alice greeted him, thankful for the distraction. Gerald had always been a favorite of hers. Almeria's guests were sitting up, the older ladies beaming, and the two young ones blushing and smoothing their skirts. Alice suddenly realized why Almeria was entertaining two very young ladies and their mothers.

"Your aunt claims she is sponsoring a young lady for the season," Almeria said as Gerald sat down.

"That sounds exciting, Aunt Alice."

"I hope so," Alice agreed.

"A young lady's come-out is an expensive matter. How can you possibly afford it?" Almeria said.

Alice ignored her. It was none of her business, and to ask such a question before guests was the height of rudeness.

"Mother," Gerald said in quiet reproof.

His mother pouted. "Well, it *is* expensive."

Gerald turned to Alice with a warm smile. "I hope you're coming to my party next week, Aunt Alice."

"Party?" Alice said blankly.

"For my birthday." Gerald turned to his mother. "You did invite Aunt Alice, didn't you, Mother? I particularly asked you."

"Of course I invited her." Almeria shrugged. "It must have gone missing in the post. In any case, it's a small family party, a simple 'at home', hardly worth her attending."

Since all Almeria's invitations were hand delivered, the excuse fooled no one.

"In that case, I'll invite Aunt Alice, and her guest, myself," Gerald said.

His mother's thin lips thinned further.

At that point the other guests reluctantly acknowledged their visit had, sadly, extended past the time generally accepted for morning calls. They rose and took their leave, pressing invitations on Lord Thornton to parties and visits to the theater and rides in the park—to all of which Gerald responded with charm while at the same time managing to avoid accepting any of them.

Alice seized the opportunity to escape with them. Explaining that she had errands to run, she hurried away.

As soon as the guests had left, Gerald turned to his mother. "That was not well done of you, Mother. You know Aunt Alice is not well off."

His mother pouted. "So you constantly claim, but sponsoring a young lady is an expensive enterprise, so you see, she must have money. Your father was right not to give her an allowance."

"Uncle Thaddeus didn't leave her a penny. It's a damned disgrace."

"Gerald! Such language."

"Well, it is." Gerald was unrepentant. "Father inherited everything, so it's his responsibility to make the provision for his brother's widow that his wretched brother failed to."

"Nonsense! If Alice can waste money bringing out some girl nobody's ever heard of, she clearly has money to spare. Unless the girl really is a lodger, which wouldn't surprise me in the least, Alice having no sense of what is appropriate to her position."

Gerald blanched. "Lodger? What makes you think—"

"And if she actually is short of money, she can do what everyone else does—find herself another husband and get out of our hair."

"Mother!"

His mother lifted a hand. "That's enough, Gerald! I've had quite enough of dreary Alice for today. I won't hear another word about her." She patted the seat beside her. "Now come over here and tell me how you found Lady Elizabeth. Or do you prefer her cousin, Miss Pumphrey?"

"Neither," he said absently. If his aunt really had taken in a lodger, she was in worse straits than he'd thought. He'd argued repeatedly with his father about the need to make her an allowance—Uncle Thaddeus had cheated Alice and her unworldly father in the matter of marriage settlements, and as far as Gerald was concerned, it was a stain on the family honor to have the dowager countess left in such dire straits. Besides, he was fond of her.

But his father was a complete penny-pinch and even made Gerald—his heir and only son—a miserly allowance, hoping to make him dance to his tune. And his mother despised Alice and wouldn't hear of giving her any support.

"Both young ladies seemed very taken with you," his mother continued.

Gerald repressed a sigh. His mother was forever throwing eligible young ladies at his head, citing his need to beget an heir, but at twenty-seven, he was in no hurry to settle down. His early adulthood had been spent overseas, part of an army at war. Having sold out after Waterloo, and then finding himself raised to the peerage, courtesy of his uncle's death, he was enjoying the diversions of peacetime London. And was in no mood to find a leg shackle just yet.

He rose. "Thank you, Mother, I'm off." He wanted to catch Alice for a private word.

"Won't you stay for dinner? We have guests and you'd be most welc—"

"Sorry, Mother, I have other plans." He didn't, but he knew what kind of dinner his mother would arrange: one with a blushing young lady seated on either side of him. He'd taken lodgings in town for this very reason—he valued his independence. And it limited his mother's opportunities to thrust potential brides at him.

Gerald hurried out into the street, ran to the corner and looked both ways. Yes, there was Alice, crossing Berkeley Square, all on her own. She ought to have a footman or maid with her, but he doubted she could afford it. Her situation was a disgrace.

He ran after her. "Alice, Aunt Alice!"

She turned and watched his approach with a faint frown. "Is something the matter?" she said when he arrived.

"I'm not sure—is there?"

She blinked. "What do you mean?"

"Mother said—" He broke off as a sudden spatter of drops fell. "Look, it's going to rain. Let us go into Gunter's. We can talk while we wait out the rain."

She opened her mouth as if to argue, but the heavens opened, and they ran the short distance to Gunter's and entered with rain pelting down behind them. They found a table, and Gerald ordered a pot of tea and some almond biscuits.

When their tea arrived, Gerald said, "Mother said you've taken in a lodger. Is that true?"

She made an annoyed sound. "Oh, what nonsense. Almeria was just making mischief. You know her way. I do have a young lady staying with me, and it pleased your mother to call her a lodger. But she is a guest."

He lowered his voice. "Are you sure, Aunt Alice? Because if you are in financial difficulties, I could speak to Father again and—"

"I said I wasn't, Gerald." She laid a gloved hand on his arm. "It's kind of you to trouble yourself, but really, my situation is not your responsibility."

"No, it's my father's," he said bitterly. "But he will do nothing. But if she's not a lodger, who is this girl? Mother said nobody has ever heard of her."

"Lucy Bamber is my goddaughter. I'm perfectly all right, and there's no need for you to worry. Now please, let us drop the subject." She fixed him with a bright, determined smile. "Tell me, how did your race go?"

Lady Charlton had gone out, which meant Lucy was free to do what she liked. She finished unpacking her things—it didn't take long: she didn't have much. She prowled around the room, picked up a novel, put it down, picked up another one. Both were books she'd been planning to read, but that garden, so green and private, enticed her.

Who did it belong to? It was spacious and beautiful, but each time she looked, it was empty. Typical of rich people: they had all these beautiful things just for show and didn't use them.

She crept down the stairs and slipped out into the back courtyard while Mrs. Tweed's back was turned. There was a black wrought iron fence and gate at the end of the small courtyard. She tried it. Locked. Of course. People locked everything in London.

She peered through the railings. Nobody in the garden at all. What a waste. A big tree grew just inside the garden, with one large branch hanging over the fence. She eyed it thoughtfully.

She never had been one for following the rules, and who cared anyway? If the owners of this gorgeous garden weren't using it . . .

A small, round wrought iron table stood in the corner of the courtyard. She dragged it to the fence, climbed onto it, tucked up the skirts of the horrid orange dress, and used the branch to swing herself over the fence. She dropped to the ground, grinning. She was in.

She walked the paths carefully, keeping an eye out for an owner, or an angry gardener, but there was not a soul, only the birds and a red squirrel that eyed her cheekily before bounding up an oak.

Time disappeared as she explored, lost in a new world, until a few heavy drops of rain startled her back to awareness. The clouds overhead loomed thick and slaty: this wasn't a quick shower then. Bother.

She ran to the pretty little glass building and tried the door, but it was locked. The rain grew heavier. Her wet skirts clung to her, cold and clammy against her legs.

She tried to shelter under a big tree, but lightning flashed and thunder rumbled, and she recalled something about how lightning was attracted to trees.

She returned to the tree that overhung Lady Charlton's courtyard, but it was wet, and the trunk was too slippery to climb, and she had nothing to climb on to reach the branch. Feeling like a fool, she nerved herself to call out. "Mrs. Tweed? Tweed? Is anyone there?"

Eventually Mrs. Tweed poked her head out the back door and, exclaiming distressfully, she hurried out with a large key. Tweed followed with a big black umbrella.

Mrs. Tweed unlocked the gate, clucking over Lucy like a mother hen. "Oh, my dear, however did you get locked out? Look at you—you're soaked to the skin. Come in, come in. Tweed, fetch hot water for the young lady's bath. She'll take it in the kitchen, where it's warm and toasty."

Lucy stared as Tweed relocked the gate and hung the big

iron key just inside the back door. There was a key. Why hadn't she asked?

"I don't need—" she began.

But she was shivering, and Mary, the maid, said, "You'll have a nice hot bath, miss, and no arguing. Lady Charlton would never forgive us if we let you catch a chill."

Lady Charlton would probably be delighted if she died of pneumonia, Lucy thought. She didn't want Lucy living with her, just as Lucy didn't want to be here.

Tweed placed an enamel bathtub in front of the fire and filled it with steaming water. Mrs. Tweed and Mary then shooed him out and turned to help Lucy undress. Lucy stepped away, wrapping her arms around herself.

"No need to be shy, miss. We're all women here."

But it wasn't shyness or modesty that stopped her; it was shame. As usual, Papa had only concerned himself with the appearance of things. The ugly orange dress might look expensive, but her underwear was a disgrace: worn, patched and repatched, barely even suitable for cleaning rags.

Oh well, she supposed, no use putting off the moment. They'd soon realize. Nothing was secret from servants.

She turned her back, stripped off her dress and then her underwear, and stepped into the bath.

Lucy could practically hear the silent looks Mary and Mrs. Tweed must be exchanging, but there was nothing she could do. Finally Mary said, "I'll see what I can do with this dress. I just hope it hasn't shrunk." Lucy hoped it had.

After her bath, Lucy wrapped herself in the large, toasty-warm towels Mrs. Tweed had heated for her and, with a muttered thanks, hurried upstairs to her bedchamber.

Ten minutes later Mary knocked on her door. "Mrs. Tweed sent this up for you, miss." She brought in a tray containing a large cup of hot chocolate and a slice of Dundee cake and placed it on the dressing table.

Lucy's cheeks were hot. "Thank you, Mary."

The whole episode had been an exercise in mortification. And kindness.

Evening fell and hunger was beginning to rumble in Gerald's belly. But where to dine? The landlady of his bachelor suite provided an excellent breakfast, but that was all. He had a number of friends he could call on who'd be happy to join him for dinner, but truth to tell, he was becoming a little weary of the company of young men his own age. They were all too often . . . callow. Fine for a frivolous evening out, but right now he was not in that sort of mood.

Particularly since he'd lost the race by a whisker. Brexton would be crowing about it all over London. Brexton was not a gracious winner.

Gerald was a member of White's, but so was his father and his father's friends, and in their company he was the one who felt callow. The way his father spoke to him—especially in front of his friends—as if Gerald knew nothing and understood less—it grated. Anyone would think him a schoolboy, not a man back from years commanding troops at war.

So his preference tonight was for the Apocalypse Club, a club formed specifically for officers returned from war. He headed for St. James.

He entered the club and, to his surprise, spied a tall, dark-haired man he hadn't seen since Waterloo. "Colonel Tarrant, well met."

Of all the men Gerald might have run into, Tarrant was the most welcome. He'd been Gerald's commanding officer, a fine leader and, despite the gulf between a colonel and a captain, a friend.

The tall man rose and held out his hand with a welcoming grin. "Paton. Good to see you. Join me for a drink before dinner?" They settled back in comfortable leather armchairs and prepared to catch up.

"I thought you were still on the continent, colonel. How long are you back for?"

"For good, I hope," Tarrant said. "And I'm a colonel no longer. I've sold my commission and am returning to civilian life." He added gruffly, "And it's Lord Tarrant now."

"Oh yes. I heard about your brother. My sincere condolences. You were close, weren't you?"

Tarrant nodded. "My best friend as well as my brother. Stepping into his shoes has not been easy." He sipped his wine and grimaced. "Every time someone addresses me as 'Lord Tarrant,' I turn my head, expecting to see Ross."

Gerald nodded sympathetically. "I'm still not used to people calling my father 'Lord Charlton,' when that's always been his brother."

"Oh yes, and you're a viscount now, aren't you? Lord . . . ?"

"Lord Thornton, for my sins."

Tarrant raised a brow. "Not enjoying your rise to the peerage?"

Gerald shook his head. "No, it's—it's . . . oh, nothing." He shouldn't have said anything about his new position. He wasn't one to wash his family's dirty linen in public. Not that his father's miserliness and determination to control every aspect of his newly inherited estate was dirty linen, precisely. Just endlessly frustrating for his heir.

He pulled a face. "It's nothing—just that now there is a title in play, my mother is after me to take a wife and start breeding an heir. She and my father never fail to remind me that my uncle died without issue. His wife was barren, you see."

"Ah." They sipped their drinks and stared into the flames.

Gerald glanced at Tarrant. "I suppose you'll be doing much the same."

"Lord no. I have no interest in marrying again. I have my daughters."

"But no heir."

Tarrant shrugged. "The title won't die out: there are male cousins around."

Gerald envied him his freedom to do as he chose. "So, tell me, what's the news from Europe?"

Tarrant filled him in. Europe, in the wake of Napoleon's ravages, was still a mess, with much rebuilding to be done, physically, economically and politically. "Every man and his dog jockeying for power," Tarrant said, shaking his head. "The process won't be over for years yet—if ever."

"So what will you do now?"

"Apply myself to the running of my brother's—no, my estate. And become a family man again."

"Yes, the two little girls. You won't be bored, leaving such a busy and exciting life to settle in the country?"

"I won't be bored. To be honest, I was weary of death and destruction, and now the endless negotiation and devious stratagems." He shook his head. "It's not for me. Not any longer."

Gerald thought it all sounded fascinating.

"And there are now three little girls to keep me busy," Tarrant added, and Gerald belatedly recalled hearing that the colonel's wife had died in England after giving birth to their third child. Was it four years ago? Or five?

"A gallant and lovely lady, your late wife," Gerald said quietly. Young Mrs. Tarrant had traveled with the army, camping in tents, sharing the difficulties and the privation and the danger, but always with a smile for her husband's men. "You knew, of course, all we junior officers were in love with her."

Tarrant smiled. "Perfectly understandable. I was myself."

"How old are the girls now?" She'd given birth twice in the middle of an army at war. Afterward, the two little girls had traveled with them. They'd been the darlings of the regiment.

"Judy's eleven—can you believe it?—and Lina is seven, and the baby, Deborah, is four."

So, four years since the colonel had lost his wife.

"I haven't seen them yet," Tarrant added. "They're in the country with their grandparents, Lord and Lady Fenwick." Seeing Gerald's surprise—Tarrant had always been devoted to his children—he explained, "I only arrived in England a few days ago, and I'm getting Tarrant House prepared for them. It's been closed up for several years, and I found leaks in the roof, birds' nests in the chimneys and all sorts of other problems. Ross was never one for coming to London. As soon as the house is fit for habitation, I'll drive down to collect them—I'm hoping by the end of the week. But we shall see."

They went in for dinner then, and over steak and kidney pie and roly-poly pudding with custard—the Apocalypse Club catered to no-nonsense, hearty appetites with food that stuck to the ribs—they caught up on the last few years. The time flew—they had many acquaintances in common, and having worked together so closely for so many years, the two men knew each other well.

They talked of many things, but Gerald kept thinking about the current European situation. The fighting might be over, but so much was still unresolved. Disputes and dissension continued, but now they were handled through diplomatic channels.

Then, over cheese and biscuits with port, Gerald described the peacetime pleasures he'd been enjoying, even mentioning the curricle race in passing, skipping the part about the goose and the maidservant. It still galled him to have lost the race for such a reason.

Afterward, one of those silences fell—the contemplative sort, broken only by the murmur of other diners and the clink of glassware and cutlery.

Tarrant swirled the brandy around his glass. "So, Thornton, this is your life now, betting on races and card games and boxing matches."

Gerald ruefully acknowledged it. His life was so superficial by comparison. He knew it—had felt it even before he'd run into Tarrant. And now, with the tales of his frivolous exploits still hanging in the air, he found himself viewing his life from the point of view of a man well used to doing important work, a man with a purpose in life.

As he had once been . . .

But what else was a man to do when his every attempt to be useful was blocked by a jealous father? "Actually, since you're in town, my mother is holding a small party, supposedly to celebrate my twenty-seventh birthday. It's mainly family and a few close friends. I'd be very pleased if you'd come."

Tarrant eyed him doubtfully. "An intimate family party? I wouldn't like to intrude."

Gerald grimaced. "A 'family' party with a lot of unrelated but eligible young females present—I did mention my mother is trying to shove me into parson's mousetrap, didn't I?" He added in a confiding rush, "I'd be very grateful for a bit of masculine support."

Gerald knew very few of his current friends would attend—either they were also bent on avoiding parson's mousetrap, or they were the kind of friends his father called "fribbles and wastrels" and wouldn't be invited. But Mama would hardly refuse to invite his former commanding officer, a military hero who was now a lord.

Tarrant sipped his brandy. He was going to refuse, Gerald knew it. And why wouldn't he? An insipid family party with a room full of marriage-minded chits was hardly likely to appeal to a man of Tarrant's sophistication, especially having come straight from the drawing rooms and diplomatic circles of Europe.

"Please? It would mean a great deal to me."

"Very well, if you don't think I'll be intruding, I'd be delighted."

"Excellent!" Gerald sat back, pleased. He knew Tarrant was only being polite, but he didn't care. "I'll get Mama to send you an invitation."

Alice met Lucy coming down the stairs just as the final reverberations of Tweed's dinner gong were dying away. "Oh, Lucy, how did your aftern—" She broke off in surprise. Lucy looked quite different. Her hair was no longer a mass of careful, elaborately lacquered curls but was pulled up into a loose, simple knot that suited her much better. And she'd changed her dress, the same overbright pink of the day before, but looking more elegant, less fussy.

"I like your hair like that." She stepped closer, eying Lucy's dress. "Is that the same dress you were wearing the other day, because if it is—"

Lucy bristled. "I unpicked all the frills. And I don't care if you think I ruined it. I hate frills and—"

"You haven't ruined it at all," Alice interrupted her firmly. "In fact, it looks much better on you now than it did." She wasn't being tactful, either. Without the frills, Lucy looked less . . . less bunchy and more graceful. Good dressmaking would make quite a difference.

"Oh." Lucy paused, still prepared for combat. "I hate the color, too."

Alice nodded. "It is rather a garish shade. Something in a softer pink would suit you better. We shall see. I've arranged a private consultation with my dressmaker for tomorrow morning. Shall we go in?" She gestured toward the dining room. She was looking forward to a glass of wine with her dinner.

The calls she'd made after Almeria had gone from bad to worse. Everyone seemed to assume she was resuming her place in society in order to find a husband—apparently Almeria had spread the word. Everyone had suggestions—

elderly widowers for the most part. And when she said she was not planning to marry again, it was greeted with polite laughter, as if she couldn't possibly be serious. So then she'd mentioned Lucy.

Your *goddaughter*? The questions flowed thick and fast. Who was this goddaughter? From where had she sprung? Who were her people? Where was her mother? *Who* was her mother? Why had Alice never mentioned this goddaughter before?

"I was hard-pressed to come up with acceptable answers," she told Lucy over the first course. "Until people asked, I hadn't realized quite how little I know about you and your background."

"Doesn't matter." Lucy spooned up her soup. "Make something up."

"It does matter," Alice said, exasperated.

"Only to you," Lucy said. "I don't care what you say. Just tell me, and I'll say it, too." She buttered another slice of bread.

The depth of the girl's indifference was frustrating. Did she think that lords—even husbands, for that matter—were so easily come by? That she needn't even bother to *try*?

Tweed entered with the next course, a raised chicken pie with vegetables.

Alice said, "Mary tells me you got caught in the rain this afternoon."

Lucy gave her a wary look. "I tried to shelter in that pretty little building, but it was locked."

"The summerhouse? Sorry, I didn't think to tell you. It's always kept locked, ever since the residents of one of the other houses on the garden square had houseguests, a group of unruly young men who got frightfully drunk one night and left the place in an absolute shambles. Because of that, the key is only made available to residents who have proved themselves to be completely trustworthy."

"Oh."

"Did you notice the small stone Japanese lantern on the flags by the summerhouse doorway?"

Lucy thought for a moment. "Do you mean the thing that looks a bit like a stone birdhouse, except it's sitting on the ground?"

Alice nodded. "Inside it you'll find the key. Just remember to lock up when you're finished and return the key to the same place."

Lucy eyed her doubtfully, as if she didn't quite believe that Alice would trust her with the key, but all she said was, "I've never seen anything like—what did you call it? A summerhouse?"

"Summerhouse, folly, temple—people call it different things."

"I'd call it a fairy palace," Lucy said softly, then seeing Alice's expression, added dismissively, "or I would if I were a child."

"I'm sorry you got drenched," Alice said.

Lucy touched her hair. "I had to wash my hair."

Alice didn't think that was the only reason. It was becoming clear that Lucy preferred a simple, unfussy style in all things, but Alice didn't want to make the girl any more self-conscious than she already was, so she simply nodded and said, "Mary told me your other dress is ruined."

"Good."

"Good? Didn't you like it?"

"I hated it. It was badly cut and ridiculously fussy, and the color made me look like a—like a sick canary."

Lucy smiled. "I think you might enjoy meeting my dressmaker. She's also a woman of robust opinions, particularly when it comes to matters of fashion."

Chapter Four

The cab turned into Piccadilly and pulled up in front of an elegant shop with a large picture window. With green velvet curtains draped behind the window and a single long white-satin glove and a length of silk draped over an elegant black wrought iron stand, it looked quite classy, Lucy thought. The name *Chance* was lettered in elegant gold script with a simple white-and-gold daisy painted on the glass.

Chance meant *luck* in French. Lucy hoped Lady Charlton was right about the dressmaker listening to her opinions. It would be the first time ever, she thought sourly. But then Papa—and his latest mistress—weren't in charge here.

Inside, the shop was modern and elegant. Lucy looked around approvingly. A short, fashionably dressed woman came limping toward them, a wide smile on her face. Some kind of assistant, Lucy assumed.

"Lady Charlton, delighted to see you again. It's been a while."

"It has, Miss Chance," Lady Charlton said warmly.

Lucy stiffened. *Miss Chance?* This was a mistake, surely?

Lady Charlton continued, "But today your client is my goddaughter, Miss Lucy Bamber, who will be making her come-out this season."

The little woman's brows rose. "This season, eh?" She gave Lucy a long, thoughtful look, then gave a decisive nod. "Bit of a rush, but we'll manage. If you'll step through here, ladies, we'll 'ave this consultation inside." She turned her head. "Polly, love, bring tea and biscuits through for Lady Charlton and Miss Bamber, will you? This will take a while."

A discreetly dressed young woman nodded and disappeared through the green velvet curtains.

The short woman gestured. "Through here, if you please, my lady, Miss Bamber."

Lucy didn't budge. She grasped Lady Charlton by the sleeve. "A word in private, if you please." She jerked her head, indicating outside.

Lady Charlton gave her a quizzical look. "Very well. A moment please, Miss Chance. My goddaughter and I need a word."

Lucy led her out onto the footpath. She didn't want that woman to overhear the conversation.

"Well, Lucy, what is it?"

"That woman isn't French at all. She's a . . . a Cockney!"

Lady Charlton raised her brows. "Yes, and . . . ?"

"My father promised me a proper French dressmaker. Not some Cockney." And he'd paid Lady Charlton well for it, so if she was trying to cheat by having Lucy dressed by some second-rate cheap Cockney dressmaker, Lucy wasn't going to stand for it. She'd had enough of being badly dressed. For the first time ever, she was going to have what she wanted, not what Papa and his latest woman chose for her.

Lady Charlton said coolly. "Really? I see. And which French dressmaker would you prefer?"

"I don't know, but Papa said—"

"It will, of course, alter our arrangements quite considerably if we have to travel."

Lucy blinked. "Travel?"

"To Paris."

"I don't understand. Papa said you would take me to the best French dressmaker in London."

"Ah, I see." Lady Charlton's expression softened slightly. "The trouble is, there are no genuine French dressmakers in London at the moment. Oh, there are some very good dressmakers who call themselves French, who display in their shops French magazines containing the latest fashions from Paris. They call themselves French names and speak English with a French-sounding accent, but try speaking to them in French . . ." She shook her head. "Miss Chance is one of the rare few who refuses to pretend she is anything other than she is."

"Oh."

"And what she is, is an excellent and original dressmaker, patronized by some of the most elegant ladies in the ton. Now, I don't wish to foist my choices on you, Lucy, but why don't you come in and see what you think of Miss Chance's ideas and creations? If you're not happy, we'll go elsewhere and try out some other dressmakers."

Lucy gave a reluctant nod. "Very well."

Miss Chance smiled at them as they reentered the shop. "All sorted? Right, through here, if you please, ladies."

The next two hours passed in a flash. First, over tea and thin, crisp almond biscuits, Miss Chance pulled out sketches and drawings and designs cut from magazines and questioned Lucy about her thoughts.

Miss Chance really seemed to listen and was so interested in Lucy's opinions and preferences that Lucy's stiffness soon passed. From time to time, Miss Chance called to her assistant, Polly, to fetch this dress or that for Lucy to look at—and under Polly's supervision, a variety of young women displayed various unfinished dresses for Miss Chance to make a point about or for Lucy to examine.

Next she took Lucy into a room that Lady Charlton laughingly called Aladdin's Cave. It was filled to the brim with swathes and rolls of fabric.

Miss Chance then stood Lucy in front of a large mirror and began to drape fabrics over her, muttering comments that Polly noted down. "See, that color doesn't do anything for you, but this"—she whipped off one shade and replaced it with another—"see how this one brings out your pretty eyes and makes your skin glow? Lovely complexion. Plenty would kill for skin like this, so we'll be making sure the gentlemen notice, eh, Miss Bamber?" She chuckled as Lucy fought a blush. She wasn't used to compliments.

Then the discussion moved beyond color, to examining weight and drape and all kinds of other qualities Lucy had never considered. By the time they came to the discussion and selection of several designs, Lucy's reluctance to let Miss Chance dress her had completely dissolved. This whole process was fascinating. She was learning so much.

The only awkward part was when the assistant, Polly, led Lucy into a private cubicle to disrobe and have her measurements taken. Lucy hadn't expected that at all.

She'd tried to make excuses, to suggest that it could be done later, but Miss Chance and Lady Charlton looked at her in such surprise that the excuses died on her tongue.

She stood stiffly as Polly helped her out of her clothes. She'd felt quite pretty while Miss Chance had been trying out fabric colors and textures and talking about the styles that would suit her best, but now, as layer by layer her horrid old, shabby, worn-out, too-tight, heavily patched underclothes were revealed, Lucy felt herself shriveling with shame.

But Polly didn't bat an eyelid. She simply took various measurements and noted them down in a special book.

When she was finished, she gave Lucy a bright smile, quite as if she hadn't noticed a thing out of place, saying, "There now, miss, that's all done."

Lucy had reached for her old clothes, but from outside the cubicle, Miss Chance thrust several almost-finished dresses through the curtains, saying, "Pop her in these, Polly, see how they go."

The first one fit perfectly. "Come on now, Miss Bamber, let's see you," Miss Chance commanded, and shyly, Lucy stepped out of the cubicle.

Miss Chance examined her with a critical expression, then stepped forward and tucked in the visible portion of Lucy's chemise. Lucy felt herself blushing again, though not with pleasure this time. She'd told and told Papa she needed new underclothes, but . . .

"Turn around." The little dressmaker twirled her finger, and Lucy obediently turned.

"Needs taking in at the back there, Pol." She produced some pins, and pinned and tucked, then stepped back. "What do you think, Miss Bamber? Lady Charlton?"

Lucy eyed her reflection in the big looking glass, and swallowed. She looked . . . she looked elegant. The dress was now a perfect fit thanks to Miss Chance's pins. It was light and soft, in the palest sage green muslin, embroidered here and there with tiny white sprigs. There were no frills, though there were three narrow bands around the base of the skirt that no doubt stopped the hem from flying up. She swished back and forth experimentally. "It's lovely."

"Isn't it on order for someone else?" Lady Charlton asked.

Miss Chance shook her head. "It was, but we'd barely started on it when the girl's mother changed her mind. This was already cut out and tacked together, so we part finished it in case we found another buyer. If you like it, Miss Bamber, we'll do the alterations and have it ready for you by this afternoon."

Lucy did like it. It was the nicest dress she'd ever worn.

Finally, they drove back to Bellaire Gardens. Lucy's head was in a spin. Miss Chance had promised to deliver two more day dresses, two evening dresses and a beautiful, smart pelisse by the end of the week. And that was only the start.

She'd lost track of what they'd ordered. All she knew was that she'd never seen so many beautiful dresses in her life.

Lady Charlton had overseen the whole process: all Lucy had to do was to approve the design and the fabric. The only thing that disturbed Lucy was when, at the end, Lady Charlton had handed over what looked like a substantial amount of cash. She asked her about it in the cab.

"You paid her up front?"

"Yes, a part payment."

"Papa says you never pay tradesmen up front. They should send you a bill, and you pay at your leisure."

Lady Charlton nodded. "In general that's true. Miss Chance is an oddity in that she usually demands payment up front before the goods leave the premises. Some people refuse to patronize her for that reason, but she's so good, she has her pick of clients, so it doesn't bother her."

Lucy mulled that over. It made sense to her. Papa hardly ever paid his bills. It was one reason why they moved so often.

I am expecting several morning calls this afternoon," Alice told Lucy at breakfast several days later. "I would like you to make yourself available." She'd thought that the visit to the dressmaker had been a turning point in her relationship with Lucy. The dresses had delighted the girl, and she'd actually been quite pleasantly behaved.

But the moment Alice mentioned parties and balls and the possibility of vouchers for Almack's, the sulky, ill-behaved creature returned. Alice was getting very tired of it.

Lucy didn't look up from buttering her toast. "Why are they called morning calls when they're in the afternoon?"

"I don't know. They just are. Wear one of your new dresses—the sage green muslin, I think."

Lucy spread her toast with plum jam. "Who's visiting then?"

Alice hung on to her patience. "I don't know. That is the nature of morning calls. People drop in at the accepted hour, stay chatting for twenty minutes or so—it's not polite to stay much longer—and then leave. It is an excellent chance for you to begin getting to know people." It had been the reason she'd done the rounds of morning calls over the past few days, calling and leaving cards and letting people know that she was resuming her social life, so people would begin calling on her—and Lucy—in return.

Lucy, chomping on toast, said, "What if I don't want to meet them?"

"Don't speak with your mouth full," Alice said evenly. She was sure the girl was doing it to annoy her. "And I don't care if you want to meet them or not. Your father has asked me to introduce you to the ton, and introduce you I will."

Lucy pulled a face. "Even if I don't want to?"

"Even if you don't want to."

Lucy gave her a flat look from under her lashes and bit into her toast.

By four o'clock that afternoon, Alice heartily regretted making Lucy meet her guests. Of the many fashionable society ladies who had called, one was a mother with several marriageable sons and one was a grandmother whose titled son had passed his thirtieth birthday and was showing no sign of wanting to marry and settle down. They'd come especially to meet Lucy.

The girl had behaved abominably—slouching in her seat, responding to polite questions with a monosyllable or a grunt, making no attempt to initiate conversation, yawning in an openly bored manner and loudly slurping her tea. She even scratched under her arm several times, as if she had fleas or something. Which she most certainly did not.

Alice would have been mortified if she weren't so furious. Lucy's behavior was both deliberate and provocative.

The minute the last guest had left, Alice rang for Tweed. "Tell any further callers that I am not at home, thank you, Tweed."

"Thank God for that," Lucy said and made to leave.

"Not so fast, young lady." Alice shut the door. "Sit down. I want a word with you."

Lucy gave her an insolent look. "About what?"

"About your appalling behavior."

Lucy leaned back in her chair, her expression speculative. "You know the solution to that, don't you?"

Alice frowned. "What do you mean?"

"My father is paying plenty for you to bring me out. It's perfectly clear that you don't want me here, and I certainly don't want to be here, so give me half the money Papa paid you, and I'll be out of your hair."

It was the last thing Alice expected. "You don't want to do this?"

"No."

"You're not aiming to marry a lord?"

Lucy's answer was a contemptuous snort.

"Then why . . ?"

"Why did Papa arrange this? Because he wants to make himself sound important—to be able to speak of 'my daughter, Lady Fancypants' or, better still, 'my daughter, the Duchess of Stiff Rump.' Because he doesn't listen to me, because he doesn't care what I want, because it isn't about me; it's all about him!"

The contradictions in Lucy's behavior began to make

sense. Alice said curiously, "What would you do if I did give you the money?"

"Make a life for myself."

"What kind of a life? Where would you go? What would you do?" The girl had no family that Alice knew of. Only her father. And the world was a harsh place for a young girl alone.

Lucy made a frustrated gesture. "I don't know, but it wouldn't be this, pretending to be someone I'm not, cold-bloodedly hunting a lord, all to live a life where I'll never belong, never be happy. I don't belong in high society, and I know it, if Papa doesn't. He's not the one who'll suffer. He won't be rejected and scorned and humiliated and looked down on."

"What makes you think it will be like that?"

"It was at school—every one. Papa always chose really exclusive schools, the kind that only take girls from aristocratic families. He lied. He told them I was the granddaughter of a baron." She rolled her eyes. "The girls invariably knew, of course. First it was my accent—"

"But your accent is quite good."

"It is now," Lucy said. "After five fancy schools it should be."

"Oh."

"And it'll be the same here. People will soon find out I'm not 'one of them,' and it will be just like school. So I'd rather not go through any of it, if it's all the same to you." She leaned forward, her expression pleading now. "So will you do it, my lady—give me the money, I mean?"

After a short silence, Alice sighed. "I'm sorry, Lucy, I can't do that. Your father and I made an agreement and I—"

Lucy flung up her hands. "Oh! You're just like Papa! You don't care about what I want at all! It's all about money with you people, isn't it? A person's happiness doesn't matter to you at all!" She stormed out of the room, furious and, if Alice was any judge, on the verge of tears.

Alice sank onto the nearest chair, shocked by the outburst and what it had revealed. The reasons for Lucy's atrocious behavior were clear to her now—and in retrospect, she should have realized. But she'd assumed that Lucy was merely spoiled and indulged and used to having her every whim met.

Some frank talking was required. And an apology.

Because understanding Lucy's reluctance to enter the ton didn't make Alice's situation any better. If anything, it made it worse. Somehow, she had to get those letters back. But how?

Maybe she could talk Bamber into changing his mind about a lord. But in that case, would he still give her the letters? She didn't know, but she couldn't do nothing.

The first step was to find out where Bamber was living. And where he kept the letters.

Lucy," Alice said at breakfast next morning, "Do you know where your father lives?"

Lucy looked up sharply. "Why? Are you going to tell him—"

"It's just in case I need to contact him. He never left me his address."

Lucy sniffed. "That's because he hasn't got one."

"What do you mean?" He must have one. Everyone had an address.

"I told you I never had a home, didn't I? Not since Mama died. That's because Papa doesn't stay anywhere very long."

Alice was troubled, and not just by what Lucy was telling her. There was a brittleness beneath the girl's seemingly careless outlining of her situation. "But how do you contact him?"

Lucy shrugged. "I don't."

"But what if you were ill or in desperate need of him?"

Again she shrugged. "I survive or I don't. But he finds out eventually. He seems to have eyes and ears all over the place."

"What about letters? Doesn't he have an address to which people can send correspondence?"

"He had to leave an address with the headmistress when I was at school," Lucy admitted.

"Well then—"

"But it was a different address every time."

There was a short silence. "So there is no way of contacting him."

"No."

"You're not lying to me, are you?"

Lucy snorted. "Would it make any difference if I was? But no, I really don't know where he is, or how to contact him. I never have."

Alice's tea was cold. She drank it anyway. So much for her plan to steal the letters back.

Lucy continued eating her breakfast, feigning indifference, but Alice was filled with unexpected compassion. What must it be like to be so alone? Her only relative a father who arranged her future without consultation, a father whose whereabouts was unknown—even to his daughter.

Alice glanced at the door. No sign of the servants. "Lucy," she said quietly, "I would give you all your father's money"—Lucy looked up, hope shining in her eyes—"if I could, but I can't. Our agreement wasn't about money."

"But—"

"Yes, he gave me money, but that was just to cover your expenses. He did promise me a bonus once you were married, but the reason I agreed to bring you out in society was . . . was nothing to do with money."

"But if you don't care about the money, you could give me whatever is left."

Alice shook her head. "No. I'm afraid the consequences for me would be . . . unbearable." There was a short silence, then she added, "Your father has some . . . documents that will ruin me if he releases them."

"Blackmail?" Lucy's mouth twisted. She gave a harsh laugh. "That's more like it. He wants me off his hands, so—"

"He wants you settled and happy." Alice was learning not to be shocked at Lucy's acceptance of her father's less-than-sterling qualities.

Lucy snorted. "No, he just wants me off his hands. I know my father. But at least I understand now. You're as unhappy with this situation as I am, but we're stuck with it."

Alice nodded. She refilled her cup, the tea now not only cold but bitter. It suited the moment.

"We have to find some way to go forward, Lucy—something that will not upset you or endanger me."

Lucy gave her a sharp look. "He hasn't threatened you, has he? Because he's never—"

"No, no, nothing physical. It's a . . . it's a different sort of threat."

"I'm sorry. I wish he wouldn't do this kind of thing but—"

"It's not your fault, Lucy. Now, think—could you bear to continue with this scheme?"

Lucy wrinkled her nose. Alice's tension mounted. Without Lucy's cooperation, she'd never get those wretched letters back.

"I like the clothes," Lucy said after a minute. And then added, "But I'm not very good with all that society stuff."

"I wasn't either when I was your age. I was frightfully shy." Lucy might not be confident, but she wasn't shy. "Believe me, all of that can be learned. As long as you're willing, I can teach you how to go on."

Lucy absently folded and refolded her napkin. "I suppose it might be all right—as long as I don't have to marry a *lord*." She said *lord* the way most people would say *snake*.

"What have you got against lords?" Alice asked curiously. For most young ladies, the idea of marrying a lord was a dream. "I can see how marriage to a titled gentleman would be a daunting prospect, but you never know wh—"

"I'm not *daunted*. I just don't like them and their high-and-mighty attitudes. They all think they're God's gift."

"Have you met many titled people?"

Lucy sniffed. "Plenty. Nearly all of the comtesse's visitors were titled. The ladies were—well, *high in the instep* doesn't begin to describe them. Some of them were right cows! And as for the men, a peasant like me was just something to help themselves to, whether I wanted it or not." She snorted. "But I showed them."

"I see," Alice said. Thaddeus had been much the same. It was the reason she'd never been able to keep young maidservants.

"And some of the girls I was at school with were titled and they were complete bitc—er, cows as well."

"It seems you've been very unfortunate in the titled people you've met so far, but not all titled people are the same. And people without titles can be equally unpleasant."

Lucy eyed her in silence, her chin jutted stubbornly, unmoved by Alice's argument.

Alice stomach knotted at what she was about to do. But she couldn't in all conscience force this young girl into a marriage with the kind of man she found abhorrent. Even though her father had given Alice specific instructions: *I want a proper lord . . . I won't stand for nothing lower than a baronet.*

But surely what Bamber truly wanted was for his daughter to be happily settled and secure. A title was no guarantee of happiness. She took a deep breath and took the plunge. "What if I accept that you don't wish to marry a lord?"

Lucy's eyes narrowed. "You will?"

Alice nodded. "It will make it easier."

"Why?" Lucy flared. "Because I'm not beautiful?"

My, but she was quick to take offense. Alice said in a calm voice, "No, because the number of unmarried titled gentleman is limited, but if we include all eligible gentlemen, you would have a much wider choice."

"Oh."

"Presuming, of course, that you want to find a husband." There was a short silence. "Do you, Lucy?"

Lucy shrugged. "I suppose so. What else is there for me to do? I'm not clever enough to be a governess, and anyway, I hated school." Beneath the would-be indifference, Alice thought she could detect a faint note of hopelessness.

What else was there indeed? The options for unmarried women, especially those with no income, were few, and not very pleasant.

"But I don't want to marry someone high and mighty. I don't want a husband who'll look down on me."

"Understood." And Alice did understand, having experienced it herself.

"What about you?" Lucy said. "Are you happy about having me here and taking me about?"

Alice was about to assure her politely that she was only too delighted, but stopped herself. Lucy had already shown herself to be cynical and suspicious. She would see through any false assurances.

"I wasn't at first," she admitted. "To be honest, I was angry and resentful. And your behavior didn't help. You were hoping I'd want to be rid of you, weren't you?" She'd probably done the same at all those schools she'd been expelled from.

Lucy's expression was a grudging admittance.

"But now that we've brought our differences into the open, I feel more positive." Alice was starting to feel some sympathy for this awkward, uncommunicative girl. "If you're willing, we could regard this as an opportunity."

Lucy eyed her cautiously. "What sort of opportunity?"

"I've never had a young lady to sponsor into society. I had no children of my own, and I'm lamentably lacking in relations. And now, here you are, and while it wasn't what either of us planned, or particularly wanted, we can choose how we want to go forward—endure it or enjoy it."

There was a short silence, then Lucy said, "You mean it could be fun?"

"Exactly." Alice smiled. The girl was quick. "And I promise you that I will never try to push you into an unwanted marriage—lord or no lord." A chill thread of doubt wound through her as she spoke. She ignored it. Bamber wanted his daughter to be happy; he must. She would lose the bonus that he had promised, but that didn't worry her. All she cared about was getting the letters back.

"So, what do you say?"

"It depends." Lucy tilted her head. "What was all that godmother stuff about? You're not planning to launch me with rats and lizards and pumpkins and glass slippers, are you?"

Her dry, slightly caustic delivery surprised a laugh out of Alice. So the girl had a sense of humor. "I've always thought glass slippers would be horridly uncomfortable—so cold, and with no give in them at all."

Lucy raised a sardonic eyebrow. "But you're fine with rats and lizards?"

Alice chuckled again. "Becoming your godmother was your father's idea." She explained the difficulty she would have had trying to introduce Lucy as a relative, however distant. "Besides, I'm a terrible liar. People who know me well can always tell."

"Really? That's awkward."

"So, are you willing to enjoy this whole thing?"

Lucy shrugged. "Very well. I'll try."

"I'll try" was hardly an enthusiastic response, but Alice was grateful for what she could get. "Good. Now, I'll need to know a great deal more about you and your background."

Lucy eyed her cautiously. "Why?"

"Because people will ask, of course—they've already started. The ton is quite a small and rather closed society, and people like to understand how we are all connected.

It's the reason I became your godmother—so we'd be connected in a way people could appreciate."

"I see."

"So far I've managed to imply to people that your mother and I were girlhood friends—luckily I had a very obscure girlhood, so nobody could contradict me—and that we had lost touch over the years because your family moved quite often. That your mother had died, and it was for her sake I was bringing you out."

"Sounds good to me." Lucy seemed indifferent to the conversation. She was folding her napkin into some intricate shape.

Alice smacked her hand on the table. "No, it's not nearly good enough, Lucy. You don't seem to understand. To most of the people in the ton, background is everything. If anyone suspects I never saw you or any of your family before this week, and that I'm trying to pass you off—falsely—as my goddaughter and a friend of the family, we'll be ruined."

Lucy looked up. "We?"

"Yes, *we*—both of us. You for not being who they think you are—the ton can be very unforgiving of people who try to deceive them in order to gain access to the highest levels of society. As for one of their own who aids and abets such a deception . . ." She shook her head.

"Oh."

"Yes, *oh*."

"We'll have to agree on the story then," Lucy said, quite as if this were an everyday occurrence for her. And perhaps it was.

"Exactly, but we should keep it as close to the truth as possible. Now, what was your mother's name?"

"Louisa."

"And her surname—her maiden name?" Alice prompted.

Lucy's brow furrowed in thought, then she shook her head. "I don't remember."

Alice was shocked. "You don't remember your mother's maiden name?"

Lucy gave a careless shrug. "She never talked much about the past, never mentioned her parents. And if ever I raised the question, she'd change the subject."

"What about your father? Surely he knows."

She shook her head. "I asked him once and he got so angry, I never asked again."

"I see." How strange not to know such basic information about one's parents.

"Do you know where your mother grew up?"

Lucy shook her head. "No. What about where you grew up? Was that in the country?"

"Yes, in the village of Chaceley, in Worcestershire. My father was the vicar there. I implied this afternoon that your mother and I knew each other as girls, but had lost touch after she married and moved away," she said.

Lucy nodded. "That'll work. We moved a lot. Papa has what he calls 'itchy feet'—he always likes to keep moving."

Alice couldn't imagine not having any place to call home. Even if home wasn't very comfortable.

"What should we tell people if they ask about your father?"

"That he's away, traveling. It's what I usually say."

"I suppose that will have to do." It was all very peculiar, but then this was a very peculiar situation. For all Alice—or Lucy—knew, her mother could have been Romani. This whole wretched business was a fantasy. Or a nightmare, if it got out.

Chapter Five

Alice paused in the doorway of the Charlton House reception rooms. They'd arrived late on purpose. As she explained to Lucy, it was easier to enter a room full of people than to be standing awkwardly, waiting for everyone else to arrive. Besides, it was fashionable to be a little late.

"Don't be nervous, it's just a small family party," Alice murmured.

"I'm not nervous." Lucy gazed around the room curiously.

No, if anyone was nervous, it was Alice. She'd attended very few social events since Thaddeus's death—none at all during her year of mourning, and very few since she'd gone into half mourning. She hadn't enjoyed them.

At each event, some so-called gentleman had sidled up to her and, after some token conversation, had made her an improper proposition. How could they imagine she'd be interested? She'd given them no reason to think so—she didn't even flirt!—but it was apparently a widespread belief that a widow must be desperately missing her husband's marital attentions.

Alice was relieved to be spared them.

But tonight she was here *en chaperone*. All she had to worry about was Lucy, because surely, at a family party—her late husband's family at that—nobody would approach her with indecent suggestions.

That was why she'd allowed her maid, Mary, to persuade her into the new dress that Miss Chance had made her. The design of the dress was perfectly respectable and the color quite comme il faut for a widow of eighteen months, and yet it felt like a gorgeously frivolous froth of a dress, a gleaming smoky cloud of lilac silk and taffeta—too pretty, no doubt, for a small family party, but who cared? It had been ages since she'd worn anything new, and in this dress she felt somehow lighter, younger. Ready to go dancing, though there would be no dancing tonight. Almeria's parties were invariably dull.

She knew, she just knew that Almeria would disapprove of the dress. If Almeria had her way, she'd have Alice wearing black widow's weeds for the rest of her life. And just the thought of that put a smile on Alice's face.

She glanced at Lucy, who was scanning the crowded room with a faint anticipatory smile on her face. She, too, was feeling the magic of a pretty new dress and the confidence that came with the knowledge that she was looking her best in pale gold muslin and a lacy cream shawl.

Alice could hardly believe the difference between the girl who stood beside her now and the one she'd first met—sullen and withdrawn in the unflattering, overly elaborate dress and the heavy, fussy lacquered mass of ringlets.

Mary had braided Lucy's tawny hair in a simple coronet around the crown of her head and tucked in some tiny yellow faux rosebuds. The simple style showed off Lucy's lovely complexion and bright eyes. Her face had the roundness of youth, and now that it wasn't half drowned in a mass of fat corkscrew curls, you could see the cheekbones that would emerge as she matured. She wasn't a beauty, but she was quite arresting.

As long as she behaved herself, Lucy couldn't fail to make a good impression.

Alice glanced around, looking for her hostess. It was rather more crowded than she'd expected. Not quite the intimate little "at home" gathering Almeria had indicated. Alice knew about half the people there, and as for the others, some she'd seen before, though never met, and quite a few were complete strangers. Not as many young gentlemen as she'd expected, though, which surprised her. One would have thought a party to celebrate a young man's birth would have attracted more men of his age.

Alice found her sister-in-law, resplendent in puce silk and gold lace, and greeted her cordially. "Almeria, what a very pleasant gathering. Thank you for inviting us." Strictly speaking, Almeria hadn't invited them at all. Gerald had.

Almeria's mouth pinched as she eyed Alice's dress. After a brusque greeting she pulled Alice aside and said in a low, angry voice, "I don't want this nobody of yours setting her cap at my son. Is that understood?"

"Perfectly," Alice said calmly. "If it's any comfort, Almeria, my goddaughter has no designs on Gerald or any other titled gentleman."

Almeria made a scornful sound. "You always were a fool, Alice. Just keep her away from him, all right?" She turned away to speak to her other guests.

James was restless. He should never have accepted Gerald's invitation. A family party, as insipid as he had feared. As Thornton had warned him, the company was heavy on hopeful young unmarried misses and their mamas. He knew a few of the other gentlemen, some from the army and one or two acquaintances from school days, but there was nobody he particularly wanted to talk to.

He sipped the wine, which was inferior, made small talk and found he was surprisingly popular—until he realized that for some of these females he was as much a target as Thornton. Married ladies on the hunt for a lover, and unmarried ladies on the hunt for a title.

James had no interest in either. All that was behind him now. He'd had the best with Selina and had no interest in second best.

He was aware that his daughters might need a mother figure, so he'd sent for Nanny McCubbin, who was as motherly a figure as anyone could want. And as the girls grew older, a good governess could provide all the female guidance they would need.

He surreptitiously checked his fob watch. How soon could he make his escape?

He observed the hopeful young misses clustered in groups, following young Thornton with their eyes.

He'd met Thornton's parents—they'd invited him for dinner before the party—and now he understood why Thornton seemed so restless and unsettled. They treated him like a schoolboy instead of a man who'd commanded troops—damned well, too, keeping a cool head under fire and showing a talent for tactics and strategy.

Musicians began setting up in the other room. Time to leave. He was a good dancer, but he wasn't in the mood tonight, especially here, with the eyes of ambitious ladies on him.

He drained his glass, set it on a nearby side table and prepared to make a discreet exit. And halted.

She must have only just arrived: he would have noticed her earlier. Tall and slender, she was dressed in a soft lilac dress that clung in all the right places. As she walked forward to greet her hostess—with an unselfconscious grace that caused his mouth to dry—the dress seemed to caress her limbs, floating around her like a cloud.

"Who is that?" he breathed. But there was no one near to answer.

Her companion was a younger lady, a girl with light brown hair wearing a yellow dress. Her daughter?

The woman glanced around the room, saw someone she knew, gave a little wave and smiled. He swallowed. The sweetness in that smile lit up the room.

Her dark hair was arranged simply in a loose knot on her crown, revealing the graceful line of her neck. Her neck was bare—she was the only lady there who wasn't draped in jewels—revealing smooth, creamy skin. He wasn't close enough yet to tell the color of her eyes, but they were striking, framed by lashes that were long and dark.

And her mouth—dear lord, her mouth. Lush, soft, vulnerable. Rich, dark rose against the creamy pallor of her skin. A mouth made for kissing.

And why the hell was he thinking about kissing a woman he'd never even met, when not two minutes before he'd been telling himself that all that was behind him now? And believing it.

He couldn't drag his eyes off her.

His gaze dropped to her left hand, but of course she was wearing evening gloves. Was she married?

She had to be. A woman like that would never be left on the shelf. And she wasn't in black, and though lavender was considered by some to be a color for half mourning, that dress was very far from being widow's weeds. So, not a widow. Damn. He didn't dally with married women.

From the corner of his eye, he spotted Thornton and his mother passing—his mother gripping her son's arm like an arresting sergeant and towing him determinedly along. Going by Thornton's resigned expression, their destination was some young lady his mother particularly favored.

"Thornton." His arm shot out, and Thornton came to a grateful halt. James indicated the tall lady on the other side of the room. "Who is that lady?"

Thornton followed his gaze. His eyes narrowed. "I don't know," he said slowly. "She looks vaguely familiar, but . . ."

He shook his head. "Mother"—he turned to his mother, who hadn't relinquished her grip on his sleeve—"who is that young lady with Aunt Alice? The one in yellow."

His mother snorted. "Some nobody that Alice has befriended. She claims the gel is her goddaughter, but I've never heard of her. Ignore her, Gerald—she's not worth your time or attention. She comes from I know not where, I don't know her people, she has no fortune that I can ascertain, and she's no beauty. I'm very cross with Alice for bringing her along, but of course, you know Alice—she lives to vex me. Now come along. I want you to meet Lady Ledbury's daughter, Lally." She tugged on her son's sleeve.

Thornton didn't move. He stared, his expression intent. "I'm sure I've seen that girl before."

"You can't have," his mother said impatiently. "She's a complete nobody and new in town. Now come *along*, Gerald." They moved off.

So, his tall dark lady was Thornton's aunt Alice. James couldn't take his eyes off her. If he'd had any expectations of an aunt of Thornton's, particularly one who was a dowager countess, it would have been an older lady, a kindly old gray-haired dear.

Not . . . *her.*

Alice moved through the room with Lucy, nodding to this person and that, and offering brief greetings, but not really engaging in conversation. Alice knew many people here; Lucy knew no one. Then she noticed a small group of young ladies, some of whom she knew slightly. She led Lucy toward them. Lucy needed to make some friends her own age.

"Good evening." A tall, grave-faced gentleman stepped into their path. Dressed in severe dark evening dress, the same as every other man in the room, there was, nevertheless, something about him. Perhaps it was his height or his broad shoulders, or maybe it was his unconscious air of command. Among the soft, pampered company, he stood out like an eagle among pigeons.

Alice didn't know what to say. She was aware of thick dark hair cropped short; a bold, aristocratic nose, which looked as if it had been broken at least once; a firm chin and piercing gray eyes that bored into her. They were almost hypnotic.

His skin was tanned, as if he'd lived an outdoor life. It wasn't at all a fashionable look. It made him look tough. Hard. Ungentlemanly.

And yet she found him disturbingly attractive.

She felt a blush rising. It stiffened her spine. She didn't know this man, had never been introduced and didn't like the way his eyes met hers without a trace of self-consciousness. She'd had enough of arrogant men to last a lifetime. She lifted her chin and met his gaze full on. She would not be intimidated.

His mouth quirked. His eyes darkened.

"Excuse me, please." She waited for him to step aside.

He didn't move, just watched her with a faint smile playing around his firm, well-shaped mouth.

She gave him a cold look and stepped pointedly around him. She was aware, as she walked away, of those gray eyes following her shamelessly. It was like a warm, unsettling touch.

She presented him with a straight spine in return.

"Who was that?" Lucy whispered.

"No idea. Whoever he is, he needs a lesson in manners." She felt cross and ridiculously flustered. Those bold glances, that air of assurance, as if he had every right to accost her when they'd never even been introduced.

All these years she'd been invisible to men. Now, because she was widowed . . . Or was it the dress? Was it too revealing after all? She glanced down. It wasn't. The neckline was restrained and discreet.

But she couldn't shake the feeling that she should have worn her old dove-gray gown. Or one of her dusty blacks.

"He seemed to know you."

"Well, I don't know him." She'd never seen him before in her life; she was sure of it. He was not the sort of man one forgot.

"Perhaps, but he obviously *wants* to know you." Lucy glanced back, eyeing him curiously. "How is it that a man can be—well, he's rugged more than handsome, and yet somehow he's more attractive than the really handsome men here. He makes them look, I don't know, *pretty*. And a bit useless."

Alice gave her a sharp glance. Was Lucy interested in him? Young girls did often look to older men for a husband.

"A pity he's so old," Lucy finished.

"*Old*? He can't be above forty," Alice said crossly.

"Yes, as I said, 'old.'" Lucy gave her a mischievous look. "Besides, he's interested in you, not me."

"Me? Nonsense!" Alice said briskly. "Now, let me introduce you to these girls."

The girls were clustered together near the window, talking and laughing hilariously. Lord, had she ever been so young and carefree? And why were there so many young ladies at a supposedly small family party. Only two of the six were in any way related to the family, and they were both distant—second or third cousins.

Alice greeted the girls she knew, and after the various introductions had been made, she edged quietly back, so as not to inhibit them.

After a few minutes of initially tentative conversation, the girls started to relax. Then Lucy said something that made them all laugh, and after that they were all talking and laughing happily. Alice smiled to herself: their silly, lighthearted chatter made her feel positively ancient.

Several of the girls' mothers were sitting at the side of the room, keeping a weather eye on their daughters while having a cozy chat. Should she join them? None was particularly a friend, but perhaps it was time to start making friends of her own, other than the ladies Thaddeus had instructed her to cultivate.

Not onc of them had called after Thaddeus died.

Two older gentlemen approached the group of girls, flirting ponderously—no danger there. The other mothers didn't give them more than a glance. Alice was pleased to see that while Lucy made no effort to put herself forward, going by the attention both gentlemen paid her, she was making a good impression.

It seemed the badly behaved Lucy really was a thing of the past.

Feeling thirsty, Alice signaled to a footman who was gliding through the crowd bearing a tray of gently fizzing glasses. He didn't see her. She looked around for another footman and lifted her hand, but he, too, didn't notice. Why was it that women of a certain age seemed to become invisible?

The chattering girls suddenly fell silent. Had Lucy made a mistake? Alice glanced around. All eyes were turned in her direction, and there was a sudden fluttering of fans and eyelashes. One girl gave a nervous giggle, hastily stifled. What on earth?

"Aunt Alice," said a voice at her elbow.

She turned. "Oh, Gerald. Many happy returns of the day. Are you enjoying your party?" She glanced briefly at the tall man who stood at her nephew's elbow. Him again.

"I'd like you to meet my former commanding officer, Colonel—Lord Tarrant. Tarrant, this is my aunt, the dowager Lady Charlton."

The tall man bowed over Alice's hand. "Delighted to meet you, my lady."

"Colonel Lord Tarrant," she murmured.

"Just Lord Tarrant," he said. "I'm no longer a colonel. I've sold out. And you look far too young and pretty to be a dowager." His gray gaze didn't shift. She felt her cheeks warming.

Was he one of those—the kind of man who thought a

widow was up for anything? She knew perfectly well she was neither young nor pretty.

"Allow me to fetch you a drink." He lifted a finger—one finger!—and immediately two footmen glided up—two!—presenting her with a choice of ratafia, champagne or lemonade. Trying not to feel aggrieved, she accepted a glass of lemonade and drank thirstily.

The girls behind her were still whispering and giggling.

Gerald leaned toward Alice and said quietly, "That girl you came in with—the girl in the golden gown—would I have met her somewhere?"

"I doubt it," Alice said. The colonel's intense regard was unsettling her. She wished he'd go away. "She's only just come to London. Her name is Lucy Bamber, and she's my goddaughter."

Gerald hadn't taken his eyes off Lucy. "Will you introduce us?"

She hesitated, recalling Almeria's demand, but she could hardly refuse to introduce them when Gerald had specifically asked her. "Yes, of course. Lucy?" She beckoned.

Lucy turned and noticed Gerald, and her bright smile abruptly faded. For a split second Alice could have sworn there was a panicked look in her eyes, but before she could be sure of what she'd seen, Lucy was approaching with nothing more than an expression of mild inquiry.

The girlish whispering and giggling stopped. Looks were exchanged, and the small group of young ladies focused intently, like pointers scenting prey. Their mothers' heads came up, and all conversation stopped.

Ohhh. Of course. These girls and their mothers were here for Gerald.

Feeling like a sparrow watched by a circle of cats, Alice introduced Lucy to her nephew, and he introduced her to his former colonel, Lord Tarrant. But it was clear that Gerald had eyes only for Lucy.

"Have you been in London long, Miss Bamber?" he asked.

"Not long." Lucy plied her fan and gazed across the room, apparently uninterested.

"Have you seen many of the city sights yet?"

"Not yet."

"Perhaps I could show you some of them—with Aunt Alice, of course, or some suitable companion." Alice was surprised by his offer. Gerald never squired young ladies around. He couldn't possibly be interested in Lucy, could he?

"Perhaps," Lucy said vaguely. Her gaze wandered over the crowd.

"Are you interested in art? I'm told the Elgin Marbles are very popular." Then, when Lucy didn't respond, he added, "Or perhaps you prefer flowers. Kew Gardens has some remarkable specimens from all over the world.

"Mmm? Flowers? My godmother has flowers in her garden," she said in a seen-one-flower-seen-them-all kind of voice.

Alice didn't know whether to laugh or weep. On the one hand, she was relieved that Lucy was showing no interest in Gerald. But oh, she was being so naughty.

Gerald persisted. "Perhaps Astley's Amphitheatre would be more to your taste. They put on some quite spectacular shows."

Lucy gazed at something over to the right and didn't answer.

"Miss Bamber? Did you hear me?" Gerald sounded annoyed. He was not used to young ladies ignoring him. Quite the contrary. "I asked you about Astley's Amphitheatre."

For a moment Lucy didn't respond at all, then said in an awed voice, "That woman over there is wearing the largest turban I've ever seen in my life. I wonder how she makes it stay on." All eyes except Gerald's swiveled toward the lady with the enormous turban.

Gerald's gaze didn't shift from Lucy's face. "You know, I have the oddest feeling that we've met before."

Lucy sighed. "So many gentlemen use that line. It's not very original."

"No, I'm serious. I'm sure I've seen—"

"Have you met these ladies, Lord Thornbury?" Lucy turned and beckoned her erstwhile companions forward. They closed the gap in seconds, shoving and elbowing one another with genteel, ladylike determination.

"Thorn*ton*, it's Lord Thornton," Gerald began but quickly found himself surrounded by fluttering, chattering, bashful and flirtatious young ladies. Lucy slipped to the edge of the circle, looking pleased with herself, and began talking again to the two elderly gentlemen who'd been abandoned.

By sharing Gerald with her new friends, she'd made a good impression on them—and their mothers, Alice observed. It seems Lucy really wasn't interested in lords. Not in Gerald, at least. That would please Almeria.

Only what on earth had got into her that she would behave in such an impudent and mischievous manner toward Gerald—who was, after all, the guest of honor? It verged on the insolent.

Over the bobbing heads of the eager debutantes, Gerald gave Alice and the tall colonel a hunted look.

Lord Tarrant laughed softly. "Ah, the perils of being young and eligible. Another lemonade, my lady? Or perhaps an ice?"

"Thank you, no." Alice suddenly realized that she was more or less alone with this big, looming colonel. Former colonel. Lord Tarrant. He presented his arm and said, "Shall we take a turn around the room?"

She looked around for an excuse to escape, someone needing to be talked to, but there was nobody, not a single person looking in her direction. Even Lucy seemed happily occupied, chatting to the two elderly gentlemen and observing her new friends parading their charms to a harassed-looking Gerald.

Trapped, Alice glanced back up at her tall companion.

He looked amused. "No urgent appointment? Nobody needing your exclusive attention? Then, shall we?"

"Thank you," she muttered and took his arm.

They strolled around the room.

"I understand you are a widow."

She tensed. "Yes."

"My condolences."

Alice inclined her head in acknowledgement. She could hardly admit she was glad to be free of her husband, and it felt hypocritical to be accepting condolences.

They strolled on. "I knew your late husband slightly," he said after a few minutes.

"Indeed?"

"Yes, at school."

"Mmm." She made a vague, polite, indifferent noise.

Another few minutes passed, then he said, "We were not contemporaries, of course. He was in his final year, and I was a small boy in my first year."

"Mmm."

"I was not an admirer."

She had no intention of discussing her husband with anyone, let alone this big, unsettling stranger. If he wanted to fish for information, he would be disappointed. "The weather has been very pleasant lately," she said. "It augurs well for the harvest."

"Indeed. Are you interested in agricultural matters, Lady Charlton?"

"Not in the least."

The smoky gray eyes glinted with amusement. "You grew up in the country, I understand. Whereabouts?"

"Worcestershire."

"A pretty part of the country. I myself am from just outside Kenilworth in Warwickshire. Do you know it?"

"No." She pressed her lips together. She was being horridly uncivil, she knew. Normally she was quite good at keeping a conversation bubbling along. With any other man, she would be asking questions—men always liked to talk about themselves—and encouraging him to talk about his home or the harvest or his military career or his horses or whatever he was interested in, but she didn't want to offer this man any encouragement.

What was it about him? Apart from the way he had initially accosted her, his manners had been unexceptional. She'd been prepared for an improper suggestion, or at least a hint. Instead he'd been all consideration.

But he unsettled her. The way he looked at her. And the way he refused to take a hint, apparently indifferent to her patent lack of interest in him or his conversation. And that look of . . . of amused understanding in his eyes, as if he knew what she was thinking. But he didn't. He couldn't.

Some men were so wrapped up in their own importance that they didn't notice when a woman was bored or uninterested or even—she thought of Thaddeus—quietly furious. They just talked on, confident of their intrinsic fascination.

But this man wasn't like that, she was sure. He seemed perfectly aware that she was doing her best to freeze him out. And it seemed to amuse him. Which was very annoying.

She was also very aware of the warmth and strength of the arm on which she'd laid her gloved hand. Just to be polite. And that was irritating, too. She didn't want to be aware of him. She just wanted him to go away.

Somehow he's more attractive than the really handsome men here. It was true. She would feel much more comfortable with a useless, pretty man. This one . . . His mere physical presence unsettled her. As for those all-seeing gray eyes that kept capturing hers and making her forget where she was. She was too . . . too conscious of him.

They finished their second circumnavigation of the room, and she was determined it would be their last. Just as she was casting around for a reason to excuse herself, music began in the second reception room. She started. Almeria hadn't mentioned any dancing. Where was Lucy?

Lucy had told Alice that she knew how to dance, but that she'd never been to a proper dance or a fashionable ball.

Alice knew from her own experience that there was a wealth of difference between country dancing as it was done in the actual country and the way people danced country dances in society.

She scanned the room quickly. There was no sign of Lucy.

"Would you care to dance, my lady?"

She shook her head. "Thank you, no. I am here tonight *en chaperone*."

"Ah, yes, the goddaughter who has so intrigued young Thornton. Looks like she's joined the dancers in the other room. We'd better follow them in." Before she could say a word, Alice found herself being propelled toward the second reception room, his hand lightly resting in the small of her back. "There she is, with your nephew," Lord Tarrant murmured.

Alice made a small sound of dismay. Almeria would be furious.

Gerald and Lucy were on the dance floor, the dance quite lively, but their expressions told a different story. Lucy looked perfectly indifferent, even bored. Gerald was obviously frustrated.

"Miss Bamber doesn't look as though she's enjoying the dance," Lord Tarrant said.

"She'll be minding her steps," Alice murmured. She hoped it was true.

"Our hostess looks even unhappier about it," Lord Tarrant observed.

Alice followed his gaze. Almeria stood at the side of the dance floor, glaring at her son and Lucy. Almeria swung her gaze around the room, fixed it on Alice, standing at the entrance, and stalked toward her.

"Oh dear," Alice murmured.

Lord Tarrant glanced down at her. "Trouble on the way?"

"I'm afraid so." Alice took a deep breath and braced herself for Almeria's tirade.

"Right then." Lord Tarrant took Alice by the hand and, without warning, swung her into a nearby set of dancers.

"What on earth?" she gasped. But the dancers around them happily adjusted to an extra couple in the set.

He swung her around masterfully. "Do you dislike dancing?"

"No, but—"

He twirled her in a circle, and she was too breathless to speak.

The top couple danced down the row, and everyone clapped to the beat. After a quick glance at Almeria, fulminating on the sidelines, Alice clapped along obediently.

"I told you I had no intention of dancing tonight," she told Lord Tarrant when they met in the next movement. Almeria would be even more furious now, imagining that Alice had deliberately thrown Gerald and Lucy together. And was now avoiding her.

"I know, but the situation called for action," he said solemnly. His eyes gleamed with amusement.

She snorted. "Action?"

"Retreat and regroup—an old army tactic. Avoid a confrontation unless you can be sure of winning."

"Since when is dancing an army tactic?"

"Oh, Wellington is all for dancing—all his staff officers were excellent dancers. It's a very healthful—and strategic—exercise," he said with a virtuous air that fooled her not at all.

She wanted to laugh, but she didn't want to encourage him.

"Besides," he added as they came together again, "did you really want to stay and listen to whatever that woman has to say to you? She looks ready to explode."

Alice didn't, of course, but Almeria would say her piece eventually. She always did.

"As for being here *en chaperone*," he continued, "isn't

this a much more agreeable way of keeping a close eye on your charge?"

"Agreeable for whom?" she said tartly as she circled gracefully around him.

Those gray eyes had a wicked gleam in them. "For me, of course. I wouldn't dare speculate about how you might feel. I don't yet know what pleases you."

Yet. As if he planned to discover what pleased her. No one had ever cared to discover what pleased her.

He was flirting. He was definitely flirting. And she had to nip it in the bud before he got ideas. She wasn't that sort of widow.

Her first ever ton party, and she was dancing with a lord. Papa would be thrilled. Lucy was decidedly unthrilled.

Of all the lords in all the houses . . . And for him to be Lady Charlton's nephew!

Had she known this party was for the arrogant fellow she'd encountered on the Brighton road, she'd never have come; she would have pretended she had the headache or something.

As it was, she'd done her best to avoid talking to him. She'd deliberately caused him to be swamped by marriage-minded debutantes, distracting him from looking too closely at her. And had turned her back on him and flirted madly with the two old fellows. Old sweethearts they were, too.

She'd been about to quietly slip away, but the minute the music sounded in the next room, Lord Thornton looked at her over the heads of the other girls—he was annoyingly tall—and asked her to dance. By name, so there would be no mistake.

Curse him. If he hadn't been a lord, and she hadn't encountered him on the Brighton road that day, she would have accepted like a shot. He was rather good-looking, and despite the fuss the other girls were making of him, he didn't seem too big-headed.

But he was wrong for her in every way possible.

She'd pretended not to hear, but the clot of eager debutantes had parted like the Red Sea, leaving a clear path for Lord Thornton to step forward and repeat his invitation.

She'd looked around for Alice, but she was occupied talking to her tall admirer. So with all eyes on her, and it being the first dance at a birthday party for this wretched lord, Lucy had no option but to accept.

He led her into the next room, where people were beginning to form sets. "So, Miss Bamber, you've only just arrived in town."

"Apparently so." Imitating the haughtiest of her former schoolfellows, a girl she'd christened Lady Languid, Lucy gave him the sort of smile she hoped looked both cool and enigmatic. And repellant.

"Are you enjoying living in London?"

"It's tolerable." Lady Languid always spoke in an affected drawl. Nothing was ever fun or even enjoyable; everything was tolerable or intolerable or barely tolerable or insipid or dreary.

They danced on.

"Where were you living before?"

Lucy gave him a cold glance, but otherwise ignored him.

Apparently unaffected, he continued, "You're quite a mystery, aren't you? Everyone is wondering where you've sprung from."

She arched a brow and said languidly, "They must have very dull lives to be so easily intrigued."

They separated in the dance, and when they came back together, he seemed to have dropped—thank goodness—his interrogation about her origins. "You're very light on your feet, Miss Bamber. You clearly enjoy dancing."

"It's tolerable."

"What else do you enjoy? Music?"

"It's tolerable."

"Do you play an instrument?"

"No." Would the man never give up?

"Sing?"

"No." Only for her own enjoyment. Never for performance. What was it Frau Steiner had told her? *Your technique is execrable, your instrument barely mediocre*—Lucy's "instrument" being her voice. Opera singers. What did they know? Singing was for joy, not just for performance.

She glanced over to where Alice was dancing with her tall admirer. If she knew how Lucy was treating her nephew at his own birthday party, she'd probably be appalled. Lucy was a bit appalled herself, but she had to ensure Lord Thornton wanted nothing to do with her in future.

And to give nothing away.

But Lord Thornton seemed unaffected by her haughty behavior. Perhaps he was used to this kind of conversation. He probably knew lots of much haughtier ladies—the haughtiest lady Lucy had met here tonight was his mother, which made sense. The other girls she'd met had been quite friendly—especially after she'd called them over to talk with Lord Thornton.

The dance continued. He circled around her, regarding her thoughtfully.

"You know, I have the strongest feeling we've met before."

Curse the man. Couldn't he take a hint? Lucy sighed ostentatiously. "That line didn't work the first time, and to repeat it is really rather . . . sad." How long would this wretched dance go on for? Any minute he was going to work out where he'd seen her before, and then it wouldn't just be embarrassing for her; it would be awful for Alice.

"I mean it," he continued. "Your face is oddly familiar to me. I just can't place it."

"Nonsense, I have a very ordinary face. There are girls like me everywhere."

He seemed to take that as an invitation to look at her in quite a personal manner. "I don't find you ordinary at all."

Lucy felt her cheeks warming, and it was with relief that

she launched into the next stage of the dance, "stripping the willow," in which she had to twirl around all the other men in the set, and conversation was impossible.

But the minute conversation became possible again, Lord Persistent said, "Perhaps I've met some of your relatives, and what I'm noticing is a family resemblance."

It wasn't easy to shrug while dancing, but Lucy managed it. "Perhaps."

"Would I have met any of your relatives?"

"I've no idea." She gave him a wide-eyed, limpid look. "Would you?"

His eyes narrowed, and at that point Lucy decided to give up on the Lady Languid imitation. It wasn't putting him off in the least. Time to change the subject.

"I understand you were at Waterloo, Lord Thornbroke. What was that like?"

"Thornton," he corrected her. "Lord Thornton. War is not a pleasant subject for ladies. The best I can say of it is that it put an end once and for all to the depredations of Napoleon."

"You're not worried he will escape again?"

"No, his rule is well and truly broken. His time is over."

"And so you've sold your commission and returned to civilian life. How are you finding that?"

"Tolerable." His expression made it clear he'd chosen the word deliberately and was indicating that what was sauce for the g—no, she wasn't even going to *think* about geese.

"And so today is your birthday?"

"Yes."

Was he being deliberately difficult? She tried a different subject. "So, tell me, Lord Thorncliffe, are you a sporting man?"

"Thorn*ton*, it's Lord Thorn*ton*," he said grimly. "I played cricket at school, of course, but if by 'sporting' you mean riding to hounds, no. I don't hunt. I'll shoot game, as long as it's for the pot, and I enjoy fishing when I get the chance."

"And where do you like to go fishing?"

He glanced at her. "Are you really interested in my fishing habits?"

She smiled sweetly. "Not at all, but one must make conversation, mustn't one?"

He let out a huff of laughter, which wasn't at all her intention. Then, thankfully, what had felt like the longest dance in the history of dances finally ended. "Thank goodness that's over," she said as they bowed and curtsied to each other.

One dark brow rose. "You didn't enjoy the dance?"

She smiled. "It's just that I'm frightfully thirsty." She glanced around and saw the other Lady Charlton signaling him, a grim expression on her face. "Oh, look over there—your mama wants you. Hadn't you better run along?" As if he were eight instead of eight-and-twenty.

He didn't even glance in his mother's direction. "I did not survive years at war with Napoleon's forces only to dance to my mother's tune," he said, escorting Lucy to a nearby seat. "I'll fetch you a drink. And then, perhaps you'll grant me a second dance."

Lucy had to admit she liked his matter-of-fact attitude, but she couldn't afford to let him get to know her any better. The minute he'd gone, she jumped up and hurried across the room to where Alice was standing with her tall admirer.

"Godmama," she said, "excuse me for interrupting, but I feel the most horrid headache coming on. Would it be possible for me to go home early?" She fixed Alice with an intense look, hoping she got the message.

"Yes, of course," Alice responded instantly. "You poor dear, you're looking quite pale. We must leave at once, get you into bed with an eau de cologne compress."

Lord Tarrant glanced at Lucy. His mouth quirked. "Dear me, yes, that's the palest flush I've seen in a long time."

Alice's lips compressed. "Come along, Lucy dear, we will just make our apologies to our hostess and be off. Goodbye, Lord Tarrant, so . . . interesting to have met you."

They hurried away.

"Do I really look pale?" Lucy whispered.

Alice glanced at her. "No, but it was the first thing that came to mind. Drat him."

"You wanted to leave early, too?"

She nodded. "Now hush and try to look ill," she said to Lucy as they approached their hostess, who was also called Lady Charlton. Lucy found it very confusing.

"Almeria, I'm very sorry but—" Alice began.

"So you ought to be!" The other Lady Charlton gave Lucy a scathing look. "I warned you about attempting to entice my son with your . . . your *guest*." The way she said *guest* it might have been dipped in vitriol.

"Gerald asked to be introduced. I could hardly refuse," Alice said calmly.

"And then they *danced* together." Lady Charlton glared at Lucy as if she'd committed the crime of the century. Old bag.

"Yes, because Gerald asked her in front of others. She could hardly refuse that, either," Alice said. "And now, Almeria, we're leaving. Miss Bamber has the headache."

Lady Charlton sniffed.

Lucy tried to look pale and wan. She was impressed with Alice's cool responses. If anyone had spoken to her like that, she would have snapped back, and probably lost her temper. But Alice had responded so calmly and reasonably, the other Lady Charlton had nowhere to go—you could see the frustration on her face.

Even more impressive was that Alice had defended Lucy. Nobody had ever defended Lucy.

"Thank you for inviting us," Alice said. "It's been a delightful party."

"Yes, thank you so much," Lucy murmured. She glanced back and saw Lord Thornton holding a glass of ratafia and looking around. She slipped an arm through Alice's, and they quietly slipped away.

* * *

Did my nephew upset you in some way?" Alice asked once they'd reached home.

Lucy was embarrassed to explain, but it had to be done. "No, I'm not upset—but oh, Alice, he's going to be a problem."

"In what way?"

"I've met your nephew before—and not in the best of circumstances." She told her about their encounter on the Brighton road.

Alice regarded her wide-eyed. "You mean *you're* the reason Gerald lost his race?"

Lucy nodded. "Well, it was the goose, really. He'd stopped because of her. I just collected her off the road." And held him up further, by giving him a piece of her mind as well.

Alice let out a muffled snort. "A *goose*? Gerald lost his race because of a goose? Oh, he won't like people knowing that."

"No, and the way I was dressed, in my old clothes and an apron, and with my hair down and blowing about—I'm sure he thought me some kind of maidservant or farm girl. And the way he spoke to me, ordering me off the road as if he owned it—well, it was so, so *lordly*, it made him want to cheek him. And so I did." He'd been furious.

Alice was still chuckling. "A goose. No wonder he didn't explain. But what were you doing with a goose anyway?"

"She's the comtesse's pet goose."

"Your comtesse has a pet goose?"

Lucy nodded. "Apparently back in France at the height of the Terror, the comte was imprisoned in Paris—she heard later they chopped his head off—and the comtesse was alone in their castle in the country. One night something had stirred up the local peasants, and they marched on the castle carrying sickles and pitchforks and burning brands. The castle geese started hissing and honking like mad, and when she looked out to see what the matter was, she saw the peasants coming for her. She managed to grab her jewels and escape, but her castle was burned to the ground.

"And ever since then she's kept a pair of geese—Ghislaine and Gaston—to protect and warn her. But Ghislaine is naughty and likes to wander, and she wandered onto the road when your nephew was coming."

"It was lucky he missed her."

"He stopped, actually." Lucy hadn't expected that. Most lordly types she'd encountered would have driven straight over a goose. But then he'd shouted at her, and still shaken by the close encounter, she'd snapped and shouted back.

She wished now she hadn't, because he obviously recognized her, even if he didn't yet realize why.

"Ghislaine and Gaston, what a tale." Alice sobered. "So you and that goose were the reason poor Gerald lost his precious race. Oh dear. He's not likely to forget that. Or forgive."

Lucy nodded. "I know. I'm going to have to avoid him. He already thinks he knows me from somewhere."

"Yes, I see. It does make things rather awkward."

"That's why I wasn't very polite to him tonight. I tried to give him a disgust of me so he won't want to have anything to do with me in future."

"It won't be easy, seeing he's my nephew." Alice glanced at Lucy, her expression faintly embarrassed. "I wasn't particularly polite to his friend, either."

"The tall colonel?"

"He's not a colonel anymore."

"Is that why you were rude to him?"

"No, of course not. And I wasn't rude, exactly, just not very encouraging."

Lucy was perplexed. "But he liked you, I could tell."

"I don't care. I don't want to encourage him."

"Why not? What's wrong with him? Was he too forward? Coarse? Suggestive?" Men often were, in Lucy's experience. Especially lordly types. But surely they wouldn't behave like that to a proper, gentle lady like Lady Charlton, would they?

"No, no, nothing like that. He was a perfect gentleman." Alice sighed. "It doesn't matter. I'm tired. I'm going to bed."

Hours later Alice lay in bed, sleepless, twisting, restless between her sheets. She couldn't get Lord Tarrant out of her mind. He'd behaved perfectly politely—apart from initially addressing her without being introduced. So why had she reacted to him that way?

He hadn't made any kind of nasty proposition—he'd just looked at her with an expression in his eyes, an expression she didn't even know the meaning of—and she'd fled from his presence like a nervous virgin, which lord knew she wasn't.

Somehow, he'd stirred sensations in her—with just a look from those hypnotic eyes, like a winter lake, silver against the tan of his skin. Sensations she'd never felt before. Sensations she didn't want to feel.

I don't yet know what pleases you.

Yet. As if it were some kind of promise. No one had ever cared to discover what pleased her.

She turned over and punched her pillow.

Why couldn't she stop thinking about him? And how could a mere glance from those eyes feel like a . . . like a caress? It was . . . unsettling. Wrong.

She was too . . . too aware of him. His height, his strength, the faint fragrance of his shaving soap. The indefinable air of masculinity about him.

As if he were some kind of tall, well-made magnet and she some feeble creature made of iron filings.

She punched the pillow again. She was no feeble iron-filing creature. She refused to be.

Chapter Six

The morning after the party, Gerald's manservant brought up a note with his morning coffee, a message from his mother requesting him to call on her urgently. The fact that it was just after nine o'clock and his mother was sending notes made him think it must indeed be urgent: Mama rarely rose before eleven.

On the other hand, it was Mama sending the note. Gerald finished his breakfast, washed, shaved and dressed, and set off shortly before ten.

His mother's butler ushered him into her bedchamber, where she sat in bed, swathed in a sumptuous silk dressing gown, propped up with half a dozen pillows, with her writing desk over her knees and correspondence scattered around her.

She presented her cheek to be kissed. "About time, Gerald. I sent that note at quarter to nine."

He obediently touched his lips to her already powdered and rouged cheek. "What's this about, Mother?"

"You danced with that gel last night."

"I danced with a dozen girls," he said in a bored voice. "I understood that was the point."

"Don't be facetious, you know very well which gel I mean—Alice's foundling."

"Alice's *foundling*?"

His mother made an impatient gesture. "She might as well be. Nobody has ever heard of her. She has no fortune, no looks to speak of and nothing to recommend her. I am told you even asked her for a second dance. Is that correct?"

"I intended to, but she'd already left."

His mother sniffed. "I warned Alice I would not tolerate her throwing the wretched gel at you. I'm glad to see she listened, for a change."

"Aunt Alice didn't have anything to do with it."

"She introduced you, after I'd specifically ordered her not to."

Gerald stiffened. "You ordered her not to?"

"Of course. I don't want you having anything to do with that gel. She is not the sort of gel I want my son to associate with. Is that understood?"

"Perfectly, Mother," he said crisply. He turned on his heel and, fuming, stalked from the room. How dare she think she could tell him who he could and could not see? Or dance with. Or anything.

He set out immediately to call on his aunt. And her so-called foundling.

Really, Mama was outrageous. He didn't know much about Miss Bamber—and, it had to be admitted, the girl had given him no encouragement—but as for *no looks to speak of*, what utter rubbish. Miss Bamber was both lively and pretty. In fact, he found her disturbingly attractive. And intriguing.

Lucy was on her way downstairs when the front doorbell sounded. She paused on the landing and drew back out of sight, clutching her old carpetbag to her chest. Alice had warned her that after their attendance at her sister-in-law's party the previous evening, there were likely to be morning calls and that Lucy should be prepared.

But morning calls were conducted in the early part of the afternoon, and yet here it was, not yet eleven o'clock, and someone was at the door.

She glanced down at herself. She was wearing one of her old dresses, worn and faded, too tight across the chest and short, showing her ankles. She hadn't expected to meet anyone. It was a lovely morning and she planned to spend a few hours painting.

So far she hadn't met a soul in the garden, only a gardener who'd nodded but otherwise ignored her, which pleased her greatly. Privacy and time to herself were a gift she'd had little of in recent years.

Tweed opened the door. "Good morning, Lord Thornton."

Lucy drew back, listening.

"Is my aunt in?"

"She is, my lord, but I'm afraid she is not yet ready to receive visitors. However, if you would care to wait a few minutes, I'm sure she will want to see you." Lucy watched as the butler ushered Lord Thornton into the front drawing room, then mounted the stairs in his usual stately manner.

Lucy crept down the stairs on tiptoe.

"Miss Bamber."

Blast! Lord Thornton stood in the doorway of the drawing room. Lucy pretended not to hear and hurried on.

"Miss Bamber." Louder now.

Cursing silently, she turned, clutching her bag to her chest, and gave him a blank, 'Do I know you?' kind of look.

"Lord Thornton," he prompted after a moment. "Good morning, Miss Bamber." His gaze ran over her, and though he gave no sign that he noticed her shabby old dress, the faint cleft between his brows told her he did. She tensed. It was too close to the clothing she'd worn at their encounter on the road.

What was he doing here, making a morning call at eleven o'clock like some kind of ignorant bumpkin? Lords were supposed to know these things.

He inclined his head. "I trust you enjoyed yourself last night."

"Last night?" she echoed, as if she had no idea what he was talking about.

His frown deepened. "At the party given by my mother." And when she didn't respond, he added, "Almeria, Lady Charlton."

"Lady Charlton is upstairs," she said helpfully. "I don't know anyone called Almeria."

"My aunt is the *dowager* Lady Charlton. Almeria, Lady Charlton, is my mother." He sounded annoyed. Good.

Lucy smiled vaguely. "Really? How nice for you. Now, I must be going. Nice to meet you, Lord . . . er."

The furrow between his brows deepened. "Thornton," he grated. "We were introduced last night. You danced with me."

"Of course," she said in an unconvinced manner. "So we did." Footsteps on the stairs above indicated his aunt was on her way. "Goodbye, Lord Thornfield. So nice to meet you." Hiding a smile, Lucy hurried away.

Behind her, she heard Lord Thornton say, "Thorn*ton*." Lucy grinned. She waited out of sight and listened as Alice greeted her nephew.

"That so-called goddaughter of yours, has she got rats in her attic?" Lord Thornton said bluntly. Lucy bristled at the "so-called." The rest of the question made her smile.

Alice responded. "What on earth do you mean, Gerald?"

"I just saw her in the hall. She had no recollection of meeting me last night."

"Oh, well, she probably forgot you. She came down with the headache, and we had to leave early."

"Really?" He sounded quite skeptical.

"Yes. Also there were a great many people at the party.

Many more than your mother had suggested to me beforehand. I expect poor Lucy was just overwhelmed."

"Overwhelmed?" He snorted. "If that girl was overwhelmed, I'm a Dutchman."

"She wasn't? Oh, I'm so pleased. It's quite difficult when you're a young girl meeting so many people for the first time, having to be on your best behavior at your first ton party."

"She danced with me," Lord Thornton reminded her.

"Yes, I saw. Very prettily, too, I thought. I was worried she hadn't been adequately instructed, but her performance was all that anyone could wish for."

"Her conversation, on the other hand, left a great deal to be desired. Like getting blood out of a stone."

"Really? And yet Sir Edward Platt told me my ward was charming, and Lord Anthony Pellew sent us each a posy this morning." Listening from behind the stairs, Lucy was touched to realize that Alice was defending her. Again.

"I'm talking about the way she spoke to *me*."

"Perhaps you intimidated her. You military fellows can be quite intimidating, you know. That tall friend of yours, for instance."

"I did not intimidate her!" Lord Thornton snapped. "I doubt anyone could intimidate that chit." Lucy smothered a giggle.

"You're not suggesting she was rude to you, Gerald, are you?" Alice sounded shocked.

"No, not exactly rude, just . . . uncooperative."

"I expect she was minding her steps," Alice said in a soothing voice.

The grinding of Lord Thornton's teeth was almost audible.

"Was there some reason you called this early?" Alice asked Gerald.

He gave her a blank stare, then re-collected himself. "I intended to invite you and Miss Bamber to drive out with me this afternoon."

"I'm so sorry," Alice said, "but we are both engaged this afternoon. But thank you for the thought."

"Perhaps another time?"

"Perhaps," she said vaguely. "Though if you're just being polite, Gerald, and only showing hospitality toward Lucy because she is my goddaughter—and because I suppose your mother has warned you off her—there is no need to bother. Sir Edward Platt and Lord Anthony Pellew have both offered to show Lucy some of the sights of London."

"Those old roués!" he exploded. "Each one is old enough to be her father—Sir Edward could even be her grandfather!"

"Which doesn't mean they can't be perfectly charming hosts," Alice said in mild reproof. "It's a tour of city sights we're talking about, not marriage."

Lord Thornton gave a cynical snort. "Anyway, she said she wasn't interested in seeing the sights."

"And yet she accepted both invitations," Alice said gently.

Lucy could almost hear the brooding silence coming from the drawing room. Laughing softly, she took the big iron key and let herself out into the garden.

She found herself a quiet, sunny corner, opened her bag and set out her paints.

The following day, James, temporarily fed up with the demands of roofers, plasterers, painters, plumbers and chimney sweeps, headed out in the afternoon on horseback for some fresh air, exercise and peace. As he approached the park, he heard his name called. "Tarrant, I say. Colonel Tarrant!"

Turning his head, he saw Chichester, a young military gentleman of his acquaintance, also on horseback, approaching and waving as he threaded through pedestrians and carts and hawkers.

"Heading for the park?" Chichester asked, and suggested they proceed together. "Ride there most days. Devilish pleasant."

James fell in with him, and as they talked and caught up on news and mutual acquaintances, he took little notice of their route. It had been an age since he'd ridden in London, and he assumed Chichester would know the best places.

The moment they entered the park, however, he realized that not only had he chosen his time poorly, he'd also chosen the wrong companion—and the wrong park entrance.

It was obviously the fashionable hour in Hyde Park. Throngs of fashionably dressed people jammed the pathways, strolling and talking. Smart carriages moved along Rotten Row at a crawl, as did plenty of riders on horseback.

"Splendid sight, what?" Chichester said, beaming. "All those pretty ladies."

James nodded. Curse it, he'd forgotten Chichester's penchant for flirtation. They wove slowly between barouches and phaetons, and men and ladies on horseback, and pedestrians impeding their progress. Carriages stopped without warning to take up or put down passengers or hail acquaintances on foot. Some people seemed to think nothing of holding up the traffic while they chatted to friends in other carriages, blocking the road entirely. James resigned himself to slow progress and silently plotted his escape route.

Then he noticed a particular pair of ladies strolling along, one tall and slender, dressed in a claret-colored pelisse and wearing a straw bonnet tied with a simple claret-colored ribbon. The other was younger and curvier and wore a green pelisse and a hat adorned with daisies.

"I'll see you later, Chichester," he said, directing his horse to the side. Throwing his leg over the saddle, he dropped lightly to the ground just as Lady Charlton and her goddaughter came level with him. As he greeted them, he heard a voice behind him saying, "Oh, I say. Fast work, Tarrant."

Chichester, curse him, had followed and also dismounted. He stood there grinning expectantly at the ladies. James, having no choice, introduced him, but once he saw which lady Chichester was beaming at, he said, "It's very crowded here. Lieutenant Chichester, why don't you walk ahead with Miss Bamber, and I will escort Lady Charlton."

Chichester and the girl happily agreed. Lady Charlton, however, hesitated. Her creamy complexion grew rosy under his gaze, her sea blue eyes were pools of doubt. Was she simply shy or was there something about him that disturbed her? She certainly disturbed him. Not since he was a young man had he been so instantly and powerfully drawn to a woman.

He presented his arm, and she gave his horse a nervous glance. "Don't you need to mind your horse?"

James smiled to himself. Her apparent reluctance to further their acquaintance did not extend to snubbing him in public.

"He's used to being led." He nodded ahead to where Chichester and Miss Bamber were walking and chatting while Chichester's mount ambled placidly along behind.

She glanced at his arm and with a sigh accepted it. They strolled along, his horse following behind. She glanced back several times.

"You're not fond of horses?" he asked.

She shook her head. "It's not that. I've never had much to do with them." She glanced back again. "They're very big, aren't they?"

Yes," he agreed solemnly. "Being rather tall, I need a taller horse. So you've never ridden?"

"No."

"I'm surprised. Most ladies I know who were brought up in the country ride to some extent."

"My father was a country vicar. Both he and my mother were brought up to ride and hunt, but Papa gave it up when he took orders—he didn't approve of it anymore—and Mama never rode again after she got married. Besides, the only horse we could afford was the one that pulled Papa's gig, and that was necessary for his parish visits. Papa took his vows very seriously, and every spare penny went to the poor of the parish. Or to 'the unconverted.'"

"'The unconverted'?"

"They were Papa's passion in life—he believed their souls were endangered unless they converted to Christianity. He and Mama sailed for the Far East shortly after my wedding."

"And are your parents still abroad?"

"In a manner of speaking," she said after a moment. "They died within months of arriving."

"I'm sorry." James hoped they weren't eaten by headhunters or boiled in a pot or another of the grisly fates so often encountered by missionaries attempting to force their foreign ways on perfectly contented native peoples, but there was no way he could ask such a thing. Especially when he was trying to charm a most reluctant lady.

She glanced at him and seemed to read his mind. "A tropical fever carried them both off."

"I see," he said, slightly relieved. "That must have been very difficult for you." Newly married, orphaned and with only her husband to support her. He couldn't imagine Thaddeus Paton supporting anyone except himself.

They strolled on in silence. Ahead of them, Chichester and Miss Bamber were chatting and laughing, clearly getting on well.

"Your Lieutenant Chichester," she said. "What's his background?"

"Not *my* Lieutenant Chichester," he stressed lightly. "Merely a chance-met acquaintance from my army days. But to answer your question, he's well-enough born, but a second son. He'll inherit no money or land and is destined to be a career soldier, though between you and me, he's not the kind of lad destined for greatness." He glanced at her and added in a lowered voice, "Unless your goddaughter is an heiress, I wouldn't encourage that connection. He's a gazetted flirt. When Chichester weds, which I expect won't be for a good few years, he'll undoubtedly marry for money."

She gave a slow nod, then turned to him with a smile that took his breath away. "Yes, that's exactly what I needed to know. Thank you."

He couldn't think of a thing to say. All he could think of was how lovely she was when she smiled. And how he wanted to make her smile more often.

She added, "I don't want Lucy to make the kind of mistake that—to make a mistake in her choice of husband."

The kind of mistake that she had made, he wondered?

"It's rather daunting," she continued, "being responsible for a young girl's future happiness."

"I'm sure she's in the best of all possible hands," he said. It was a commonplace response, a mere polite nothing, but for some reason the light in her eyes died, and she looked away, as if troubled. What had he said?

A slight breeze sprang up, stirring the leaves and the ladies' dresses. "We'd better go," Lady Charlton said abruptly. "We have an engagement to prepare for this evening." She called to Miss Bamber, bid James and Chichester goodbye and vanished into the fashionable throng, leaving James gazing after her.

"Are we in a hurry?" Lucy asked breathlessly as they wove swiftly through the crowd, nodding to acquaintances and calling out brief greetings but nothing more—which was quite uncivil. "Is there an appointment I've forgotten?"

Alice hurried on without answering. She had no reason for their flight—no reason she could acknowledge, that is, except to herself.

Panic, that was it.

Lord Tarrant had smiled down at her with such a look in his eyes. Intense and yet warm and approving and . . .

It had set off such flutters inside her.

She'd had no idea what to do.

And so she'd run.

Which was utterly pathetic!

But what else was she to do? She couldn't encourage him.

"It's going to rain," she told Lucy.

Lucy glanced at the clear blue sky. "I see. A bit like my pallor the other night, then. Only in your case, it was brought on by a certain tall former colonel."

"Nonsense," Alice muttered and hurried on. Lucy was uncomfortably perceptive at times. "What did you think of Lieutenant Chichester?"

Lucy snorted. "A silly rattle and too full of himself, but entertaining enough for a walk in the park."

Alice nodded. And then there were times she was grateful for Lucy's sharp mind.

To Alice's faint discomfort, Lord Tarrant called the following afternoon. Discomfort because, on reflection, she'd decided that she'd behaved foolishly the previous times she'd met him. She wasn't a green, impressionable girl; she was a sensible widow who knew exactly what she did and didn't want.

Just because a man had never sent her into a flutter before by his mere presence. And the way he looked at her . . . And his smile. It was no reason to get all hot and bothered.

She'd fallen out of the habit of socializing, that was all, and had read too much into the looks Lord Tarrant had given her. She wasn't ever going to marry again, and even if he did intend improper overtures, it was nothing to be anxious about, because she was most definitely not interested in having an affair. All that horrid bedroom activity was, thank goodness, behind her.

She was a mature, grown woman, and she would behave like one.

Lord Tarrant was her third male caller that afternoon.

Two of Thaddeus's friends had visited—separately. Word had obviously reached them that she was receiving again. The first had suggested with a leer that he was more than willing to help assuage her loneliness. The arrival of other visitors prevented her from sending him off with a flea in his ear, and though she itched to smack his oily, presumptuous face, she had to make do with an icy response.

The second of Thaddeus's friends, Sir Alec Grafton, had arrived just as several ladies were leaving, and just after Lucy had excused herself for a moment. He took advantage of her brief lack of company to lean forward, place a heavy hand on her knee and make an even more blatant offer.

She'd brushed away his hand like a repellent insect, and was in the process of coldly informing him that she was perfectly content as she was, thank you, and she'd be grateful if he never troubled her again—ever!—when Tweed announced Lord Tarrant.

He must have overheard her delivering the last part of her little speech. He gave Sir Alec a hard look as the man took his leave, but his expression was smooth as he greeted her and took the seat she waved him to. On the opposite side of the room.

There was a short, tense silence. If he so much as hinted that she might be lonely and in need of male company . . .

He rubbed his hands together. "Brrr, pretty chilly in here at the moment."

Alice blinked. It was a sunny afternoon, and if anything, it was rather warm.

His expression was an odd mix of rueful amusement. "Finding some of your visitors tedious, I gather."

"Not simply tedious—obnoxious, offensive and unwelcome."

"Dear me. If any more of that kind arrive, give me a wink and I'll toss them out on their ear."

Was he serious? Or was he making fun of her? She couldn't tell from his expression. Lucy returned, and two other ladies arrived. They exchanged greetings and made polite chitchat.

It quickly became clear that Lucy wasn't the focus of these ladies' visit. Alice was their target. Lady Fanstock, the older lady, was a grandmother, and she and her daughter had come with a view to presenting Lady Fanstock's middle-aged son, Threadbow, as a potential—nay, ideal—husband for Alice.

Lady Fanstock waxed long and lyrical about Threadbow's many fine qualities, and whenever she paused to draw breath, Threadbow's older sister filled the gap with more encomiums. Threadbow was clever, he was sensitive, he would cause her no worries of the wandering sort—he'd never been in the petticoat line—and it was a complete fabrication on people's part to suggest that he had weak lungs.

Alice nodded, murmured polite, noncommittal responses and wondered whether the clock was broken. The hands were moving so very, very slowly.

In the middle of one of these torrents of Threadbow praise, Alice happened to catch Lord Tarrant's eye. He raised a dark, sardonic brow, winked, then jerked his head toward the door in query.

Give me a wink, and I'll toss them out on their ear.

A bubble of laughter rose in her. She managed to turn it into a cough.

Tea and little iced cakes were then brought in.

Eventually Lady Fanstock and her daughter finished their tea and left. Lord Tarrant should have gone, too, but he made no move to depart, possibly because there were several little cakes remaining. It seemed Lord Tarrant had a sweet tooth. Before she could delicately suggest to him that his visit was well overdue to end, two more ladies arrived. He rose, greeted them politely and sat down again.

Alice resigned herself and called for a fresh pot of tea and more little cakes—somehow they'd all been eaten.

These lady visitors were visibly delighted with Lord

Tarrant and pelted him with questions—attempting to discover, none too subtly, his marital status, fortune and plans for the future, as well as his war experiences. She was amused to see how he deflected the more intrusive questions by changing the subject so adroitly that the ladies didn't realize it.

She wasn't surprised by their interest. There was something about him, something compelling. It wasn't just that he was tall and ruggedly attractive; he had an air of command—not the kind of swaggering arrogance that she associated with her late husband and some of his friends, but a quiet assurance. As if he were perfectly comfortable in his skin and had nothing to prove.

And of course there was the title and the fortune to go with it.

While his attention was on the other ladies—and the cakes—she took the opportunity to look at him, really look at him. Without those disturbing, knowing gray eyes observing her interest.

And that's all it was, she told herself—interest. Curiosity. Nothing else.

He was not heavy, as Thaddeus had been, but lean, with a body well used to hard exercise. And fighting, she reminded herself. He'd arrived wearing fine brown leather gloves. He'd removed them and now drew them through his long fingers over and over, as if restless—though in every other way he seemed relaxed.

He was closely shaved. The thought prompted the memory of the faint scent of his cologne the evening of the party. His thick, dark hair was cut short, almost brutally so. She thought she detected a slight hint of curl.

Alice repressed a smile. A number of men of her acquaintance cultivated a head of artistically arranged curls. She suspected some went to bed with their hair in rags, or perhaps their valets used curling irons. Lord Tarrant cut his curls off.

He was plainly dressed in immaculate buff breeches, which clung to his long, lean legs, with their hard, muscular thighs. His linen was pristine, his neckcloth was neat but not ostentatious, and his dark blue coat, clearly cut by a master tailor, hugged his broad shoulders. His boots gleamed with polish, and unlike most fashionable gentlemen of her acquaintance, there were no fobs dangling from his waistcoat, just a plain gold watch chain.

He'd stopped speaking, and she glanced up and found him watching her. Watching her watching him. Her cheeks warmed. Amusement glimmered in his eyes. And then she realized it wasn't just him—everyone in the room was looking at her. Expectantly.

"I'm so sorry," she said, addressing the ladies. "Were you talking to me? I'm afraid I was woolgathering."

"Quite all right, my dear," the older lady said, with a knowing sidelong glance at her companion. "I was just wondering whether you and your goddaughter are planning to attend the Peplowe masquerade ball next week."

"Yes, indeed, we're looking forward to it, aren't we, Lucy?" Alice said, willing her blush to fade. "Lady Peplowe and her daughter called here earlier." Lady Peplowe had very kindly sent a note the previous day adding Lucy to Alice's invitation, and assuring Alice that had she known Lucy was visiting, she would have been included in the original invitation. Alice was delighted. Penny Peplowe was a thoroughly nice girl, the kind that she hoped Lucy would become friends with.

The talk then turned to costumes, but as nobody wanted to reveal their costume plans in advance, the conversation soon dwindled. The two ladies rose to take their leave. Lord Tarrant rose also and bid them a courteous goodbye but made no move to follow them out.

The two ladies exchanged glances once more, and Alice, hoping Lord Tarrant would take the hint, took Lucy with her as she escorted them to the front door, leaving Lord Tarrant alone in the drawing room.

James leaned back in the very comfortable chair, crossed his legs and settled down to await her return. He was perfectly aware she wanted him to leave, but he had something to say to her first.

He'd learned a few things about her in the time between dancing with her at the party the other night and calling on her this afternoon. From what he could gather, she'd had a number of men sniffing around her skirts and had given every one of them short shrift.

From the prickly way she'd reacted to him on the previous two occasions, she was expecting more of the same from him. Even though he suspected she was feeling much the same attraction to him that he felt to her.

Which was interesting. For a woman who'd been married for eighteen years and was now widowed, there was a strange kind of innocence about her.

He needed to get to know her better. But first he had to get her to relax around him. He had a plan for that.

"Still here, Lord Tarrant?" she said as she entered the drawing room. She looked at the clock on the mantelpiece, a pointed reminder that he'd stayed nearly three quarters of an hour. And most enlightening he'd found it. The old tabbies were trying to match her off, trying to foist some spineless nonentity onto her. And she was trying to match her goddaughter up with whoever she could.

The goddaughter—now, she was a bit of a mystery. A minx, he thought, and sharp enough to cut herself. She'd lead some man a merry dance.

He'd risen to his feet as she entered. "Thank goodness. I thought they'd never leave." He also thanked goodness—silently—that the goddaughter hadn't yet returned. He had

Alice all to himself. He couldn't think of her as Lady Charlton, not when that harpy, Gerald's mother, had the same title. But convention had to be observed.

"It is polite to stay for no more than twenty minutes," she said crisply. He sat down again, but this time took the chair next to hers. Alice gave him a startled look and edged slightly away, smoothing her skirt.

"I know, but I wanted to ask you something. In private."

She stiffened, took a deep breath, then said in a rush, "Thank you for your interest, Lord Tarrant, but I must—I wish to make it clear that—" She broke off, her cheeks delightfully rosy. She took another deep breath and continued, "I must tell you that I am not interested in any, um . . . in any kind of liaison—respectable or . . . or otherwise." She met his eye. It was some kind of gauntlet then.

He raised a brow, and she added firmly, "In other words, I have no interest in marrying again, or in pursuing any, um . . . anything else."

"I see." James kept his voice solemn. She was adorable. And charmingly flustered. "You've made your position very clear," he assured her. "No 'um' or anything of that nature. Understood. What about friendship?"

She blinked. "Friendship?"

"It can happen between consenting adults of the opposite sex, I believe."

"You don't mean . . ."

"I'm talking about simple, everyday, out-in-the-open friendship. Of the completely respectable kind."

She gave him a doubtful look. "It's not a euphemism?"

"For 'um'? Definitely not."

"Oh." Was that disappointment he heard in her voice? Or relief?

She still appeared wary of his motives. Time to play his three little aces. "The thing is, I have three small daughters who I haven't seen for four years—I've never even seen the youngest. I'm planning to bring them to London to live with me. They're living with their maternal grandparents at the moment, but I want them with me."

"Daughters? You have three young daughters? You're married, then?"

"Widowed these four years."

"Oh." Quite a different kind of *oh* from the previous one.

"I've sent for my old nanny, and I suppose I'll hire a governess eventually, but"—he gave her a frank, manly look—"I'm a man, a former soldier, and out of my depth with young females. It would be good to have a friend—a female friend—to talk things over with and to advise me from time to time."

"Ohhh. You want a friend to advise you about your daughters? A female friend."

"Exactly." He leaned across and placed his hand over hers. "So, Lady Charlton, would you consent to be that friend?"

She looked at his hand and hesitated. "Of course I would be glad to advise you about your daughters but—" She broke off as Miss Bamber came skipping into the room.

"Sorry, I— Oops. Have I interrupted something?"

Alice snatched her hand away. "Not at all. Lord Tarrant was just leaving."

James, who had risen to his feet after Miss Bamber entered, said. "Not quite yet. I have something to ask you first."

Lucy immediately turned to leave. "I'll go."

"Stay right where you are, Lucy," Alice said. The girl glanced at her godmother in surprise.

"Yes, stay, Miss Bamber," James said easily. "This concerns you as well."

Lady Charlton gave him a surprised look. Lucy sat down. James sat as well.

"I wondered if you'd like to go to the theater," he said. "It's Shakespeare, *A Midsummer Night's Dream*—quite an entertaining production, I'm told."

Lucy's face lit up. "The theater? I've never been to the

theater." She turned to her godmother. "What do you say Ali—I mean, Godmama?"

Lady Charlton visibly hesitated. So cautious, even about a simple visit to the theater. Was she like that with everyone? Or every man? Why? Still grieving for her husband, perhaps.

James had plans for Alice, Lady Charlton, but he meant it about being friends with her. He definitely wanted to get to know her better. A lot better. "I'm putting a small party together for tomorrow night. I have the use of a box and—"

Alice said, "It's very short notice," at the same instant that Lucy said eagerly, "We're not doing anything tomorrow, are we?"

James pretended not to notice Alice's chagrin. "It has to be tomorrow night," he explained. "I'm leaving London the next morning."

"Leaving London?" Lucy echoed. She glanced at Alice. James didn't miss the exchange. Interesting.

"Yes, I'm collecting my daughters from their grandparents' home in Bedfordshire." To Lucy he explained, "My wife died four years ago, not long after she gave birth to my youngest. I've never seen her—my youngest, that is."

"Why not?" Lucy asked, her voice sharp with disapproval.

James wasn't offended. "I was overseas, away at war when she was born—in England. Then there was Waterloo. Later I was caught up in the mess that results in the aftermath of war. The army is a demanding master, Miss Bamber, and we officers have little say in where we are sent. But I found I missed my girls too much, and so I decided to sell out and come home."

"Why didn't you go straight to Bedfordshire?" Lucy demanded. "If you missed them so much."

"Lucy, it's not our business—" Alice began.

"No, Lady Charlton, it's quite all right," James said. He turned to Lucy. "That was my original plan, Miss Bamber. But I stopped to break my journey overnight in my London house and discovered chimneys blocked with birds' nests, a leaking roof, peeling wallpaper and more. So for the last week or so I've been setting the house in order to make it fit for my girls."

He gave a rueful smile. "They might have started their lives in tents and peasant cottages, but for the last four years they've become accustomed to something much finer. But it's almost all done now, and the final touches will be completed while I'm in Bedfordshire. I hope to have them with me in London by Friday week. So, will you join my small party at the theater tomorrow night, Lady Charlton, Miss Bamber?"

Alice hesitated, but Lucy was gazing at her with such a naked plea in her eyes that James wasn't surprised when she sighed and said, "Thank you, Lord Tarrant. We'd be delighted."

"Excellent. I'll send a carriage to collect you." James rose and took his leave.

He stepped out into the street feeling mildly triumphant. Now, who did he know who had a box at Drury Lane Theatre?

The moment Lord Tarrant left, Alice heaved a sigh of relief. His presence made her feel so strange: prickly and hot, and oddly tense. And yet, apart from overstaying his visit, his behavior had been perfectly proper.

It was kind of him to invite them to the theater.

Still . . . how was it that he could dominate a room simply by sitting quietly on a sofa? Was it those polished-pewter eyes? No matter who was talking, no matter whom she was looking at, she'd been aware of him the whole time. Each time he'd crossed his legs, she'd noticed.

His buckskin breeches weren't that tight, and yet she was very aware of the hard muscularity of his legs. She'd never really looked at a man's legs before. She hoped he hadn't noticed her staring but she feared he had. For almost the entire length of his visit, she'd felt the warm touch of his gaze resting on her.

Friends, she reminded herself. He just wanted friendship from her, because she was a woman and he had three small daughters. And because he didn't know many people in London. It sounded quite appealing—as long as she could get past these unsettling feelings.

It wouldn't be for long, she was sure. He'd be looking for a wife soon, once he was settled and knew more people. With a title and three daughters, he'd want someone young who could bear him a son. Not a barren woman past her prime. Not that Alice wanted to marry again.

She'd never had a male friend before. She didn't have many friends at all. Between them, Thaddeus and Almeria had managed to alienate any friends Alice had made.

A male friend might be interesting. She felt a small frisson of excitement.

"Thank you for accepting Lord Tarrant's invitation." Lucy broke into Alice's chain of thought. "I can't wait to see inside a real theater. Frau Steiner talked about theaters all the time. She was an opera singer—retired, of course. But, oh, she had so many interesting stories. Lord Tarrant definitely likes you."

Alice blinked at the abrupt change of subject. "Oh no, I think he's just being polite. He's been out of society so long, he doubtless doesn't know many people."

"It sounds as though his daughters have had a very strange upbringing."

Alice began to place the tea things onto a tray. "Yes, I wondered about the tents and peasant cottages, too."

Lucy moved to help her. "Well, I like him. In fact, I think he's charming. I can't understand why you were uncivil to him the other night."

"I wasn't uncivil, just . . ."

"Worried about how I was behaving?" Lucy suggested.

"Perhaps a little," Alice admitted. "But now that I know why you did what you did, I think everything went quite well. You already have several admirers." She gestured toward the bouquets that had arrived the morning after the party. They were still fresh.

Lucy wrinkled her nose, apparently unimpressed by the senders of the bouquets. Admittedly they were rather old. "The main problem was your nephew almost recognizing me."

"Yes, well, I doubt we'll see much of Gerald. Young bachelors don't generally frequent the kind of events we'll be attending, and you gave him no encouragement." Alice picked up the tea tray. "And if we do run into him, we'll just have to hope he doesn't remember."

"My lady!" Tweed said disapprovingly from the doorway. "That's my job."

Alice let him take the tray from her. She didn't have nearly enough servants, and collecting a few teacups and plates to take to the scullery was hardly a job that was beneath her, but it clearly offended Tweed's notions of what was proper.

Chapter Seven

Gerald lounged against the wall of the box, idly observing the comings and goings of the people in the stalls below. He wasn't terribly fond of the theater, but Tarrant had invited him, and Gerald had nothing else planned.

Voices outside the box alerted him to the imminent arrival of the rest of Tarrant's party. The door opened, Gerald straightened, and as the first person stepped into the box, she came to a dead halt. It was that girl. Her excited expression faded, and for a moment she looked dismayed.

Seconds later his aunt bumped into her. "Lucy, whatever are you doing—oh, Gerald. We didn't expect—how lovely to see you." She gently pushed the girl aside and came forward to greet him.

"Evening, Aunt Alice. I didn't realize you were to be one of Tarrant's party, either." He nodded at the girl. "Good evening, Miss Bamber." Swathed in a green velvet cloak trimmed with snowy swansdown and wearing a green-and-cream-striped turban, she looked like one of Persephone's handmaidens.

She inclined her head graciously, all signs of dismay gone. "Lord Thorndike."

"Thorn*ton*," he grated. The wench was doing it deliberately.

She touched a white-gloved hand to the side of her face in an unconvincing gesture of regret. "Of course. So shatterbrained of me." Her sherry-colored eyes danced.

Gerald eyed her balefully. She wasn't the slightest bit shatterbrained. Or the least bit sorry. And he was sure he'd seen her somewhere before. That cheeky expression, those eyes, that attitude . . . That mouth . . . But where?

The orchestra began, and the audience settled—as much as it ever did. "Are we waiting for any more people to arrive?" Aunt Alice asked Tarrant.

"No, as I said, it's a very small party." He seated Aunt Alice and took the seat beside her. Gerald seated Miss Bamber and placed himself a little behind her. For some reason he felt he needed to keep an eye on her.

Tarrant hadn't invited a party at all, Gerald realized. He was only interested in one person: Aunt Alice. He'd invited her goddaughter for the sake of propriety, and Gerald so he'd keep the girl occupied.

Tarrant was pursuing his aunt. But for what purpose? Men did chase after widows. But not Aunt Alice, surely. She'd always been the soul of virtue.

Tarrant. Gerald had always thought him a man of honor. The chivalrous type. A man of integrity. He'd make her a good husband.

But he'd told Gerald quite clearly that first night at the club that he had no intention of marrying again.

Aunt Alice was busy scanning the crowded theater through her opera glasses. Tarrant leaned back lazily in his seat, watching her with an indulgent expression.

What were his intentions? Gerald felt very protective of his aunt. She'd always been kind to him, and his family had treated her so unkindly. She was all alone. Someone had to look after her.

The hairs on the back of his neck prickled. Someone was watching him. He turned his head to find Lucy Bamber regarding him with narrowed eyes. She immediately switched her attention to the stage, pretending she hadn't noticed him.

Something nagged at the back of his mind. Who the devil was she?

The play began, and she leaned forward, as if entranced. At first Gerald thought she was putting it on, but soon he realized she really was entirely caught up in the foolishness onstage—of course she would sympathize with the rebellious daughter. And then the comedy . . .

Her laughter was . . . distracting.

Most young ladies he knew tittered or giggled, or else cultivated a world-weary air of ennui, thinking it frightfully sophisticated to appear bored with everything.

Lucy Bamber's laughter was wholehearted, spontaneous and annoyingly infectious. Gerald found himself smiling at stage antics he'd seen a dozen times and hadn't thought funny the first time. But she found them hilarious. And he couldn't help but smile in response.

Which was irritating. He didn't want to smile along with her.

When the first act ended, she clapped ecstatically and turned to Aunt Alice with an expression that took his breath away. "Oh, Alice, isn't it wonderful?" Then she saw him watching her, and the bright animation dimmed. She raised a brow as if to say, "Well? What are you looking at?"

Gerald stomped away to fetch refreshments.

He returned with champagne to find the box full of several visiting ladies and far too many visiting gentlemen. Tarrant, he noticed, hadn't moved an inch from where he'd been sitting beside Aunt Alice. Gerald's lips tightened. Tarrant had always been clever tactically.

Lucy Bamber was surrounded by young gentlemen—including two of his friends. She was sipping champagne and smiling. His friends were behaving like besotted fools, flirting and flattering. And she was lapping it up, dammit.

A small table had been brought in and spread with drinks, glasses and a range of appetizing refreshments. Of course Tarrant would have arranged provisions beforehand. He'd always been efficient.

The realization did nothing for Gerald's mood. He drained his glass of champagne, poured another, leaned against the wall and watched his friends competing to make Lucy Bamber laugh. He wished he'd never come. He hated the theater.

They were well into the third act, and Gerald had lost all interest in the play. He sprawled moodily in his seat, legs crossed at the ankles, hands stuffed in his pockets, watching Lucy Bamber through half-closed eyes. The candlelight limned her profile. It wasn't a classic profile by any means; she wasn't a beauty. But something about her drew him, though he was damned if he knew what.

It was warm in the theater—all those candles and the heat of a thousand bodies—and she'd removed her long white gloves. Her cloak hung loosely over the back of her chair, as if she'd shrugged it off unthinkingly, letting it lie where it fell in folds around her. Her attention was wholly on the stage; they were at the part where everyone was pretending to be somebody else—stupid story—as if that would fool anyone. She stroked the swansdown edging of her cloak rhythmically, as if she were patting a cat, stroking the soft feathers between her fingers. Stroke . . . stroke . . . stroke.

He sat up frowning, a thought picking elusively at the edge of his brain. An image of another slender hand stroking something soft and white . . . Feathers . . . A long white neck . . .

And then it burst upon him. "The goose girl!" he exclaimed. "You're that goose girl!"

Lucy Bamber didn't respond. Her hands stilled. She gazed at the stage, frozen, lifeless as a statue.

"That's where I saw you before. The goose girl!"

"Shhh!" Several people hissed at him.

"But I tell you—"

"Ssshhhhh!" Louder now. Heads were turning. Aunt Alice turned around, caught his eye and made a hushing gesture. Gerald hushed, but the knowledge wanted to burst from him.

He waited impatiently until the end of the act. The moment it did, he turned on Lucy Bamber. "I knew I'd seen you before. You're that goose girl!"

She raised a slender, incredulous brow. "I'm the *what*?"

"That goose girl!"

She gave him a puzzled look, fingered the fluffy trimming on her cloak and said, "It's swansdown, not goose feather."

"I'm not talking about the blasted cloak. You're that goose girl. I know you are, so don't try to wriggle out of it."

"Gerald dear—" his aunt began.

"I'm not mistaken, Aunt Alice. When I met this—this female, she was a goose girl."

Lucy Bamber shook her head in a show of bewilderment that made him want to throttle her. "I dressed up as a shepherdess for a costume party once, so perhaps—"

"Don't prevaricate!"

"But I really did dress up as—"

"We met on the Brighton road, not two weeks ago. You were carrying a goose. I knew I'd seen you before, and it only just came to me."

"*I?* Carrying *a goose*?" She sounded utterly incredulous. She glanced at his aunt and Tarrant, as if inviting them to join in her incredulity. "What were you doing on the Brighton road, Lord Thornthwaite, when this goose and I supposedly met you?" Her voice and expression were serious, but her eyes glinted with knowing mischief.

"I was—" he broke off and felt himself redden slightly. He hadn't told anyone how a goose and an impertinent chit of a farm girl caused him to lose his race. If it got out, his friends would never let him hear the end of it. "It doesn't matter. What I want to know is why a common goose girl is attending the theater with my aunt."

"Is she?" The wretched girl looked around eagerly. "Where? Point her out to me."

Aunt Alice had a sudden coughing fit and buried her face in her handkerchief.

"I'm talking about you," Gerald snapped. "As you very well know. You had a goose called . . . Ger—Ghislaine. That was it. Ghislaine."

"A *goose*? Called *Ghislaine*?" She gave him a worried look. "Are you sure you didn't hit your head or something when you were on the Brighton road?"

"No, I—"

"Gerald dear, that's enough. You're making a scene," Aunt Alice said, apparently recovered from her coughing fit.

In a low, furious voice he said, "I'm *not* making a scene, Aunt Alice, but that girl—"

"Is my goddaughter. In any case, this is neither the time nor the place for such a discussion. Now please go outside, have a glass of something and breathe in some fresh air."

It was the last straw. She was treating him like a schoolboy. With a last glare at the wretched goose girl, who looked both smug and mischievous at the same time, Gerald flung himself out of the theater box. And ordered a brandy. A large one.

So what if he recognized me? I don't care." Lucy said as she plumped down into an overstuffed chair. Lord Tarrant had just dropped them home from the theater. Alice hadn't invited the gentlemen in. Gerald had come with them in the carriage. He'd been silent, brooding and glowering for the rest of the evening, and she simply couldn't deal with him at the moment.

"In fact," Lucy continued, "I quite enjoyed it. Did you see his face?" She chuckled.

Alice stared at her. *Quite enjoyed it?* She didn't understand Lucy's complete about-face. At the party she had fled from Gerald's presence in case he recognized her. Now that he had, Lucy was claiming she didn't care. Alice was, frankly, rattled. "But what will happen when he tells everyone? We'll be ruined."

"No, we won't," Lucy said confidently. "He won't tell anyone."

"But—"

"Didn't you see how he stopped himself? He doesn't want to admit he lost that race because of a goose."

Alice pursed her lips thoughtfully. Lucy was right. He had stopped himself. "But knowing that it was you he met is only the start of it. He'll be busy unraveling the rest. I know Gerald—once he gets an idea in his head, he won't give up."

"Pooh! What's there to discover? So what if he met me on the road? So what if I was carrying a goose? I can have done all those things and still be your goddaughter—and I *am* your goddaughter. That was smart of Papa, even if he is a scheming rotter. And I'm here by your invitation"—she caught Alice's look—"as far as he knows, at any rate. He doesn't need to know that Papa forced you. Or how."

"I suppose so," Alice said uncertainly. Knowing Gerald, she figured he'd be around here first thing in the morning demanding to know the truth, and what was she going to tell him?

"It doesn't matter what your nephew knows or thinks he knows, Alice—he can't tell you what to do. He's just a nephew."

She was right, Alice knew, but Alice didn't have Lucy's

brash confidence. And she hated telling lies. "You really don't care, do you?"

Lucy shook her head. "No. He can't hurt me. It's pride. He's angry that he lost that stupid race, and so he wants to bring me down. But I won't let him."

Alice frowned. "What makes you think he wants to bring you down?"

"The way he looks at me, as if I'm the lowest of the low. Lords are like that. But I don't care." Lucy rose. "I'm for bed now, Alice. Thank you for a lovely evening. Goodnight—and stop fretting. It'll all turn out all right." And with that she went up to bed, apparently without a worry in the world.

The worries stayed downstairs with Alice, who sat staring into the fire, mulling over the situation and trying to decide what to do.

Part of the trouble was that she had no real idea who Lucy was. Oh, she'd had some education and training in ladylike behavior—when she chose to use it—but for all Alice knew, she could be illegitimate or the daughter of a prostitute or a convict or anyone. All she knew for certain was that Lucy was the daughter of a scoundrel.

If the ton learned she had been trying to pass off a girl like that as a true-born lady . . .

For Alice, the consequence would be social disgrace—even without Bamber's releasing those letters. The consequences for Lucy? Social disgrace in a society that she didn't much care about. But she'd be on her own again.

The more Alice came to know her, the more she liked Lucy. There was a kind of reckless courage about her—she supposed it came of having to manage for herself for most her life. Lucy thought that Lord Tarrant's daughters had had a strange life, but from Alice's point of view, Lucy had had just as strange an upbringing. No permanent home, five schools, two foreign ladies and a father she couldn't even contact? And who knew what else?

Yet despite it all, Lucy was a kind girl. The minute she'd learned about her father blackmailing Alice—and even though this masquerade was the last thing Lucy wanted—she'd accepted Alice's position and tried to make the best of it.

The servants liked her, too, despite her initial truculence and bad behavior. Servants were usually excellent judges of character.

If only Lucy hadn't run into Gerald on the Brighton road.

He was as stubborn as his father. He was also quite protective of Alice. What to do? Tell him the truth, or try to stick to the story they'd concocted? Or take him into her confidence and enlist his help in trying to trace Bamber and get the letters back?

Oh, the indecision.

James's carriage drew away from Bellaire Gardens. "What the devil was up with you tonight?" he said to Thornton. "I don't know what all that goose girl nonsense was about, but—"

"It's not nonsense," Thornton insisted. "And it confirms the uneasy feeling I've had about my aunt and that girl since the beginning. I *did* meet her on the Brighton road in some small, obscure village. I talked to her, face-to-face, as close as you and I are now. She was shabbily dressed and carrying a goose. So why is a girl like that living in my aunt's house, being introduced to the ton?"

"I'm not sure what I think of Miss Lucy Bamber," James said. "She's a minx, that one. But I can't believe your aunt would be party to such a—"

"Didn't you notice Aunt Alice's reaction? She was worried, on edge, but *she wasn't surprised.* She *knew* that girl was a goose girl. Oh, she tried to pretend she didn't know what I was talking about, but she's a hopeless liar, always has been. And I can always tell."

James said nothing. He had noticed Alice's reaction. There was guilt there, as well as anxiety.

Thornton hurried on. "When I was ten, I broke my leg—fell off my horse—and was laid up for weeks. I was bored to death, but Aunt Alice read to me by the hour and played endless games of cards and other games. I can *always* tell when she's bluffing or trying to trick me. Always." He met James's eyes. "Something fishy is going on. I'm sure of it."

"I see." James nodded. It was an outrageous claim, that a titled lady would take in a goose girl and try to pass her off as a lady—for what purpose?—but Thornton had always been levelheaded. "Have you asked her directly about it?"

"No, but until I worked out where I'd seen that girl before, all I had to go on was nebulous suspicion. I'm going to speak to her about it first thing tomorrow morning."

"Just be sure of your facts then, because as things stand, it's your word against that of Miss Bamber. And frankly, hers is more believable. A goose called Ghislaine?"

They drove through the London streets in silence. Several times Thornton glanced at James, opened his mouth, then shut it again. He glanced out the window, shifted uncomfortably, opened his mouth but again said nothing. Clearly, he had more on his mind.

The carriage pulled up in front of Thornton's lodgings. He opened the door, jumped down, then turned back and said in a rush, "Tarrant, I need to ask you something."

"Yes?" James had a fair idea of what it was.

"I'm very fond of Aunt Alice, so I must ask, what are your intentions?"

"To fetch my daughters and bring them back to London," James said smoothly. "'Night, Thornton." He rapped on the roof of the carriage, and it moved off.

James knew perfectly well what Thornton was asking him, but he was damned if he'd answer to her nephew. Alice was a grown woman, a widow in her middle thirties. James only needed to explain his intentions to her.

She was going to have to confess. Alice had decided. The idea of trying to continue the bluff with Gerald was impossible. She'd never been a good liar and to attempt it would strain her nerves horribly.

Once she'd made that decision, a weight lifted off her shoulders.

Gerald arrived at ten, still faintly smoldering and obviously prepared for an argument. She greeted him calmly and served him coffee and gingernuts—his favorites.

"Aunt Alice, that girl—" he began.

"I know what you're going to say, Gerald," she interrupted.

"No, you don't. I really did meet her on the Brighton road where—"

"She and a goose called Ghislaine caused you to lose your race."

"I know it sounds ridic—" He broke off. "How did you know?"

"Lucy told me all about it."

He stared at her. "So you did know all along. I knew it!"

"Yes. Now drink your coffee, Gerald, and I'll explain the whole thing. And I hope I can trust you to keep a confidence."

He didn't like that, she saw, but the appeal to his gentlemanly instincts did its job. He gave a curt nod. "Of course."

Alice explained the situation: the unexpected appearance of Octavius Bamber, the blackmail, Bamber's requirement that Alice sponsor Lucy's come-out, the baptism—everything. It was quite a relief to get it all out in the open, even if it was to a disapproving nephew.

When she'd finished, he said, "These letters, Aunt Alice, are they, er . . . ?"

"Deeply embarrassing. You don't need to know any more."

"No, no, of course not," he said, reddening. No doubt his imagination was working overtime, but she couldn't help that. She had no intention of explaining their contents to anyone.

"Well, the solution to that is obvious. I'll confront that swine Bamber and force him to give the letters up, and then you can be rid of that girl and—"

"And how, pray, will you find Bamber?" His assumption that it was all so easily fixed was irritating.

He looked at her in surprise. "Don't you know where he lives?"

"No, of course not. Otherwise I would have acted sooner."

"I'll ferret him out," Gerald said confidently.

"I wish you would try. But be warned, even Lucy has no idea how to contact her father."

"Her! She'd lie her way out of anything."

"I believe her, Gerald. I admit, I disliked and resented her at first, but I've come to know her better, and I believe she's almost as much a victim in this as I am."

He gave a scornful snort. "You're too softhearted for your own good, Aunt Alice."

"Lucy has no desire to enter society, no desire to marry a lord."

"Hah! So she claims."

"You must admit she's been at pains not to attract *you*. Perhaps that's the reason why you—"

He frowned. "Why I what?"

Alice shook her head. "It doesn't matter." Gerald had taken an unusual amount of interest in Lucy—the two seemed to strike sparks off each other whenever they met, and Alice didn't think it was just about a race and a goose.

With almost every young unmarried miss in London falling over herself to please and flatter Gerald, the one girl who showed no interest in him whatsoever was bound to stand out.

She continued, "The point is, Lucy had as little say in the situation as I did. I like the girl, Gerald, and I want to help her as best I can. But I will need your assistance."

"My assistance? Aunt Alice, this is ridiculous. I have no intention of helping—"

"Me?" Alice interjected. "You won't help *me* out of this situation, Gerald?" She waited.

He looked uncomfortable. "It's not that, I just—"

"Just what?"

"Dash it, Aunt Alice, I don't want her getting away with it."

"Getting away with what? She's as stuck as I am. If this gets out, we'll both be disgraced. It won't matter as much to me," she lied. Other people's good opinion had always been important to her. "My situation will remain unchanged, though it will be embarrassing and uncomfortable for a time. But imagine the repercussions for Lucy, a girl with no fortune, no home and no family—unless you count her scoundrel of a father, which I don't. From all I can make out, he has a history of dumping her with strangers and leaving her to sink or swim."

Gerald looked slightly perturbed. Good, he was finally considering Lucy's situation.

Alice rammed home her argument. "That girl is effectively all alone in the world. And for a single woman without support, that means poverty and destitution—or worse. Would you really wish such a fate on that bright, funny girl?"

There was a short silence, then Gerald said, "Very well, Aunt Alice, you've made your point. I don't have to like it—and I don't have to like her—but I suppose I'll have to help. Apart from tracking down her father, what do you want me to do?"

"Help me find Lucy a husband."

Gerald's jaw dropped. "What the h— What on earth do you imagine I can do?"

"I don't know many young bachelors. You do. Most of

your friends are eligible, in fact. You're in an excellent position to bring them to meet Lucy."

He stared at her. "Dash it, Aunt Alice, I can't go around dragging my friends into parson's mousetrap. I'd soon have no friends at all."

"Nonsense! Nobody's saying they have to marry Lucy, just that she needs to meet a number of suitable young men, and hopefully find one who will suit." She added in a steely voice, "A man who values her for who she is, not for her bloodline or what fortune she can bring. A kind man who can make her happy." Lucy would have what Alice had not, she was determined on it.

He scowled. "How would I know what would make a chit like that happy?"

"Don't be difficult, Gerald. Just bring around some nice young men, and Lucy—and the young man, of course—will do the rest."

"I suppose I could try," he said morosely.

"Excellent. But don't bother bringing any of your titled friends."

"Why? What's wrong with them?" he said stiffly.

"Lucy isn't interested in anyone with a title."

"The devil she's not!"

Alice shrugged. "The girl is entitled to her opinion, and you will respect it, if you please."

"And if I don't please?" he muttered.

Alice looked at him. "You know, Gerald, you've complained that your parents treat you like a schoolboy instead of a former army officer. I'm beginning to see their point."

He made a face. "I'm sorry, Aunt Alice. It's just that I'm no blasted matchmaker. I'd much rather go after that scoundrel Bamber, wring his neck and wrest those letters from him."

"You're welcome to do what you can about the letters," Alice told him. "And if you do manage to retrieve them, I'll be most grateful. In the meantime, please bring your friends around to meet Lucy."

Have you thought about what we're going to wear to Lady Peplowe's masquerade ball?" Lucy said to Alice later that day.

Alice gave her a blank look. "I hadn't given it a thought." She frowned. She didn't want to spend money on a fanciful costume that would only be worn once—the money Bamber had given her for Lucy's expenses was dwindling rapidly. It was not nearly what he'd promised her, and there was no sign of any more forthcoming.

Another reason for Gerald to track him down.

"I think we're going to have to wear dominos."

Lucy's face fell. "Oh no, we can't. Dominos are so dreary. The only people who wear them are those who are too staid and dull to dress up."

"We can't afford a proper costume, Lucy."

"Isn't there something we can improvise with?"

Alice thought about it. It had been years since she'd attended a costume ball. Thaddeus didn't like them. But she did recall at least one occasion . . .

"I suppose we could. I'm fairly sure some of my old costumes are in a trunk in the attic. But goodness knows what condition they'll be in. Some of granny's old clothes are stored up there, too, I think."

"Ooh, I love old clothes," Lucy said. "Can we go up now and see what's there?"

Pleased by the girl's easy acceptance of her budget limitations, Alice agreed, and they immediately went up to the attic to see what they might find. She hadn't been up there since she was a little girl.

The attic was dusty and contained all kinds of forgotten items—a battered and balding rocking horse, a dollhouse with faded wallpaper and small dusty carpets that she remembered with fondness. There was old-fashioned furniture in need of mending and several large trunks and chests, as well as hatboxes and all kinds of mysterious objects discarded over the years.

"Oh, how sweet," Lucy exclaimed, finding a box containing dollhouse furniture and other tiny items, all looking well used and in need of repair.

"Let's not get too distracted," Alice said, laughing. "We're after costumes, remember?" Lucy reluctantly put the dollhouse items aside and went back to searching through the trunks.

"Look! A treasure trove," Lucy exclaimed, opening a box and pulling out a glittering tangle of costume jewelry. "And what's this?" She lifted out a tissue-wrapped bundle and unwrapped it to reveal a slightly dented papier-mâché headdress in faded gold.

"Oh, it's my old Cleopatra outfit," Alice exclaimed. "I'd quite forgotten about it." It was from very early in her marriage. She'd dressed for her first costume ball, all excited, but when she came down in her outfit, Thaddeus had taken one look at her and ordered her back upstairs: he wasn't taking her anywhere dressed so outrageously.

She never did go to the ball.

She found the dress that went with the headdress and shook it out. It was a long, floaty garment made of layers of gauzy blue and green fabric, but it wasn't *outrageous*—there were too many layers for even the shape of her body to be visible. The neckline was scooped low, but it was not at all immodest. Looking at it with fresh eyes, she was indignant on behalf of her younger self. Thaddeus was just being mean.

Somewhere there was a belt of gold medallions that cinched around her waist—yes, there it was, along with a couple of bangles shaped like snakes that wrapped around her upper arm. She'd worn gold sandals, she recalled. She still had them somewhere.

"It's perfect," Lucy exclaimed.

Alice shook her head. The headdress, belt and armbands were sadly tarnished. "I can't possibly wear these. They're far too shabby."

"I can fix them," Lucy said confidently.

"How?"

"Wait and see. And Mary will be able to freshen up that dress so it will look as good as new. Now, that's your costume sorted. I thought this might do for me."

She held up a filmy white muslin dress.

Alice frowned. "But that's not a costume. It's just one of my old muslin dresses from years ago. It's very old-fashioned."

"Yes, from the days when London ladies dressed a bit like Greek and Roman goddesses," Lucy agreed. "And that's who I'm going as—someone from the ancient world. I'll make a headdress of leaves and add a few draperies. Wait and see—it'll be perfect."

Alice gave it a doubtful look. "The muslin is a bit yellowed, isn't it?"

"Mary will know how to fix that, too. And if she doesn't, who cares?" Lucy added gaily. "I'll be an ancient, slightly yellowed Grecian goddess."

The following morning Lucy woke to a world bathed in sunshine. "I've received a note from Gerald," Alice told her at breakfast. "He's arranged for one of his friends to take you for a drive in the park this afternoon."

Alice explained that she'd taken her nephew into her confidence and that he'd agreed to help Lucy find a husband. Lucy was feeling rather cynical about Lord Thornton's miraculous about-face, but she didn't tell Alice that.

"What friend is this? Will he collect me from here?"

"No, you and I will promenade in the park at the fashionable hour," Alice said, "and Gerald will drive up with his friend, a Mr. Cornelius Frinton. Gerald will step down and accompany me on my walk, while Mr. Frinton takes you for a circuit of the park in his phaeton."

Lucy frowned. "Won't I need some kind of chaperone?"

"Not for a drive in the park in an open carriage in full view of everyone," Alice assured her. "Besides, I expect Mr. Frinton will have a tiger or a groom in attendance."

"Do we know anything about this Mr. Frinton?"

"Not really. Just that he's a friend of Gerald's from school, and that, according to Gerald, he's eligible and reasonably well-off."

"Very well then. What shall I wear? The bronze walking dress?" Lucy was still learning the various kinds of dress suitable for different activities. A dress was not simply a dress. Apparently.

"Perfect. And the olive green pelisse—it's sunny now, but it's bound to change. And if it's still sunny this afternoon, take a parasol—that lovely skin of yours needs protecting. Or if there are clouds building, we'll take umbrellas."

Hyde Park was full of fashionable people sauntering along, dressed to the nines, seeing and being seen. The sunshine was in intermittent evidence, concealed by fluffy white clouds from time to time, so no parasol was necessary. Lucy's straw hat tied with a gauze net scarf in bronze was deemed sufficient protection for her complexion.

She strolled along with Alice, feeling rather smart. Alice made a point of stopping to chat with anyone she had the slightest acquaintance with, warmly introducing Lucy each time as her goddaughter.

Alice was a truly generous soul but Lucy had mixed

feelings about it. On the one hand, it was what they'd agreed, but she was beginning to feel guilty about the trouble Alice was going to on her behalf. Not that Lucy could change anything.

How had Papa found anything to blackmail Alice with? She was the nearest thing to perfect that Lucy had ever met: kind, ladylike, moral, modest, careful with money but generous with her possessions—right now Lucy was wearing Alice's hat, kid gloves and earrings, which went perfectly with her outfit.

And even when Alice was furious—and Lucy was well aware that she had driven Alice's temper to the limit early on—she'd never yelled or anything. She'd just spoken firmly and made her position very clear.

Above all, she had never once blamed Lucy for what Papa had done. It would have been so easy for her to have taken her temper out on Lucy, but she hadn't, and for that more than anything, Lucy was enormously grateful. All her life she'd received some blame, if not all, for her father's actions. But not from Alice, not once.

Alice had even promised Lucy that she wouldn't try to force her into marriage, that she wanted her to find a kind man she could love. Reading between the lines, Lucy guessed that Alice hadn't married that sort of man. In fact, she never talked of her husband at all. Which made her concern for Lucy's welfare and happiness all the more generous and touching.

She owed it to Alice to find a husband as quickly as possible and stop Papa's blackmail from hanging over her. That Lord Thornton had decided to help her find one was surprising—more than surprising, really—but Alice had assured her most sincerely that he was trying to help.

Lucy was yet to be convinced.

"Here they are now," Alice said as Lord Thornton and another young man drove up in a smart black-lacquered phaeton drawn by two high-stepping gray horses. Lucy was impressed. They stopped and Lord Thornton jumped lithely down.

After introductions and a brief conversational exchange, Lord Thornton helped Lucy climb into the phaeton, and she and Mr. Frinton drove off.

Mr. Cornelius Frinton was not a handsome fellow, with his ginger hair, a bony face, and a large, beaky nose. He made up for his lack of looks by dressing immaculately in the very latest fashions; in fact, his shirt points were so high that he had some difficulty turning his head.

At least that was what Lucy assumed at first, when, after several conversational openings, he had failed to look at her once. Nor had he responded with anything other than a choked kind of gurgle, or a murmur of assent and a convulsive twitch of his rather prominent Adam's apple. And every time she spoke and he failed to respond, he blushed.

He wasn't deaf. She briefly wondered if he had a speech disorder, but after he'd greeted several masculine acquaintances in perfectly clear English, she finally realized what the matter was: Cornelius Frinton was cripplingly shy with women.

Oh, but she'd like to strangle Lord Thornton.

She set out to put Mr. Frinton at his ease, chattering about his lovely horses, about the weather, about life in London. Noticing that he bowed or nodded or doffed his hat to quite a few people, she said, "You seem to know a lot of society people, Mr. Frinton. I know practically no one in London. Could you point me out some of the more well-known ones?"

That worked a treat, and from time to time he'd indicate someone and say a name, and even, once or twice, give a little more information. "Lady in blue hat. Silence, Lady Jersey. Almack's patroness. Silence, because she never stops talking." And then he blushed beetroot.

Lucy laughed. "Not your problem then."

He turned his head and looked at her, and when he realized she wasn't being critical, he gave her a shy smile.

They ended up circling the park twice, then drew up to where Alice and Lord Thornton were waiting. Lord Thornton helped her down. "Did you enjoy your drive?"

Lucy wanted to smack his smug face. "Yes, indeed," she said blithely. "Mr. Frinton and I had a lovely chat, didn't we Mr. Frinton?"

"Chat?" Lord Thornton looked quite disconcerted.

Mr. Frinton nodded, bowed to Lucy. His Adam's apple bobbed frantically, and he said in a strangled voice, "Delighted. Take you up anytime, Miss Bamber."

Lord Thornton gave her a narrow look. She bared her teeth at him in a bright smile. With a set jaw, he climbed back into the phaeton. As the carriage moved off, Lucy called, "Thank you for a delightful drive, Mr. Frinton. Goodbye, Lord Thornbottom."

He didn't even bother to correct her.

"How did it go?" Alice asked. "I must say, I'm a little surprised by Gerald's choice. Mr. Frinton is hardly the most prepossessing of men."

"Yes, not blessed by the looks fairy, and dreadfully shy, poor boy, but perfectly sweet all the same." Alice might believe that Lord Thornton was trying to help Lucy find a husband. Lucy knew better.

As if she needed his help anyway.

Chapter Eight

Twilight was fading into darkness as James rang the doorbell of his in-laws' country home. He'd been traveling all day, only stopping to change his horses, and was glad to have reached his final destination. He couldn't wait to see his daughters.

The butler opened the door and said in surprise, "Colonel—" He broke off. "I beg your pardon, it's Lord Tarrant now, isn't it? My condolences on the loss of your brother, my lord."

James nodded brusquely. "Thank you, Sutton."

"Welcome back to England, my lord. I didn't realize we were expecting you."

"You weren't. Lord and Lady Fenwick are in, I presume? But it's the girls I've come for." He glanced up the stairs. "In the nursery, are they?"

James took several steps forward, but the butler stepped in his way, his expression troubled. "I will let Lady Fenwick know you have arrived. If you would care to wait in the drawing room, my lord, I will have refreshments brought in." He gestured.

"I don't need to wait, I just want to see—" But the butler had gone. Damned formality. He was half tempted to run up the stairs to the nursery anyway, but he supposed a few extra minutes wouldn't hurt. It wasn't as if the girls were expecting him.

He ran his hand over his stubbled chin. He probably should have stopped at an inn and shaved and changed his clothes, but dammit, he wanted to see his daughters. They wouldn't care if he was rumpled and unshaven. They'd seen him in worse condition than that. At least, Judy and Lina had.

Little Deborah. He wondered what she'd look like, whether she'd take after her mother or him.

"Tarrant." His mother-in-law greeted him from the doorway. He rose and would have bowed over her hand, but she waved him back to his seat. His father-in-law followed her in and gave James a curt nod as a greeting. James nodded back.

"You didn't tell us you were coming." His mother-in-law wasn't smiling, but some things never changed.

"I apologize for any inconvenience, Lady Fenwick." He'd tried once, as a newly married man, to call her *mama-in-law*, but she'd frozen him out so severely that he'd never tried again.

His in-laws had never approved of him. They hadn't wanted him—a younger son, and a soldier in time of war!—for their daughter, but Selina only gave the appearance of being gentle and biddable. She'd stood firm until her parents had no choice but to give in. And then she'd insisted on going to war with him, following the drum, sharing the discomfort and the difficulties and the danger. She'd loved every moment of it, and he'd loved having her with him.

She'd born him two healthy children under unimaginable conditions. The two little girls had relished army life as much as their mother did.

But four years ago Selina had been experiencing a difficult third pregnancy and on medical advice had reluctantly agreed to return to London, taking the two little girls with her.

The baby had lived, but Selina had died shortly afterward. Childbed fever, they said. Her parents blamed him, even though he'd been a continent away, risking his life for king and country, and Selina was in London in the care of her parents, with the best medical attention available.

James dragged his thoughts back to the present. He neither wanted nor needed his in-laws' approval. He was here for one thing only: his daughters. He glanced at the doorway. "Where are the girls?"

"Would you like tea?"

"Later, perhaps, but first I would like to see the girls."

Lord and Lady Fenwick exchanged glances. "They're not here at the moment."

James frowned. They wouldn't be outside at this time of the evening. "Where are they?"

There was an awkward silence.

His voice hardened. "Where are my daughters?"

"Attending Miss Coates's Seminary for Young Ladies. It's a very genteel establishment—"

"At *school*? Judy and Lina?" Judy was eleven and Lina only seven. They were far too young to be sent away to school.

James tamped down on his anger. He was here for his girls, not to argue with his in-laws. "Then I'll just see Deborah."

His mother-in-law glanced away. "She's with her sisters, of course."

He rose to his feet, rage coursing through him. "Deborah? In a boarding school? Dammit, she's only four years old!"

His mother-in-law shrank from him. His father-in-law bristled with righteous indignation. "Language, sirrah!

And you cannot expect a frail, elderly lady like my wife to care for someone else's children."

James cast his mother-in-law a scornful look. "Frail and elderly, my foot! As I recall, you turned fifty-four last month. In any case, I haven't noticed a shortage of servants in this establishment. And they're not 'someone else's children'—they're your grandchildren!"

Lady Fenwick snorted. "They're a trio of young hoydens, more like—and no wonder, dragged up in the wake of an army of rough soldiers, living in frightful conditions in close proximity to foreigners instead of being raised as decent Christian young ladies. School was the only possible alternative."

"And yet Deborah has been entirely in your charge since birth."

"Yes," she said disdainfully, "but she carries your blood."

He clenched his jaw. "I doubt very much whether you had the raising of her anyway. Your own daughter was raised by nursemaids and governesses—oh yes, I know all about her upbringing. But at least you never sent her away to live with strangers."

She shrugged a thin shoulder. "There was no need. Selina was a quiet, well-behaved, well-bred gel—until she met you."

He let that pass. The woman knew next to nothing about her own daughter. "There was no need to send the girls away from all they knew, especially since they'd lost their mother."

She dismissed that with an airy wave. "Children adjust. They're perfectly happy there."

He pulled a worn, stained letter from his breast pocket and held it up. "And yet these 'perfectly happy' girls wrote to me saying they were miserable and begging me to come and get them."

Lady Fenwick frowned and sat forward. "They can't have. They were given—" She broke off.

"Given letters to copy?" He nodded, remembering the short, bland, almost formal letters his daughters had written each week. "I thought as much. They didn't sound at all like my lively little Judy, and Lina used to draw pictures all the time. I haven't had a single picture from her in months—until this." He held up the letter showing a brief letter in childish script and a drawing of three small girls of varying heights, all looking sad.

"Children always complain—" his father-in-law began.

"Enough." James cut him off with a curt gesture. "I have no interest in your excuses. Just give me the address of that school, and I'll be gone."

Lord Fenwick glanced at his wife, then rose and took a pen and paper and ink from the drawer in a nearby table. He scribbled the address and handed the paper to James.

James glanced at the address and almost crushed it in his fist. It was another day's travel away. He stalked to the door.

Lady Fenwick rose and followed him. "What are you planning to do with my grandchildren?"

James snorted. "It's too late to pretend any concern for them. You've shown your hand. Goodbye. My daughters and I shan't bother you again."

She drew herself up indignantly. "You—you can't mean to deny me their company, surely?" There was a thread of anxiety in her voice.

He knew the real source of her concern: How would it look to outsiders for a grandmother whose only granddaughters had nothing to do with her? He let her stew for a minute, then said evenly, "If the girls want to see their grandparents, of course I will allow it. Despite what you seem to think, children need family."

James gave instructions to his driver, and the coach headed off into the night, the coach lights glowing gold against the darkness. He would stop at the first decent inn he came to; he refused to spend a single night with his in-laws.

Brooding, he stared through the coach window at the shifting shadows of the passing countryside. He thought of his daughters, the last time he'd seen them. Seven-year-old Judy and three-and-a half-year-old Lina, with her shabby, much-loved dolly, standing at the rail of the ship, clinging to their mother's hands, Selina standing straight, red-eyed but calm, the swell of her pregnancy outlined by the wind pressing her dress against her.

Now Selina was dead, and Ross and his parents, too, drowned in a boating accident. Not to mention all the friends he'd lost during the war. So much death . . .

James's girls were all he had left. Sending them away at such a young age, when they could have stayed with family—that he couldn't forgive. Three little girls in a seminary for young ladies, one of them just four years old—still a baby.

Why, why, why had they been sent away? He couldn't understand it.

He knew his girls weren't hoydens—or if they were, it was a reaction to their mother's death. But that was no reason to send them away. Servants could be hired who would care for children with all the warmth their grandparents lacked.

His daughters had been born into a rough and unsettled life, traveling with an army, but they'd thrived. They might have lived in tents and billets and slept on the ground or in the back of a wagon, but between Selina and himself—and his batman and the woman he'd hired to help Selina—they'd had a home, a home made of people and love, not bricks and mortar.

He'd missed them damnably, had thrown himself into his work to ease the ache of loss.

He pulled out the letter and read it for the umpteenth

time. Short and to the point, just like Judy. *We hate it here, Papa. We miss you. Please come and get us.*

Judy's writing. He settled back in the corner of the carriage, remembering her birth.

He'd been waiting outside the tent, pacing anxiously while Selina labored within, giving birth to their first child. One of the camp followers was acting as midwife. She was a burly, no-nonsense woman who'd birthed six of her own and attended the birth of many more. She'd pushed back the tent flap, saying, "It's a girl," and handed him a tiny, blood-smeared bundle wrapped in a towel. Then she disappeared back into the tent, saying, "Stay outside. We ain't finished yet."

James stared down at the tiny bundle, the little red scrunched-up face, the impossibly small starfish hand with fingernails like small pink jewels.

Holding her carefully, terrified of dropping such a small, delicate creature, he'd used the end of the towel to clean her face, wiping off smears of blood and some waxy substance. And then she'd opened her eyes.

She'd stared up at him, so intense, like an ancient, wise little soul, and he'd stared back, hardly able to breathe, and it was as if she'd reached her little starfish hand into his chest and squeezed his heart. Emotion swamped him, and he knew he would die to protect this little scrap of newborn humanity, his daughter.

And as she grew and flourished, gave him her first real smile, took her first steps, spoke her first words, the feeling only grew stronger.

He was there too when Lina was born, this time in a tumbledown peasant cottage. He took delivery of the naked, squalling, red-faced, kicking, angry baby, and this time he knew what to do. He'd bathed her, pink and slippery, in a basin of warm water, which, as well as cleaning her, somehow calmed her. And when she'd curled her soft, tiny fist around his big rough-skinned finger and stared up at him, he was gone, just as before.

He'd shown the baby, clean and pink and quiet now, to her big four-year-old sister. Judy had gazed at the little face with wonder and said, "She's awful ugly, isn't she?"

James smiled recalling it. He'd grown up believing that children belonged to their parents, and that was true of some. But not James: he belonged, heart and soul, to his daughters.

Alice was fast losing patience with her nephew. So far he had brought four young gentlemen to meet Lucy, none of them in the least bit suitable. Mr. Frinton—sweet boy or not—could barely get out a word in female company. After him had come Sir Heatherington Bland, a morose fellow who, far from being bland, had a distinctively pungent body odor.

Then there was Mr. Humphrey Ffolliot, who had Opinions, which he shared at the slightest provocation—in fact with no provocation at all. The country was Going to the Dogs! Too Many Blasted Foreigners! As for Women, they'd got completely Out of Hand and no longer Knew Their Place!

Lucy appeared to listen demurely to every word, murmuring a comment every now and then. It seemed to Alice that far from agreeing with him, Lucy was gently mocking him. Not that Mr. Ffolliot noticed. He informed Alice as he was leaving that her goddaughter was a Fine Example of Womanhood.

And yesterday Gerald had introduced his friend Tarquin Grimswade, a very pretty young man dressed in rainbow shades. He claimed to be a poet and an artist, but he was so self-absorbed that Alice thought for all the notice he took of other people, he might as well be performing in front of a mirror.

Lucy had behaved very naughtily and had faintly mirrored his flowing hand movements and facial expressions as they spoke. Mr. Grimswade had found her charming.

And now this evening, they were to meet prospective suitor number five. Gerald had invited Alice and Lucy to Vauxhall Gardens, where there was to be a concert, followed by a gymnastic display and then fireworks. Alice always enjoyed fireworks, and Lucy had never seen them, so they were both looking forward to the outing.

It was a lovely evening, clear and warm, with a faint breeze. Gerald collected them in a carriage. He had hired a box for the evening, and as they arrived, a stout young man in tight yellow inexpressibles rose to his feet. Number five.

Gerald introduced them. "Mr. Cuthbert Carswell," he said. "A friend from my school days."

Mr. Carswell bowed ponderously. "Delighted to meet such lovely ladies." From the faint creaking sound that accompanied his bow, he was wearing a Cumberland corset, like the Prince Regent. Alice glared at Gerald. Gerald avoided her eye.

They seated themselves, a waiter instantly appeared, and Gerald ordered refreshments. Shortly afterward he spotted some acquaintances, excused himself and disappeared, leaving Alice and Lucy alone with Mr. Carswell.

Alice watched him striding away and disappearing into the crowd. Outrageous behavior for a host.

Unlike Mr. Frinton, Mr. Carswell had no difficulty carrying on a conversation. In fact, it soon became clear that, like Mr. Ffolliot, he was quite capable of carrying one on without involving anyone else.

"Did Lord Thornton happen to mention that I recently discovered that I am the presumptive heir for Lord Buttsfield, who owns a barony in Yorkshire?" He smirked at Lucy. "Lord Buttsfield is an elderly gentleman, a confirmed bachelor with no plans to marry, so it is my expectation that before very long I will become Lord Buttsfield. And when I marry"—he added in case she missed the point—"my wife will become Lady Buttsfield."

"How exciting for her," Lucy said.

"Yes. I fancy quite a few ladies will be setting their caps at me."

"Naturally," Lucy agreed coyly.

"In the meantime I have a snug little property of my own, in Yorkshire, where I am involved in conducting some very exciting developments in pig breeding."

"Pig breeding, reeeally?" Lucy repeated with every evidence of fascination. Alice wasn't fooled for a moment.

"Yes," he continued enthusiastically. "I'm crossing the best of my Old Yorkshire sows with some Chinese pigs—I was after the famous Chinese Swimming Pigs, but sadly couldn't find any reliable source. But these other Chinese pigs are well suited to my purposes," he enthused. Without waiting for any inquiry as to his purposes, he continued, "They are small, but they mature early and put on a great deal of fat very quickly. Which is just what one wants in a pig." He nodded in satisfaction.

Lucy glanced at her escort's rounded stomach and pudgy thighs, and winked at Alice, her eyes dancing. Alice didn't find it at all amusing. What on earth had Gerald been thinking, inviting this man? He couldn't possibly believe that Lucy would be attracted to such an insensitive bore. Boar. Boor.

"And the best thing about the pigs I'm breeding—do you want to know?" Nobody said a word or moved a muscle. Alice decidedly did not want to know. "It's their color," he said triumphantly. "Guess what color they are?"

"I couldn't possibly," Alice said repressively. Had nobody taught this young man that it was not polite to prattle on forever, let alone dwell on the intricacies of pig breeding to ladies? Especially ladies he'd only just met.

"Go on, guess!"

"Puce!" Lucy guessed.

Mr. Carswell laughed heartily. "No, no. Try again."

"Blue!"

"Ha-ha. Try again."

Alice looked around, hoping for some release from what promised to be an endless guessing game. But there was no sign of Gerald or the refreshments, she could see nobody else she knew, and the concert hadn't yet begun. The fireworks would come later.

"Pink?" Lucy said.

Mr. Carswell sniffed. "Pink? Common everyday, ordinary pigs are pink," he said disapprovingly. "My pigs are special."

"Then put us out of our misery and tell us what color your very special pigs are," Lucy said.

"White!" he said triumphantly. "Pure, glorious white from snout to tail. They are refined pigs, you see, bred by refined people."

"Is the flesh white too?" Lucy asked. "I can't imagine eating white ham. Or white bacon."

"Oh, we don't eat them," Mr. Carswell declared, shocked. "They are purely for show."

"Then what's the point?" Alice asked crossly.

"My dear lady," he began, "the breeding of pigs is a complex and delicate process, rather beyond the lesser understanding of our dear females, but I shall try to simplify it for you." He then embarked on a long and dreary explanation.

Alice gazed out over the throngs of people wandering through the pleasure gardens and wished Gerald would come back so she could strangle him for inflicting this appalling fellow on them.

Gerald finally returned at the same time as a waiter bearing a tray with champagne. Gerald glanced at Lucy, who was listening to Mr. Carswell with every appearance of fascination. She looked up, gave him an absent little wave and turned back to Mr. Carswell with a rapt expression.

Scowling, Gerald handed the drinks around, then said loudly and heartily, "Well, how are you all getting on?"

"Famously," Lucy said. "Mr. Carswell has been telling

us all about his fascinating pig-breeding program. Do you have any idea of the complex process in getting bacon onto your plate, Lord Thornbroke?"

"No."

"Then you must tell him aaaall about it, Mr. Carswell," Lucy said. "I'm sure he'll be as fascinated as I was."

"Oh, I will, I will," Mr. Carswell said.

Gerald's mouth tightened. Alice narrowed her eyes. So, he knew perfectly well the kind of man he'd inflicted on them. She would have words with Gerald.

"And did you know," Lucy said, bright-eyed, "that Mr. Carswell is in line to become the Baron of Beef?" Alice choked on her drink.

"No, no, dear lady," Carswell corrected her with an indulgent smile. "I'm to be the Baron of *Buttsfield*."

"Silly me, my mistake," Lucy said gaily. She raised her glass at Gerald. "Good health, Lord Thornbottle."

The waiter then returned bearing more refreshments, including bread and butter, some chicken, an onion tart, some cheesecake and a dish of the shaved ham that Vauxhall was famous for.

"Call this ham?" Mr. Carswell picked up a slice with his fork and held it up disdainfully. "Paper thin. And not near enough fat on it." He then embarked on a long-winded explanation of how other pigs he'd bred in the past produced a much finer ham than the stuff they were being served. He had just begun to describe the various breeds of pig and their entrancingly different qualities, when the concert began.

"Hush now, everyone," Alice said crisply. "I very much dislike it when people talk through musical performances." She directed a beady eye at Mr. Carswell.

He swallowed and the flow of porcine information abruptly stopped. The music swelled, and under cover of the sound she had a quiet word with Gerald. "What on earth do you think you're playing at?"

"Playing at, Aunt Alice?" Gerald said with an innocent expression.

She eyed him narrowly. "You know very well what I'm talking about."

Mr. Carswell leaned forward and gave her a reproachful look.

Alice leaned closer to Gerald. "I'll speak to you later."

"I'm going to strangle Gerald," Alice declared after he'd delivered her and Lucy home from Vauxhall. "I've asked him to call on me first thing in the morning. I was too angry to speak to him tonight."

"Didn't you enjoy yourself, Alice?" Lucy asked. "I did, immensely. Especially the fireworks."

Alice looked at her. "You can't possibly have enjoyed Mr. Carswell's conversation."

Lucy gave a gurgle of laughter. "The Baron of Beef? I did, in a way."

"But the man was such a bore!"

Lucy giggled. "I hope you spell it *b-o-a-r*."

Against all inclination, Alice laughed. "Exactly! But how could you have possibly enjoyed talking to him—or listening to him, I should say. You looked quite rapt."

"I wasn't. I was just pretending to listen. Men like that only need the appearance of an audience."

"Then why—"

"Didn't you notice your nephew's face?" Lucy said with a mischievous smile. "The more I doted on Mr. Porker's conversation, the crosser Lord Thornton got. It was the same with Mr. Ffolliot. I cooed agreement with that dreadful man while Lord Thornton sat there glowering. It was so entertaining."

"So you think Gerald is doing it deliberately?"

"Offering me impossible men? Yes, of course. I must say, he's showing a great deal of ingenuity in coming up with them. I expect he'll be running out of impossible gentlemen soon and will have to dig up some poor creature out of the gutter. Or debtor's prison." She laughed.

"Don't you mind?"

"Not at all. It's vastly entertaining."

"But why is he doing it?"

Lucy's smile was like the cat's that ate the cream. "Perhaps to punish me for making him lose his race. He certainly gets cross when I seem to enjoy these men's company, doesn't he? And they enjoy mine."

Alice doubted it had anything to do with the wretched race. "Well, you might not mind these ridiculous stratagems, but I do," she said with asperity. Getting Lucy safely married was not a joke to her. Her future peace of mind rested on it.

Lucy seemed to realize this. She leaned forward to place a hand on Alice's arm. "Please don't worry, Alice. I promise you I will find myself a husband, and quickly. It just won't be with your nephew's help, that's all."

"But, Aunt Alice, you said you wanted your goddaughter to meet suitable eligible men."

"Don't try that flummery on me, Gerald," Alice said. Gerald had called on her, as she'd requested the previous night. Lucy had gone off with Lady Peplowe and Penny to visit Hatchards bookshop, so Alice had her nephew to herself.

"Not one of the men you've produced has been in the slightest bit suitable—eligible, perhaps, but you can't possibly believe that a girl like Lucy, who is bright and lively, could be interested in marrying a man who never speaks or one who never stops speaking, and then only about pigs! Or one with the kind of attitudes that Mr. Ffolliot espouses? Or the rest? Honestly, Gerald, you couldn't possibly have dredged up any worse candidates if you tried!"

"Nevertheless, she seems to have made a conquest of them all," Gerald muttered.

"Is that disappointment I hear in your voice, Gerald? Because *if* Lucy has made a conquest of any of those impossible gentlemen, it is simply because she is a polite, kindhearted girl. She might appeal to them, but none of them could ever appeal to *her*."

Gerald snorted. "Polite and kindhearted? She's just trying to annoy me."

Alice wasn't going to argue with that. Lucy was playing her own deep game, as was Gerald. "At least now that we're getting more invitations to balls and parties, she's starting to meet suitable gentlemen at last."

"Does that mean you no longer have need of my services?"

"If you were in the least bit serious about it, I would, but since you seem to want to make a mockery of my difficulties—"

"I'm not."

Alice merely looked at him with brows raised.

"Oh, very well. I might not have chosen the more suitable of my acquaintances for Miss Bamber, but—"

"They were, I have no doubt, the *least* suitable, and if you are determined to waste our time, I beg you will desist. Now, how have you been doing with your search for Lucy's father, or have you been spending all your time on finding ridiculous matches for Lucy?"

Gerald grimaced. "I've made inquiries all over, but it's as you said: the man seems to have no permanent address. He's as slippery as an eel. I've tracked him to several different addresses, but at each one he's been long gone. Have you thought about hiring a Bow Street Runner?"

"Are you mad? Word would be out in no time. No, we need to make discreet, private inquiries, not have it on public record."

"Then may I share the problem with Lord Tarrant."

Alice looked at him in horror. "Lord Tarrant? No! Why on earth would you want to tell him my private business? I barely know the man." Bad enough that he haunted her thoughts with his offer of *friendship*. She didn't want him involved any deeper in her life.

"No, but *I* know him very well," Gerald said. "And there's no one I'd trust more with my problems."

"It's not your problem, though, is it?"

"You're family, Aunt Alice, and your problems are my problems."

"That's all very well, but Lord Tarrant—"

"Has connections."

Alice eyed him cautiously. "What sort of connections?"

"There's a fellow in the Horse Guards who runs the most extraordinary network of investigative agents. They're famed for efficiency and discreet inquiry. They don't usually do private work—the network was built during the war to gather wartime intelligence—but there's not as much work for them in peacetime, and there might be a possibility that one of the agents could track down Bamber's whereabouts on your behalf. If anyone can swing it, it would be Tarrant. He's a friend of the fellow who runs it."

Alice didn't like the sound of it. She didn't want Lord Tarrant to be involved. She hardly knew him. She didn't want him to know she was being blackmailed, didn't want him to think badly of her. And she would die if he ever read those dreadful letters.

"You can trust Tarrant, Aunt Alice. He's the most honorable, capable, trustworthy man I know."

"Perhaps, but I don't want him to—"

"Don't you *want* Bamber found?"

"Yes, of course I do. It's just . . ." She took a breath and tried a different tack. "What would you do to Bamber if you found him?"

"Force the swine to give up those letters."

"Yes, but how? You wouldn't hurt him, would you?"

"What do you care if I did? The man deserves a dam—a dashed good thrashing."

"Yes, but it could get you into terrible trouble. People go to gaol for that kind of thing. Besides, scoundrel as he is, he's also Lucy's father."

Gerald gave a derisive snort.

"And none of this is her fault."

"It's not yours, either. Now, may I tell Tarrant about the problem or not?" She hesitated, and he added, "It's the best chance we have, and if Miss Bamber is refusing to have anything to do with lords, you're effectively breaking your agreement with her father. Finding him and getting the letters back is your only hope, and for that we need Tarrant and his connections."

Alice sighed. It made sense, but she really, really didn't want Lord Tarrant to know. He would never look at her in the same way again.

"I know you're uneasy about it, Aunt Alice, but it really is the best solution. Tarrant is off fetching his children at the moment, but he should be back in London soon."

"In that case, give me until then to think about it. When Lord Tarrant returns, I'll let you know my decision."

Gerald then took his leave. Alice took herself outside to walk in the garden. Fresh air and greenery always helped her think more clearly.

But from the uncomfortable question of allowing Gerald to tell Lord Tarrant about her problems, her thoughts drifted to notions of a friendship between a man and a woman. Exactly what did Lord Tarrant imagine it would entail?

What did she know about bringing up young girls anyway? She'd never had anything to do with children.

Miss Coates's Seminary for Young Ladies was a tall, gray, stone building just outside the village of Daventry. Surrounded by a neat green garden, it didn't really look like a prison for young hoydens. Though appearances could be deceptive.

Inside, James met Miss Coates, a tall, thin spinster with a calm, intelligent mien. Once he'd established his identity and shown her his credentials, her attitude warmed considerably. "I've never before taken in a child as young as Deborah," she told him, "but her grandmother was adamant that the girls had to stay together."

"Her grandparents were of the opinion that the girls were difficult to handle. I believe 'hoydens' was the word they used."

"'Hoydens'?" Miss Coates laughed. "Far from it. They have all the usual energy of children of that age." She eyed him. "I understand that Judith and Selina spent their earliest years traveling with Wellington's army."

"That's correct. Their mother returned to England for Deborah's birth."

She nodded. "That explains why they follow orders so well. They're lively and high-spirited—at least Judith and Deborah are—but they've never caused me or my staff any real difficulty."

He wondered again at his mother-in-law's description of them as hoydens. "And Lina?"

She hesitated, then said, "Selina is a dear, sweet child, but quite shy and withdrawn."

James wondered what that might mean, but he said nothing.

Miss Coates continued, "Your daughters don't sleep in the dormitories, as the other girls here do. They have their own bedchamber. During the day, my servants care for Deborah, but outside of class time and in the evening, she is with her sisters."

"I see." He was agreeably surprised by the woman's good common sense.

She gave him a thoughtful look, then said, "May I speak frankly, Lord Tarrant?"

"Please do."

"Judith and Selina take good care of their little sister, but it is far from an ideal situation. Judith seems to feel she is responsible for both her younger sisters, and though she handles the responsibility well, she needs to be a child again, not be a little mother at the age of eleven."

"I quite agree."

"What are your intentions for the girls, then?"

He raised a brow. It was not for this spinster schoolmistress to question his intentions—he was their father. For a moment he was tempted to give her a sharp set-down, but he had to admit she had impressed him, and it did seem as though she had attempted to do her best by his daughters.

Though there was that letter . . . He pulled it out and placed it on the desk in front of her. "How do you explain this?"

She glanced at it and nodded. "I'm afraid that was my fault."

"In what way?"

She sighed. "Judith had fallen behind on her evening assignments, claiming she was too busy with Deborah to do them. I informed her that if that was the case, perhaps Deborah would be better off sleeping with Betty, the maid I'd hired to look after her during the daytime. I was bluffing, of course—I would never have separated them—but Judith didn't know that, and she was, naturally, furious." She gave him a rueful glance. "Quite a temper your eldest daughter has."

He tapped the letter. "This letter is completely different from all the others I've received from the girls."

She grimaced. "I know, they copied the others from model letters. You probably won't believe me, but that's not the common practice here—their grandmother gave strict instructions as to how they should communicate." She lifted her chin and looked him in the eye. "I caught Judith trying to smuggle this letter out. I confiscated it, read it, and then posted it myself."

His jaw dropped. "*You* posted it?"

"I did," she said composedly. "And it achieved what both Judith and I intended."

"And what was that?" This woman was surprise after surprise.

"It brought you here." She leaned forward across her desk. "Those girls need a home, Lord Tarrant, not a room of their own in a boarding school, no matter how good the school, and I pride myself that this is one of the best. I'm quite willing to keep them—they are dear girls, one and all—but it is my opinion that they need to be part of a family, to belong, to have a home and to feel loved."

He blinked. "I couldn't agree more. While I thought they were happy and being well looked after by their grandparents, I was content to leave them. Life in the army was no life for small girls, not without their mother."

"And what has changed?"

He refolded the letter and tucked it away. "My older brother died recently, and I inherited the estate and the title and the responsibilities. I now have a home to offer my children, and the income to support them. I have resigned my commission and intend to make my life here in England, with them."

She sat back, smiling. "I am so glad." She picked up a small bell and tinkled it. A moment later a young woman appeared. "Would you bring down the Tarrant girls, all three of them, please." The young woman's gaze slid to James, but the headmistress said, "Don't explain—just tell them they're wanted in my office." The young woman left.

James waited. Impatient and absurdly nervous, he rose to his feet and began to pace around the headmistress's office. The door was open. He could hear footsteps and voices on the stairs. He glanced at the headmistress. "If you don't mind, I'll . . ." and he was out in the lobby, gazing up the stairs, waiting for his children.

They came down the stairs in a group, three across, Judy

and Lina on the outside, little Deborah in the middle, holding their hands. The teacher or assistant, or whatever she was, brought up the rear. Not that James even noticed her. He had eyes only for his daughters. They'd grown so much.

They saw him and came to an abrupt stop halfway down the stairs. "P-Papa?" Judith said uncertainly. Then, at his smile, "*Papaaaaaa*!" she shrieked, and letting go of her little sister's hand, she leapt down the stairs and flung herself at him, just as she always used to. He caught her and managed not to stagger back.

"Oh Papa, Papa, Papa!" she said, hugging him in a death grip around his neck. "You came, you came!" She was laughing and sobbing at the same time.

He hugged her to him, his little girl, all legs and arms now. So tall. Eleven. He couldn't speak for the lump in his throat. Oh, those lost years. He ached for them.

Eventually Judy loosened her grip on him and slid down to resume her own two feet. Smoothing her hair back, he turned to greet his other two daughters.

There was Selina, the image of her mother, staring at him with big blue eyes—her mother's eyes. She waited on the stairs, making no move to approach.

"Lina, it's Papa. It's *Papa*!" Judith shouted.

But when Lina had last seen her father she was not quite four.

"You don't remember me, do you, Lina?" James said gently.

She just looked at him, her forehead furrowed. And then she shook her head.

"But it's Pa—" Judy began.

"It's all right, Judy," he said. "Lina was a very little girl when you left. She was not quite Deborah's age. It's not surprising she doesn't remember me."

He glanced at Deborah, the child he'd never met, and took a swift breath. Dark-haired little Deborah didn't resemble her mother in the least. She was the image of his brother, Ross, at the same age. There was a portrait somewhere of Ross as a child, with the exact same expression. She eyed him suspiciously, then, scowling, plonked her bottom on the stairs and folded her arms, making it clear she had no intention of coming closer.

He almost laughed; Ross, too, had had that same stubborn expression.

A hesitant tug on his coat drew his attention. It was seven-year-old Lina. After an intense, troubled scrutiny, she held up her arms, the way she used to as a toddler. "Up?" James said softly, as he used to.

She nodded, and he picked her up, a stiff, wooden doll in his arms. And then she suddenly softened and leaned forward and pressed her face against his neck. "Ohhhh, you smell just the same," she whispered and hugged him tightly. "I do remember you, Papa, I do."

James just held her for a long, long moment, fighting back unmanly tears.

And then it was time to meet his third daughter. He approached the stairs and knelt down so that their faces were more or less level. "Good afternoon, Deborah. We've never met, but I'm your f—"

"Debo," she muttered.

"I beg your pardon?"

"I'm Debo, not Deborah."

He nodded. "I see. Well then, Debo . . ."

She leaned sideways and looked past him at Judy and Lina standing behind him. "You sure this is Papa?"

They assured her he was. She examined him carefully. She didn't look too impressed. Her scowl was as black as ever. She leaned forward and hit him on the shoulder. "You left us."

"I did," he admitted. Technically they'd left him, but he wasn't going to argue.

"Why you left us?"

"I had to. I was a soldier, and the king needed me. A soldier works for the king."

"The king?"

He nodded.

"Because of the king . . ." She considered that. Her scowl deepened, and her lower lip pushed out. She hit him on the shoulder again. "Then I hate the king."

And there it was, another piece of his heart given over to a small, helpless, angry creature.

"We're all going to be together now. I've come to take you and your sisters home."

"Where is home?" Debo demanded.

"With me, with all of us together." He hadn't yet taken control of the country estate—he still thought of it as Ross's estate, Ross's home. But he'd lived there as a boy, and it was his now. "I have a house in London and a house in the country, but we're going to live in London first." There was work to be done in London, documents to be signed, reports to consider and act on.

And a lovely, skittish lady . . .

Debo considered the possibilities, then tilted her head and narrowed her eyes. "You got a cat in London?"

"No." Cats made him sneeze.

"Hmph!" The scowl was back.

Behind him Miss Coates spoke, "Deborah has a great fondness for cats. She has been waiting for the kitchen cat to have kittens." She added softly, "The kitchen cat is a very fat tom."

James turned back to his smallest daughter. "There might be a cat in one of the houses, Debo—I don't know."

The frown didn't lift. Clearly "might be" wasn't good enough for this small, adorable despot.

"I suppose we could get a kitten."

"Good." Debo stood up. "We going now?"

Chapter Nine

Alice sat at her desk, doing the accounts, as she did at the end of each month. She'd always done the domestic household accounts—Thaddeus considered them women's work; he'd dealt with everything else. His allowance to her for the household had never been generous, and Alice had been taught by her mother to keep strict account of everything.

After Thaddeus died and the extent of his personal debts was discovered, Alice had worked hard to clear herself of debt and bring everything back into balance. But now the money Bamber had given her for Lucy's expenses was all gone, and she was sliding once more into debt.

She hadn't been extravagant; the money had mostly gone on clothing and shoes—and Alice didn't begrudge a penny of it. A young lady entering the marriage mart needed to look stylish and fashionable if she were to have any success—and everything depended on Lucy marrying well.

Both she and Lucy were used to making ends meet, and Miss Chance, too, had done her best, designing several evening dresses with removable gauze overdresses so that three dresses could become nine. And wherever possible, Alice had lent Lucy shawls, hats, gloves and other accessories.

Neither of them wore much jewelry, either. The pearls Lucy had worn that first day were so obviously false it was better to wear nothing. In any case, Lucy favored a pretty gold locket her mother had owned.

Bamber had promised to send Alice more money, but none had been forthcoming. And with no way to contact him, it didn't look promising.

Alice closed the account book, locked it away in her desk and went looking for Lucy.

She found her, as usual, in the garden, under her favorite tree, the big old plane tree, with her sketchbook. Seeing Alice coming, she hastily shut it. Whether she actually ever did any drawing, or whether it was a ploy to enjoy some free time, Alice didn't know. Lucy had never offered to show her drawings to Alice, and Alice didn't want to pry.

"Lucy dear, I've been wondering about those five schools you attended."

Lucy said cautiously, "What about them?"

"Why did you leave?" There was a short silence. Lucy shifted uncomfortably and avoided her eyes. Alice added gently, "It wasn't because you misbehaved, was it?"

Lucy swallowed. "No."

"Was it something to do with money?"

Lucy nodded.

"Every time?"

Again, Lucy gave a shamefaced nod. Alice felt a sharp spurt of anger at the father who had consistently put his growing daughter in such an invidious position. She hadn't intended to press Lucy any further, but suddenly out it all came.

"He always picked the most exclusive schools he could get me into—he lied, you know, giving me grand imaginary relations. And he was always very openhanded with money at the start." As he had been with Alice.

"But the money always ran out," Lucy continued bitterly.

"It was so embarrassing. The headmistress would call me down for little talks in her office—whatever address Papa had given her no longer worked. Her letters and bills were returned. It was so uncomfortable—none of them ever believed that I knew as much as they did about Papa's whereabouts."

"So what happened then?"

"They gave me jobs to do to pay my way: helping in the kitchen, looking after the younger pupils, cleaning—you name it."

Alice cringed on her behalf. The snobbish girls would have shown her no mercy at her fall in status. No wonder Lucy hated "ladies."

"But your father always came for you in the end."

Lucy nodded. "Usually weeks later. He'd swan in with no apology, declare his daughter 'too good for this rubbishy institution' and announce that he was withdrawing me to place me in a much better school." She grimaced. "Which he did."

"And the same thing happened again." It wasn't really a question. Five different schools, and each time, nothing at the end but humiliation for Lucy. Alice had no doubt that this had also happened with the Austrian opera singer and the French comtesse. And now her.

"Yes." A slight breeze rustled the leaves. Lucy folded her arms and shivered, although it wasn't cold. After a minute she turned and faced Alice. "The money's run out, hasn't it?"

"I'm afraid so," Alice said regretfully. "Of course, your father might be arranging to send more even now—"

"He won't. He never does. He flashes it around at the start, but that's it." There was a long silence, then she took a deep breath. "I suppose you want me to leave now."

"Of course I don't," Alice said indignantly. "You forget, I made a vow when I became your godmother."

Lucy said dully, "Yes, but that wasn't real. It was just one of Papa's schemes."

"It was real to me. I made a promise before God, and I meant every word."

Lucy stared at her a moment, then her confusion cleared. "Oh, of course—the blackmail. I'd forgotten for a moment. You can't afford to let me go."

"It's not that at all. Of course I am worried about what your father will do with the letters, but it's your father I blame, not you. Money or not, you are staying right here."

Lucy bit her lip, then took Alice's hands in hers. "I'm so sorry for all this trouble, Alice. I promise you, I'll find a husband as fast as I can and get out of your way" She took a deep breath and added, "I'll even marry a lord if you can find one who'll have me."

Alice would have laughed if the poor girl wasn't so bitterly ashamed and in earnest. "There's no need to go that far," she said in a bracing voice. "Blackmail or not, I'm not letting you go to anyone but a gentleman who will love and cherish you as you deserve to be loved and cherished."

Lucy's eyes shimmered with unshed tears. "You are so good to me, Alice. I can't thank you enough."

"You don't need to thank me. We might have started off badly, but my life was quite drab and uneventful when we first met. Now scarcely a day goes by without something exciting happening, and I've met all sorts of interesting and unusual people."

Lucy gave a cynical snort. "Blackmailers, liars—"

"Yes, indeed, not to mention poets, pedants and passionate pig breeders."

It surprised a reluctant laugh out of Lucy. "You can blame your nephew for those ones."

"Oh, believe me, I do. But my point is, your coming to live with me has brightened my life immeasurably. And despite the difficulties—and the blackmail—I've enjoyed it more than I would have believed possible. In fact"—she linked her arm through Lucy's—"I've come to love you like a daughter. So I won't hear another word about your leaving—unless it's on the arm of a handsome, thoroughly besotted man. Now, shall we go in and see what Mrs. Tweed is preparing for luncheon?"

"Oh, Alice." Lucy's eyes flooded with tears and she hugged Alice tightly. "No one has ever been as good to me as you, and yet you have every reason to hate me."

Alice hugged her back. "Nonsense. You've done nothing to be blamed for, and besides, there's enough hate in the world. I refuse to add to it. Now come along and wipe your eyes. It's time for luncheon!"

After luncheon, Alice called on her nephew at his lodgings. It was one thing to refuse to allow Lord Tarrant to help her when it was just about the blackmail. But to let Bamber abandon his daughter to poverty and humiliation again? No indeed. She wanted the wretched man tracked down and called to account.

And if that was at the expense of her own dignity, so be it.

"You've made the right decision, Aunt Alice," Gerald said when she explained.

She'd given him her permission to take Lord Tarrant into his confidence and was still feeling quite hollow and a bit sick at the thought of Tarrant's reaction. But it had to be done. Bamber had left her with no choice.

"When do you think you'll speak to him?"

"Tarrant? Oh straight away, I should think." Seeing her surprise, he added, "He arrived in London last evening—I saw his carriage pull up outside Tarrant House last night and three little girls tumble out. He's had plenty of time to get himself and his daughters settled in." He glanced at the clock on the mantel. "I'll call on him this evening."

It was well after the dinner hour. James's girls were tucked up in bed under the supervision of Nanny McCubbin, who'd arrived in London before them and had taken control of not only the nursery but also the whole house, apparently. The servants jumped to her command. The girls were reserving judgment, but as their former headmistress had said, they knew how to follow orders. James had every faith in Nanny McCubbin.

He was in the library sipping brandy by the fire, having a quiet night in, when young Thornton dropped by. Over a brandy, Thornton explained his aunt's problem, after first swearing James to secrecy.

"And you say this villain is using these letters to blackmail Lady Charlton?" James said.

"Yes."

"Do you know what's in them?"

Thornton shook his head. "She wouldn't say. Just that they were very personal and private, and she would be devastated if they were made public."

Love letters, then, James thought. It surprised him. She didn't seem the type to conduct an illicit affair. He couldn't deny that he felt a little disappointed. It wasn't the impression he'd had of her.

Still, she was in trouble, and he'd agreed to help.

"What have you done so far to track him down?"

Thornton outlined everything he'd done, ending with, "He's a slippery damned weasel."

"And are we sure that Miss Bamber isn't involved? She's not hiding her father's whereabouts, for instance."

Thornton pursed his lips. "Aunt Alice is convinced that Miss Bamber is as much a victim as she is, but I'm not so sure. What kind of man would blackmail a stranger to take in his daughter and then give her no way of contacting him? It's not credible. What if something went wrong? Bamber has no way of knowing that Aunt Alice has a heart as soft as butter."

James nodded. It did seem most unlikely.

"Did you question Lady Charlton's butler?"

"About any letters posted? Yes, but Tweed said Miss Bamber hasn't left any to be posted. I suppose she could have posted something herself, but she goes nowhere unaccompanied, so it would be quite difficult to slip away and contact her father."

But needs must, James thought. His eleven-year-old daughter had managed to get a letter to him, even if she'd been caught doing it. Or maybe, as things stood at the moment, Miss Bamber felt no need to contact her father.

"You seem to have done everything possible to find the man," James said. "What do you think I can do?"

Thornton looked a little self-conscious. "I was thinking that fellow you know in the Horse Guards—Radcliffe, isn't it?—might be able to help."

James considered it. Radcliffe didn't usually involve himself in private matters like this, but he supposed there was no harm in asking his advice. He knew people, did Radcliffe.

"There's no guarantee he'll be able to help."

Thornton nodded. "I know, but I'd feel better knowing we have explored every possible avenue. Alice is a good person. She doesn't deserve to be under someone's thumb like this. Not now, when she's finally free."

Finally free. An interesting turn of phrase to use about a relatively recent widow, James thought.

"What can you tell me about her marriage?" Thornton hesitated, and James added, "It would seem to have a bearing on the blackmail."

Thornton acknowledged the truth of that with a long sigh. "Uncle Thaddeus was . . . I think he was a bit of bully."

"Think?" James remembered him from school. He was a nasty piece of work back then.

Gerald wrinkled his nose thoughtfully. "The thing is, he could be quite charming in public. The ladies seemed to love him. But the way he treated my father—Papa was a younger son, you know, and Uncle Thaddeus used to, I don't know, rub Papa's nose in it. Papa was dependent on him for everything—he'd been left nothing in Grandpapa's will—but Grandpapa expected Uncle Thaddeus to make over one of the lesser estates to Papa's management and use. That's the way it's always been done in our family. Only Uncle Thaddeus didn't."

James could see that the issue rankled. From what he gathered, Thornton's father had done exactly the same to Thornton as his uncle had done to him. But that wasn't the issue that concerned him at the moment. "And how did your uncle treat his wife?"

"He wasn't . . . kind. When there was only family present, he treated her, oh, like a servant. Dismissively. As if she didn't matter. Quite cruelly at times."

James stiffened. "Physically?"

Thornton shook his head. "I don't think so." His lack of certainty set James's teeth on edge. "It was a different kind of cruelty, like a cat toying with a mouse. Embarrassing her, making cutting comments, humiliating her in front of others."

James's hands closed into fists. To treat such a gentle lady so . . .

"For instance, he never lost an opportunity to belittle her, especially in front of my mother. Alice is barren, you know, and I don't recall a single occasion when Uncle Thaddeus didn't mention the fact, directly or indirectly. He had a very cutting tongue."

"Why particularly in front of your mother?"

Thornton gave a shamefaced grimace. "Mama used to encourage him. She's never liked Aunt Alice, I don't know why. It's not fair. Alice doesn't deserve any of it; she's the kindest person."

There was a short silence. James thought that Thornton was probably wondering the same thing he was: If Charlton had been openly cruel to his wife in company, what must he have been like in private?

"But if she did have a lover," Thornton burst out, as if he'd been having a silent argument with himself, "I, for one, don't blame her. She deserved some happiness in her life. Didn't she? Well, didn't she?"

His words hung in the air. James didn't respond. He wasn't sure what he thought about it at the moment. He was appalled by what Thornton had told him about her marriage. But infidelity? His emotions were all over the place.

"Any idea who this lover might have been?"

Thornton shook his head. "I don't think I ever even saw her with a man, except at balls and parties. But that doesn't prove anything, I suppose."

"I don't really care about the lover," James said, surprising himself, "but if we knew who he was, we could follow him up. He must surely know something about Bamber, if he gave—or sold—him the letters." And if he did hand over private love letters from Lady Charlton, the man deserved a damned good thrashing.

"So will you speak to Radcliffe?"

"Yes, I'll call on him tomorrow. Do you want to come?"

"Of course." They made arrangements to meet the next morning, then Thornton thanked him and left. James poured himself another brandy and pondered the question of Lady Charlton and her secret lover.

He couldn't help feeling a little disappointed. But that was foolish. At his age, he should know better than to put people on pedestals.

So she was human. But he'd stake everything he owned that she wasn't a wanton. In fact he'd thought her quite shy of men. He'd flirted with her in the mildest way, and she'd practically run a mile.

And as far as he could see, she made no effort to encourage the attentions of other men. Quite the contrary.

So if she'd had a secret lover—and he wasn't sure of that, though what else could those letters be about?—it must have been for love, rather than the boredom or neglect that drove many wives to infidelity. And given the shameful way her husband had treated her, who could blame her for that?

It was a mystery. But it wasn't going to hold him back from doing everything he could to help her.

And did this revelation of her past change how he felt about her? Did it make him want her any less? He swirled the last of his brandy, inhaled the potent fumes and considered the question.

The answer he found was, quite clearly, no. Well, then . . .

The following day Lord Tarrant sent a note to Alice, informing her he was back in London and adding that he was looking forward to introducing her to his daughters.

Alice read the note through several times, looking for some hidden meaning, but there was none. She responded with a note inviting him and his daughters to afternoon tea the day afterward.

As soon as it had gone, she felt absurdly nervous. She was being ridiculous, she told herself. A daytime visit by three small girls and their father was nothing to be nervous about. Besides, Lucy would be there.

She'd thought of him far too often for her peace of mind, the image of his tall person and those mesmerizing gray eyes popping up in her thoughts at odd moments throughout the day. And especially at night.

But it was ridiculous to imagine she'd missed him. She hardly knew him.

He'd made it clear that he just wanted friendship from her, she reminded herself. *Friendship!* Which suited her perfectly.

But did friendship mean the same thing to him that it did to her? There were times when she'd noticed an intense look in his eyes that seemed to indicate more than just friendship. It was that look that disturbed her, and generated unsettling feelings in her, feelings she'd never had before, sometimes when he wasn't even there. Feelings that seemed to be guiding her to the edge of some unknown cliff.

Oh, what nonsense. She was a mature woman, past her prime, and he knew she wasn't interested in marrying again. She'd also made it plain to him that she wasn't the kind of widow who'd welcome men to her bed. It was just afternoon tea, for heaven's sake.

Mrs. Tweed was thrilled when Alice told her there would be a gentleman and three small girls coming for afternoon tea. She immediately went into a frenzy of baking plans, which only exacerbated Alice's nerves. "Whatever you think best, Mrs. Tweed. I'm sure you'll do us proud," she said and scuttled out of the kitchen in fine cowardly form.

The day of the visit by Lord Tarrant and his children dawned clear and sunny. Lucy was up early and disappeared into the garden, as she did most mornings. Delicious scents floated from the kitchen, as did the sound of singing, loud and slightly off-key. Mrs. Tweed was in a good mood. Children in the house, at last.

Alice pushed that thought from her mind. It wasn't a reproach. Mrs. Tweed was just happy. She liked children, and she enjoyed baking. And it was a lovely day, and not too hot.

Tweed, too, had been fussing around all morning, making sure everything was in perfect order. Fresh flowers in the hallway and drawing room. Floors polished and smelling faintly of beeswax, cushions plumped, windows washed, the silverware shining—all days before the usual household routine.

One would imagine the King was coming to call.

As the time grew closer, Alice dithered about what to wear. She didn't want to appear to be dressing up for him. She *wasn't* dressing up for him. It was just an ordinary afternoon visit. With small children, who would no doubt end up with sticky hands from the delicacies that Mrs. Tweed was making.

But she didn't want to look drab, either. Neat and quietly à la mode would do, she finally decided, then emptied her wardrobe looking for something neat but not too stylish. She finally settled on one of her old mourning dresses, a dove gray dimity frock. It was a little on the drab side, but if there were any doubt about her intentions, it would send a subtle message. She was *not* trying to attract.

Her maid, Mary, eyed the chosen dress disapprovingly. "You're not wearing that, are you, m'lady? Not for afternoon tea with his lordship and the little girls." Clearly Alice's entire household was taking a very different view of the purpose behind the visit.

"Yes, Mary, I am. I don't know why everyone is making a fuss. We have visitors for afternoon tea all the time."

Mary sniffed, and fastened the dress with an expressionless face that fooled Alice not at all. "At least wear this, m'lady," she said, draping a lacy cream shawl around Alice's shoulders.

Alice pushed it off. "No, I don't like wearing shawls when taking tea. They always slide off me." Or the ends fell into her teacup.

"Then what about this?" Mary brought out a three-quarter-sleeved, dark-cherry-pink spencer. It was an old favorite, and Alice had almost forgotten she owned it, but she had to admit it suited the dress perfectly, without making her feel as though she'd gone to any special effort. She gazed at her reflection in the looking glass and nodded. It would do.

Alice paced restlessly around the drawing room awaiting the arrival of Lord Tarrant and his children, and she was rearranging the flowers for the fifth time when Tweed knocked on the door.

"This communication just arrived, m'lady." He held a silver salver, on which sat a letter. "Delivered by an Unknown Person. I found it slipped under the door. Shall I burn it, or do you want to read it?" His expression made his own preference clear.

Alice held out her hand. "No, I'll read it. You didn't see who delivered it?"

"No, m'lady."

Tweed retreated. Alice could think of only one person who would send her a letter by such means. She broke open the seal, unfolded the letter and another piece of paper fell out. She picked it up, set it aside and read the letter. Just as she thought, it was from Bamber.

Lady Charlton,

I am extremely disappointed. So far my daughter has been seen being escorted by various undistinguished Misters, one Viscount—your own nephew—but no Earls or Dukes. It is Not Good Enough. I made it Very Clear to you that she is to marry a Titled Man. To refresh your memory of our agreement, I have enclosed a Reminder—a copy only. I hold all the originals.

Octavius Bamber, esq.

She unfolded the enclosed paper and glanced at the contents. Bile rose in her throat. She crumpled the copy in her fist. She did not need to read the whole thing. She remembered the occasion . . .

She walked over to the fireplace and threw the letter in the fire. She watched as it briefly flamed then slowly turned to ash. Oh, that all her problems could so easily be destroyed.

But what to do?

She is to marry a Titled Man . . .

It seemed she'd been unduly optimistic in assuming that

Bamber's main desire was to see his daughter settled securely and happily. This letter made it clear that all he cared about was a title.

If only the wretched man had called in person, she would have talked to him, tried to convince him that Lucy's happiness mattered more than any title. But he'd probably paid some urchin to deliver the letter. He must know that the money he'd given her for Lucy's expenses had run out by now.

She had promised not to force Lucy into an unwelcome marriage and she utterly refused to break that promise. And since Lucy was as determined as ever to eschew lords, it was more important than ever that Bamber's hiding place was found and the letters retrieved and destroyed. He had, after all, broken his side of the agreement by not providing her with the money he'd said he would.

She sat down and penned a quick note to Gerald, then drank a cup of coffee to brace her nerves.

Octavius Bamber would *not* ruin her day.

Lord Tarrant and his daughters arrived right on time. He introduced Alice and Lucy to each girl in turn, starting with the oldest, Judith. She curtsied and greeted Alice with faint reserve, as if wondering just who Alice was and what their relationship was to be. Or maybe Alice was ascribing her own foolish imaginings to the child.

Simple friendship, she reminded herself.

The next daughter, Lina, also curtsied—it was clear the girls had been well trained—and murmured her greetings in a shy almost-whisper. She was a pretty child with blonde hair and wide blue eyes, and Alice wondered if she resembled her late mother. Judith's gray eyes obviously came from her father, but otherwise there was no strong resemblance.

Of the three girls, the littlest, Deborah, looked most like

him, with curly dark hair and wide gray eyes. She bobbed a quick, crooked curtsy and rattled off, "HowdoyoudoLadyCharltonMissBamber." She glanced cautiously at her father, then added, "Yougotacat?"

Lord Tarrant gave Alice a look that was half amusement, half apology.

Alice gave a rueful smile. "Why, no, I'm sorry, Deborah. I'm afraid we haven't."

"Oh." The small person scowled.

"There's one that's often in the garden," Lucy said. "I'm not sure who it belongs to, but I often see it out there. A ginger tom, very friendly and well fed, so it obviously belongs to someone."

Deborah's eyes lit up. "Can we go see?" Judith nudged her, and Deborah added, "Pleeeeease."

Lucy glanced at Alice for permission. Alice raised a brow in query at the children's father. He sighed and nodded, "If it's not too much trouble."

"No trouble at all," Lucy assured him. "It's a glorious day. Shame to waste it by being inside. Come along girls." She whisked all three girls away, leaving Alice alone in the drawing room with Lord Tarrant. Which had not been the plan. At all.

Those smoky-gray eyes . . .

She invited him to sit. "Sherry?"

"No, thank you."

"Your daughters are charming."

"Even 'Yougotacat?' Debo?"

She laughed. "She does seem rather more interested in cats than people."

His eyes crinkled with amusement. "It was practically the first thing she said to me when we met. And now the first thing she says to me each morning is 'Wegettingthatkittentoday?' Which she repeats at intervals throughout the day." His mouth quirked. "At that first meeting I did mention a vague possibility of getting a kitten. How was I to know she'd take it as a sacred oath signed in blood—my blood."

Alice laughed.

"In my defense," he added, "I had no idea quite how determined a person that small could be. She's utterly relentless." It was clear he adored the little despot.

"So are you going to get her a kitten?"

"Of course, if only to save my own sanity." He gave a snort of amusement. "The headmistress of the school she was at told me that Debo had been checking the kitchen cat every day, waiting for it to give birth. 'It' being a very fat tom."

She chuckled.

"The difficulty is in finding suitable kittens in London. It seems very few kittens are allowed to grow to a size ready to be given away—most people, unless they want one for themselves, drown them at birth."

"Oh dear. How very sad for the mother cats—and the kittens, of course," she added. Thaddeus had never allowed her any kind of pet. It suddenly occurred to her that she could have a cat or a dog now—in fact she could fill the house with pets if she wanted.

It was odd how these random reflections kept popping into her mind. She supposed after eighteen years of having the law laid down to her—and in a way the eighteen years before that had been just as strict, though Papa's law had been slightly more benevolent—she was only just getting used to her freedom.

She suddenly became aware that he was looking at her with a quizzical expression. "What?" she said.

"You went away, somewhere else. Somewhere not very pleasant, I suspect." His voice held no criticism or accusation, just a quiet observation.

She felt herself blushing. "Sorry, I was just . . . just thinking about cats and keeping pets. I've never had one."

"Never? Don't you like animals."

"Oh, I always wanted one—a dog rather than a cat, but I would have been happy with either."

"Then why did you never get one?"

"My father didn't approve of unnecessary animals—which was his definition of a pet—and my husband didn't like them, either. Cats made him sneeze."

"They make me sneeze, too."

"And yet you're going to get one?" she said in surprise.

His mouth twisted with wry humor. "Of course. Can you imagine my little 'Yougotacat?' Debo being happy without one? What are a few sneezes compared with the happiness of my daughter?"

Alice swallowed, touched by his complete willingness to endure discomfort for the sake of his child's pleasure. For a moment, she couldn't say anything.

He gazed back at her, his eyes darkening. His eyes dropped to her mouth, then he leaned forward, his expression suddenly intense. "Lady Charlton," he began.

At that moment the clock in the hall chimed the half hour. Alice jumped, suddenly tense, though why she had no idea. "Speaking of your daughters," she said hastily, "we'd better go and see what they're up to. My cook has been preparing a feast to delight a little girl's heart, and I'd hate us to be late."

With a rueful look, he rose and held out a hand to help her up. She took it without thinking, though of course she could rise perfectly well unaided.

Neither of them wore gloves, and as they touched, skin to skin, a shiver ran through her: it wasn't at all unpleasant. Quite the contrary. She released his hand and brushed her skirt down self-consciously.

"Through here." She led the way to the back gate and the garden.

Lord Tarrant paused at the gate, his gaze taking in the wide expanse of greenery, the winding pathways, bright flower beds and mature trees. "Good lord, I had no idea there was such a large garden behind all these houses. There is no indication of it from the street, though now, I come to think of it, you can see a few treetops. It's your own private park, isn't it?"

"Yes, the garden is the reason my maternal grandmother bought the house. She was a countrywoman at heart, but my grandfather was much involved in politics and had to live in London for a good part of the year. This was their compromise.

"I share it with the other house owners." She gestured to the houses that enclosed the garden square. "Several are owned by the Earl of Salcott, who lives in that large house on the corner. The old earl recently died, so I suppose his son will be taking over. Otherwise few people seem to use the garden except as a backdrop. Lucy comes out here most mornings and says she rarely sees anyone other than the occasional gardener."

"It's a beautiful retreat. You're very lucky."

"Believe me, I am very aware of it, and very grateful to Grandmama for leaving me the house in her will. Now, shall we seek out your daughters and Lucy?"

"Yes, of course." He presented his arm, and after a brief hesitation, Alice placed her hand on it. It was warm and strong, and she tried not to be aware of it.

They walked the various pathways, looking for the children, but there was no sign of them. "They can't wander off," Alice assured him. "The garden is very secure, and the only exits are through the private houses that enclose the garden. And Lucy is with them."

He smiled down at her. "I'm not worried. I'm enjoying our time together."

They rounded a corner and saw a small figure standing alone beneath a large, spreading plane tree, staring up apparently talking to the tree. "That's Lina." Lord Tarrant picked up his pace. "What's she doing on her own?"

They hurried up to her. "Lina, what's the matter?" he said. The little girl turned, her face distraught. "I'm s-s-sorry, Papa," she said. "I t-t-tried." She burst into tears.

Without hesitation her father scooped her up into his arms. Lina clung to him, sobbing and trying to explain in jerky, incoherent phrases. Murmuring soothing reassurances, he held her, smoothing back her hair and rubbing her back while the little girl sobbed herself out.

The sobs slowed, but remnants kept coming in jerky bursts. Lord Tarrant pulled out a handkerchief and dried her face. "Now, do you think you can tell me what has upset you so?"

"I t-tried to s-stop them . . . but D-Debo . . . the cat . . ." She clung to his neck like a little limpet. "P-p-lease don't send us awaaaay, Papa. We're not hy-hydons. Truly we're not."

"Hydens?" Alice wondered. She glanced up into the tree and saw three faces looking worriedly down. Four faces, actually—Lucy's, Judy's and little Deborah's, and in her arms, a furry-faced ginger cat.

Over the shoulder of his sobbing daughter, Lord Tarrant glanced at Alice, sending her a silent message of apology. She directed her glance upward, and he followed her gaze, closed his eyes briefly and nodded in understanding.

"Hush now, Lina," he murmured, his voice deep and reassuring. "Of course I'm not going to send you away. I've just got you back."

"P-p-promise?" Lina choked. "Even if we're h-hydens?"

"Even if you're hoydens, I promise." Lord Tarrant dried the fresh burst of tears. "Now stop crying and listen to me, Lina." He took her chin in his hand and made her look at him.

She inhaled a jagged breath and eyed him with wide, tear-drenched eyes, her mouth trembling.

In a clear, firm voice, audible to the listeners in the trees, he said, "Selina Louise Tarrant, I hereby promise you that

I will *never* send you or your sisters away, no matter what you've done. Do you understand me?"

The little girl nodded.

"Good. Now, I suppose all this upset is because your sisters—and Miss Bamber—climbed this tree."

Lina nodded. "It's very unladylike. Only the veriest hydens climb trees—hydens are very bad girls. And before, when Grandmama caught us . . ."

"I know, you were sent away to school," her father said. Alice's brows shot up. Lord Tarrant nodded in grim acknowledgement. "But that's never going to happen again."

He looked up at the other three girls in the tree. "Let me guess, that cat was up the tree."

Debo nodded and clutched the cat tighter. "He was lonely."

"More like trying to escape my little monster," Lord Tarrant murmured to Alice. "And you others followed?"

"It's my fault, Lord Tarrant," Lucy called down. "I encouraged the girls to climb the tree. I often sit up here to read. It's very peaceful. I didn't realize it was forbidden. I'm sorry. Please don't blame the girls."

"It's very unladylike," Lina repeated, parrotlike. "Isn't it, Lady Charlton?"

Lord Tarrant turned to Alice, his eyes glinting with humor. "Well, is it, Lady Charlton?" Alice looked from him to the tear-stained child in his arms.

"Some people might think so, but I think it's perfectly acceptable for young ladies to climb trees, especially in the privacy of their own garden," she said firmly.

"Or a friend's garden," Lord Tarrant prompted.

"Or a friend's garden," she agreed.

"And it's not hydenish?" Lina breathed.

"It's not in the least hoydenish," Alice said. "In fact, when I was your age, I spent many happy hours sitting in the apple tree at home. Of course, if I'd thrown apples at anyone, that would have been hoydenish. Naturally, I didn't do any such thing."

Lina nodded solemnly. "No, because you're a lady—Lady Charlton."

Alice regarded her thoughtfully. "No, Lina, the 'Lady' in my name is just a title, like Miss or Mrs. Any girl, no matter what her background, can become a lady—it's all in how you behave and how you treat others. Of course, a lady should consider the feelings of others, but otherwise she can do whatever she wants, as long as it doesn't hurt anybody else."

Lina regarded her with wide, solemn eyes, absorbing that. Alice glanced up at the girls in the tree and saw that Lucy had also received the message. Good.

"And is it only young girls who can climb trees, Lady Charlton?" Lord Tarrant asked smoothly, his eyes dancing. It was a dare, plain and simple.

Alice had no desire whatsoever to climb a tree. It had been years since she'd even tried, and even as a young girl, she didn't often do it. One could tear one's clothes for a start, and new clothes weren't easily come by at the vicarage.

On the other hand, there was this tall, handsome devil with a look in his eyes that made her itch to take up his unspoken challenge. And a tear-stained little girl looking to her for reassurance, with an expression that almost broke Alice's heart.

All her life, Alice had strived to please others and do what she was told was "the right thing." And where had it gotten her? Endlessly trying to please others, and finding it a thankless task. Did she really want to set this earnest little girl on the same path?

She made up her mind. "Turn your back," she told Lord Tarrant.

He promptly did a military-style about-face that made

Lina, still in his arms, giggle. The little girl squirmed around and watched Alice over his shoulder.

Luckily the tree was an old one, and unlike most of the planc trees in London's streets and parks, it had never been pruned or pollarded. The trunk was broad and lumpy with handholds and branches sticking out. The larger branches began about three feet off the ground.

Alice carefully gathered the skirts of her dress, thanking the impulse that had caused her to wear an old dress she didn't particularly care for. She rolled the skirt and petticoat up and tucked them into the waist of her drawers.

She eyed the tree cautiously. It was going to be a bit of a scramble. Four pairs of eyes—five if you counted the cat—watched her eagerly. Why had she ever agreed to do this mad thing?

"Need a hand?" a tall devil with his back to her murmured.

"Not in the least." She took a deep breath and started with a jump, to reach the first branch she judged strong enough to support her. It was so thick, it was hard to hold on to. As she stretched up, she heard a ripping sound. A cool breeze under her arm told her she'd ripped a seam in her spencer. Too bad. She wasn't going to stop now. It was an old spencer, and seams could be resewn.

Scrabbling with her feet to gain purchase on the lumpiest part of the trunk, she tried to swing her leg up to hook it over the first big branch. Once, twice . . . she almost managed it, then suddenly a large warm hand placed itself on her bottom and shoved—Alice squeaked with indignation—and there she was, sitting on the branch.

She glared down at him, her cheeks on fire, and not just from the effort of climbing. Her whole body was hot and flustered. Even her bottom was blushing—she could feel it. "You, you—"

"Helped, yes, I know." He was grinning. "It's not against the rules, is it?"

It was very much against the rules of gentlemanly behavior—watching her climb in her drawers when she'd *told* him to turn his back. As for putting his hand on her bottom! Her almost-naked bottom! She could still feel the warm imprint of it on her skin.

She so wanted to ring a peal over his head, but she couldn't do it in front of his daughters—and he knew it, the rogue.

"Can you go on from there by yourself?" he asked with a solicitude that didn't fool her for a moment. His eyes gave him away every time. He was enjoying this.

She stood and scrambled up to the next branch, pulling and heaving. *Riiip!* The second sleeve of her spencer went. Ladies' clothing was not designed for energetic activities like climbing trees. Or even raising their arms.

The girls above called encouragement and advice, and slowly Alice climbed until, panting but triumphant, she finally seated herself on a broad, thick branch well above Lord Tarrant's head. He looked up, grinning. She wished she had an apple to throw at him. But by her own account that would be hoydenish.

It might be fun to be a hoyden. All her life she'd been so well behaved. How dull. But it was another of those possibilities that now stretched temptingly before her.

She looked across and found Lucy and Judy grinning at her. Debo's whole attention was on the rather martyred-looking ginger cat clutched firmly in her arms.

Down below, Lord Tarrant was lifting Lina up to the first branch. "Go on now, Lina, up to Lady Charlton with you."

The little girl scrambled up the tree far quicker and with less effort than Alice had. She plonked herself down on Alice's branch and smiled shyly up at her. "We're two ladies in a tree," Lina said excitedly.

Alice shook her head. "No." She indicated the others above them. "We're five ladies in a tree."

"Anacat," said Debo.

"And a cat," Alice agreed.

"Actually," said a deep voice very close below her, "we're five ladies, a cat and a gentleman in a tree." He pulled himself effortlessly onto the same broad branch and, over his daughter's head, grinned at Alice like the veriest urchin. "How long since you climbed a tree, Lady Charlton?"

"Years." She eyed his long legs, enclosed and protected by supple buckskin breeches. "Ladies' clothing is not conducive to tree climbing."

He glanced at the ripped seams of her sleeves. She was immediately aware of his gaze. "So I see. Perhaps I should get breeches made for the girls."

Between them, Lina gasped. "Girls can wear *breeches*?"

"Only in private," Alice said hastily. "And when there are no gentlemen around."

Lina turned and looked accusingly at her father.

"It's all right," he said. "Fathers are not gentlemen."

Alice spluttered. "Very true."

His eyes darkened. His smile was full of dark promise. "And you can take that as fair warning."

Alice swallowed. "Time to go inside now," she announced to the occupants of the tree. "Mrs. Tweed has a lovely afternoon tea ready for us. I trust you are all hungry."

His gray eyes dropped to her mouth and stayed there. "Ravenous."

One by one, they all scrambled down from the tree. Alice insisting on going first so that she didn't have to endure Lord Tarrant standing below her, looking up. Or helping her down.

He helped his daughters down, swinging them by the hands for the last little distance. Debo was the most difficult: she didn't want to let go of her feline captive.

"Pass it to me," he told her. "I'll keep it safe."

She hesitated, and her hold must have loosened, for with a wriggle, a yowl and a leap, the cat was away, bounding down the tree and vanishing into the shrubbery. With a wail, Debo tried to grab it and would have fallen had her father not managed to grab her in time.

"Thassmycaaaaat!" she wailed.

"It's *not* your cat," he told her and brought her down far enough to hand her down to Alice, waiting on the ground. "Hang on to her," he told Alice, "or she'll disappear after that wretched animal."

"S'not a wretched animal," Debo grumbled.

"No," Alice agreed as she set her on her feet. "He's a very handsome cat. But he does belong to somebody else. They'd be very sad if you took him away. You wouldn't want to make them sad, would you?"

Debo shrugged. Anonymous cat owners moved her not at all.

"Your father will get you a kitten very soon, I'm sure," Alice said, as he came slithering down the tree.

Debo gave him a cynical look. "S'what he said back at Miss Coates's. But still, I got no cat."

He brushed twigs off his coat. "I'm doing my best, Debo."

The little girl sniffed.

"Come along, there's a lovely tea waiting for us inside," Alice said. "Wash your hands in the scullery first."

As they walked back toward the house, Alice felt a small, cold hand slip into hers. She looked down and smiled. Lina was walking along beside her, giving a happy little skip from time to time.

Mrs. Tweed had outdone herself. There were dainty triangular sandwiches with their crusts cut off—cucumber, egg and watercress, ham, and chicken. There were little sausage rolls, hot from the oven, the pastry golden, crisp and flaky. In the center of the table sat a large, luscious sponge cake oozing with cream and jam. There were tiny individual number cakes, each one just large enough for a small girl to hold in her hand. There were wafer-thin almond biscuits—crisp, nutty and sweetly bland—and to finish, a dish of fruits, including fat, sugar-encrusted purple grapes that crunched deliciously as they bit into them.

Thc girls—and Lucy—oohed and aahed over the sight, and for the first ten minutes there was no sound at the table other than "Please pass the . . ." and the sound of chewing and blissful sighs.

Mrs. Tweed had provided a large pot of tea, but there was also milk for the children or lemonade, cold, tart-sweet and refreshing, which Alice chose. Lord Tarrant drank the tea but accepted a glass of wine when Tweed offered it to him.

He ate some of everything but particularly favored the sausage rolls, as well as the cream-filled sponge and the number cakes. He was finishing his third sausage roll when he looked up and caught her watching him.

"You *were* ravenous," she said.

He gave her a slow smile. "Yes, but I wasn't talking about food." Again his gaze dropped to her mouth.

What was he looking at? She had a weakness for cream cakes, and she also loved the sugar-coated grapes. Was cream or sugar stuck to her lip? Fighting a blush, she picked up a napkin and scrubbed at her lips.

His smile deepened, but all he said was, "Your cook is very good." Three little girls looked up and nodded, their mouths full.

"Papa," Judy said after swallowing a mouthful of cake, "it wasn't really Miss Bamber's fault that we climbed the tree. I went up first and the others followed."

"Not true!" Debo said. "I was first! I won."

"Actually, the cat went up first, and Debo followed," Lucy interjected.

Lord Tarrant held up a hand, stopping a babble of argument. "Enough. Neither Lady Charlton nor I have any interest in who climbed what. The rule from now on is that there must be a responsible adult present before anything like that happens again. It could be dangerous."

"Is Miss Bamber a responsible adult?" Judy asked.

"Yes," he said. "Now, I'm assuming you don't want any more of this delicious food, so shall I ask Mr. Tweed to take it away?"

His answer was immediate silence, and a renewed attention to the food at hand. Alice laughed softly. He certainly knew how to handle children. "You said you were having trouble finding a kitten of a suitable age," she said quietly, aware of the small ears further along the table. "I might have a suggestion."

A dark brow rose. He gave an encouraging nod.

"An acquaintance of mine, Beatrice, Lady Davenham, runs a literary society that I occasionally attend. She has several cats, and often has kittens. She's too softhearted to drown them, and is forever foist—er, bestowing them on her friends. I could make inquiries, if you like."

"That would be wonderful. Thank you." In the same low undervoice, he said, "Did you hear that, Debo?"

The little girl nodded and said with her mouth full of cake, "Yes, Lady Charlton's getting me a kitten from a Bee lady with lots of cats. When?"

"Ears like a bat when it comes to Things Feline," he told Alice.

Alice chuckled. "The literary society meets tomorrow. I'll take Lucy."

Lucy pulled a face. "Literary society?"

"You'll like it. I promise."

Chapter Ten

"That swine Bamber has been threatening Alice again, damn his impudence!" Thornton told James. It was early morning, the dew was still on the ground, and James and Thornton were on horseback. After a good fast gallop to sweep the cobwebs away, they were now walking their mounts and talking. Hyde Park was almost deserted, except for a family that rode out together most mornings.

James gave him a sharp look. "Threatening? How?"

"Sent her a note complaining that the girl wasn't being seen with enough lords—can you believe the fellow's insisting his daughter must marry someone titled?" He snorted. "He also sent a copy of one of the letters he's blackmailing her with, threatening to make it public."

To whom had she written those letters, James wondered again. "Did you see it?"

"No, she burnt it."

They rode on. James was thoughtful. Why would Bamber send Alice a copy of one of her own letters? To frighten her? It obviously had, if she'd told Gerald about it. But she'd burnt it, so she obviously was too ashamed to let him see it.

"Has Radcliffe's man—what was his name again?—discovered anything yet?"

Thornton nodded. "Heffernan. He's good, I'll give him that. He hasn't found Bamber—he's a slippery bastard—but he's already discovered a number of men who've been cheated by Bamber."

"Cheated? How?"

"All kinds of cheats and swindles. You name it—financial schemes that turned out to be false, counterfeit deeds and certificates, fraudulent share schemes, card cheats, the sale of land he didn't own. Quite inventive, really."

"And blackmail?"

Thornton's mouth twisted. "Harder to tell, according to Heffernan. Blackmail is the kind of thing people are more likely to deny, to hide. Cheat them out of their life savings and they'll scream the house down, but blackmail them and they'll deny there was ever anything to be blackmailed about. Understandable, I suppose."

A breeze sprang up as they were passing under a spreading oak, and drops of water spattered down on them.

"None of the men we questioned knew anything about his daughter, howev—"

James twisted in his saddle to stare at Thornton. "Good God! You didn't ask them directly?"

"Of course I didn't," Thornton retorted irritably. "I know better than to draw the attention of angry, vengeful men to Bamber's daughter. Lord, they'd have the girl for breakfast." He brushed water droplets off his coat. "I simply asked whether they knew of any family—as a way of contacting him. None of them knew a thing."

"And you believe them?"

Thornton nodded. "If they had any way of contacting him, they would have done so, believe me. His victims are out for his blood. The fellow has to be one step away from a one-way journey to Botany Bay, if not a lynching. No wonder he's so hard to find."

"All the more reason to keep these inquiries discreet. I won't have Lady Charlton and Miss Bamber bothered any further by Bamber's nonsense than they already have been."

Thornton gave him a quizzical look. "*You* won't have *my* aunt bothered?"

James gave him a level look. "No."

"Then perhaps I should ask you again about your intentions in that direction."

"My intentions?" James responded. "Breakfast. My girls will be up and dressed by now. I don't want to keep them waiting. We always take our breakfast together. 'Morning, Thornton. Thanks for keeping me up to date with the investigation."

"But I meant—" Thornton began, but James was already cantering away.

Gerald's visit to the Horse Guards had been an eye-opener. He'd found it fascinating working with Heffernan over the last few days, but it had been even more interesting listening to Tarrant and Radcliffe discussing the situation in post–Napoleonic Europe, on which they'd spent quite some time in that initial visit, before moving on to the question of Bamber.

He'd never given much thought to what happened after a war was won—or lost—but it was clear from their talk that a war of a different kind was being conducted on a number of different fronts, only now it wasn't called *war*—it was called *diplomacy*.

Gerald had always assumed diplomacy was a dull kind of career, where dull people attended dull functions and made or listened to endless dull speeches. He hadn't realized that under that smooth, polite surface appearance, all kinds of exciting things could be happening.

Several times during the discussion he'd felt Radcliffe's gaze resting on him with a thoughtful expression. Once this Bamber problem was dealt with, he might investigate the possibilities of the diplomatic service. It would be a change from frittering his life away with curricle races and card games and boxing matches, endlessly waiting for his father to allow him some responsibilities.

But first, the hunt for Bamber. It was all very well for Aunt Alice to assure him that the Bamber girl knew nothing about her father's whereabouts, but Gerald wasn't convinced. Aunt Alice was a soft touch, and Lucy Bamber—well, she was a tricky, twisty piece. He didn't know quite what to think of her. She attracted and annoyed him in equal quantities. And she occupied far too much of his thinking time.

He decided to ask her straight-out, face-to-face. He fancied himself a reasonable judge of character: if she lied to his face, he would know.

To that end, he sought out her and Alice in Hyde Park at the fashionable hour. His aunt was in her favorite burgundy pelisse, and Miss Bamber was walking on the arm of a large, neatly attired gentleman, smiling up at him with every appearance of interest.

Gerald ground his teeth. What the devil was she doing with that crashing bore Humphrey Ffolliot? And what the devil was he doing to make her smile up at him like that, curse him?

She was looking exceptionally pretty in shades of yellow, a breath of sunshine beneath a flower-trimmed straw bonnet that framed her face charmingly.

This was an investigation, he reminded himself sternly. He was not swayed by charm—hers or any other female's. He drew up beside them, greeted the ladies, gave a curt nod to Ffolliot and invited Miss Bamber to take a turn around the park with him in his curricle. Her creamy complexion flushed with surprised pleasure and, assisted with pompous ceremony by Humphrey blasted Ffolliot, who acted far too possessive for Gerald's liking, she climbed up lightly to take the scat beside him.

Part of her dress floated up and settled over his boot. He carefully removed it and shifted his leg so that they didn't touch. He needed no distractions for this, and as it was, Miss Lucy Bamber was all too distracting for his peace of mind.

"Ffolliot, eh?" he said as the curricle moved off. "Can't imagine what you could possibly see in that fellow."

"Can't you?" she said with a provocative glance. "And yet you introduced him to me as an eligible prospect."

Damn. He'd forgotten that.

She added in a dulcet tone, "Mr. Ffolliot has been setting my opinions right. I had no idea how ignorant I was, being a mere foolish female. Such a masterful man."

Gerald snorted. If that's the sort of fellow she admired, more fool her.

They drove on in silence. She sat beside him looking pretty and guileless and all butter-wouldn't-melt, a little smile playing around her delectable mouth. But he knew—he just knew—that underneath that angelic exterior, she was as devious and deceitful and disingenuous as her scoundrel of a father. She had to be. She was the whole purpose of his vile scheme. The contrast, the cheek of her, infuriated him. He wanted to shake her until her teeth rattled. Or kiss her senseless. Which would be madness.

She sat there smiling gently to herself as if she knew something he didn't, and enjoyed knowing it, all the while pretending to be simply enjoying the park and the sunshine and the wretched tweeting birds. Little Miss Innocent.

They reached a quiet corner of the park, and Gerald brought his horses to a stop and turned to her. "Miss Bamber."

She turned to him and the soft, expectant light in her eyes caused him to catch his breath.

Female wiles. He hardened his heart. "I've met several

men recently who knew your father." He had to know whether she was involved with her father's schemes, or if she even knew about them. And if she was involved, how much?

Her eyes narrowed. "Checking up on me, Lord Thorncrake?"

He refused to react. "Checking up on your father."

"You mean raking up dirt." Her mouth twisted cynically. "And hoping to find some dirt on me, too, I suppose."

He arched a sardonic brow. "If the cap fits."

Her mouth tightened. She gazed out across the park, saying nothing.

"You will admit, I hope, that I have a right to investigate your father, considering what he's doing to my aunt."

"You mean the blackmail."

His brows flew up. "You know about that?" Alice had given him no indication that Miss Bamber knew anything about it.

She gave a careless flip of her hand. "Only that it exists, not what it involves." She gave him a sidelong glance. "Why so surprised? There had to be some reason why Alice took me in, a perfect stranger. She told me about it when I tried to wriggle out of the whole mad scheme."

"Mad scheme?"

"To marry me off to a lord." She gave a scornful huff. "Ridiculous."

Why ridiculous, he wondered. Most girls wanted to marry into the aristocracy. He had the evidence of his own sudden popularity after his uncle died and his father became Lord Charlton and Gerald became Viscount Thornton. Females who'd never given him a second thought now hung on his every word and gave every indication that he was the finest fellow in the world.

He wasn't sure he believed her claim. "Why would you want to wriggle out of it?"

She turned her head and met his gaze squarely. "Because I don't like lords, and I can't think of anything worse than to be married to one."

He blinked. "How do you know you don't like lords? We're not all the same, you know. 'Lord' is just a word, a title—it doesn't tell you anything about the man who bears it."

She snorted. "It's not just a word. It's an attitude, a belief about one's importance in the world. A lord thinks—no, he *knows*—that the world is his oyster. And that everyone else is some kind of lesser being put on this earth for his pleasure and convenience."

"That's a revolting attitude!"

"I know, which is why I could never bring myself to marry a lord."

"No, I meant your attitude toward lords. How do you that that's what they think?"

"I've met plenty of lords, and I know."

Her certainty annoyed him. "Where? How have you met this vast profusion of lords? You've only been in London a short while."

"Lords also infest the countryside, you know. I met dozens when I lived with the c—a grand lady I was living with."

"Another grand lady?" he said sarcastically.

"Yes, a French comtesse," she said coolly. "And she had grand visitors—lords and ladies, marquesses and dukes—coming to stay with her all the time."

"A French comtesse," he repeated in a flat voice. What nonsense. "In France, was it?"

"No, in England, not far from Brighton. She kept a pet goose." Her sherry-colored eyes taunted him. "The goose you tried to run over."

"I did not try to run the blasted thing over. I stopped!"

She gave an indifferent shrug, dismissing his words as she so often seemed to do. Gerald held on to his temper. She was trying to annoy him, and he refused to let her win.

"And did your father blackmail her too?"

She sent him a scathing look. "No, he made a different

arrangement. Do you think it will rain later?" she said, making clear the conversation was closed as far as she was concerned.

Gerald begged to differ. They drove down an avenue of trees, and something else she'd said occurred to him. "You said Alice took you in, 'a perfect stranger,' but I thought you were my aunt's goddaughter. Was that a lie?" If so, he'd be surprised. Alice never told lies.

"No, she really is my godmother."

"Then in what sense were you a stranger?"

"Oh, work it out yourself," she snapped. Color rose in her cheeks. "Is this what this drive is all about? Getting me alone so you could confront me about the sins of my father? Looking for reasons to blame me? Because if so—"

"I have the right to look out for my aunt's interests. She is family, after all."

"Oh, 'family,' is it?" she flashed. "Then why has the current Lord Charlton—your father—done nothing to help Alice out of the financial difficulties her husband—his brother, your uncle, the previous Lord Charlton—left her in? Yes, of course I know about it. And don't you dare imagine that Alice has breathed a word of it. She's far too proud to say anything, but servants let things slip, you know. And I have eyes and a brain. It's obvious."

Gerald shifted uncomfortably on his seat. He completely agreed, but he wasn't going to give her the satisfaction of admitting it.

She continued in a low, vehement voice, "As for your mother"—Gerald winced in anticipation—"she loses no opportunity to belittle Alice in front of others. A fine family you can boast of. But do I blame *you* for your uncle's selfishness or your father's miserly neglect of his duty or your mother's bitchiness? No! So don't blame *me* for my father's dirty dealing! *I* blackmailed no one, *I* stole nothing, and I've never cheated anyone in my life!" Unshed tears glittered in her eyes.

She breathed in a deep, ragged breath. "So how do you think I feel, knowing my father has made me the instrument of ruin for a dear, kind lady like Alice? And the only way I can prevent it is by marrying the kind of man I most despise!"

Gerald stared at her. That aspect of things hadn't even occurred to him.

"Oh, look—there is Mr. Frinton." Leaning out of the curricle, she waved vigorously.

Corney Frinton, dressed up like a dog's dinner, spotted her and, beaming, maneuvered his phaeton to come up beside them.

"Miss Bamber, Gerald," he managed, his Adam's apple bobbing furiously.

"How splendid to see you again, Mr. Frinton," Miss Bamber said warmly. "And what a very smart outfit you're wearing. So stylish and elegant."

She was practically gushing, Gerald thought sourly, overdoing it, lavishing compliments on his friend just to annoy him, not that poor old Corney would realize. Corney Frinton would be over the moon if any female under eighty noticed him, let alone a pretty young thing like Lucy Bamber.

Corney swallowed, ran a gloved finger around his immaculately arranged collar and neckcloth, then gestured silently toward the seat beside his.

"Take a turn around the park with you, Mr. Frinton?" she said. "Why, thank you. I'd be delighted." And before Gerald had time to blink, she was clambering across from his curricle—without even setting foot on the ground—and Corney was solicitously helping her into his rig. As if she were some kind of delicate flower, which, Lord knew, she wasn't.

"Thank you for taking me up, Lord Thorncross," she said across the gap. Her voice was flat and brittle and she didn't even bother to look at him. "And for the lesson in family honor. Next time you think to invite me, don't bother. Goodbye."

Corney blinked, gave Gerald a reproachful look, tipped his hat and drove away.

Gerald watched her drive off with Corney. He owed her an apology, he knew he did. He didn't want to apologize—he was still annoyed with her for reasons that weren't clear to him—but he knew he'd gone too far. Alice had *told* him that Lucy wasn't responsible for her father's machinations, that Lucy was as much a victim as she herself was.

But Gerald hadn't believed her. Alice was such a soft-hearted woman.

Now . . . The memory of Lucy Bamber's pale, tense face, her eyes glittering with anger and indignation and . . . it looked almost like hurt, but it couldn't be that, could it?

Do I blame you *for your uncle's selfishness or your father's miserly neglect of his duty or your mother's bitchiness? No! So don't blame* me *for my father's dirty dealing!*

He'd almost made her cry.

I *blackmailed no one,* I *stole nothing, and I've never cheated anyone in my life!*

It rang shockingly true.

He watched the phaeton disappear, swallowed up by the crowd of fashionable carriages and horses, and a hollow feeling of shame—or was it loss?—lodged in his chest.

What had he done?

It being a fine day, James had decided to bring his daughters to the park, to see the fashionable people and horses—he caught himself up on the thought. Might as well admit it to himself. He was hoping to meet Lady Charlton again.

He couldn't stop thinking about her.

He'd hired a barouche—he was trying out various carriages to see which would suit his enlarged family. Nanny McCubbin sat with a girl on either side of her, with Debo's hand firmly clasped in hers, in case the little girl spied a cat somewhere and jumped out.

Judy sat up beside her father, eyeing the colorful throng with interest, in particular the ladies on horseback. "Papa, when may I get a horse?"

When, he noted, not *may*. But it was a reasonable question. All the girls needed to learn to ride. He'd had to teach their mother from scratch—Lady Fenwick had refused to allow her delicate daughter such a dangerous activity. Selina had taken to horseback like a duck to water. And as small children, both Judy and Lina had ridden up in front of their parents numerous times.

"I'll organize lessons for you first. Riding in London is not the same as riding in Spain." Judy bounced on her seat with excitement.

"Me too, Papa?" Lina asked.

"You too," he agreed.

"Idonwannahorse. I. Want. A. Kitten," said a gruff little voice.

Up ahead, James spotted Lord Thornton's curricle, pulling up beside Lady Charlton and Miss Bamber. Thornton took up Miss Bamber, leaving Lady Charlton alone in the company of that frightful bore, Ffolliot.

"Look, there's Lady Charlton," he said, and the children and Nanny McCubbin craned to see her. He pulled up beside her. "Out you hop, girls. Stretch your legs," he told the children, and helped Nanny McCubbin down.

"Lady Charlton, would you care to take a turn around the park?" he said after the greetings were completed. Her look of thankfulness almost made him laugh. She climbed in with alacrity, and the barouche set off at once, leaving Nanny McCubbin and the children staring after him with mixed expressions.

Ffolliot, having no interest in children and underlings, stalked off.

"Thank goodness you happened this way," Lady Charlton said. "I was ready to murder that man."

"No 'happened' about it. I saw you in the company of the biggest bore in London and came racing to the rescue, callously abandoning my children and their nanny in the process."

She laughed. "Thank you. But he's not the biggest bore in London, I'm afraid. You clearly have not yet had the pleasure of the company of Mr. Cuthbert Carswell, pig breeder extraordinaire, who can talk for forty minutes at a stretch about the breeding of pigs—without ever being asked a question about anything! I promise you, he could outbore Mr. Ffoilliot."

He gave her a shocked look. "No! Ffoilliot is a member of one of my clubs, and I promise you nobody can empty a room faster. And you say this Carswell fellow is worse?"

"Infinitely," she said with feeling.

"But how is it you are acquainted with these appalling windsuckers in the first place?"

"My nephew introduced them to Lucy as likely prospects," she said grimly.

"Likely prospects? For what? Murder?"

She laughed. "For marriage. Honestly, when I think of the gentlemen Gerald has introduced us to, I wonder what on earth he thinks *eligible* means!"

"Impossible?"

"Completely! Oh, they're all wellborn, and each of them is well-off, I gather, but not one of them is the slightest bit likely to appeal to a lively girl like Lucy. I cannot imagine what Gerald was thinking."

"Can't you?" he asked dryly.

"No, I—" She gave him a thoughtful look. "You don't mean . . ."

He nodded. "Your nephew is no fool, so if he's introducing impossible men to Miss Bamber, there's a reason for it."

A faint crease appeared between her brows. "You don't mean he wants her to fail, surely? When he knows the situation I am in."

"It's more likely he wants them to fail—the impossible men."

"Ohhh," she said on a long note. "I see what you mean. Do you know, several times I've thought those two were playing some sort of deep game. But honestly, if they have feelings for each other, why not say so—why not act on it instead of all this contrary rigmarole?"

"Why not indeed," he said meditatively. He gave her a thoughtful sidelong glance, opened his mouth, shut it, opened it again and decided not to say what was on the tip of his tongue. Instead he said, "I don't know Lucy well enough to guess, but as for your nephew, I'm not sure he realizes it himself. He just knows who he doesn't want her to marry. And thus, all these impossible men."

"What a devious boy he is. I am still cross with him, however. Do you know, at Vauxhall the other night, Gerald had the temerity to abandon Lucy and me to *hours* of Mr. Carswell lecturing us on pig breeds, the creation of and uses of—all with absolutely no encouragement! Gerald just walked off, leaving us stuck with Mr. Carswell in full porcine flight!"

James couldn't help laughing. "Flying pigs, were they?"

Her lips twitched, but she managed to say with a fair attempt at indignation, "You, sir, are a callous beast, laughing at my misfortune. You may put me down at once."

"Here? In the middle of nowhere? Now that would be abandonment. Now, how shall we punish your nephew? String him up by his thumbs? Place him in the stocks? Or, better still, lock him in a cell with Ffolliot and your bacon-brained pig man."

"He is not *my* pig man." She tried to keep a straight face but failed miserably. "An hour with Carswell would teach you."

He patted her hand. "Poor love, you have endured some dreadful people, haven't you?"

There was a short silence. "What did you call me?" she said quietly.

Ah. "When?" he said unconvincingly.

"You must not say such things," she said after a moment. "It is not appropriate."

James took a deep breath. He hadn't meant to raise this now, but the word had slipped out and the time had come. "I think it's entirely appropriate."

She looked away from him, her gloved fingers knotting restlessly. "I told you when we first met that I wasn't interested in anything other than friendship."

"Yes, but—"

"And using words of . . . of endearment is not fitting for a friendship between a man and a woman."

"What if I want more than friendship?"

She shook her head distressfully. "No, no. It's not possible." He couldn't see her face for the damned bonnet. He wanted to pull it off and toss it away.

He placed a hand over her twisting fingers. "Look at me, Alice."

She stilled. "And you should not be calling me Alice. I have not given you permission."

"Look at me, please. We cannot discuss this with your face turned away from me."

"We're not going to discuss it at all." She finally turned her head, and he saw at once that she was distressed, more than he'd imagined. And it wasn't simply a matter of propriety, so what was it?

"It's marriage I'm talking about, nothing dishonorable."

She shook her head. "I can't—I won't marry again."

"Why not?" he asked softly, and then when she remained silent, he added, "Can you not trust me a little? I promise you, I won't bite."

She didn't answer, just shook her head, her lips pressed

together—to hide their trembling, he thought. What could be so distressing about an offer of marriage?

"I don't mean to press—"

"Then don't. Please take me back. Lucy will be back by now."

"Very well. I haven't made this offer lightly, but I acknowledge that I've sprung it on you and that I could have chosen a more appropriate time and place. But we *will* talk about it again," he said with gentle emphasis.

"It will make no difference. My mind is made up." And if he wasn't mistaken, that sounded like flat despair.

The carriage turned around, and they headed back toward the busier part of the park, where the fashionable people were parading. An awkward silence hung between them.

Alice breathed slowly, trying hard to appear calm. Her hands were cold, her fingers trembling. She smoothed the fabric of her gloves over them and recalled the touch of Lord Tarrant's hand over hers just a few moments earlier.

She darted a sideways glance at him and found him watching her. The look in the eyes told her he was recalling it, too. And was puzzled by her abrupt rejection of him.

She tried desperately to think of something ordinary to say. And remembered the card in her reticule. She pulled it out. "Oh, by the way, I spoke to Lady Beatrice—Lady Davenham, I mean; the lady with the cats—and she said she'd be delighted to give Debo a kitten. She gave me this card to give to you. It has her direction. There's a note on the back." She handed him the card.

He examined it and chuckled. "I gather I'm to present this to her butler." He read the writing on the back. "*Admit Lord Tarrant and daughters on important kitten business.*"

"She said to call on her as soon as you liked."

"We'll go today."

They reached Lucy, who was standing talking to a

young man, with Lord Tarrant's daughters and their nanny standing close by. The nanny was chaperoning Lucy, too, by the look of it. "Nanny McCubbin takes her duties seriously," he commented. "She's enjoying caring for the girls. My brother and I weren't nearly such fun, I suspect."

Alice would have liked to learn more about Lord Tarrant and his brother, but the time for such confidences was gone, destroyed by his wretched intention to offer her marriage. Oh, why had he done it? They could never go back to their easy friendship now.

"I'll call on you tomorrow," he told Alice. "At eleven?"

She made an indifferent gesture. "If you must." She climbed down, and the girls scrambled into the carriage, talking nineteen to the dozen. A passionate argument was in progress between Judy and the plump, motherly-looking nanny about some of the hats they'd seen ladies wearing and whether they were elegant or horrid with so many birds cruelly deprived of their feathers. The whole question hung on whether the poor birds would have survived their plucking or not. Nanny McCubbin was unable to state categorically that they did. What did Papa say?

Lord Tarrant glanced at Alice with a humorously resigned expression, but she turned away, pretending not to see it. They couldn't share such intimate glances any longer. But oh, it hurt.

They waved the carriage and the girls off. "Are you all right, Alice?" Lucy said as it disappeared from sight. "You're looking rather pale."

"A slight touch of the headache, nothing to worry about."

"Do you want to go home?"

"No, a stroll in the fresh air will revive me. I'm fine."

But she wasn't. *Marriage!* How could he deceive her like that when he'd offered her friendship? She'd been so enjoying their friendship, too—she'd never experienced anything like it. But it was all spoiled now. They could never go back to how it had been. She'd have to sever the connection.

They strolled on. Ladies and gentlemen greeted them, bowed, made small talk. Alice went through the motions,

Marriage. The whole idea appalled her. Under a man's thumb again, subject to his whims and fancies, her own desires ignored, her opinions trampled underfoot. Belonging to a man, her body his to use as he willed, whenever and however he wanted.

The marriage bed. She shuddered.

"Are you cold?" Lucy asked.

She shook her head and forced herself to pay attention. "Did you enjoy your drive with my nephew?"

"Him? Hah!" They walked on, brooding in silence, stopping from time to time to exchange a brief greeting with an acquaintance.

Alice responded absently, her mind wholly taken up with Lord Tarrant's proposal. He wasn't at all like Thaddeus, she told herself. But when she'd first met Thaddeus, he'd seemed charming—until after the marriage had taken place.

Lucy suddenly said, "Lord Thornton didn't invite me for a pleasant drive in the sunshine—it was to question me about my father. He's been investigating me, did you know?"

Alice did know, and it was her fault Gerald was looking into Lucy's father's background. Guiltily, she wondered whether she ought to confess to Lucy what she'd asked Gerald to do.

"He's trying to implicate me in Papa's actions."

Alice gave her a sharp look. "But he can't. You're not complicit in your father's actions—are you?"

"No, of course I'm not." Lucy gave her a hurt look. "Though I doubt your nephew, with his nasty, suspicious mind, believed me. He's doing his best to paint me as some kind of an adventuress, which, to be fair, I suppose I am, though not"—she kicked at a stone on the path—"by my own choice. And then he had the cheek to lecture me about family!"

"What about fam—?"

Lucy rushed on, "You would have been proud of me Alice. I so wanted to hit him and knock that stupid, smug, superior expression off his face, but I managed to control myself. I was a lady—on the outside, at least. Luckily Mr. Frinton came past just then. He invited me to take a turn in his phaeton, so I went off with him, and I don't care if it was rude to change carriages like that. He deserved it—Lord Thornton, I mean."

"I see. And how did you get on with Mr. Frinton?"

"He was quite sweet. It was much pleasanter driving with him than it was with your horrid nephew—oh, I'm sorry, Alice. I know I shouldn't say such things about your nephew, but honestly, he can be so infuriating."

Alice nodded. Men often were, in her experience. Promising a nice, safe friendship when really they were planning on marriage.

"And it's so much easier talking to Mr. Frinton than with that arrog—er, than to Lord Thornton."

"You mean Mr. Frinton actually spoke?"

"At least twenty-eight words," Lucy said. "And after spending fifteen minutes in a curricle with your nephew, I'm inclined to think I'd be better off with a man who *never* spoke."

They strolled on, heading for the gates now. "Did you tell Lord Tarrant about Lady Beatrice's kittens?"

"Yes. He's probably gone straight there."

"Debo will be thrilled."

"Mmm." She was going to have to break the news to Lucy. Those little girls, he'd used them to entice Alice into his so-called friendship. And all the time, he'd just wanted a mother for his daughters—it was clear to her now. Men! Why could they not simply say what they wanted? Why did they have to lie?

She was going to miss those girls. Lucy would, too. She'd opened up so much more with them. The role of big sister suited her. She was going to make a lovely mother one day.

"I doubt we'll scc much of Lord Tarrant and the girls in the future," she told Lucy.

Lucy turned to her in surprise. "Why? Are they going away?"

"No, but . . ." Alice swallowed. "Lord Tarrant and I have had a . . . a disagreement. I fear we've reached a parting of the ways."

Lucy gave her a searching look, but all she said was, "What a pity. I liked him and his daughters." There was no reproach in her voice. After a moment she sighed and added, "What a day, eh? I quarrel with your nephew, and you quarrel with Lord Tarrant. Men! Why are the wretches so impossible?" She linked her arm with Alice's and they crossed the road into Mayfair.

Lord Tarrant had said he would come at eleven. Alice had been restless and pacing all morning. She'd slept badly and had woken in the wee small hours and lain in the dark, waiting for the dawn to show through the crack in the curtains, going over the speech she would make to him.

She would be calm and quietly resolute. She would explain her reasons—no, she wasn't required to justify herself. A simple yes or no would do, and there was no question about which it would be: no. She wasn't playing coy or hard to get. She meant it.

She would never marry again.

Oh, why had he gone and ruined everything? It wasn't fair, making her feel safe with friendship when all the time he was plotting marriage. She was halfway to loving his daughters already, thinking perhaps she could be like an aunt or a godmother to them, or simply an older friend, as she was now with Lucy.

She recalled the feeling when little Lina had slipped her hand into Alice's and skipped along beside her. She'd never had a child hold her hand like that before. Such a simple thing, unthinking childish trust, but it had moved her unexpectedly.

She would miss him as well, more than she could say. His presence in her life—and that of Lucy—had dispelled some of the loneliness she'd lived with most of her life. He'd given her the kind of adult companionship, understanding and acceptance that she'd never really experienced.

But as she'd feared, there was simply no way a single woman could be friends with an unmarried man. Oh, why did men always want more than she could give?

The front door bell jangled. Lord Tarrant had arrived on the dot, as usual.

Alice smoothed down her dress, took a deep breath, turned to face him and, for a moment, lost her breath.

He looked magnificent. Immaculately attired in fawn buckskin breeches, gleaming boots, a dark olive coat and a subtly patterned olive waistcoat, he strode across the room to greet her. His neat, unfussy neckcloth and crisp white shirt contrasted with the slight tan of his complexion. His short dark hair was casually tousled. His presence filled the room.

"Don't you look lovely this morning? Like a sea maiden." His smile went all the way to his eyes. It pierced her heart.

She mustered her composure. "Good morning, Lord Tarrant." She waved him to a chair and seated herself on the sofa. He was freshly shaved; she could smell his faint masculine cologne.

"Well, you've made one little girl very happy."

Alice blinked at his unexpected opening.

"And almost shortened my life," he continued in a light, relaxed tone. "Why didn't you warn me?"

"Warn you of what?" she asked, all at sea.

"That there were three kittens. Three! And there I was

with three little girls, all oohing and aahing over these, squeaking, climbing, purring, tiny fluffy creatures." He gave her a mock-indignant look. "Did I tell you that cats make me sneeze? I don't suppose I did, otherwise you might have warned me that there are I don't know how many cats in that house. Twenty-five at least."

She couldn't help laughing. "Three grown-up cats plus the kittens."

"Perhaps," he said austerely, "but I sneezed for twenty-five!"

She laughed again. "Oh dear. And how many kittens do you now own?"

"Just one!" he said triumphantly. "But it was very expensive."

"Expensive? But I thought Lady Beatrice gave them away."

"Yes, and the cunning old dear did her best to foist all three kittens on me—she's a charmer, isn't she, when not trafficking in kittens? But I foiled her! I told Judy and Lina that they could have either a kitten or a pony. The ponies won by a narrow margin—tiny kittens are disgustingly cute, and they were *there*. But though stabling horses in London will cost me an arm and a leg, horses don't make me sneeze, so I consider it a victory."

She laughed again. "And Debo was happy?"

"Delirious with joy, except that she wanted to take all three home. But it was explained to her that with three kittens in the house, she would have to share, which is not a word in Debo's vocabulary yet—though Nanny McCubbin is on a mission to change that. So after much anguished deliberation, she finally chose the black-and-white kitten with three white paws, or rather, the kitten chose her by climbing up onto her shoulder and refusing to budge. Its name is Mittens, and she and Debo are in love. And yes, sadly, Mittens is female—I checked—so it seems my future will include flocks of small cats and a great deal of sneezing." But he didn't seem too distressed by the prospect.

It sounded hilarious. She wished she could have been there to watch it. "I'm so glad it worked out." She smiled at him and suddenly realized that they were leaning rather too close to each other, and that not only was she smiling up at him, he was smiling back at her with a warmly intimate expression in his eyes.

And she had been so determined to remain cool and rational and firm.

Biting her lip, she straightened and looked away.

"Oh now, don't poker up on me again," he said. "When we were getting on so well."

He reached out to her, but she waved his hand away, saying, "Don't."

"Why not?" He said it gently, inviting her to explain rather than demanding it.

"Because I can't, that's why. I will never marry again. I simply can't."

"But—"

She began her rehearsed speech. "You're a baron with three daughters—"

"And a cat."

"If you're not going to take me seriously—"

"I'm sorry. I take you very seriously. It's just . . ." He made a helpless gesture. "I don't want to hear this nonsense."

"It's not nonsense. Now please let me finish. You're a baron with three daughters, and you're going to need an heir to inherit the title."

He opened his mouth.

"Pfft!" She glared at him and held up a minatory finger. "I'm not finished. I can't give you an heir because"—she took another deep breath and forced out the painful words—"I'm barren. I was married eighteen years, and I never once quickened with child."

"But—"

"And before you suggest that maybe my husband was the

one at fault, his mistress, whom he kept exclusively before and all throughout our marriage—he even died in her bed—did bear him a son." And Thaddeus had never let her hear the end of it. "So, you see, I *was* the one lacking."

She sat back, weaving her shaking fingers together. Foolish that she found it so upsetting to talk about—Thaddeus had rubbed her nose in it often enough over the last eighteen years, and Almeria, too—but still, admitting it left her trembling. But at least it was out now.

He sat for a moment in silence, just looking at her. "Finished?"

"Yes."

"Good. To start with, I don't need an heir—I have half a dozen cousins who would be delighted to step into my shoes."

"But—"

"Pfft!" He held up a stern finger in imitation of her earlier gesture. "My turn. Second, I don't want children from you, Alice, though if they happened, I would, of course, be delighted. So you see, your worries are groundless. What's more—"

"Stop, just stop." Tears flooded her eyes. She blinked them away, shaking her head in repudiation of his words. "It's very kind of you to say so—"

"'Kind'?"

"But I can't do it. Can't marry you, can't marry anyone. I couldn't bear it. I'm not the—not the sort of woman made for marriage."

He took out his handkerchief, moved beside her on the sofa and, cupping her chin, gently blotted her tears. "Alice, my dear, I don't know what maggot you have in your mind about marriage, but if there's one thing I'm certain of, it's that you're exactly the sort of woman made for marriage."

"Ohhh . . . Don't . . . I'm not . . ." She shook her head, rejecting his words, though they pierced her very soul.

"Yes, you are." He tilted her chin and, very gently, pressed his lips to hers.

She stilled. Cupping her face between his big, warm hands, he feathered tiny kisses over her mouth, her cheeks, her eyelids, as if tasting her tears. She couldn't move, could hardly breathe.

Her mind went blank. The warmth of his body soaked into her.

Brief, fleeting, tender touches. It was like nothing she'd ever known. Almost as if she were being . . . cherished.

She put a tentative hand to his face, feeling the faint prickle of bristles under the firm, smoothly shaven skin, and breathed him in. The light fragrance of his cologne mingled with a darker, more masculine scent. It was addictive.

Still feathering her with kisses, he stroked along her jawline with one hand and slipped his fingers into her hair, loosening her pins and letting her hair fall out of its careful knot. One long, strong finger stroked the tender skin of her nape. Faint shivers ran down her spine, warm and enticing.

His mouth closed over hers, and she recoiled in surprise as his tongue ran along the seam of her lips, gently insistent. She pulled back, startled.

Gray eyes, dark with some unknowable emotion, met hers. "Alice?" he murmured. He leaned forward again to capture her mouth, and again she pulled away.

"I'm not . . . Oh, stop it." She pushed feebly at his hands and said in a choked voice, "Don't you see? I can't."

He released her at once. "Can't what, sweetheart?" His voice was low, understanding.

"Can't be married. Ever. Not ever." She crushed his handkerchief in her hands and fought to regain her composure. She'd allowed him to kiss her. It was a mistake. Giving him the wrong idea.

"Not even to me?" As an attempt at lightness, it fell sadly flat.

Despairing, she shook her head. "It would only make us both miserable in the end." Sooner than later.

"I don't see why."

"Perhaps you don't, but *I* know. I cannot be a wife to you, or any man." Her voice cracked, and a few more tears trickled down her cheeks. She scrubbed at them with his handkerchief. "Marriage, for me, was . . . was . . . unbearable. So please, let us drop the subject."

"But—"

"No. Just . . . no." In a stifled voice she added, "Please leave."

He hesitated, then rose slowly and stood, troubled as he gazed down at her. "I'm sorry, Alice, so sorry I have upset you. I'll leave you now, my dear. I have no wish to distress you any further." His voice was like a caress, warm and deep and sincere, and it brought on a fresh flood of useless tears.

Eyes squeezed closed—she couldn't bear to look at him and see the reproach, or hurt, in his eyes—Alice shook her head. *He* hadn't distressed her; it was the situation, the resurgence of old pain, the reminder of hopes crushed and dreams shattered. All because, foolishly, she had let herself dream again, just a small, timid, hopeful dream that she could be content with half a loaf—with friendship. But that had turned out to be just as painful, if not more so.

She held out his handkerchief, and when he didn't take it, she looked up.

Lord Tarrant was gone.

James walked home, his thoughts back in that room with Alice. What was going on? *I cannot be a wife to you, or any man.* What did she mean by that?

Did she mean she was repulsed by the opposite sex? Some women were attracted more to their own sex than to men. But he didn't think Alice was one of them.

He thought about their kiss—well, it was barely a kiss.

She'd stiffened at first, like a wooden doll, wary, as if expecting . . . expecting what? He had no idea. But he'd felt her trembling and knew she was taut and on edge.

So he'd taken it gently at first, slow and reassuring.

And she hadn't repudiated him or his attentions. In fact, after a few moments she'd softened in his arms and started to unfurl, like a flower opening to the sun. She'd begun to relax against him, savoring his caresses, mild as they were. The way she'd hesitantly stroked his face—she wasn't repelled by him, he was sure of that. In fact, he was pretty sure he'd felt the first few shivers of arousal rippling gently through her.

She was attracted to him, he was certain—well, as certain as a recently rejected man could be.

Marriage, for me, was unbearable.

Lord, but that husband of hers had a lot to answer for. Thaddeus Paton had been an insensitive bully at school, and James doubted he'd changed much. Any woman would be miserable with him.

But she'd said "unbearable." What part of marriage was unbearable for her?

He thought about the moment she'd jerked back, pulling away from him. What had he done to cause her to startle like a wild bird? He tried to remember. It wasn't easy, as he'd been losing himself in her, the taste of her entering his blood, the hunger in him growing.

The taste of her—that was it.

It was when he'd stroked the seam of her lips with his tongue.

She'd pulled back, surprised. A little shocked. As if . . .

No, surely not. She was a married woman. She'd been married for eighteen years. And yet . . .

He picked up his pace. Part of him wanted to turn around, march back into her house and get to the bottom of it, but she'd had enough upset for the day. He wanted her in his life and in his bed, and the last thing he wanted to do was to bully her.

Chapter Eleven

I'm sorry, Gerald dear," his aunt said as she came down the stairs, "but she doesn't want to speak to you."

Gerald clenched his teeth. It was his second time asking to see her, but Lucy Bamber refused to do him the courtesy of letting him explain. It was infuriating.

After that drive in the park, he couldn't get the look in her eyes out of his mind. It disturbed him. He needed to speak to her, to set things straight.

But she had this absurd prejudice against anyone with a title.

Anytime in his first twenty-six years he would have been perfectly acceptable to her—unless she was also prejudiced against army officers. For the first two decades of his life, he'd had no title, nor any expectation of one. But eighteen months ago, he'd become a viscount, and thus was persona non grata for Miss Lucy Bamber.

Miss Lucy Bamber of no particular background. In fact, of a particularly shady background.

Blast her. He was in a mood to storm off, but his aunt

had other ideas. "Come into the drawing room, and we'll have a nice cup of tea, and you can tell me what you've been up to." She smiled. "And I have something particular to tell you."

He followed her in, hoping she had some more information about that wretch Bamber. He and Heffernan kept coming up against dead ends. Heffernan was widening the search, tracing Lucy's background in the hope that it would lead to something, some hint that would lead them to Bamber.

He'd started with the place he'd met her, on the Brighton road. There couldn't be too many Frenchwomen there—comtesses or not—who had a pet goose.

"Dear boy," Alice said as she seated herself in her favorite chair. "I want to thank you for taking the trouble of introducing your friends to Lucy. I must also apologize for thinking you meant the introductions spuriously."

Gerald blinked. He had meant them spuriously. "What do you mean, Aunt Alice?"

She smiled at him. "It seems to have answered after all."

"Answered what?"

"Mr. Frinton wishes to court Lucy."

"*What?*" For a moment he couldn't breathe. "Are you telling me that Corney Frinton, the man who cannot string two words together within twenty yards of any pretty female—no, make that any female—has plucked up the courage to court a girl? To court your goddaughter?"

Alice nodded vigorously. "Yes. He asked my permission."

"Intending marriage?"

"Well, of course, intending marriage, what else, you foolish boy?"

Corney Frinton. Gerald sat down heavily on the sofa, as if his legs had suddenly given way.

"He's a very sweet boy, of course, perfectly eligible and very rich." Alice paused, a slight crease between her brows. "Though if she took him, I suspect it would be for my sake, to get me out of her father's clutches. I hope she won't make such a sacrifice."

Sacrifice? If Lucy married Corney Frinton, she'd be rich, would have the best of everything, fine clothes, a position in society—Corney might be as articulate as a rock, but he was very good-natured and very well connected. She'd be set for life.

"It won't do," he said firmly. "It would be a very unequal match."

The faint crease turned into a decided frown. "Gerald Paton, I never dreamed you could be as horridly toplofty as your mother. I'm disappointed in you, really I am. Lucy might not be born to the aristocracy, but she's a perfectly lovely girl, and any gentleman ought to be—"

"I meant," Gerald interjected hastily, "unequal in personality. Old Corney is a fine fellow, but he's not up to scratch with women. Your goddaughter would run rings around him."

His aunt just looked at him, her soft blue eyes seeming quite flinty.

"Besides," he added, dredging up another reason why the match would be all wrong, "she's probably the first female Corney's ever been able to talk to. It would be a mistake to marry only because of that."

She considered it, then nodded. "Perhaps Sir Heatherington Bland would be better."

"*What?* You mean Bland is also—"

"He asked my permission at the Carter-Higgins ball," she said smugly.

"But damn it all, the fellow's titled! I thought she refused even to look at a lord."

"Language, Gerald." He muttered an apology, and she continued, "It's a fine line, I admit, but Sir Heatherington's a knight, not a baronet, and therefore not really a member of the aristocracy. But it might be sufficient for her father to accept, though he did say a baronet was as low as he was prepared to go. And you must admit, Sir Heatherington is quite good-looking and very rich."

Gerald didn't have to admit anything of the sort. "But good God, the man stinks."

"Oh, a wife will soon fix that," his aunt said placidly, then added after a moment, "Gerald dear, your mouth is hanging open."

He shut it with a snap.

James called on his reluctant lady again the following day. Alice received him with a blank look of surprise. "What are you doing here? I thought . . ."

"You thought I'd go away and stay away?"

"Yes."

"But we agreed to be friends, didn't we? And friends don't abandon each other—not in my world."

A crease appeared between her silky arched brows. "But we can't be friends, not since . . ."

"Since I proposed marriage?"

"Yes."

"I see. Does that ban extend to my daughters? I must say, they'll be very disappointed not to be allowed to visit you or play in your garden. They haven't stopped talking about it ever since you climbed that tree with them." She gave him a troubled look, and he added sadly, "I would have brought them today, but I was worried you'd send them away."

"I would never send them away!" she said, shocked.

"So you would still welcome their visits?"

"Of—of course." She'd finally perceived his trap.

He glanced out the window. "Perhaps we could talk in the garden?"

"In the garden? Why?"

"Because it's spring, and the sun is out, and who knows how long that will last?" And because he wanted her to lose a little of the tension that currently held her as tight as an overwound clock. He presented his arm, and, with a bemused expression, she allowed him to escort her into the garden.

They strolled along, the woman on his arm pretending to enjoy the delights of the garden in the intermittent mid-spring sunshine and filling the silence with determinedly inconsequential chatter. They admired the flowers, picked some catmint for the kitten's basket, observed the budding lavender where she explained, in detail and rather desperately, how she made lavender bags to keep her linens fresh and fragrant, a subject in which he wasn't the slightest bit interested.

Since the garden wasn't doing the job, James decided to get straight to the point. "You know, marriage with one man might be unbearable, but it could be quite different with another—with me, in fact. Because you must admit, as friends we've done quite well."

"Yes, but there is . . . a distance between friends that makes it . . . easier."

"And that's what troubles you about marriage? Its intimacy?"

She flushed and looked away. "I wish you would not—"

"I'm fighting for my future happiness here," he said. "*Our* future happiness. And I don't wish to distress you, but if some plain speaking will help—" At that moment large raindrops started to fall. He glanced up. Where had the sun gone? It was all dark clouds and—blast this wretched climate!—rain, getting heavier by the minute. He glanced around. "Here, that summerhouse."

Taking her hand, he ran with her toward the summerhouse. He tried the door. "Blast. It's locked." Rain pelted down.

"The key is here." She took an ornate key out of the nearby stone lantern, and he unlocked the door. They fell inside, breathless, laughing and damp from the sudden downpour.

She shook out her skirts, which were clinging to her

shape in a most enticing—and deliciously improper—way. James simply stood and watched her.

Her hair clustered in damp curls framing her face. Her complexion, burnished by the rain and the exercise, glowed like a pearl. Damp, disheveled, unselfconscious and natural, she purely took his breath away.

"Lord, but you're beautiful," he murmured, and without thinking he stepped forward and cupped her face between his hands. Her skin was like cold silk, her mouth lush and damp and sweetly curved, and he was drowning in her eyes, her sea-deep, sea blue eyes. James couldn't help himself

Slowly he lowered his mouth to hers, watching her eyes widen and then flutter closed. She was tense, but she made no move to pull away as he brushed his mouth across her lush, tender lips. He nibbled gently on them, teasing and tasting, and she pressed against him, her mouth closed tight, her lips pursed as she pressed baby kisses on him.

He ran his tongue along the seam of her lips, seeking entrance. Her eyes flew open, her breath hitched, and her lips parted, and he was in, and oh, the glory of her. She tasted of surprise and rain and sweet, sweet woman.

Heat sizzled through him, setting his body alight. He wanted to take her now, here in the summerhouse, with the rain all around them, cocooning them in their own private world.

He deepened the kiss and felt her hesitation, and then the first shy touches of her tongue against his.

He pressed deeper, pulling her pliant body against him, feeling himself hardening.

Awareness finally trickled through to his brain and hit him like a dash of cold water. It wasn't just shyness here, not just inexperience; it was a level of innocence that shocked him. *Baby kisses.* She had no idea how to kiss. Eighteen years of marriage, and she had no idea how to kiss.

That bastard!

He eased back.

* * *

Alice pressed her hands against his chest, not quite sure whether she was pushing him away or just . . . not wanting to break all contact. His chest was warm and firm, and she fancied she could feel his heart beating under her fingers.

It couldn't possibly be beating as fast as hers.

It took a few moments to clear her head. She had no idea kissing could be so . . . Like that.

He waited, gazing down at her with an unreadable look in his mist-dark eyes.

She moistened her lips. His eyes dropped to her mouth and darkened further.

She looked away—the intense look in his eyes was too distracting—and tried to gather her scrambled faculties.

He stroked a lock of hair away from her face. "It occurs to me that perhaps the aspect of marriage you disliked so much is the thing you call 'um'—the activities in the marriage bed."

Alice gasped. She didn't know where to look. Stunned by his bluntness, she floundered before managing to say, "You should not— My marriage is—was private."

"I'm right, aren't I?"

She opened her mouth, closed it and looked away.

"I'll take that as a yes," he said.

His calm demeanor was irritating. "This conversation is not appropriate. I wish you would stop."

He gave her a rueful smile. "I'm not trying to upset you, just . . . clear the air. So, how many men have you lain with?"

The question shocked her. She pressed her lips together, refusing to answer. She looked toward the door, but the rain was pelting down heavier than ever. The windows were starting to fog up. She ought to remove herself from this conversation, rain or not. But she didn't move.

He frowned. "None? Really? What about the fellow you wrote those letters to? Your secret lover."

"Letters? What letters?"

"The ones Bamber is blackmailing you with."

"*I* didn't write those letters! My husband did, to his mistress." She added indignantly, "I've *never* had a lover, secret or otherwise. I was a faithful wife."

He gave her a thoughtful look, then nodded slowly. "I didn't think you were the straying kind. And I suppose you were a virgin when you married."

She didn't answer. Of course she'd been a virgin. She was—had always been—a virtuous woman. It was outrageous of him to suggest otherwise.

"So," he continued, "if you disliked the 'um' you experienced in the marital bed, and you've only ever lain with your husband, it's clear with whom the fault lies."

She felt herself flinch and turned her face away.

"Oh lord, don't look like that. I didn't mean you." He caught her cold hands in his big warm ones. "I meant the fault lay with your husband, the late earl," he said softly.

"Oh." Thaddeus had never let up about her inadequacies as a wife. In all ways.

Lord Tarrant's warm thumbs caressed her chilled fingers. "Most women find 'um' also known as sexual congress—pleasurable unless—"

She snatched her hands away. "They do not! My mother warned me it would be unpleasant, and it was— Oh why are we even talking of such matters? It is quite reprehensible of you. Not to mention inappropriate and unseemly."

He placed a finger on her lips, stilling her. "You interrupted me."

She blinked and pulled away. It was just a touch, but it was too . . . distracting. "What?"

"I hadn't finished. Women generally find sexual congress pleasurable unless their male partner is clumsy, ignorant or utterly selfish. I'm guessing your husband was the latter."

Her cheeks were on fire. She pressed her cold hands against them to try to cool the heat, but it was in vain.

What was she to say to such a thing? Never in her life had anyone spoken to her in such a way, so frankly, so openly about matters that should remain behind closed doors—closed *marital* doors—not in a summerhouse in a shared garden with a man she'd only known for a relatively short time.

His voice deepened. "You have a dislike of 'um' because your experiences with your husband made it more like 'erk.' But with me, I promise you, it would be quite different. Marry me and I will turn 'um' into 'yum.'" His eyes danced.

She stared at him, torn between laughter and tears. "This is not a subject for joking."

"Indeed it is not—except that I fear you have yet to discover that sexual congress can be fun and lighthearted, as well as extraordinary and intense and moving and . . . earth-shattering." He waited a moment, then added, "Anyway, think it over."

Think it over? She couldn't think at all. His words had stirred up such turmoil in her brain, she couldn't think of a thing to say.

The rain was slowing. "I—I must go. Lucy and I are planning to go . . . er, out." She had no idea. There were no plans.

"By all means, run away," he said with an infuriatingly understanding smile. "But think about what I said. The 'um' you've experienced is not the 'um' you deserve. We'll resume this conversation another day."

"No! That we will not!" She opened the door and looked out. The rain had slowed, and it was only a short distance to her house, but she would still get very wet.

A warm hand closed around her arm and a deep voice

said, "No need for you to get any wetter. I'll go. I'll send Tweed back with an umbrella."

She turned to thank him, and he bent and kissed her, his mouth firm and warm. "Just think about what I said." He kissed her again, swift and possessive, and it seared her to the bone. Then he stepped out into the rain.

Alice plonked bonelessly onto a bamboo chair and stared unseeing through the open door into the rain-washed garden. She put a shaking hand to her mouth. Her lips tingled. She could still taste him. Her whole body was . . . a tangle of sensations.

So that was what a kiss—a proper kiss from a man—felt like.

No wonder the poets rhapsodized so. She'd never quite understood it before.

The raw intimacy of it. His tongue inside her mouth . . . It should have been unpleasant, but instead it was . . . exciting. Addictive. She could still taste it, the sharp, dark taste of a man—of this man. The unleashed coil of wanting it—him—swirled deep within her.

Rocking gently, she wrapped her arms around her body. It was an ache, a need, but for what?

She might not know about kissing, but she understood what that masculine hardness pressing against her meant. And yet it hadn't repelled her.

It was as if his kisses had somehow melted something inside her. She'd never felt such tenderness, such an affinity with another person. It left her aching, yearning.

And deeply confused.

Sharp, damp air from the open door cooled her cheeks. The rain was easing.

He'd shocked her, had trampled over her delicate sensibilities and blasted her assumptions about men and women wide open.

Women generally find sexual congress pleasurable un-

less their male partner is clumsy, ignorant or utterly selfish.

Could that possibly be true? *Pleasurable?* She couldn't imagine it.

I'm guessing your husband was the latter.

She had no difficulty believing that. Thaddeus had been selfish in all things. He took what he wanted with no care for anyone else.

She thought about what her mother had told her the night before her wedding. Mama had not found sexual congress in the least pleasurable. *The marriage bed is something women must endure with as much grace as possible. The activity is deeply distasteful to any lady, but remember, once you have conceived a child, it will cease. The child will be your reward.*

Alice had never been rewarded with a child. And the unpleasantness had gone on for years.

But Lord Tarrant claimed most women found pleasure in the act.

Alice could not imagine how. But Papa was a vicar and a rigidly moral man, and Mama had always been quite prudish. It was likely that both he and Mama had come to their marriage bed as virgins.

Clumsy, ignorant or selfish? Perhaps all three, if what Lord Tarrant said was true. Certainly Papa had never been an affectionate man. She recalled the way Lord Tarrant had picked up Lina in her distress and soothed her, making the child feel loved instead of shamed. And the way he'd given little Debo her much-longed-for kitten, even though cats made him sneeze.

Papa would never have done that. Nor would Thaddeus.

Lord Tarrant's children were in no doubt that they were loved and valued. Alice had never felt like that. All through her childhood she had tried to earn her father's love by being good and obedient, by doing the right thing. But no matter how hard she tried, she'd never managed to measure up to Papa's standards. She was never good enough.

She'd gone to her wedding with such hope, such tender dreams, determined to find the happiness that people said came with marriage. But whatever Thaddeus had wanted in a bride, he'd made it very clear, almost from the first day, that she wasn't it. And as time went on, he'd reminded her regularly that she was as far from a satisfactory wife as a woman could be.

Her barrenness had only reinforced it.

The rain had stopped, but raindrops still dripped from the trees. She could hear footsteps crunching on the crushed limestone path: Tweed coming with an umbrella.

Alice stood, smoothing her hair and straightening her skirts, hoping the turmoil inside her wasn't visible. She moistened her lips, and remembered the way his gaze had focused on her mouth and intensified. Her lips tingled at the memory, as did other parts of her body that were nowhere near her mouth.

Marry me and I will turn "um" into "yum."

Lord Tarrant had shaken her foundations to the core. In more ways than one.

Chapter Twelve

It was the night of Lady Peplowe's masquerade ball. Alice had donned her flowing blue-green gown and her maid, Mary, had dressed Alice's hair in what she imagined was an Egyptian style—close around the head, then flowing loose with beads and gold cords plaited in. She'd also painted Alice's face with crimson lips and shadowed, almond-shaped cat's eyes.

The woman in Alice's looking glass didn't look much like her at all. She looked glamorous and mysterious.

"You look gorgeous, Alice," Lucy said, entering the room. "Here's the rest of your outfit. Mary, that hairstyle is perfect—the headdress will fit over it beautifully."

Alice stared at the gleaming gold headpiece, armbands and belt Lucy had brought in. "These look wonderful, Lucy—just like new. However did you do it?"

Lucy grinned. "Oh, papier-mâché is easy. I couldn't afford proper gold leaf, but eventually I found some paint that produces a very good imitation. The shine won't last long, but that won't matter for something you wear once or twice.

And if in five years' time you want to wear it again, I'll just paint it again. Now try it on."

Mary carefully fitted the headpiece on Alice. The thick gold band, embossed with Egyptian-style motifs, enclosed her head. On her forehead was a large jewel glittering in the center of a sunburst shape entwined with snakes.

"It's perfect and lighter than I remember," Alice said, adjusting it slightly. She slipped the snake armbands on and fastened the belt of Egyptian-style medallions around her waist. It, too, had new glittering "jewels" glued on. There was also an elegant gold mask with large cat's-eye eyeholes with gold ribbons to tie it on.

She turned to Lucy to thank her again and frowned. "You'd better hurry and get dressed. I hoped we'd leave in half an hour." Lucy was wearing a wrapper, and she hadn't even dressed her hair.

Lucy dimpled. "Don't worry, I'll be ready. I just need Mary's help with a few things."

Mary smiled. "Be with you in a minute, miss." Lucy danced out, and the maid added, "If that's all right with you, m'lady?"

"Of course. You're enjoying yourself, aren't you, Mary? Dressing us up like dolls."

"I am and all, m'lady. This old house has really come to life since that young miss came to live here. Her, and having Lord Tarrant's little girls come to visit. Like a breath of fresh air, it is, having young life about the place." As she was leaving, she turned in the doorway and said, "And you, m'lady, I can tell you're happier—you look ten years younger. And dressed like that you look . . . stunning. Lord Tarrant's eyes are going to fall right out when he sees you."

"Oh no, you're mistak—" But Mary had gone.

Alice viewed herself in the looking glass. Mary—all the servants—had the wrong idea about Lord Tarrant and her. They were all expecting a betrothal announcement, and that wasn't going to happen.

She wasn't dressing for him, she really wasn't. She was dressing for herself. And so that the night wouldn't be spoiled for Lucy. And Lady Peplowe. And because this was the only costume she had.

Besides, she wasn't even sure he was coming. Lady Peplowe might not have invited him.

She stood in front of the looking glass and swished her skirts gently back and forth. A smile slowly grew. She did look quite unlike her usual self.

She tied on the slender gold mask. Her eyes glinted mysteriously through the cat's-eye slits. Her smile deepened.

He probably wouldn't even recognize her. If he came, that is.

Half an hour later, Alice watched Lucy coming gracefully down the stairs. "You look wonderful," she exclaimed. "I would never have recognized that as my old muslin dress."

Lucy, smiling, pirouetted on the landing, skipped down the last few steps and made Alice a deep curtsy. She was clearly looking forward to the ball.

The dress was pure white—Mary had worked wonders—and it seemed looser, floatier and less structured than the dress Alice remembered. A Grecian-style pattern had been stenciled around the hem in gold, and gold braid sewn around the neck. Gold buckles were fastened at the shoulders, to which a length of gauzy, gold-edged fabric was fastened, floating about her, adding to the impression of a statue come to life.

Around her waist Lucy wore a braided girdle of gold rope, with ivy and other creepers from the garden woven in. Her tawny hair was arranged in a vaguely Grecian style, loosely pulled back and bound in places with more gold rope. A headband made of fresh leaves crowned her brow. She wore a pair of light sandals and carried a simple white satin mask. Alice noticed with a jolt of shock that her toes were bare and her toenails were painted gold. It was very daring and wonderfully bold.

The difference between this young, happy, excited girl and the sulky, badly dressed creature she had first encountered was heartwarming. It might have started as blackmail, and Alice still fretted about the consequences of that, but she couldn't regret having Lucy come to live with her. Mary was right: Lucy had brought life and liveliness to all their lives.

"You're so clever! I never could have created such a costume," Alice exclaimed. "You could have stepped straight out of a mural in a Greek temple. And you look beautiful." It was true, too. Lucy glowed with health and youth and excitement.

"We both look beautiful," Lucy said.

Alice helped Lucy tie on her mask and arrange her cloak over her costume, being careful of all the greenery, then they climbed into the carriage and were on their way.

Alice looked around her. There was no doubt about it, Lord and Lady Peplowe knew how to throw a ball. Carriages lined the street, waiting to drop off their occupants. The front of the house was lit with blazing brands tended by liveried footmen, the dramatic leaping flames lighting up the night. A temporary porte cochere had been erected in case of rain, and a red carpet laid from inside the house to the edge of the road, ensuring that neither hem of dress nor sole of shoe need touch the common pavement.

Inside people milled about, passing their cloaks and hats to servants—though not those people wearing dominos, who were mostly men. The crowd moved slowly up the stairs, where they were greeted by Lord and Lady Peplowe.

Lord and Lady Peplowe looked magnificent dressed as an oriental potentate and his queen, in sumptuous colorful silks and satins, glittering with gold and jewels. Both wore large, splendid turbans, and Alice felt a little dull by comparison, but Lady Peplowe was extremely complimentary. "The perfect partner for you is waiting inside, Queen Cleopatra," she said with a wink to Alice. "And any number of young gentlemen will be lining up to dance with this lovely Greek goddess."

Alice hoped so. Bamber's deadline was creeping ever closer.

They passed the receiving line, entered the ballroom and stopped to admire the scene. It was decorated with colorful silks draping the walls, potted palms and sprays of greenery placed at intervals around the room, and pierced-brass lanterns studded with colored glass throwing patterns of colored light across the crowd beneath.

"Isn't it wonderful?" Lucy breathed. "I've never seen anything like it."

Alice had to agree. The Peplowe ball was going to be talked about for months to come. It was already "a sad crush"—the ultimate accolade.

People were dressed in every variety of costume one could imagine. There were harlequins and pirates, knights of old, several devils with horns, Cossacks and Turks, Neptune with his trident, ladies in last century's fashions, with high powdered hair and wide pannier skirts, creatures from mythology with strange heads and human bodies, jesters, medieval ladies with high pointy headdresses, Spanish ladies in mantillas, and dainty milkmaids and shepherdesses.

Lucy leaned over and murmured in Alice's ear, "No self-respecting shepherdess or milkmaid would be seen dead in an outfit like that." Then she added with sardonic humor, "Maybe I should have come as a goose girl."

Alice followed her gaze and saw her nephew, Gerald, threading his way through the crowd toward them, a grim expression on his face. Not another quarrel, not again, surely?

"Greetings, O divine lady goddess." A young man dressed as a medieval page bowed to Lucy. His outfit was an unfortunate choice: his legs, clothed in white hose, were bandy and very skinny. But what he lacked in musculature, he made up for in confidence. "Grant me a dance, O Fair One. Are you Athena, perhaps, or maybe Aphrodite?"

Lucy shook her head.

"Artemis, perhaps? Or Venus?"

"Venus was Roman, you cloth-head." Another young man in a Viking outfit joined them. He bowed to Lucy. "Would you be Hebe, perhaps, goddess of youth and beauty?"

At that point, Gerald, who was dressed as a Spanish bullfighter, arrived, just as the first young man said to Lucy, "I give up. Tell us, O Fair Lady, which goddess you are. And then grant me a dance."

Lucy pretended she was answering her pageboy admirer, but she looked straight at Gerald as she said, "I am no goddess, good sirs, but a priestess of Apollo." Her gaze clashed with Gerald's. "I am Cassandra of Troy, cursed to speak the truth but never to be believed."

Gerald's jaw tightened. "About that, could I have a word, please?"

"Hey, we were first," the two young men objected.

"Indeed you were," Lucy cooed, and ignoring Gerald completely, she placed a hand on each young gentleman's arm, and they strolled away.

Gerald watched them disappear into the crowd, then turned to Alice. "She's never going to forgive me, is she, Aunt Alice? Perhaps you could intervene on my behalf."

"You are mistaken in me, young man," Alice said, a little irritated that she'd been so easily recognized. She supposed being with Lucy had given her away. But she didn't want to intervene on Gerald's behalf, so she clung to her current identity. "I am Queen Cleopatra, aunt to no one here, and you must sort out your own tangle."

"Indeed you must," said a deep, amused voice behind her. "Take yourself off, young fighter of bulls, and make your own amends to yon cold and angry lady. I have an appointment with my queen."

"You have no such—" Alice began, turning. Her words dried up at the sight that greeted her.

A tall Roman soldier bowed. "Mark Antony at your service, Queen Cleopatra."

Over his mask, he wore a gleaming gold helmet topped with a crest of red feathers. Over a short red tunic, he wore a leather cuirass that was molded to his powerful chest and hard, flat belly. A symbolic gold eagle covered his heart.

Instead of trousers he wore a kind of kilt made of strips of leather studded with brass medallions. It ended at his knees—his bare, brawny, naked, masculine knees.

She dragged her eyes away, but couldn't help wondering whether Roman generals wore the same thing under their tunic as Scotsmen were reputed to. She clamped down on the thought. She should not be thinking of such things.

A short red cloak hung from gold buckles at his shoulders, dangling rakishly behind him. His tanned, powerful arms were bare, and a broad gold armband was clasped high on one muscular arm, while thick leather bands encircled his wrists. On his feet he wore red three-quarter-length boots.

He looked powerful, barbaric and magnificent. The sight of him took her breath away.

Mark Antony, Cleopatra's famous lover. He couldn't have known what she was wearing to the ball, could he? That gleam in his eyes told her otherwise.

"Who told you?"

He pretended puzzlement. "Told me?"

"What I was going to be wearing tonight."

He laid a dramatic hand over the eagle on his breastplate. "There was no need for anyone to tell me, O Queen. It was in the stars—we are fated to be together."

"Nonsense." She told herself he was just playing a part, but there was a note underneath the playfulness that sounded worryingly sincere. "It can't be a coincidence. Somebody must have told you what I was wearing tonight."

"You're right. It was a little bird."

"What little bird? Not Lucy?" She'd be very disappointed if it were.

"No, your goddaughter didn't give anything away, not knowingly at least." He tucked her hand in the crook of his arm, and they strolled around the room.

"If you recall," he continued easily, "you had a troop of small visitors the other day—it is very kind of you to allow them to visit the garden whenever they want, by the way—and they saw certain gold-painted items drying in the summerhouse. Later, when they told me about their visit, they asked a lot of questions. Questions like 'Who was Cleopatra, Papa, and why would she wear snakes on her head and arms?' Which was interrupted by, 'Shhh, it's supposed to be a secret!' which received the indignant rejoinder, 'I'm not talking about the *costume*, just the lady. It's history. We're *supposed* to learn about history!'"

She couldn't help smiling at his vivid re-creation of the scene. "And so you put two and two together."

"And sent my valet out to scour London for a costume. You will be astonished to learn that uniforms for Roman generals are quite thin on the ground." He glanced around and murmured in a secretive tone, "Don't tell a soul, but this costume is actually Caesar's."

She laughed. And feeling bold, she directed a pointed glance at his legs in the short tunic. "Don't you find it rather drafty? That short skirt thing."

"Skirt thing?" He leaned back in feigned horror. "Would you call a proud Scotsman's kilt a 'skirt thing'?"

She shrugged. "If I didn't know what it was called, probably."

"This"—he touched the red fabric—"is called a tunic." He paused. "And these dangly leather straps are called, I believe, 'dangly leather straps.' The official term, you understand."

"Ah, I see," she said, attempting solemnity through a bubble of laughter.

"As for whether I find it drafty, I don't, here in this crowded ballroom—though I suspect it might be wise to eschew the more vigorous of the country dances. But on a windy day I suspect these dangly leather straps would come in handy. Protection in more ways than one."

They strolled on. "Do ladies find them drafty?" he asked. "Dresses, I mean."

"Our dresses are much longer."

"So they are, but what about ladies who have not yet adopted the newfangled underwear our late, lamented princess popularized . . ."

Alice felt her cheeks warm. Princess Charlotte had scandalized some and thrilled others when she'd adopted the wearing of drawers. Most ladies wore them these days, but not the old-fashioned types, or those whose parents were rigid moralists, like Papa. The church considered the wearing of drawers by ladies as scandalous and immoral, drawers being items of clothes designed for men.

Then there were people like Thaddeus, who subscribed to the medical opinion that drawers overheated ladies' female parts and thus made it more difficult for them to conceive.

Alice had worn her first-ever pair of drawers to Thaddeus's funeral.

"I have no idea," she murmured. Deciding this conversation was heading into awkward areas—she still didn't know what he was wearing under his tunic and wasn't going to ask, *and* she wouldn't put it past him to ask whether she was wearing drawers or not—Alice glanced around in search of some distraction.

"Fretting about young Cassandra?" he asked. "That has to be a first."

"What is?" She constantly worried about Lucy.

"Cleopatra playing chaperone to a priestess of Apollo." He smiled. "Don't worry, that young lady is more than capable of looking after herself."

"That's not the point," she began.

"Looks like she's occupied with young Thornton." He nodded to one of the balconies at the back of the room, where Lucy and Gerald were standing, face-to-face, radiating tension. As they watched, Lucy flung up her hands and stormed off, leaving Gerald staring after, frustration evident in every line of his body.

"Oh dear, I'd better go and—"

A large hand closed around her forearm. "No, leave them to it. They've been circling around each other forever. Best let them get it out in the open."

"Forever?"

He shrugged. "It feels like that anyway. Now come, let me procure you some refreshment, and then we shall dance."

"Shall we?" she said dryly.

"Shall we not, my queen? And why would that be? Have I stepped on your toes in some way? Do you fear my tunic flying up? Worried about my dangly bits?" How she knew he was quirking an amused eyebrow at her under his golden helmet she couldn't say, but she was sure he was. His dangly bits indeed.

She wished she knew how to flirt back at him and maintain a witty, lighthearted conversation, but instead all she could do was blush and feel hot and flustered. But was determined not to show it. "A lady likes to be asked."

"Of course." He swept her an instant bow. "My dear Queen Cleopatra, would you grant a humble soldier a dance?"

She looked around. "I might. Where is he?"

He snorted. "Minx. Very well then, will you grant me a dance?"

"Yes. Which dance would you pref—"

"The first waltz. And the second."

"But—"

"I would take every dance, except there is some stupid rule about limiting oneself to two dances with one lady."

Alice decided not to argue.

* * *

Lucy prowled through the crowd furiously, peering between the clumps of gorgeously attired people, looking for the culprit. Hah! There he was, the arrogant beast, in his sinfully tight black breeches and his glittery matador's coat, thinking he looked so fine, surrounded by ladies all cooing and gushing. She marched up and poked him in the shoulder—hard. "How dare you drive away my partners!"

Lord Thornton turned, rubbing his shoulder. "I didn't!"

Aware of his circle of admirers avidly listening, she allowed him to steer her a short distance away.

"You didn't, eh? Then why did Mr. Frinton and Mr. Grimswade both come to me in the last half hour and withdraw from the dances they had reserved?"

He shrugged. "How would I know?"

"Liar!" she snapped. "They both told me it was at your request—as my guardian's nearest male relative!"

He didn't answer, didn't even look the slightest bit guilty.

She poked him again, this time on the bead-and-sequin-covered chest. Matador indeed! She could happily throw him under a bull right now. "Understand me, Lord Thornroach, you have *no* authority over me. None whatsoever, and if you ever try to arrange my dances or any other aspect of my life again—"

"What else was I to do? You refused me even one dance earlier."

"As is my right!"

"I only took your waltzes."

Such smugness. She wanted to hit him. "They were *my* waltzes to give!"

He shrugged again. "You don't have permission to waltz yet."

"So? I planned to sit them out with the partners of my choice."

He snorted. "You planned to sit one out with Corney Frinton and what—talk?"

"Mr. Frinton can talk. Sometimes. Anyway, what business is it of yours how we pass the time? I'd rather sit in total silence with Mr. Frinton than with an arrogant lord who thinks he knows everything."

He cocked an unimpressed eyebrow. "And what did you plan to do with Tarquin Grimswade? Listen to his poetry? I can assure you, it's utter drivel."

"You introduced me to both those gentlemen as potential husbands. So what has changed? Or is it just a case of dog in the manger?" Hah! He looked uncomfortable at that little gibe. The hypocrite.

"I simply wanted to talk to you. I've been trying to talk to you since that drive in the park, but you've been avoiding me—"

"I can't imagine why, when you're such delightful company."

"And then tonight, when you refused me even one dance—" He broke off as the opening bars of a waltz sounded. "Let's go outside," he said, "where I can say my piece, you can berate me in relative privacy, and then we'll be done."

Cupping his hand around her elbow, he escorted her across the railed terrace and down into the courtyard. Wought iron chairs and tables were arranged around the perimeter, large potted palms and other plants had been clustered to give privacy to the tables, and multicolored lanterns were hung here and there, giving the scene a softly foreign appearance. Everyone had made their way inside for the much-anticipated first waltz of the evening. The courtyard was deserted.

"Well?" She turned and faced him, her arms folded across her chest. "What is it you are burning to tell me? More disgraceful family secrets you have unearthed about me? More slanders against my character? More baseless accusations about how I'm plotting with my father to ruin Alice?"

"No." He ran a finger around his tight matador collar, and swallowed. "I want to apologize."

Lucy blinked. "Apologize?" It was the last thing she'd expected.

"You're right. I did suspect you of working with your father, of plotting against Alice and taking advantage of her kind nature."

"Did?"

He nodded. "I don't think that now. You . . . you convinced me of your innocence that day in the park."

She raised a cynical brow. "So I told you I wasn't working with my father and you believed me, just like that."

He looked uncomfortable. "More or less."

She snorted. "I don't believe you. You've uncovered more dirt on Papa, haven't you? Something that exonerates me, isn't that it?"

A small nerve in his jaw twitched rhythmically. He eyed her grimly as he considered her question. "More or less. I learned about your school experiences."

Her stomach clenched. "What school experiences would those be?"

"Five—or was it six—different schools in how many years? And you never went home for the holidays."

She lifted an indifferent shoulder, but a sour taste flooded her mouth.

"And then you were sent to live with some old German opera singer for a year, and then that French comtesse with the goose for another year. Although whether you were a guest or a maidservant isn't clear."

Because, depending on the comtesse's whim, she was both. "I suppose Alice told you all this." It was a painful betrayal, but Lord Thornton was, after all, Alice's nephew. She supposed Alice's first loyalty must go to him. Even knowing that, it hurt, more than she would have imagined. Which made no sense. She didn't even know Alice until a few weeks ago.

He shook his head. "No, Alice is ridiculously close-mouthed about your background. All she will ever say is that you are her goddaughter—though how that came about is still a mystery to me." He eyed her speculatively and waited.

Lucy pressed her lips together and looked away. She wasn't going to enlighten him. If Alice wanted to tell him, that was her right.

A burst of laughter floated out from the ballroom. Strangely, it emphasized their isolation. "You haven't lived with your father for more than a few days at a time, have you? Not since your mother died."

Lucy gave him a flat look. "So what if I have? What business is it of yours? Why are you so interested in my history?"

He frowned. "Don't you know?"

"Know what?"

"Your father has been threatening Alice again. I'm trying to trace him."

Lucy blanched. "Threatening her?"

He nodded. "I gather she didn't tell you."

"Not a word." She felt sick. How dare Papa threaten Alice? She was doing all she could to help Lucy find a man she could happily marry.

She sank onto one of the chairs. As she had dreaded from the start, this latest scheme of Papa's would result not just in her own mortification and ruin but in Alice's as well.

And the terrible irony was that the very woman her father was blackmailing and threatening was trying to protect Lucy.

She took a deep breath and hoped her voice sounded calm. "What is he threatening her about?"

The furrow between Lord Thornton's brows deepened. "About you, of course. He's complaining that Alice isn't doing what he asked—arranging your marriage to a member of the nobility. Apparently someone has been reporting back to him that you've only been seen accompanied by men with no title or any expectation of one."

Her fingers turned into a fist. "I've told him and told him that I hate the very idea of marrying a lord!" She looked up at Lord Thornton and said bitterly, "Alice was sure that what my father really wanted was for me to be secure and settled happily, that the title didn't really matter."

She smacked her knee. "Like a fool I allowed her to persuade me. I should have known better. Papa is stubborn, and foolishly pretentious. Being related to a title obviously matters far more to him than my happiness."

Lord Thornton said nothing.

Inside the ballroom the last strains of the waltz finished. Lucy rose, feeling weary and disheartened. "I have to go. My partner for the next dance will be looking for me."

She took a few steps toward the terrace and the French doors leading into the ballroom, then turned back to face Lord Thornton. "There's really no point in looking for my father. He's as slippery as an eel. I've never known how to contact him, and you won't be the only person trying to trace him, I'm sure. If you really want to help Alice and get Papa off her back, there's only one thing you can do."

"What's that?"

"Find me a lord to marry. Any lord, I don't care which. He can be a hundred years old, for all I care."

His frown deepened. "But you said yourself that it was the last thing you wanted."

"It is."

"Then why would you do such a thing?"

She looked at him. "For Alice, of course. Why else? Alice is a darling, and I won't let Papa ruin her."

The orchestra played the introductory bars of the waltz. Gentlemen led their partners onto the dance floor. Lord Tarrant held out his hand—his bare hand. Unlike English gentlemen, Roman generals wore no gloves at a ball.

Neither did Egyptian queens.

His hand was big and warm and strong; hers felt cold. The sensation of skin against skin was thrilling. He held one of her hands in his and placed his other hand on the dip of her waist. She hesitated about where to place her hand and decided that the safest option was on his epaulettes, or whatever Romans called them.

The dance began, and he swept her into it with complete assurance. It was far from her first waltz, and though he was holding her with perfect propriety, he felt very close, much closer than she'd expected. All that bare masculine skin . . .

The scent of him wrapped around her, the sharp tang of his shaving cologne, the earthy scent of leather and, beneath it all, his own distinctive clean masculine smell. Soap and man—this man.

It was disconcerting to realize that she'd probably recognize him blindfolded and in the dark by his smell alone. His enticing masculine smell.

He twirled her around, his big, powerful body dominating hers, the two of them moving as one to the music. She felt as though she were flying. It didn't feel safe. It was exhilarating.

Inch by inch, he drew her closer. She felt the press of his thigh against hers. Heat sizzled through her—and it wasn't because of the dancing. She felt breathless—and it wasn't because of the dancing.

Every inch of her was aware of him. The heat of his body, the powerful arms, his hand on her waist, his bare thighs beneath the short tunic. She clung to him, allowing herself to simply twirl and spin to the music as he willed it. She felt almost dizzy and yet sharply, gloriously alive.

"And they say the waltz is a scandalous dance," he murmured. "Such nonsense."

She glanced up at him. Didn't he feel it?

His eyes danced with knowing laughter, his mouth curved, and he drew her even closer.

He felt it. She closed her eyes, unable to meet the intensity in his, and gave herself up to the music, the dance and the man.

Eventually the waltz ended, and he led her to a seat. "Thirsty?"

She nodded.

"Ratafia, lemonade or champagne?"

She was already intoxicated and she hadn't had a drop of wine, but she found herself saying, "Champagne, please."

She watched as he crossed the room in search of refreshments, his stride powerful and easy, his shoulders broad and almost bare. He was magnificently at home in his costume.

She shivered, unable to drag her gaze off his long, muscular legs in that short, red tunic. Waves of heat rippled through her. So this was desire . . .

She'd felt pale echoes of it before, but nothing like this, never anything this strong. It had been building between them, she realized, ever since that first kiss. No, even before that.

Women generally find sexual congress pleasurable . . .

She couldn't stop thinking about it.

He disappeared into the crowd, and she sat and watched people enjoying themselves. The masks and costumes seemed to have encouraged more overt flirting, and some were definitely stepping very close to the line. If not over it, she added mentally, noticing one of the shepherdesses slide her hand into the folds of a Roman senator's toga.

She blushed and looked away, feeling a little out of her depth. How many of the ladies here enjoyed sexual congress? The ones who flirted? Was that why she didn't know how to flirt? Because she had disliked the marriage bed?

Oh, how could she be so old and still feel so ignorant? Lucy was better at this than she was, and Lucy was half her age.

Lady Peplowe, superb in her enormous turban, moved among her guests, talking and chatting, bringing people together and effortlessly putting them at ease. She was a superlative hostess and very popular.

As Alice watched her, a thought sprang to mind.

Perhaps a decade or so older than Alice—Penny was the youngest daughter—Lady Peplowe was plump, casually elegant and very sophisticated, but Alice had always found her comfortable to talk to. She wasn't an intimate friend, but she had shown a great deal of kindness to both Alice and Lucy.

She would surely not mock Alice for her ignorance and lack of sophistication.

Alice waited until Lady Peplowe began to move from one group to the next. She hurried across the floor and intercepted her. "Lady Peplowe," she began, suddenly breathless.

Lady Peplowe's brows rose. "Is there something the matter, my dear?"

"No, no, it's a lovely party. It's just . . . May I call on you tomorrow? There is something particular I would like to discuss with you." She was blushing, she knew.

"Of course. Only make it later in the day—say, five o'clock. I intend to sleep very late tomorrow."

"Oh, yes, sorry. I didn't think. Would you prefer me to come the following day?"

She smiled. "No, I can see it's something that won't wait."

"It will, of course, it's just . . ."

Lady Peplowe patted her hand. "Tomorrow at five will suit me very well, Lady Charlton. You can explain it all then. In complete privacy." She glanced over Alice's shoulder. "Now, there's a handsome Roman general waiting with a glass of champagne for you. Better go and relieve him of it before some other lady snaps it—and him—up. He's a delicious sight in that costume, barely there as it is. I do like a man with a good pair of legs, don't you? And as for those gloriously muscular upper arms . . ." She fanned herself briefly, winked at Alice and glided away.

* * *

It was time for the second waltz of the evening. Lucy watched as Alice stepped onto the floor with Lord Tarrant. Hers weren't the only eyes that watched their progress with speculative interest. They made a handsome couple.

Lucy glanced around the ballroom. Which of these extravagantly dressed people was reporting back to her father? The thought made her simultaneously furious and sick. The sooner she married some lord, the sooner this whole ghastly thing would be over.

Lord Thornton appeared at her elbow. "Shall we sit this one out in the courtyard, Miss Bamber?" It was very warm now in the ballroom, with all the lanterns and candles burning and the press of overheated bodies, so she nodded.

Outside it was blissfully cool, the night air fresh with a soft breeze stirring the leaves overhead. "You're not cold, are you?" Lord Thornton asked. He gestured to his matador's jacket with a wry smile. "I'd offer to give you my coat, but I doubt I can remove it. It took all my valet's efforts to get it on. Do you have a shawl I could fetch?"

Lucy shook her head. "I'm quite comfortable, thank you." It wasn't quite a lie. She wasn't cold, but something about sitting out here alone with Lord Thornton, not to mention the intense way he kept looking at her, made her feel a little on edge. As for his coat being tight, his whole outfit, especially his breeches, outlined his lithe, lean, muscular form almost indecently.

She could hardly drag her eyes away.

They sat for a few moments in silence, listening to the music floating from the ballroom. Then he said abruptly, "Did you mean what you said about marrying a lord, any lord?"

She looked at him in surprise. "Yes."

"Are you sure?"

"Yes." She didn't see any other way out of the fix Papa had trapped her in.

"Even an old man?"

She nodded. The very idea appalled her, but even worse was the knowledge that if she didn't, her father would ruin Alice. Besides, she might not have to endure an old man for long. Which was a horrid thing to think.

"What about a young man?"

She shrugged. "As long as he's titled, it makes no difference. Now can we stop talking about it, please? I'd rather just enjoy the night and keep these depressing realities for the cold light of day." The moon was out, hazy, lopsided and serene. The scent of flowers perfumed the air. And the music only added to the magic.

"You like this music, don't you?" he said after a moment.

"Doesn't everyone?"

He gestured to her sandaled feet. "Your feet are dying to dance. They're tapping along in time with the music. I like those gold toenails, by the way. Dashing, as well as pretty." He rose to his feet. "Shall we dance?"

She blinked at the unexpected request. "But I can't."

"You can't waltz, or you don't have permission?"

"I know how to waltz, of course, though I've never danced it in public. But I don't have permission. For some reason I'm only allowed to waltz after one of the patronesses of Almack's gives me permission. Seems ridiculous to me, but that's what I was told."

"I see. And that's why you were prepared to sit them out in wallflowery boredom with Messrs. Frinton and Grimswade."

"Both gentlemen to whom you introduced me," she reminded him acidly.

"Then let me atone." He held out his hand. "Will you do me the honor of dancing this waltz with me, Miss Bamber?"

She hesitated and looked around. The courtyard was still deserted, as was the terrace overlooking it. "Nobody will see," he said, his voice low and deep. "Come on, you know you want to."

"Very well." She rose and took his hand. It was warm

and firm. No gloves on matadors or priestesses. His other arm wrapped around her waist.

He danced well, swirling her around with grace and assurance. Dancing alone in the courtyard, in the moonlight, with the lanterns creating pools of light among the shadows—it felt strangely intimate, as if they were alone instead of only a few yards away from the loud, colorful throng inside.

Too intimate. She could smell his cologne, feel his breath against her hair. She was achingly aware of how his costume hugged every line of his lean, lithe body. And that her costume was too loose, too floaty and insubstantial. And that she was pressing up against him in a way that would not be approved of in polite circles.

She had to break this feeling of . . . intensity. Conversation, that was the thing. "What made you dress as a matador?" she asked.

He shrugged infinitesimally. "There was a costume in the shop. And I liked it. I saw several bullfights in Spain."

"Weren't they very terrible?"

He smiled. "For the bull, yes, but very exciting to watch."

She shuddered. "I could never watch such a thing. You were in Spain for the war, weren't you?"

"Yes." After a moment he added, "I'd like to go back there one day, now that peace has come. It's a fascinating country."

"You want to travel again?" It surprised her. Most Englishmen she'd met—admittedly not all that many—seemed to dislike the idea of foreign travel.

He appeared to think it over, then gave a decisive nod, as if he'd just made up his mind. "Yes. I do. I have a mind to join the diplomatic service."

"Really? Don't you have responsibilities here? I mean, isn't there an estate or something you're supposed to look after?" Not that she knew anything about a nobleman's duties.

"My father controls all that. There's nothing for me here." They circled the courtyard again, and he added, "What about you? If you had the opportunity to travel, would you take it?"

In a heartbeat, Lucy thought. But it was not to be. "I'm marrying a lordly octogenarian, remember?" she said lightly. "I doubt I'll get to travel."

"About that. I think I have the solution to your problem."

She looked up at him. "Oh yes?"

For a minute or two he said nothing, just twirled her around in the moonlight. Then, just as she was sure he wasn't going to speak, he cleared his throat and said, "Become betrothed to me."

She dropped his hand and stepped away. "What? No. Marry *you*?"

He held up his hands pacifically. "Calm down. I didn't say 'marry me'—I said 'become betrothed.'"

"No. That's ridic—"

"Hear me out. You don't want to marry a lord, isn't that right?"

"Yes, but—"

"But in order to save Alice from whatever your father has threatened her with, he needs to believe you are going to marry a lord."

She frowned. "Ye-es."

"A formal betrothal would convince him, would it not? If it was officially announced in the *Morning Post* and the *Gazette*, and the banns called in St. George's, Hanover Square."

She thought about it. If Papa believed it was a done deal, and he probably would, with it being all formal and official, it could, just possibly work. Though he did say he'd come to her wedding. "Maybe."

"Then you and I will announce our betrothal."

She shook her head. "But you can't! You don't want to marry me!"

"Don't worry. We can call it off as soon as Alice gets those letters back from your father. Actually *you* will call it off. A gentleman cannot honorably withdraw once the announcement has been made."

"Why not?"

"A gentleman cannot break his word."

She snorted. "Rubbish. Men break their word all the time."

"Perhaps, but not if they're gentlemen. I should have said a gentleman cannot *honorably* break his word. A gentleman's promise—his word of honor—is the foundation of his status as a gentleman." Seeing her skepticism, he continued, "That's why gambling debts between gentlemen are called 'debts of honor'—and are paid before any other kind of debt. It's also why being caught cheating at cards will result in a gentleman being expelled from his club, disgraced in society and, in some cases, banished by their family to another country."

"What about ladies? Isn't a lady's word of honor just as important?"

"No, ladies aren't expected to keep promises. Being the weaker sex, it is a woman's prerogative to change her mind."

She bristled. She hated that term, the "weaker sex", but she'd struggled with enough lustful lords to know it was true enough, physically, at least. It had been her brains and agility that had kept her safe, not her physical strength, not to mention her willingness to kick a man in his cods—a strategy taught to her by the father planning his absence. "You're saying that women have no sense of honor?"

"Y—no, well, not exactly. It's just, girls are raised differently and not taught about—I mean, there's no blame—" He was getting more and more tangled. "It's not what I believe, but it is how the world sees it."

The idea that only she could call off the betrothal because women were regarded as indecisive ninnyhammers was insulting. But she didn't have to like it. There were many aspects of society she didn't like. "So what you're saying is that once our betrothal is announced, I can call it off, but you can't?"

"Exactly."

There was a short silence while she thought it over. "You'd be taking a big risk, wouldn't you? What if I didn't call it off?"

"I'd be relying on your sense of honor." His eyes glinted with wry humor. "Not to mention your well-known antipathy to marrying a lord."

This suggestion of his, coming out of the blue, on the one hand seemed like a clear and simple solution. On the other, it worried her.

All the time she'd known Lord Thornton, they'd been at daggers drawn. But tonight, not only had he gone out of his way to apologize—and she was sure that didn't come easily to a man of his pride—now he was proposing. All right, so it was only a pretend betrothal, but just days ago he'd been certain she was in league with her blackmailing father. And now he was relying on her so-called honor not to trap him into marriage? She didn't trust such an instant about-face.

"Why would you do such a thing? Be willing to put yourself in my hands?"

He met her gaze squarely. "Aunt Alice was very good to me as a child. She's my favorite relative. My parents have done nothing to help her since her husband died. Now she's in trouble, and I'm determined to help her however I can."

He sounded sincere. She was inclined to believe him. Almost.

The idea was tempting. A public betrothal to a viscount who was also heir to an earldom might just bring Papa out of the woodwork. And save Alice from any further distress.

"And you would trust me to break the betrothal?"

"I would. But I should also warn you that if you did, there might be unpleasant repercussions for you. You'd need to be prepared for that."

She knew it. Because people would be furious that a girl of no background had played fast and loose with the son of an earl. "I don't care. I never set out to hook a husband in the first place. It was all Papa's idea."

He frowned. "The idea of social disgrace doesn't worry you?"

She shrugged. "They're not my people." She'd never belonged anywhere, so being pushed out of the ton would be nothing new. She'd miss Alice, though, and Lord Tarrant's little girls. And Penny Peplowe and some of the other friends she'd made. Thinking about it, it occurred to her that she'd made more friends than she'd realized.

Oh well, it was a risk she'd have to take. No matter what society believed, women did have honor, and she owed it to Alice to free her from Papa's entrapment.

Emerging from her reflections, she looked up to see Lord Thornton regarding her with a curious expression. "Who are your people?"

"Gypsies, who do you think?" She had no "people." Only Papa.

He eyed her shrewdly, but all he said was, "So, do you agree that a false betrothal is the solution to our problems?"

She took a deep breath. "All right. I'll do it. And there's no need to worry—I promise you that I won't hold you to it. If you can believe the promises of a blackmailer's daughter, that is."

"I have every faith in your honor," he said softly, and for some reason she felt herself tearing up. She turned away, blinking furiously.

He went on in a brisk voice. "I'll put notices in the *Morning Post* and the *Gazette*. Shall we keep it quiet until then, or would you like me to arrange an announcement tonight, at this ball?"

His mother was at the ball, Lucy recalled. She'd be bound to make a horrid fuss—a public fuss—and she'd blame Alice. "No, let's keep it secret until the announcement in the papers."

He nodded. "Just don't tell Alice it's a false betrothal."

"But—"

"I'm very fond of Alice, but she's a hopeless liar. She'd hate having to keep it a secret—and she'd probably botch it. Which would upset her very much."

He was right. "Very well," she agreed. "We'll tell nobody the betrothal is a stratagem."

Inside the ballroom the waltz was just finishing. "I'd better go in," she said, rising to her feet. "I promised Mr. Grimswade I'd take supper with him."

"Just one more thing." Lord Thornton reached out and detained her with a light touch. "This agreement between us, there won't be any kind of document to sign."

"No, of course not."

"So we'd better seal it in the time-honored way."

"What time-honored—mmph!"

His mouth came down on hers, firm, warm and possessive. She was so surprised she couldn't move or even think. She gasped and his tongue entered her mouth, hot, spicy and demanding.

By the time her brain had recovered from the shock, her body was pressing itself against him, her arms were twined around his neck, and she was kissing him back. He cupped her face in his hands, angling her mouth the better to explore her, to taste her.

Heat streaked through her in waves, pooling deep within her body.

Without warning he released her abruptly. She staggered back, struggling to gather her scrambled wits. It wasn't the first time she'd been kissed, but she'd never experienced anything like . . . like *that*.

Her whole body was tingling. She was panting, as if she'd run a mile instead of standing in a secluded corner.

His chest was heaving, too, she noticed. At least she wasn't the only one.

Had he felt what she did? There was no way of knowing. His eyes were in shadow, dark, intense and unreadable. Her gaze dropped to the firm, unsmiling masculine mouth. Who knew that he could kiss like that?

As the silence between them stretched, broken only by their heavy breathing and the distant hum of people talking in the ballroom, all Lucy's old insecurities came surging to the fore. Before tonight—even an hour ago—she would have sworn this man, this lord, disliked her. Only days ago he'd accused her of plotting against Alice. Then suddenly, tonight, he was talking false betrothals and trusting her. And now this?

A kiss too far?

Striving to sound calm and unflustered, she said, "What was that about?"

He said coolly, as if the answer were obvious, "As I said, it's a time-honored way of sealing an agreement."

His words, like a dash of cold water, brought her to her senses. This was what lords did. Take what they felt like, no care for anyone else. "Hah! So you kiss your horse coper like that when you buy a horse, do you? Or your wine merchant when he agrees to deliver wine?"

"Of course not. Men usually shake hands on an agreement, but ladies"—he grinned, a purely wicked grin—"ladies don't shake hands with gentlemen, do they? So what else was I to do?"

She couldn't think of a response. Truth to tell, she was still dazzled by the effects of his kiss. She tried for a withering look, but he stood there looking smug, handsome and annoyingly unwithered.

The buzz of conversation inside suddenly rose. Laughter and exclamations floated out onto the night air.

"The unmasking has begun," he said. "I'll go inside first. Wouldn't do for us both to appear together, especially with you looking as though you've just been thoroughly kissed."

She rubbed at her mouth as if he'd somehow branded her. What did "thoroughly kissed" look like anyway? She pressed her hands against her hot cheeks to cool them.

At the steps leading up to the ballroom, he turned and looked back. "And by the way, that permission-to-waltz thing? I'm fairly sure it applies only to Almack's, not at a private ball."

"Now you tell me—" she began wrathfully, but he was gone.

She sat back down, not yet ready to return to the ballroom and play her part. Some people had come out onto the terrace to cool down after the dance, but most would be going in to supper.

She was betrothed. To Lord Thornton.

It was the last thing she'd expected. No, the kiss was the last thing she'd expected. Why had he done it?

She removed her mask, ran her hands lightly over her hair and the circlet of vines, and checked the rest of her costume. She appeared to have lost a few leaves, but other than that, everything seemed quite intact.

Taking a few deep, steadying breaths, Lucy returned to the ballroom.

Chapter Thirteen

Shortly after five the following day, Alice went to keep her appointment with Lady Peplowe. She was absurdly nervous.

She'd arranged for Lucy to walk in the park with Penny Peplowe while Alice was visiting Lady Peplowe. It would ensure their privacy.

The girls headed off with a footman and maid in attendance, and Alice was shown into the drawing room. Nobody seeing this part of the house would imagine a grand ball had been held there the previous evening. Everything was immaculate. The servants must have been working since before dawn.

Lady Peplowe was seated in the bow window. She patted a chair in a welcoming gesture. "Good afternoon, Lady Charlton. I'm just watching our girls heading off to the park and wishing I had half their energy. It's going to take me days to recover from the ball, but they bounce right back, bless them."

Alice forced a smile. Her stomach was a tight knot. "I know how you feel."

"Nonsense, you're still young yourself. That peach walking dress really suits Lucy, doesn't it? I do so like it when young girls wear colors instead of the endless white so many affect."

Tea and biscuits were brought in, and while they drank and ate—or rather, Lady Peplowe drank and ate; Alice was too nervous—they chatted about the ball and the costumes and how much everyone had enjoyed it. Alice did her best, all the while nerving herself to broach the dreaded subject. Finally it simply burst from her. "I need to ask you a personal question, Lady Peplowe. Very personal, I mean."

The older woman gave her a shrewd glance and set down her teacup. "Of course." She added with a smile, "I might not answer it, but I promise I will respect a confidence."

That would suffice. "It's about the . . . the marriage bed."

Lady Peplowe's elegantly plucked brows rose. "So you can prepare Lucy, I presume. But surely, after your marriage—"

"It's not the, er, mechanics, I'm asking about. It's—" She broke off, feeling her cheeks heat. She recalled Lord Tarrant's words. "Did you ever find it . . . pleasant? Pleasurable I mean? Because I'm told most women . . ." She couldn't finish. It was too humiliating.

There was a short silence. Lady Peplowe's brows knotted, and she took a deep breath. "I never did like that husband of yours," she said briskly. "Are you saying that you never . . . ?"

Alice, face aflame, shook her head.

"The selfish pig!" The older lady reached out and patted Alice on the hand. "Well, thank goodness it's not too late to learn."

Alice blinked. "But I'll be forty in a few years."

Lady Peplowe chuckled. "And I'll be sixty. But the good

news, my dear, is that it only gets better with age and experience."

Better? Alice struggled to hide her amazement. It had never occurred to her that older ladies might still do that. Even though there was no chance of children.

"I married young, and for love," Lady Peplowe began. She glanced at the overmantel, where a family portrait hung. Alice followed her gaze. Lord Peplowe was a nondescript-looking man of medium height. These days he was balding and with a paunch, but Alice had seen the fond way his wife looked at him.

"I was just eighteen, and Peplowe had just turned one-and-twenty." She sighed reminiscently. "We were both so innocent—my mother had prepared me for my wedding night by telling me to do as my husband bid me, and Peplowe, well, his papa had died when he was twelve, and he'd never been one of those boys who chased after women—we'd grown up together you see."

She chuckled. "A pair of ignorant virgins we were. Oh, we fumbled around and managed to get the deed done, but it was awkward and uncomfortable and quite ridiculously strange. But we both assumed that was how it was done, so we persisted." She took a sip of tea, grimaced and rang for a fresh pot.

"But we both had the feeling that there ought to be something more—I mean, what the poets go on about was nothing like what we were finding, and we were in love." She glanced at Alice. "And then Peplowe had the great good sense to seek out a courtesan."

Alice gasped.

"A retired one," Lady Peplowe hastened to assure her. "You don't think I'd let him actually do anything with another woman, do you?" She laughed. "She was a good deal older, but a woman of great experience, and she explained to him just exactly how things worked, and what he should do to make it better. And even what *I* should do. Courtesans know all about how to pleasure men—some of them, the most surprising things. I don't think anyone ever asks them how to please a woman, but she was happy to instruct my darling Peplowe."

"And that made the experience more pleasant?"

"Pleasant?" She regarded Alice sympathetically. "That husband of yours really deserved a horsewhipping. No, my dear, 'pleasant' is far too bland a word. It became . . . glorious. Sometimes earthy, sometimes raw, sometimes sublime and always splendid. A true physical expression of Peplowe's and my love for each other."

Alice tried to swallow. A lump had formed in her throat. She half wanted to cry, which made no sense to her.

The fresh tea arrived, and while Alice poured and added milk and stirred in a sugar lump, she managed to get control of her emotions.

Lady Peplowe drank some tea, set her cup down and sat back. "So, my dear, now that you know, what are you going to do?"

"Do?"

"To experience for yourself some of the physical splendor your abominable husband denied you, of course."

Alice picked up her teacup, unable to think of an answer. What was she going to do? She had no idea.

"I've noticed Lord Tarrant has a certain gleam in his eye whenever he looks at you. I'll be bound a fine, strapping lad like that will know how to introduce a woman to the bliss of the bedchamber."

Alice almost choked on a mouthful of tea. "No, no, you have it wrong. I have no intention of—of—"

"Discovering what it's all about? Nonsense! For nearly twenty years you did your duty to a selfish, undeserving bully, and now it's time you paid attention to your own needs and desires. Or allowed someone else to. Get that gel of yours fired off in style and then see to your own pleasure and satisfaction." She sipped her tea and eyed Alice over the rim of her teacup. "If you don't, you'll spend the rest of your life wondering."

It took Alice a whole day and night to make up her mind. Lady Peplowe's words kept coming back to haunt her: *If you don't, you'll spend the rest of your life wondering.*

She was still far from convinced that she could experience anything like the pleasure Lady Peplowe had described. After all, Thaddeus had kept the same mistress for twenty years, and he'd obviously been satisfied with her responses in bed—and presumably she with his.

It seemed clear to Alice that she'd been the one lacking.

And if that were the case, how dreadful would it be to experience it all again after she married Lord Tarrant. James. The thought of his gradual disillusion, his growing disappointment in her, was more than she could bear.

One unsatisfied, embittered husband was enough for a lifetime.

Oh, James was no bully, as Thaddeus had been, but any man surely would come to resent a wife who was cold in bed.

But to spend the rest of her life wondering—that was no solution to her problem.

James had offered her the prospect of bliss—and she wasn't even talking about the bedroom. Companionship, and the chance to be mother to three delightful little girls—all her girlhood dreams revived. Well, most of them. One had to cut one's coat to fit the cloth. Half a loaf and all that.

Not that James was half of anything. The way he made her feel, that lurking twinkle in his eye. He could meet her gaze, even in a roomful of other people, and make her feel as though just the two of them were present. The way he so often seemed to understand more than she was saying and accept whatever it revealed about her. He could even make her laugh when she was feeling down and despondent.

Only a few weeks ago she'd been facing a lonely future, relishing the thought of her freedom but unsure about what she wanted to do with it.

And then . . . James.

He was offering marriage, family and companionship. Of course he was being practical: he wanted a mother for his girls—what widower wouldn't? And if her feelings for him were stronger than his for her, did that really matter?

How cowardly, and foolish, to reject all that because she believed she couldn't satisfy him in the bedroom. Surely it would be better to find out once and for all. What did she have to lose?

It went against the habit of a lifetime to consider what she was considering, but she could see no other solution. This endless dithering was driving her crazy. With that thought in mind, she sat down and penned a note to Lord Tarrant, asking him to call on her at his earliest convenience.

He came the following morning, bringing with him the three little girls and their nanny. "I hope you don't mind my bringing the girls," he said once the chaos of their arrival had passed. "They'd already been asking could they visit you and Miss Bamber—and the garden—again, and Nanny McCubbin seems to have found a bosom friend in Mrs. Tweed and—"

"It's perfectly all right," she assured him. After a hasty greeting, the girls had rushed out to join Lucy in the garden, and their nanny had headed off to the kitchen for a cup of tea. "As I said before, they're welcome at any time. Lucy and I love having the girls visit, and Mrs. Tweed enjoys Mrs. McCubbin's company. She even lets Mrs. McCubbin help her in the kitchen—a great and rarely bestowed honor, I'll have you know."

"You're very kind. My own house has very little

garden—it's just a courtyard with a couple of aspidistras and a few kitchen herbs—so the girls see your garden as some kind of paradise."

"It is a kind of paradise, and I'm very happy to share it. Tell me, how did you manage to pry Debo away from her cat?"

"Separate Debo and Mittens?" he said in mock horror. "Perish the thought." Then, in response to her raised brow, he added, "Can't be done, I'm afraid. Debo will go nowhere without her cat."

"But—"

"Oh, she's here all right, with the kitten—which you might not have noticed was traveling as an indignant bulge under her coat, Mittens having a strong dislike of the carriage."

"But if she lets it out in the garden . . ." Alice had visions of the kitten disappearing forever.

"Did I ever explain what a superlative nanny Nanny McCubbin is? She made a harness for Mittens, and then told Debo that she'd never manage to teach the cat to wear it—that cats cannot be trained."

"Oh, how clever. Of course, Debo rose to the challenge."

"Indeed she did, and it was a battle of wills that lasted several days and entertained us all. But now Mittens is out in your garden, wearing an elegant red harness as if to the manner born—Debo not having sufficient confidence in the manners of that ginger tom toward visiting kittens."

Alice laughed.

"Now, what was it you wanted to speak to me about?"

The bottom dropped out of Alice's stomach. He always did this to her, made her forget about whatever it was she'd been worrying about. Now all her earlier tension returned with a vengeance.

"Uh . . ." She tried to swallow. There was a giant lump in her throat.

His brows rose. "Yes."

"I've been thinking . . ."

He inclined his head and waited.

"About . . ." She could feel her cheeks heating.

"About 'um'?"

His euphemism for bedroom activities. She nodded. "Yes, I've decided to . . . to try it. Again, I mean. With you." There, she'd said it. She waited for his reaction, her stomach hollow and her pulse racing.

His eyes darkened. His brows drew together in a slow frown. He didn't say a word.

Did he not understand? Had she not been clear enough? Lord knew, her nerves were playing havoc, and she might not have made her meaning plain.

She took a deep breath. "I am willing to become your mistress."

The furrow between his brows deepened. "My mistress," he repeated in a flat voice.

"Yes."

"I see," he said after another long pause.

She waited, fidgeting nervously with the fabric of her skirt. The longer the silence stretched, the more she knew she'd made a terrible mistake. But she couldn't unsay the words. And even though she felt as if she might throw up at any minute, she wasn't going to back down from her decision.

After an age, he cleared his throat. "So, you won't be my wife, but you will be my mistress."

Put like that, it sounded terrible. Bald and blunt and ugly. And scandalous. But it was how she felt.

"Yes," she croaked.

"Even though you dislike 'um.'"

"I always disliked it with my husband." She swallowed again. "But perhaps . . ."

His frown darkened. "You're thinking that perhaps it might be different with me."

She nodded, her cheeks aflame. "You did say as much," she reminded him. *Turn "um" into "yum."*

"I did, didn't I? Well then." He rose abruptly, his expression grim. "I'm going to have to think about this. I will return in an hour to collect my children. I'll give you my answer then." He strode from the room.

Alice stared at the empty doorway, confused by his reaction. She thought he'd be pleased, thought he'd jump at the chance, but he seemed neither pleased nor eager.

The drawing room felt chilly. Childish laughter floated in from the garden.

Was he shocked by her forwardness? It was hard to tell. But the way he'd so abruptly departed, without either accepting or rejecting her proposition, must tell her something. Though what?

She smoothed the fabric of her skirt and frowned. It was a mass of wrinkles. She'd made a mess of it, twisting and crushing it without thinking. Nerves.

Did he think her offer revealed her as a strumpet? Many men would think so.

But Alice refused to be ashamed. It was her body to offer: she was a free agent now and owed fidelity to no one. If he condemned her for it, well, she would be disappointed in him—more than disappointed if she was honest with herself—but she wouldn't go back on her offer, nor would she apologize.

Lady Peplowe was right. It was time Alice discovered for herself what most other women found in the activities of the bedchamber. She wasn't prepared to spend the rest of her life wondering.

James strode away from Alice's house, oblivious of where he was going. He was as tense as a wound spring.

I am willing to become your mistress.

He pounded along the pavement, his fists clenched in hard knots, wanting to punch somebody—no, not somebody: her thrice-damned arse of a husband.

Her face haunted him, so taut and pale when he'd arrived, then later blushing and hesitant, offering herself as if she were . . . he didn't know what. All he knew was that he was boiling with frustrated rage at what had been done to this sweet and giving woman.

He wanted to marry her with all honor, but she couldn't bring herself to do it: she thought she had to debauch herself first.

The hesitation in her eyes, the uncertainty. The courage it must have taken after refusing his offer of marriage, to then offer her body, to lie down with him in an act she was sure she would loathe. Had loathed. For eighteen long, blasted years.

And she didn't even know how to kiss!

That bastard!

There were times when James caught glimpses of the hopeful young girl that she must once have been. All innocence and bright expectation. Before her pig of a husband had driven all the youthful confidence out of her.

But he hadn't managed to kill off her sweetness. Alice had every right to be bitter, but there wasn't a trace of bitterness in her.

If only James had met her back then, before she'd married that oaf. He would have married her—no, because then he wouldn't have met and married Selina, which he could never regret, and they wouldn't have had their precious girls.

But someone should have protected her from marriage to such an uncaring swine. He added her father to the list of dead men he itched to pound to a pulp. The man had been more interested in saving the souls of unknown—and probably unwilling—denizens than the welfare of his only daughter.

Crossing a road, he paused to let a wagon rumble past and realized where he was. Turning a sharp right, he headed down Bond Street to number 13, where he could get exactly what he needed: a furious bout of fisticuffs to work off his anger.

Entering Jackson's Boxing Saloon, he encountered the great man himself, who bowed. "Lord Tarrant, how may I help you?"

"I need to go a few rounds with one of your men, Jackson, but I'll warn you now, I'm in a foul mood and need to pound on someone."

Jackson chuckled and said with dry irony, "You can certainly try. Follow me, my lord."

Forty minutes later James was stripped to the waist, sluicing his heated body down with cold water. Several fast and furious bouts with one of Jackson's best men had certainly loosened some of the fierce coils of anger inside him. He was feeling calmer and more clearheaded, not to mentioned bruised and aching—but in a good way.

He'd been a fool to walk out on her like that. More than a fool—an insensitive brute. What must she be thinking? At great cost to herself, she'd offered him a very precious, deeply personal gift, and what had he done? Walked out on her. Saying he needed to think it over.

Of course he didn't need to think it over. Alice was his; she just didn't know it yet. And if she needed first to prove to herself—or rather, if she needed him to prove to her—that the marriage bed need not be something to be endured, he would do it. With pleasure.

On the way back from Jackson's, he paused by a little flower girl selling violets and bought a posy. Alice deserved better of course, but right now he needed to get back to her as quickly as possible and make up for the way he'd bungled things.

He found her out in the garden with his daughters and Lucy. They were gathered around a pair of easels.

"Look, Papa. Miss Bamber painted us a painting," Judy exclaimed.

But James only had eyes for Alice. "I'm sorry I rushed off like that," he told her quietly and handed her the violets. She thanked him, raised the posy to her face and inhaled the scent. He couldn't see her eyes, couldn't work out what she was thinking. Was she upset with him for rushing off like that? She had every right to be.

"She did one of me and Mittens, too," Debo said. "See? It looks just like us."

"Very nice," he said, and nodded vaguely at Miss Bamber.

"Lina painted one, too," Alice said, and James gave up. He couldn't possibly discuss with her what he needed to discuss, not here, with his daughters clamoring for his attention. He turned to look at Miss Bamber's paintings, and his jaw dropped.

He'd expected some kind of amateurish schoolgirl painting, but what he saw took his breath away. The main painting was an ink and watercolor of the big tree that grew in the center of the garden, as lifelike as if it were growing from the paper. "Can you see us, Papa?" Judy pointed excitedly. "Look. There we all are!"

Half hidden by the leaves of the tree and looking slightly fey, as if they were part of the tree, six faces peeped out; Judy, Lina, Debo, Alice, Lucy and himself. It was a commemoration of the Great Tree-Climbing Adventure. There was even a feline-shaped ginger smear that vividly portrayed an escaping cat.

He examined the tree painting carefully, then the one of Debo and her cat, then several others of the garden and one of Judy staring pensively up into the tree with an expression that made him want to pick his daughter up and hug her.

He turned to Miss Bamber. "But these paintings are marvelous, Miss Bamber. I had no idea you were this talented." Lucy looked down, blushing.

"None of us did," Alice said. "She's kept it a secret up to now, but Lina winkled it out of her."

Lina smiled proudly. "Miss Bamber is teaching me how to paint and draw, Papa. See?" She produced a pad filled with small sketches and paintings, and he slowly turned over page after page, examining each with solemn attention.

"They're very good for a girl her age," Lucy Bamber said quickly. There was an edge of defensiveness in her voice. Did she think he was going to dismiss his small daughter's efforts? She did, he saw. As others had done to her in the past?

"They are very good," he agreed gently. "Lina has always loved to draw, and I'm very grateful you've helped and encouraged her. Even when she was very small, she used to draw pictures on the letters Judy wrote to me. Judy wrote me all the news, and Lina brought it to life in pictures."

His two older daughters looked at him in surprise. "You remember?" Judy asked.

"Remember? I've kept every last one of those precious letters. All the years I was away at war, they were all I had of you girls. I'll show you them when we go home."

He turned back to Lucy. "Miss Bamber, may I buy that painting of us all in the tree?"

"No, you may not." She dimpled. "I've already given it to Lina."

"Buy the one of me and Mittens, Papa," Debo demanded.

"And the one of me," Judy added. "Please?"

Before he could ask, Lucy tore both paintings off the pad and handed them to him. "Please, it's my pleasure," she said when he started to argue. "I don't usually show anyone my work. You"—she gestured to the small group around her—"are the first in a long time."

"I hope we won't be the last," he said seriously. "You have a real talent. I'm going to have these framed."

"Girrrls? My lady? Miss Bamber?" a Scottish voice

called. Nanny McCubbin appeared around a corner. "Time to come in for luncheon. There's nice hot soup, so come along. You don't want it to go cold. And wash your hands," she called after them as the girls ran ahead.

"I'll be in in few minutes," Lucy said. "I'll just pack up my things."

"Then Lady Charlton and I will go ahead and warn Cook," James said before Alice could offer to help. He held out his arm, and after a moment's hesitation, she took it.

"I'm sorry I rushed off like that before," he said once they were out of earshot. "I hope I didn't upset you."

"Not at all." Her voice was cool.

"You took me by surprise."

"So I gathered."

He stopped and, taking both her hands in his, faced her. "Alice, you did me a great honor this morning, offering me the priceless gift of your trust. I'm a clumsy oaf, and I'm sorry if I offended you in any way. If your offer is still open, I would be privileged to accept it."

He held his breath as she gazed up at him. He was drowning in those sea blue eyes of hers.

After what felt like an age, she said, "I'm glad."

They resumed their walk back to Alice's house. "So what do we do now?" she asked.

"I'll make all the arrangements."

"What arrangements?" she asked, adding, "I've never done this before, so I'm unaware of the conventions."

"There are no conventions in our case," he said. "We'll make it up as we go along."

She gave him a sideways glance. "You mean you've never had a mistress before?"

"No."

"Oh. I thought all men had them."

"Not all men."

"Then what are these 'arrangements' you're talking of?"

"Do you plan to take me to your bed here, then?"

She gasped. "With Lucy in the room above me? And the Tweeds and Mary knowing? Of course not."

He smiled. "And presumably you wouldn't want to come to my bed, with my daughters sleeping upstairs—and I'll warn you now, they have a tendency to jump on me in bed at appalling hours of the morning. Generally with a cat in tow."

She laughed. "Oh dear, and do you sneeze?"

"Invariably." They'd reached her back gate, and he held it open for her. "So, my dear Alice, will you agree to leave the arrangements to me?"

"I suppose I must." She hesitated. "Do you know, er, when . . . ?"

"I'll let you know."

Lucy, having gone to sleep with her windows open, was woken early by the twittering of the birds outside. She lay there a few moments, snuggling dreamily in the warmth and comfort of her bed, contemplating the day ahead, when suddenly she remembered.

And sat straight up.

The announcement would be in the papers this morning. She was—officially, if not actually—betrothed. To Gerald, Lord Thornton. A proper lord!

Across London, people would be seeing the announcement about herself, plain Lucy Bamber, and Lord Thornton. It was a strange thought. With any luck, Papa would be one of them, reading the newspaper announcement at this very minute—well, soon; he was not an early riser—and come around here to give Alice back her letters.

When would Alice see it? It was her habit to drink a cup of chocolate and glance through the newspapers before dressing and coming down to breakfast.

Hasty footsteps sounded in the hallway outside. Alice. She knocked on the door and entered, waving her copy of the *Morning Post*. "Lucy, the strangest thing! Someone has put a notice in the paper announcing a betrothal between you and my nephew, Gerald. I don't know how it happened. It's clearly a mistake and—"

"It's not a mistake."

"We'll have to get it withdraw— What did you say?"

"I said, it's not a mistake."

Alice blinked. "It's not?"

"No. Gerald put the notice in yesterday."

"You're engaged to my nephew, Gerald?"

Lucy nodded.

Alice flew across the room and embraced Lucy. "Oh, my dear girl, that's marvelous. I'm so happy for you." She sat down on Lucy's bed, tossing the newspaper aside. "Now, tell me all about it. How did this happen? *When* did it happen? I must confess you've completely taken me by surprise. I thought you two were at daggers drawn." Beaming expectantly at Lucy, Alice folded her hands and waited for the details of the romance to be revealed.

Lucy shrugged uncomfortably. Alice had every right to feel put out at not being informed. Both of Lucy's other suitors had asked Alice's permission before proposing, and here, she and Gerald had gone ahead and announced it in the papers without informing anyone. Of course they were of age and had the right to make their own plans, but still, Alice had to feel a little hurt. And yet here she was, smiling so kindly at the girl who was deceiving her. And who was preparing to deceive her even further.

Lucy desperately wanted to let Alice in on the plot, but Gerald was right. Alice was a hopeless liar.

"It was at the Peplowe ball," she began. "Gerald took over the spots where I'd arranged to sit out the waltzes—is that right, by the way? I can't waltz anywhere until I have been approved to waltz at Almack's?"

"Oh, who cares about that? He took over your spots?"

"Yes, he told Mr. Frinton and Mr. Grimswade that, as

acting head of your family, he had the right to commandeer them."

Alice gasped and then laughed. "Head of my family indeed! What nonsense! But how wonderfully masterful and romantic."

"How arrogant, you mean. I was furious."

Alice chuckled, clearly not believing her. "What happened next?"

"He took me out into the courtyard and we talked." Having no wish to be questioned on the subject of their conversation, she hastily went on. "And later he did it again during the second waltz, only then he invited me to dance, out in the courtyard—it's all right, we were quite alone and nobody saw us. But about that Almack's question—"

"Ohhhh! A secret waltz in the moonlight. I would never have guessed Gerald had such romance in him. No wonder you were bowled over."

Lucy smiled weakly. It might sound romantic, and in her secret heart she had to admit that she had found it romantic, but really, it was just a plan to trap her father.

Alice blanched on a sudden thought. "Oh heavens! Does Almeria—Lady Charlton, Gerald's mother—know?"

Lucy shook her head. "No, we wanted it to be a surprise."

"Well, it's certainly that. Oh dear. Almeria will be around here any moment then, because of course she won't be happy—and that's an understatement if ever I've made one. She'll be furious and blame me for it, even though I knew nothing about it." She slipped off the bed. "Get dressed quickly. We'd better get ready."

"Man the battlements? Start boiling the oil?" Lucy climbed out of bed.

Alice gave a huff of laughter. "You may joke, but you don't know what she's like." At the door, she paused. "On second thought, you stay here. I'll deal with her."

"You? But you didn't know anything about it. Why should you have to deal with her?"

"Because I've been dealing with Almeria for the last twenty years. Better still, why don't you get dressed and go out into the garden as usual. I'll be able to tell her then that you're not in the house."

Alice was planning to protect her, Lucy realized. Preparing to stand up to Gerald's mother on her behalf. She couldn't remember the last time anyone besides Alice had stood up for her. She was very touched.

She crossed the floor and gave Alice a quick hug. "Alice, you are a darling, but I am not going to run off and leave you to the dragon lady. Almeria doesn't worry me. Besides, I watched how you handled her once. It taught me a lot."

Alice looked at her curiously. "Really? What did it teach you?"

"Not to lose my temper or rise to her barbs. You were quite splendid." Lucy shook out her dress and laid it on her bed. "Now, off you go. I'll be downstairs shortly. And don't worry—I'm not afraid of that woman."

"Maybe not, but Lucy, she's going to be your mother-in-law. For the rest of your life."

Lucy shrugged. Almeria would never be her mother-in-law. "She's been your sister-in-law for half your life. Has your careful politeness ever made any difference?"

Alice grimaced, then nodded. "I suppose you're right. Begin as you mean to go on. With any luck, we'll have time for breakfast before Almeria descends on us."

"Like the Black Death. Or," Lucy added mischievously, "should that be the Puce Plague?"

Chapter Fourteen

Dammit, where was Heffernan? Gerald scanned the street for the dozenth time. He'd instructed Heffernan to be on hand outside Aunt Alice's house, keeping a discreet lookout for Bamber. But there was no sign of the man.

Gerald had put the betrothal notice in several papers, not just the most popular ones, so Bamber would be sure to see it. Heffernan was supposed to be here, ready to catch Bamber when he came. Two possibilities had occurred to Gerald: either Bamber would give Aunt Alice her letters back and disappear from her life as agreed, or he'd decide he wanted more from her, blackmailers being notorious for wanting more. And if that were the case, Gerald, with Heffernan's aid, would pounce on the blackguard and force him to give up the letters.

So where was Heffernan?

A hawker had set up farther down the street, roasting nuts over a portable brazier. Gerald's stomach rumbled. He'd missed breakfast, and the smell was enticing. He gave the street another sweeping glance, then hurried down and ordered some roasted almonds.

The hawker filled a cone of newspaper with hot nuts and handed them to Gerald. "No sign of him yet, m'lord."

Gerald nearly dropped the nuts. "Good God, it's you." Heffernan looked nothing like himself. He looked shorter, fatter, grayer and hairier, not to mention scruffier.

"Don't be talking to me now, m'lord. Just take yourself off, casual-like. I have three men watching for Bamber. Don't worry. If he shows up, we'll get 'im."

"Three men?" Gerald could see no sign of them.

"Aye. All Radcliffe's men, so leave it all to us. There's no tellin' when Bamber will show—could take him all day. Might even be tomorrow, or later, depending on where he's been hiding himself. The minute he shows, we'll let you know. That lad over there, the one sweeping the street, he's my runner. He'll bring you any news quick as a flash."

Munching on the hot nuts, Gerald walked away. It went against the grain for him to leave the scene, but Heffernan was right—there was no telling how long Bamber would take to get here. And he couldn't very well turn up at Aunt Alice's house at this hour and then hang around all day without an excuse—because who knew when Bamber would come? Even a newly betrothed man couldn't get away with that.

And Alice wasn't to know that the betrothal was a ruse.

A newly betrothed man. He was betrothed to Lucy Bamber.

He smiled to himself. In her own way, Lucy was as elusive as her father. Not that there was any comparison.

Lucy and Alice had just finished breakfast and had taken a pot of tea into the drawing room when the front doorbell jangled.

"That'll be her. Are you sure you don't want to go out into the garden?" Alice asked Lucy for the third time. The fact that she was obviously dreading the encounter made Lucy feel even warmer toward her.

Lucy laughed. "Not in the least. Are you sure you won't let me deal with her by myself? I'm quite happy to." In fact she would prefer to, but Alice was determined to stay and protect her.

Moments later Almeria, Countess of Charlton, swept into the room and came to an abrupt stop. She shot a vitriolic glance at Lucy. "You!" she said in a voice of loathing.

Lucy curtsied. "Good morning, Lady Charlton," she said in a cheery voice. "What a vision you are—fifty shades of puce?"

Alice hurriedly rose, saying, "Almeria, what a surprise."

"Hah! Surprise indeed. What do you have to say for yourself, eh? Eh?" She glared at Alice.

"Would you like a cup of tea?" Alice asked and, without waiting for an answer, rang for Tweed—who appeared so quickly he must have been listening at the door—and ordered fresh tea.

"Tea!" Almeria said with loathing, seating herself in a flurry of silk and velvet. "This is not the time for tea."

"Coffee then for Lady Charlton please, Tweed," Alice said and returned to her place on the sofa.

"I want nothing! No. Refreshments. Whatsoever!"

Lucy hid a smile. Alice wasn't doing it deliberately but her attempt at soothing the savage breast—or was it a savage beast? Beastess?—was having the opposite effect.

"Well?" Almeria snapped the instant Tweed had departed. "Explain yourself, Alice. I told you most specifically that I did not wish my son to become acquainted with this . . . this . . . creature." She waved a disdainful hand in Lucy's direction.

A "creature," was she? Any intention Lucy had of being polite and conciliatory flew out the window.

"'Creature'?" Lucy looked ostentatiously around. "Oh,

you mean me? Of course you do. But you mustn't blame Alice. She was as surprised as you were."

Almeria turned a baleful glare on her. "*Surprised* is not the word."

"Delighted?" Lucy prompted brightly. "Thrilled? Jubilant?"

"I am appalled! I don't know how you managed to convince my son—"

"Oh, there was no convincing necessary. Not at all. In fact, it was all his idea."

Almeria's eyes narrowed. "I don't know how you entrapped my son into this appalling mésalliance but—"

"'Entrapped'?" Lucy interrupted. "Have you not spoken to Gerald then?"

Aleria's lips thinned. "He was not in his lodgings this morning. No doubt hiding from the consequences of his rash act."

"Or from his dear mama," Lucy said sweetly.

Almeria's eyes flashed. "Are you calling my son a coward?"

"You were the one who said he was hiding," Lucy pointed out. "I wouldn't have thought it myself, but—"

"I don't know how he was convinced to wed the likes of you, but I intend to put a stop to it."

Lucy tried to look concerned. "Is your son so weak-willed then?"

"'Weak-willed'?" Ice dripped from every syllable.

"To be so easily controlled by his mother. I confess I am surprised, especially considering how heroically he served his country, commanding I don't know how many troops and serving with distinction for—how many years was he away at war fighting the Corsican Monster, Alice?"

"Eight," said Alice.

"Six," Almeria said at the same time.

"It was eight," Alice repeated.

Almeria sniffed.

"Well, whatever it was, presumably his mama knows him best," Lucy cooed. "So, Lady Charlton, are you saying Gerald is easily led? A touch unreliable?"

"What do you mean, 'unreliable'? My son is—"

"The kind of man who gives his word without intending to keep it?"

"How dare you! My son is the soul of honor!" Almeria declared, outraged.

"Oh, good then"—Lucy smiled serenely—"so the betrothal stands."

Almeria breathed heavily through her nostrils, her eyes bulging with frustration. "I warn you, if you do not release him from this disastrous match, he will be penniless. His father will cut off his allowance."

"Like a naughty schoolboy?" Lucy said incredulously. "How very poor-spirited of him."

"Hah! That's made you think twice, hasn't it?" Almeria nodded in satisfaction. "Thought you were marrying a fortune, didn't you?"

"Not in the least. Didn't you know, we're marrying for *lovvvve*." Lucy batted her lashes and sighed romantically.

"Love? Pah! People of our order do not marry for love."

"But then, I am not of your order, am I? Isn't that your objection? In any case," Lucy continued briskly, "I doubt Gerald will need his father's financial support once he joins the diplomatic service and is living abroad."

Almeria stiffened. "The diplomatic service? Gerald? Abroad? What nonsense. He'll do nothing of the sort. I need him here."

Lucy raised a brow. "To dance attendance on you? You want to keep a grown man of eight-and-twenty tied to your apron strings? Isn't it a bit late for that?"

Almeria curled her lip. "Apron strings? Faugh! I've never worn an apron in my life."

"How odd," Lucy said. "I've always found them very useful—though not for tying people up with. Not that I've ever tried. But if you don't have many dresses, an apron is a very useful garment."

"I'm sure it is," Almeria said disdainfully.

Lucy added in a reminiscent tone, "In fact I was wearing an apron when Gerald and I first met."

"You were wearing an *apron*?" She said *apron* as if Lucy had confessed to wearing a filthy old sack.

"Yes, perhaps that's what attracted him—something a little bit different from the usual run of girls he'd been meeting."

"Why were you wearing an apron?" A filthy, old manure-stained sack.

Lucy smiled sweetly. "To protect my clothes. I was tending geese at the time."

Almeria's well-plucked eyebrows almost disappeared. "Tending geese? You were a *goose girl*?"

"Yes. But they were very well-bred geese."

A muffled sound came from the sofa. Lucy couldn't see Alice's face.

"They were French geese," Lucy added. "They belonged to a French comtesse—"

"French!" Almeria said with scorn.

"Yes, but German geese are held to be very fine, too, I believe."

"Young woman! I have no interest in geese, French, German or otherwise."

Lucy widened her eyes. "But you must. I mean, you surely sleep on a goose-feather mattress—they are the finest. And what about the Christmas goose? Do you refrain from eating that, too? Preferring pork, or perhaps chicken. Or do you eschew meat altogether? Is that how you stay so skinny? I mean, thin. No, slender—is that what you call it?"

"Cease and desist, you impertinent gel!"

"By all means, your ladyship. Just tell me what you wish me to cease and desist from, and I will gladly oblige."

"My son's betrothal—"

"Except for that."

For a long moment Almeria huffed and puffed in silence, then she rose and with freezing dignity said, "I am deeply disappointed in you, Alice, for bringing this atrocious female into our circle. As for you"—she pointed a bony finger at Lucy, who had also risen—"the only way you will marry my son is over my dead body."

"Oh surely, nothing so drastic," Lucy said chattily. "We'd have to go into blacks and that's such a gloomy color for a wedding, don't you think?"

Almeria's eyes were chips of ice. She opened her mouth, closed it, glared at Lucy some more and with a final muttered, "Abominable creature," she swept from the room.

Lucy waited until she heard the front door close behind her, then sank into her chair with a gusty sigh. "Oh, that was fun, wasn't it?" She glanced across at Alice, who seemed to have collapsed on the sofa. "Are you all right, Alice?"

Alice sat up, clutching a crumpled handkerchief. She regarded Lucy with awe. "'Fun'?" It was . . . You were so . . ."

"Brassy? Bold? Impertinent?"

"All of the above—and utterly brilliant! And so brave."

"Brave? Oh pooh. What can that woman do to me, after all?"

"She's going to be your mother-in-law."

Lucy wrinkled her nose. No danger of that. She really wished she could tell Alice it was a false betrothal, but she'd made a promise.

She almost wished she was going to marry Lord Thornton. It went wholly against the grain to give that woman what she wanted. It would serve Almeria right if Lucy married him after all.

After a moment Alice said, "You and your well-bred French geese. I thought she was going to burst." She glanced at Lucy and clapped her hand over her mouth. A snort escaped her, their eyes met, and suddenly they were both laughing uncontrollably.

* * *

It's not working," Lucy told Gerald as soon as she could grab a moment alone with him. Lord and Lady Falconer's rout was already a "sad squeeze," and more people were arriving every minute.

The news about their betrothal was well and truly out, and many people had come up to congratulate her. Some, of course, were less welcoming of the news, the Countess of Charlton being one of them. Almeria was circulating among her friends, telling people that it was a mistake, that it would be called off as soon as her son came to his senses and that "that Bamber creature," as she was calling Lucy, had entrapped him.

"Don't worry about Almeria," Alice told her. "The more people she tells that kind of thing to, the more sympathy you're getting. It's extremely bad form of her to be so obviously antagonistic toward her son's choice—particularly when *he* seems so happy. Besides, anybody who knows Gerald knows he's not the kind of man to be entrapped by anyone."

But whatever slander Almeria was spreading about Lucy didn't bother her. It was, after all, a false betrothal. Almeria would get her victory in the end, much as it would vex Lucy to have to grant it to her.

"What's not working?" Gerald asked.

"It's been two days now since the betrothal was posted in the newspapers, and there has been no word from Papa."

"I know," Gerald said.

Lucy frowned up at him. "How do you know?"

"I've had men watching the house ever since dawn that first morning."

Men watching the house? Lucy wasn't sure what she thought about that. Lying in wait for Papa as if he were a criminal.

But he *was* a criminal. He'd blackmailed Alice. He'd

also failed to give her the money he'd promised her. Lucy knew full well that Alice was now paying for all Lucy's needs out of her own pocket—a pocket that was lean at best.

And she knew he owed many people money. And that some of his schemes had resulted in serious losses for his investors, though not Papa, never for Papa. So, yes, he was a cheat and a blackmailer—a criminal. She couldn't deny it.

But he was still her father. And though he hadn't ever been much of a parent, he had done his best for her, according to his own peculiar and haphazard standards. He *had* put her in the finest schools—even if she was later expelled for his failure to pay the bills. And he *had* intended she would benefit from her time with Frau Steiner and the comtesse—and she *had* learned from them, even if most of the time they'd used her as a maidservant.

Papa always come up with schemes that sounded good. He just wasn't very good at carrying them out. Or was it that he simply didn't care about the people he involved in his schemes, as long as he benefited in the end?

Oh, Papa . . . Had he always been like this? Even with Mama? She couldn't tell; she'd been too young. But probably he was just the same. They'd moved so often, and she was sure that wasn't Mama's choice.

"How long do you think we should give it?" she asked Gerald.

"How long for what?"

"Our betrothal. If it doesn't bring Papa and the letters to us, there's not much point in going on, is there?"

"Oh, there's plenty of time yet," he said easily.

"I suppose." She glanced across to where Almeria was leaning in close to one of her cronies, whispering furiously in her ear, all the while sending dagger looks at Lucy.

Brightening, Lucy sent the woman a wide smile and twinkled her fingers at Almeria in a gleeful wave. Almeria stiffened in outrage and resumed the vehement whispering.

Lucy laughed. Yes, indeed, there was still plenty of time to enjoy the fruits of her betrothal.

"Do you have any engagements for Thursday next?" James said as he escorted Alice in to supper. Lord and Lady Falconer were known for the quality of their suppers. James was hoping for crab or lobster patties.

She turned her head sharply. "Thursday next? You mean the day after tomorrow? Is that when—we, er, you plan to, um . . . ?"

"Yes, I'm hoping for 'um' on Thursday, if that suits you."

She glanced furtively around. "And you're asking me here? In this company?"

His eyes danced but he said solemnly, "It is perfectly proper to inquire about a lady's social arrangements, whether in company or not." And then he added, for he could see his question had seriously discomposed her, "I simply wish to invite you to take a turn in my new carriage, Lady Charlton."

"Your carriage?"

"Yes, my carriage."

"Oh, your *carriage*," she said, finally understanding. She added in a clear voice, sufficient to be heard a good ten feet in any direction, "I would be delighted to take a ride in your carriage, Lord Tarrant." And then she realized the possible interpretations of that statement and blushed rosily.

James hid a smile. His beloved was not built for deception. Duplicity of any kind was simply not in her nature.

"Good," he murmured, "my horses are raring to go."

Her blush deepened.

"In that case, I will call for you at nine." He leaned closer and whispered in her ear. "Pack a bag. We will stay overnight."

"Overn—?" she squeaked and tried to turn it into a cough.

"Possibly longer."

Her eyes widened, but she said nothing as they took their places. James was delighted to see that there were both crab and lobster patties, and plenty of both. Alice just picked at her food. She was nervous, but he could do nothing about that. Not until Thursday.

"What about Lucy?" she asked in a low voice.

He served her a slice of lemon curd cake. Her favorite. "What about her?"

"I can't just go off and leave her."

"Why not? Much as I like your goddaughter, she's not coming with us."

She spluttered over a mouthful of wine. "No, but it would be most improper to leave her on her own in my house."

He wanted to laugh. But he saw her point. "What if Nanny McCubbin and my daughters came to stay? That would be adequate chaperonage, would it not."

"Y-es. Or perhaps I could ask Lady Peplowe to invite her to stay a few days. Lucy and Penny Peplowe get on very well together. I'll give it some thought."

To James's amusement, Alice raised it with Lucy going home in the carriage that evening, telling her that she'd heard this evening that an old friend of hers was ailing and Alice had decided to visit her.

No, Lucy couldn't accompany her because . . . because her friend was quite poor and lived in a very small cottage. There was no room.

Who was this friend? An . . . an old school friend.

Her name? Mary—yes, that was it. Mary.

James leaned back against the carriage squabs, enjoying the tangled story Alice was attempting to weave in order to have an excuse to get away for a couple of days. He had no doubt the darkness inside the carriage hid a positive battalion of blushes.

The possibilities of Penny Peplowe or Nanny McCubbin and the little girls were debated. Then Gerald leaned forward and said, "Actually, I have been thinking of taking Lucy to meet my grandmother, who lives outside Aylesbury."

"Your grandmother?" Lucy exclaimed. "But I can't—"

"She's heard so much about you already."

"I just bet she has," Lucy muttered.

Gerald laughed. "I promise you'll like her. She's not at all like my mother. In fact, she's been heard to say—when provoked—that Mother was a fairy changeling, and not the good sort. Grandmama would love to meet you."

"What an excellent idea," James said.

"Yes, and you can take my maid, Mary, with you," Alice agreed.

"Yes, I'm sure Lady Charlton will manage perfectly without the services of her maid," James said in a provocative voice.

A small foot kicked him on the ankle. Alice said with dignity, "Thank you, Gerald, that's the perfect solution."

James didn't think Lucy was as pleased with the idea as everyone else. In fact, he got the distinct impression she was extremely reluctant to go, but he didn't care. As long as it made Alice free to come with him, he didn't give a damn what Lucy did.

"Good, so that's all settled," he said as the carriage drew up outside Bellaire Gardens. "Good night, ladies," he said as he handed them down. "It's been a delightful evening."

The following morning a letter arrived addressed to Lucy in a flamboyant hand. Tweed presented it to her on a silver salver. She eyed it with a sinking heart. She knew that hand.

She looked at Alice. "It's from Papa."

"What does it say?"

Lucy broke open the seal, scanned the contents swiftly, then read it aloud.

My dear Daughter,

By the time you receive this letter, I shall be far away, sailing the high seas, heading for America. Congratulate me, Daughter, for I have married a Mrs. Lymon. She is a Widow from Boston, Massachusetts, the relict of an Extremely Wealthy man, so you will be Glad to know I shall be living in the Comfort, even Luxury, to which I have always aspired. I shall not be returning to England—it has become increasingly Unfriendly to me and I am glad to shake its Dirt from my boots and to start a New Life.

So, Daughter, for all your misgivings, my little Scheme was successful and you are securely betrothed to a Viscount and the Heir to an Earldom. Thus I can happily leave you, knowing I have done all I can to Assure your Future.

Please give Lady Charlton my thanks—and apologies. I had no choice.

Live well, my child.

Farewell from your Loving Father,
Octavius Bamber, esquire

She choked on the last few lines.

She ought to be used to this. How many times had he dumped her on strangers and abandoned her. This time it was forever. He was glad to go. *I can happily leave you.*

"Oh, Lucy, to leave the country—forever—without any warning, or even a personal goodbye." Alice slipped an arm around Lucy and hugged her. The warm sympathy in her voice brought a blurring of tears to Lucy's eyes. She blinked them angrily away.

She would *not* let her father bring her to tears, not again. Never again. How often as a young girl had she soaked her pillow with lonely, miserable, *fruitless* tears every time Papa had left her, assuring her that this—wherever it was, with whoever it was—would be the making of her. And then he'd drive blithely away without a backward glance. Leaving her behind to sink or swim.

And now she was alone forever, without even having the pretense of a father.

Well, better no father at all than one who regularly turned her life upside down with no warning. She could choose now how she would live her life.

And if the future stretched ahead, frighteningly blank, that simply meant she needed to make plans. She couldn't batten on Alice much longer.

"I'm all right," she told Alice wearily. "It's not as if it's anything new."

She folded and refolded the letter until it was a small square and slipped it into her sleeve. It was so typical of Papa—the self-centeredness, the self-congratulatory tone and the complete disregard of her feelings. All he cared about was his own success. So her future was assured, was it? Did he even know—or care—anything about Lord Thornton apart from his title? For all Papa knew, he could be a horrid wife beater or cat torturer or anything.

After a moment, Alice said hesitantly, "Did he even mention the letters?"

Lucy shook her head. "I'm sorry."

"Maybe he's burned them."

Lucy shook her head. Who knew, with Papa.

"But what would be the use of them now? He's got what he wanted—you're betrothed to a viscount. And he must know I have no money to buy them."

Lucy shrugged. "I don't know. Maybe it's all over. Maybe Papa's forgotten all about them. It wouldn't be unlike him. He has an enviable ability to put awkward or uncomfortable thoughts out of his mind, particularly when he has a new scheme in mind." In this case, a rich widow.

Alice sighed. "He's acting as if his 'scheme' is all over, but I would feel a lot better if he had enclosed the letters."

"It would cost more to post," Lucy said. "Papa can be quite ridiculously penny-pinching at times." She stood up and said briskly. "Now, I don't know about you, but I'm in need of fresh air. I'm going out into the garden. Do you want to come?"

Alice said gently, "No, my dear, you've had a big upset. I think you'll be happier alone to sort out your feelings."

Lucy nodded. *Happier alone.* Yes, she'd better learn how to be that.

Gerald called at Bellaire Gardens later that afternoon, ostensibly to finalize the arrangements to take Lucy to visit his grandmother, but also to bring Alice the news.

"Lucy is out in the garden," Alice told him.

"Good," he said. "But first some news. My man Heffernan sent a message. Bamber has left the country. He sailed from Bristol two nights ago, on a ship bound for America."

"I know," Alice said. "Lucy got a letter from him this morning, bidding her farewell forever. He's married a rich American widow and says he's never coming back."

Gerald stared at her, shocked. "He said goodbye by letter? Without even trying to see her? That swine. His own daughter! How did she take it?"

Alice shook her head. "She's devastated, of course, but determined not to show it. She says it's nothing new. It seems she's quite accustomed to being abandoned by that wretched man—but honestly, how could any young girl become accustomed to such carelessness? Especially as he's her only living relative. And she's such a dear girl. Oh, I could strangle him."

"You'll keep her with you of course."

"Yes, of course, though she has her pride. My guess is she'll try to insist on leaving." Alice snorted. "To go where? That man has left her with nothing. I'm just thankful she is safely betrothed to you. Were it not for that . . ." She shook her head.

Gerald frowned. The betrothal was currently as strong as wet paper. He would have his work cut out for him now. "Perhaps this visit to my grandmother might cheer her up."

Alice gave him a skeptical glance. "You think so?"

"Why not? At least it will be a change. I'll go and speak to her now." On the point of leaving, he turned back at the door. "There was no mention of the letters, I suppose?"

"None."

"Damn him—sorry, Aunt Alice."

"Don't be," Alice said. "I quite agree."

He found Lucy in her favorite spot, under the spreading plane tree, painting. Or rather, pretending to paint. He stood in the shadows and quietly watched her for several minutes. Her brush never moved. She just sat, staring blankly into the distance.

He couldn't imagine how she must feel. To be so callously abandoned, so entirely alone . . .

No matter how unsatisfactory his own parents were, they were at least there.

He must have moved or made a sound, for she turned her head and sprang up. "Gerald." She put her paintbrush down, smoothed her dress and faced him with a forced smile. "I'm glad you're here. It's time this sham came to an end."

He strolled toward her. "What sham would that be?"

"The betrothal."

"Oh, that. There's no hurry."

"You don't understand." She took a small square of paper from her sleeve and handed it to him. "I received this today. My father has left the country. As you will see, there's no longer any reason to continue this betrothal charade," she said in a colorless voice.

Gerald unfolded the square and started to read. As he did, his anger grew. The smug self-satisfaction of the man. His complete disregard for his daughter's feelings. Not even a pretense that she would be welcome to visit or that he intended to share any of his good fortune with her.

"You see?" she said when he'd finished reading. "It's time I set you free. I'm not quite sure how to proceed—do I send the notice to the papers? Or is it more proper for you to do so? Only I don't want people to think you have been in any way dishonorable."

He refolded the letter and passed it back to her. "Don't worry about it. I'm not ready to cancel our betrothal yet."

A troubled crease appeared between her brows. "Why not? We only did it to bring my father out from wherever he was lurking. Now he's on his way to America, there's no point."

"Yes, but there are other things to consider," he said vaguely.

"What things?"

"People. My grandmother for a start."

She stared at him, puzzled. "What does your grandmother have to do with it?"

"She's very much looking forward to our visit tomorrow. I'd hate to disappoint her."

"But she doesn't even know me. And won't she be even more disappointed if we break off the betrothal after the visit?"

"She's expecting us. And if you don't come with me," he added in a burst of inspiration, "Alice won't be able to go and stay with her friend—and you know how she hates to let people down. As a betrothed couple, with a maid in attendance, you and I can travel quite respectably, but if we were no longer betrothed, it would be quite scandalous."

She eyed him with a doubtful expression. "Really?"

"Yes," he said firmly. "By staying betrothed, we can make both my grandmother and Alice happy, and nobody will be put out or disappointed."

"I suppose," she agreed reluctantly.

He gave her a quizzical look. "Are you so keen to get rid of me?"

She gave a halfhearted laugh. "It's not that, it's just that— Oh, my father has embroiled us all in this dreadful tangle, and I can see no way out except to cut right through it and leave everyone free and clear." Her lovely eyes were troubled. "I am truly grateful, Lord Thornton, for your—"

"*What?*" He staggered back as if in shock.

She put a concerned hand on his arm. "What is it? Are you ill?"

"You called me Lord Thornton." And then when she didn't respond, he added, "Not Lord Thorncrake or Lord Thorndyke or Lord Thornbottle."

She looked self-conscious. "Oh. Yes. Well, I'm sorry about that."

He fixed her with a gimlet look. "Who are you and what have you done with Lucy Bamber?"

She laughed, a genuine one this time.

"That's better," he said. "I don't like seeing you all crushed and guilty. None of this mess is your fault, and your father is gone, so let us put it all behind us." Before she could argue the case, he hurried on. "Now, I plan to collect you at half past eight tomorrow morning. It's not too early for you, is it? It will take us most of the day to reach my grandmother's."

"It's not too early," she said. "But I still don't like the thought of getting her hopes up."

"Let me worry about that," he told her.

Lucy ate a hearty breakfast. Alice had toyed with a piece of toast but hadn't been able to bring herself to eat more than a mouthful. She was too tense.

She waved off Lucy and Mary shortly after half past eight. It was a rather grand affair. The smart traveling carriage had the Charlton coat of arms on the door and was pulled by a team of four fine horses. The driver wore livery, as did the footman traveling at the rear. Gerald accompanied them on horseback.

As they turned the corner and disappeared from sight, butterflies started up in Alice's stomach. James would be here in half an hour. She was all packed, but was she ready for what was to come? She had no idea.

James arrived twenty minutes later in a yellow bounder—a hired post chaise pulled by two horses. A postilion rode one of the horses.

"We're not going far," he explained, "and this is more private. No grooms or drivers to worry about or eavesdrop, no horses to stable."

Alice nodded. She couldn't even think about grooms or horses. But privacy she could appreciate. She could still hardly believe she was going to do this, even less that it was at her suggestion.

James put her valise into the boot at the back and helped her into the chaise. She'd never been in one of these conveyances before, and when he climbed in after her, it suddenly felt very small. Their bodies touched all down one side. His body felt so warm. She herself felt cold. Nerves.

They set off, and she distracted herself by looking out the window that covered the whole front of the chaise and pointing out various sights of possible interest. She feared she was babbling, but she couldn't seem to help herself.

After a few minutes it started to rain, just a soft, light spitting, but it made the window hard to see out of.

"We'll be there in about an hour," James told her. "I've rented a small cottage near a village on the outskirts of London."

"Mmm," she responded vaguely. In the small, close carriage, she could smell him—nothing strong or overwhelming, just the faint scent of his soap, clean linen, a hint of his shaving cologne and the underlying smell of his skin: the smell of James. She just wanted to lean over, press her face against his chest and inhale him.

If only that was all it took . . .

"So, how shall we while away the time?"

Startled, she turned to look at him.

He laughed at her expression. "Not with any improper activity," he said. "We'll have plenty of time for that when we get there."

"Oh. Of course." She swallowed.

His big warm hand closed over hers, and she immediately felt both comforted and yet, foolishly, even more nervous. "I meant," he continued, his thumb caressing her skin, "what shall we talk about on the journey? Let's start with you: Where did you grow up?"

She told him about her childhood at the vicarage in Chaceley and, under what she later realized was his skillful questioning, told him a great deal more than she'd intended, about her father's passion for saving the souls of denizens, about how she'd grown up lonely—she wasn't allowed to associate with the village children—and had always wished for brothers or sisters, but they'd never happened.

And all the time his thumb caressed her, moving back and forth over her hand, slow and rhythmic.

She found herself telling him how she'd come to marry Thaddeus. "I barely knew him, but both Mama and Papa were insistent that he was a good match for me—and he did seem to be good-looking and quite charming. So, two weeks to the day after we met, we were betrothed." And she, poor naive fool, had thought that Thaddeus had fallen in love with her, and she'd been so excited by this unexpected whirlwind wooing by a handsome and sophisticated London viscount that she'd imagined she was in love with him, too.

Later she'd learned that she was on a list of virtuous and eligible girls his father had given him, along with an ultimatum that if he wasn't betrothed to one of them by the end of the month, his allowance would be stopped. It was all to prevent him from marrying his mistress. She didn't tell that to James. It was too lowering.

"And six weeks after that, I was married and living in London, and Mama and Papa had departed for foreign shores—Papa's lost souls, you see," she finished.

"And not long after that, they were dead."

"Yes, it was a terrible shock. And by the time I found out, they'd actually been dead for weeks." That was when she'd finally realized she was entirely alone in the world—except for her husband, who by then had shown his true colors. "But enough about me." She forced a brighter tone. "What about you? Did you have a happy childhood?"

He told her about the estate in Warwickshire where he'd grown up—the one that was now his—and how his brother, Ross, being the heir, had been trained to take over the management of the estate. It was clear from his stories that he and his brother were very close—and that Nanny McCubbin had cared for them both. "She was more of a mother to Ross and me than our own mother was."

Alice, having seen Nanny McCubbin with his daughters, could easily imagine it.

He told her about joining the army and going to war, about how he met his wife, Selina, on leave, and how her parents were adamantly opposed to the match, but how he and Selina won out in the end. He told her how Selina had traveled with the army and how well she'd taken to that life.

As he talked and told funny and dramatic stories of their adventures, Alice became more and more aware that she could never live up to his memories of Selina. Alice couldn't even produce a baby, let alone give birth to one in the middle of a war in a tent or a dirt-floored cottage. And from the sounds of things, Selina had treated every one of those hardships as a delightful adventure.

Alice, by comparison, was dull and unadventurous: she hadn't done much with her life at all.

"The uncertain and dangerous life we lived made us both very aware that we needed to make the most of every day," he finished.

An excellent principle to live by, Alice thought. And she was having an adventure—if the definition of the word was to do something you'd never done before that felt risky and a bit nerve-racking.

There was no point in hoping that James would fall in love with her. His stories about Selina had convinced her of that. He wanted Alice as a mother for his daughters and a wife he was comfortable with, whose company he enjoyed. She could accept that, could even live quite happily with it, as long as she didn't let herself crave more than he was prepared to give.

If she could bear going to bed with him, it would be enough.

The Bible said it was better to give than to receive, and Alice had a heart full of love to give. She already loved his daughters; she would just have to take care that she didn't smother James, or embarrass him with her feelings—if she agreed to marry him, that was.

You couldn't make someone love you—Thaddeus had taught her that.

"We're here," James said as the carriage pulled up outside a small, pretty cottage. "Wait here while I open it up—you don't want to get wet."

He leapt down and splashed through the puddles to the front door of the cottage. He unlocked the front door and returned with an umbrella for her.

While he fetched their luggage and paid off the postilion, Alice looked around. The cottage was small and simple but spotlessly clean. Four rooms, by the look of it—a sitting room and two small bedrooms, with a kitchen at the back.

The floor was slate but made cozy with colorful rugs. A fire had been set in the fireplace, all ready to light. The kitchen contained a cast-iron stove, also readied for lighting, and a large table. Glancing out the back door, she saw a short path leading to an outhouse, which she made quick use of.

She washed her hands at an outdoor pump, and then explored the cottage. One of the bedrooms contained a large double bed, made up with soft blankets, fine linen and a beautiful satin-edged eiderdown. She sat on the bed—a new mattress, if she wasn't mistaken. In fact, the bed itself was too big and grand for a cottage like this. James must have furnished the whole cottage from scratch.

She swallowed. He'd gone to a lot of trouble. She hoped it would be worth it. Hoped she would be worth it.

She'd started shaking again.

"Well, what do you think?" James asked, setting down the valises and a large wicker basket. "I know it's small and simple, but I thought you'd be more comfortable with no strange servants and no neighbors. It's a five-minute walk into the village, and the post chaise and postilion will be waiting there, so whenever you want to leave, I'll walk in and fetch them."

She pressed her shaking hands together—she could do this, she could—and smiled. "It's lovely."

He took a tinderbox from the shelf above the fireplace and in a few minutes the fire was alight. "Won't be long before the room warms up."

She nodded. It wasn't cold that was making her shake. When had she become such a coward? She done this hundreds of times with Thaddeus. It couldn't be any worse.

But that wasn't what she was so frightened of.

This was make-or-break. Either she could bear to be bedded by James, or she couldn't. If she could, she would marry him. If it was as it had been with Thaddeus—proving that she was the one at fault—she couldn't marry James.

Oh, she was sure he'd say it didn't matter, but she knew it would, and she couldn't bear to see him grow more and more disappointed with a cold wife who shrank from him in bed. And then he would turn to a mistress, and she couldn't bear that, either.

"Are you hungry? I'll put on the kettle and organize something to eat." He disappeared into the kitchen, and she could hear him getting out crockery and clattering quietly about. She ought to be the one seeing to it, not him, but she couldn't even think about food at the moment.

She couldn't think about anything at all. Except for that big bed.

She glanced out the window. It was still raining, and the dismal gray light coming through the windows gave her no idea of the time. How long until the evening? An endless, unbearable wait.

Perhaps she could force herself to enjoy it—or at least make James think she enjoyed it.

No, she was not prepared to be dishonest in that way. To start a marriage with such dishonesty would be to invite further cracks and deceptions. She couldn't do it.

She paced up and down in front of the fire. She wanted to throw up. So much depended on what happened in that big bed tonight.

"You're not the slightest bit interested in food, are you?" She whirled around. He stood in the doorway watching her. His voice deepened. "You're driving yourself mad with imaginary worries."

She couldn't think of a thing to say. Her worries weren't imaginary.

"Give me a minute." He disappeared back into the kitchen.

What was he thinking? She had no idea.

He was back in two minutes. "You need to have a little faith," he said and pulled her gently toward him.

"I do have faith in you," she said tremulously.

He cupped her face in one hand and gave her one of those slow smiles that never failed to melt her bones. "I meant, faith in yourself." He stroked her cheek with his thumb. "I have every faith in you, Alice. But I can see that you need to be convinced. Can I assume you have no appetite for food at the moment?"

She nodded. "Good," he said, and lowered his mouth to hers.

Chapter Fifteen

Oh, the glory of James's kisses. Kissing. Why had it taken her so long to learn? Thaddeus had never kissed her, not like this. She was glad that James was her first.

With lips and tongue, he gently pressed her lips apart. His tongue stroked the inside of her mouth in a leisurely, sensual exploration. Every tiny motion thrummed through her body and gathered momentum. Warm shivers rippled through her, building with each stroke, pooling in the deepest recesses of her body.

She pressed her hands against his chest and slid them higher, stroking his jaw, feeling the faint underlying masculine roughness of bristles in a friction that delighted her, breathing in the scent of him even as the dark, masculine taste of him filled her senses.

She tried to copy the things he was doing with his tongue, only they dazzled her so that she couldn't concentrate, only feel. And respond without thought or purpose.

Pleasure.

She slid her fingers through his hair and pressed herself

against him—thigh against thigh, belly to belly, breast against chest. Her knees felt suddenly weak. A long shudder rippled down her spine, some deep hollow within her aching for . . . for what, she had no idea. Only a need for which she had no name . . . She clutched his shoulders, leaning against him.

He shifted his grip and swung her up off her feet. She squeaked in surprise, and he smiled. "Time to move into the bedroom."

Oh. The heat drained out of her. The kissing was over. It was time for the . . . the other.

He set her on her feet beside the bed, then sat on the other side of the bed and pulled off his boots and stockings. He stood to remove his coat, then swiftly unbuttoned his waistcoat. He draped his coat over the rail at the end of the bed and folded the waistcoat over it. She watched as he dragged his fine white-linen shirt over his head, shook it out, then draped it over the rail.

He wore no undershirt—his chest was bare and hard with a dusting of dark hair and two small, hard nipples. She tried not to stare, but she couldn't help herself. She hadn't known that men had nipples. His arms were powerful, strong and sinewy, his forearms sunburned.

She stood unmoving, gazing across the bed at him. Her mouth dried.

His mouth curved in an understanding smile. "Do you need help with that dress?"

Flushing at being caught staring, she nodded. She'd anticipated this part, and knew she'd be disrobing without her maid to help, but she hadn't expected to be undressing in front of him. Even less that he would undress in front of her. She turned her back. "Just untie the bow at the top and loosen the laces, please." She could manage from there.

Deftly he untied her laces, and swiftly pulled them not just loose but free. Cool air whispered down her spine, warm fingers brushed against her skin. She shivered, not quite understanding why. She wasn't cold.

Her dress started to slide. She grabbed at it, but, "I have it," he said, and eased it down over her hips and all the way to the floor. He knelt and looked up at her, waiting, and she had no option but to step out of it, leaving her in just her underclothes. He gathered up the folds and draped the dress over the bed rail.

She began to unhook her stays—she'd chosen front-fastening ones deliberately—but, "Allow me." His voice was slightly husky.

She could barely breathe as one by one he undid the hooks down the front of her stays. She wore a chemise underneath, but even so, she felt the brush of his knuckles through the fine lawn fabric. Her nipples were hard and tight and extraordinarily sensitive.

On the fifth hook he looked up from his task. "You can breathe, you know."

She huffed in a nervous half laugh, and he leaned forward and kissed her, lavish, leisurely kisses that sent shivers coursing through her again. Straightening, he slipped her stays down her arms and tossed them aside. He'd undone the rest of the hooks while kissing her; she hadn't even noticed.

He was breathing more heavily now. So was she. He reached for the buttons on the fall of his buckskin breeches.

"I'll get my stockings." She turned away hastily and sat on the bed. She stripped off her stockings and then her drawers. All she wore now was her chemise.

"Oh," she exclaimed. "My nightgown—it's in the valise."

"You won't need a nightgown." His voice was deep and a little hoarse. She turned to say something—but every word evaporated from her brain. He was naked. Completely, totally naked.

Alice didn't know where to look. She'd never seen a naked man before. Thaddeus had always come to her either fully dressed or, in the early part of their marriage, in a dressing gown with a nightshirt underneath. And she'd always worn a nightgown.

She glanced at him, then away, and then back again, until she was unable to look away. She was fascinated by the hard-packed masculine shape of him, so different from her.

And his male parts—was that what they looked like? She'd only felt them—it—pounding into her. She swallowed. He looked bigger in that area than Thaddeus.

Would bigger mean more painful?

She closed her eyes briefly. Stop thinking about Thaddeus, she told herself. This was James, and it was going to be different—quite different. It had to be.

James stood and let her look, seemingly quite comfortable in his bare skin.

Did he expect the same of her? She couldn't. She'd never been wholly naked in front of anyone before—only her maid when she was in her bath. She dragged her gaze off him and dived under the covers. The sheets were smooth and cold.

He slid into the bed as well, and she immediately felt the effect of his big, warm body so close to hers. He rolled onto his side, facing her, and pulled her close.

Rain spattered against the windows. Wind tossed the branches around and moaned around the chimney. The heat of his body soaked into hers.

This was it.

She opened her legs and braced herself.

He paused. "Relax," he said softly. "Let's just kiss for a while," and before she could say anything, his mouth was on hers again, and she gave herself wholly up to the delights of kissing.

As they kissed, his hands roved over her body, caressing, soothing away some nerves while at the same time arousing others. He feathered kisses everywhere: across her eyelids, in the delicate whorls of her ears, along her jawline; finding a pulse here, a sensitive spot there; causing exquisite shivers of pleasure wherever he went. He nibbled his way down her neck and she found herself arching sensuously like a cat beneath his ministrations.

He brushed a hand across her breast and the tight, aching nipple thrust hard against him. Cupping her breast in one big hand, he scratched the nipple lightly through the fabric of her chemise. She gasped as tiny sparks of sensation stabbed through her.

"You like that, don't you?"

A kind of humming noise came from her. She wanted to say something to him, but her mind was blank of words: there was only sensation. And James. She ran her hands over him, enjoying the contrast of his hard, masculine body with the softness of hers, his smooth, firm chest. She pressed her face against the skin of his chest and inhaled deeply, as she'd wanted to do in the carriage earlier. Essence of James.

His big, warm hands caressed her thighs and hips and belly. How had she never known the delight of skin against skin? She caressed him feverishly, her heart pounding, her whole focus narrowed to whichever part of her body he was touching.

He cupped her face and kissed her again—deep, drugging kisses. Then he bent and placed his mouth over her breast and through her chemise, teased her nipple with his tongue. Waves of pleasure rippled through her, and then he sucked hard, and she arched and almost came off the bed as a fierce spear of pleasure-pain spiked through her.

She lay back, gasping, and before she realized it, he was raising her chemise. Her scrambled brain focused and she braced herself for his entry. But he kept pushing the chemise up. "Lift your bottom." She lifted, and he pulled her chemise up over her head and tossed it aside. And she was naked.

"Beautiful," he murmured, and she warmed at the appreciation in his voice.

He lowered his head to her breasts again, her full and aching breasts, unbearably sensitive, and she shuddered beneath him in waves of pleasure. And slowly her body built to an aching need for . . . she did not know what.

His hand slipped between her thighs and cupped her there. Warmth spread from where they touched, and her insides rippled and clenched.

One large finger moved, stroking the delicate folds, and a spear of hot sensation stabbed through her. Then another and another. Her breath came in ragged gasps as she trembled and writhed beneath his knowing caresses.

Her legs quivered, then fell apart, loose and trembling—her body was wholly out of her control. She thrust against his hand, frantically, feverishly, grasping for something, she knew not what.

Pressure built and built inside her, she thrashed against him, and just as she was sure she was going to burst, she heard a high, wavering sound as something happened and she . . . shattered.

Slowly her wits returned. She lay against him, her breath slowing, enveloped by a feeling of lazy euphoria. And amazement. Then as she was slowly drifting back to earth, he caressed her intimately again, rose up and entered her with one slow, sure movement.

Alice's eyes flew open in surprise. There was no discomfort at all. It felt right, amazingly, wonderfully right.

He was watching her, his gray eyes intense, smoky with desire. He stroked her again in that place between her thighs, and she felt the excitement start to build again. He began to move within her, slow and deliberate, and she gasped with each thrust. Without conscious volition, she found herself lifting her body, pushing herself against him in time with each thrust.

"Wrap your legs around me," he gasped, and she did, and oh, that was better. Closer. Tighter. Harder.

The pressure built inside her as before. She clung to him, rocking in rhythm, her body clenching around his powerful male body, feeling gloriously powerful, demanding faster, harder, more, more, more. He gave one last thrust and groaned loudly. She felt a hot gush of liquid inside her and heard herself give a high, thin scream as she shattered again, this time around him.

She might have slept for a little while—she wasn't sure—all she knew was that she slowly floated back to awareness, like a feather languidly drifting to the ground. Feeling so wonderfully good. Sleepily euphoric.

She opened her eyes and found him lying on his side, watching her. "All right?" he murmured. He'd pulled the covers up over them, and she felt warm and safe and so comfortable.

She opened her mouth to tell him she felt wonderful, but instead, her mouth crumpled and her eyes filled with tears. "Oh, sweetheart." He gathered her against him and held her, rubbing her back in a gentle, soothing rhythm.

Sobs jerked through her. "I-I'm s-sorry. It's n-n-not—"

"Hush."

"I'm n-not—"

"Don't try to explain. It's all right."

"They're g-goo-good tears," she managed to choke out between sobs.

He gave a soft laugh. "I see. Just let them come. I don't mind." And he didn't. He just held her, lending her his warmth, his strength. His acceptance.

After an embarrassingly long time, the hateful sobs stopped. There was no handkerchief, so Alice found her chemise at the foot of the bed and wiped her face with it.

"I'm sorry," she said on a gulp. "I don't know why I'm crying. I—"

"Has that happened to you before? The climax, I mean."

Climax, was that what it was called? She shook her head. "I didn't even know it was possible."

He brushed damp hair off her face. "Then perhaps your emotions were a little overwhelmed."

She nodded. "But it was wonderful. I feel wonderful. I don't know why I had to go and spoil it all by weeping all over you. Men hate tears, I know."

He pulled her closer. "Usually when women cry, I want to rush out and kill a dragon for them or something, but good tears I can cope with. Just."

They lay entwined in silence for a few moments, listening to the rain and the wind outside. "Do most women experience that in the marriage bed?" she asked, thinking about what Lady Peplowe had told her.

"If the man pays attention."

Yes, that was it. Thaddeus had never paid attention. Suddenly she was angry. Eighteen years of marriage and she'd had no idea there could even be pleasure in the act, let alone . . . *that*.

She reached up and kissed him. "Thank you for showing me."

He smiled, that slow smile that always made her insides curl—and she knew now why. "Thank you for trusting me. Now—"

At that point her stomach suddenly gave a loud, long rumble.

She glanced at him, mortified, and then suddenly they were both laughing. "I think before we go any further in this conversation, I should feed you," he said. "Wait here."

He slipped out of bed, and she watched shamelessly, admiring his bare, muscular body as he pulled on his breeches and left the room. He was a magnificent specimen of a man.

Her lover.

She snuggled back down in the covers and thought about all she had learned in the last hour. It was, for her, the revelation of a lifetime. All those wasted years feeling like a failure as a woman—unattractive, undesirable, barren.

She wasn't ever going to let anyone make her feel like that again. She would not allow bitterness and regret to poison her life any longer. She wasn't even going to think of Thaddeus. She had a future. And she was the mistress of a wonderful man. Her *lover.*

She lay curled in her nest of blankets and relived the lovemaking in her mind. There was so much to learn, she realized. He'd brought her to climax simply by touching her with his mouth and hands. Did it work the other way around? With her touching him?

"Here you are." He entered with a tray. With one hand, he caught up his shirt from the rail at the foot of the bed and tossed it to her. "You might feel more comfortable in this."

She slipped his shirt over her head—it was far too big and swamped her, but she enjoyed its faint masculine smell of James. Rolling back the sleeves, she sat up and arranged the pillows to lean back on.

He passed her the tray and slipped in beside her. Her eyes widened. It was a veritable feast. "Where did all this food come from?" She hadn't noticed it before.

His eyes glinted with humor. "I knew we'd be hungry, so I had my cook pack a hamper."

Her stomach rumbled again at the sight and smell of the food. There was a pot of tea and a little jug of milk, crusty fresh bread, curls of golden butter, tender slices of ham, a pot of honey, cold egg-and-bacon pie, little lemon curd cakes and a dish of—"Strawberries?" she asked in amazement. "At this time of year?"

"Last season's, preserved in syrup. The cook at Towers, my country estate, makes them according to a secret recipe, and she sent some up to London when she heard the girls and I were living there for the moment. It's a ploy to get us to return to what she considers our proper place, which is, of course, Towers. Try one—they're delicious." He scooped one up with a spoon and popped it into her mouth. It was utterly delectable, sweet and succulent.

To Alice's surprise and secret pleasure, he fed her by hand, all sorts of delicious morsels, a little of everything, all washed down with fresh hot tea, until she was utterly sated. He took the depleted tray away and returned a few minutes later.

"I had thought we might go for a walk, but it's still pouring. Any thoughts as to what you'd like to do now? We could talk or read or even sleep if you'd like."

Alice felt herself blushing. "Could we do, um, *that* again?"

He threw back his head and laughed, uninhibited, masculine and joyous. "A woman after my own heart. Indeed we can." And he slid into bed again.

Gerald was regretting his choice of riding to his grandmother's. The fine mist of rain had stopped, but he wouldn't have minded being in the carriage. There were things he wanted to say—and do—to Miss Lucy Bamber, but her blasted maid was in the way. Which he supposed was the purpose of chaperones.

They stopped at the coaching inn at Watford for a meal and to change horses. As luck would have it, the maid, Mary, got talking to the landlady. The woman had six daughters, three of whom worked at the inn, two of whom were yet too young and one who apparently had a passion to become a lady's maid. The landlady had a host of questions to ask Mary about the life and prospects for a lady's maid, as well as the general wickedness of life in London.

"I'm sick of being stuck in the carriage," Lucy told him. "I want to stretch my legs." So he offered her his arm and they strolled to the edge of the village and turned down a shady, tree-lined lane.

"I'm calling it off," Lucy said abruptly the minute they were alone. "I can't stay with your grandmother, lying to her and getting her all excited about a wedding that will never take place. I want to go home. And the moment we get back to London, I want you to put a notice in the newspapers canceling this wretched betrothal."

Gerald was silent, trying to think of what to say. Eventually he simply told the truth. "I don't think it's wretched, and I don't want to cancel it."

"*What?*" She jerked her arm from the crook of his elbow and stepped back, staring at him, her eyes wide. "What does that mean? You can't possibly—"

"Want to marry you? I'm afraid I can. In fact, marrying you has become my heart's desire." There, it was out.

She gave him a troubled look. "But . . . but it was just a stratagem to get Papa to show himself."

"It was also a stratagem to get you betrothed to me," he admitted. "I could think of no other way to achieve it, with your determination to hold me at arms' length and your ridiculous prejudice against lords."

She shook her head, looking distressed. "But you can't. I . . . I'm Lucy Bamber, the daughter of a scoundrel—you said it yourself. Papa was a swindler, a liar, a blackmailer, a—"

"And his daughter is nothing like that. The Lucy Bamber I know is honest, honorable, loyal, spirited and beautiful."

"'Beautiful'?"

"Very." He drew her into his arms and kissed her as he'd been longing to kiss her almost from the moment they'd met. She resisted for an instant, then softened against him, sliding her arms up around his neck, twining her fingers in his hair and kissing him back with all the passion he'd hoped for.

After a few minutes she drew back. "I'm sorry—I should never have let that happen."

"Why not? Didn't you enjoy it? I did." He reached for her again.

She pushed his hands away. "I'm serious, Gerald. I'm deeply sensible of the honor you do me, but I can't marry you."

"Why not?"

She just shook her head and walked a little way along the lane. Gerald followed. "You're trying to think up reasons why you can't marry me, aren't you?" he said. "You have this ridiculous notion that you don't belong in my world."

She turned. "Well, I don't. I wasn't raised in your world, and I don't fit in it."

He snorted. "What you don't realize is that lots of people feel that way, including me."

"You? You're a viscount, the son of an earl."

"Yes, and I've been that for precisely eighteen months. Before that I was a cash-strapped captain in the army, the unregarded son of a second son, and nobody gave me a second glance."

"Maybe, but—"

"What do you think it was like to come from a life involving years of hardship and turmoil and boredom and danger and responsibility, and battlefields that stank of blood and mud and worse, with the screams and groans of the injured and dying—some of them your men and your friends—ringing in your ears? And then the war is over and you come back and try to fit into a society where people are dressed in satin, silk and lace, smelling of perfumes and their most serious problem is deciding who to dance with. Or what to order for dinner. Or how to dress their hair. Or what juicy snippets of gossip they can pass on."

Her eyes were huge. She swallowed. "I never thought of it like that."

"Nobody ever does."

She bent and picked a long stem of grass and twirled it pensively. "Why do you want to marry me, then?" She glanced at him, a faint blush on her cheeks. He didn't think it was the heat. "I was so rude to you from the beginning."

He laughed. "That's what I found so interesting. For most of my adult life I've been of little interest to anyone—certainly not a desirable marriage prospect. Then my uncle died unexpectedly, and suddenly I was a viscount and the heir to an earldom, and then everything I said or did was *sooooo* interesting, and the matchmaking mamas were all over me, and every unmarried young lady was flirting and flattering me and doing their best to hook me."

She snorted. "Not me."

"I know, and that's what first attracted my attention."

She frowned. "But it wasn't some ploy to be different."

"Oh, I know that." He let his gaze drift so somewhere over her left shoulder and murmured, "'That woman over there is wearing the largest turban I've ever seen in my life. I wonder how she makes it stay on.'"

She half turned to look, and then remembered. She blushed. "Yes, well, I was very badly behaved that night. I'm sorry."

He laughed. Her dimple gave her away every time. "I'm not. You were clever and cheeky and gorgeous and so determined to drive me away, it made me want to get to know you better."

She grimaced. "And then you found out who I really was, the daughter of a blackmailing scoundrel."

"Will you stop saying that," he snapped. "You are *not* your father, and I don't want to hear that nonsense ever again."

Their eyes met for a long, intense moment. Then a cow mooed and broke the silence.

"I might not be like my father, but that doesn't mean I'll fit into your society. Your mother hates me."

"She hates everyone. My grandmother will adore you."

She shook her head. "Not if she knows the truth. I'm

sorry Gerald. I know you think it would work, but I know that if I married you, I would end up getting things wrong and embarrassing you—and myself. And I *refuse* to be looked down on!"

"How do you know you will?"

"Because I always have been. My education is scrappy—I attended five different schools and never finished the year at any of them. I never did learn all the ladylike skills, and when people look down on me and try to make me feel small and inferior, well, I have a temper. I push back. And not always in a ladylike way."

He raised an ironic brow. "And yet, from what I heard, you handled my mother brilliantly. And in a superbly ladylike manner."

"Oh." A blush rose to her cheek. "You heard about that?"

"I did. And in the diplomatic service, brains, charm and the ability to think on your feet are just as important as society connections—maybe even more important."

She pulled a skeptical face. "Which is why most diplomats are titled."

"If you married me, you'd be titled, too. Now, let us continue this discussion after we reach Grandmama's. She's expecting us, and if we don't arrive before dark, she'll worry."

Frowning, she twisted the grass stalk into a knot, then tossed it away. "All right, I'll go to your grandmother's. But I warn you, I'm going to tell her everything."

Chapter Sixteen

Alice's idyll was over: it was time to go home. They'd spent four days in the little cottage, eating, talking and making love. Alice had never passed such a blissful time in her life. Truth be told, she never wanted to leave.

It was difficult being a mistress, she thought as she packed. Glorious, but also tough on the emotions. Once they were back in their normal lives, it would all be different. They'd have to be discreet. They couldn't see each other whenever they wanted. They wouldn't wake up together, wouldn't make love in the middle of the night and again in the morning. Wouldn't eat breakfast together—in bed—in such a delightfully decadent fashion as they had. No more evening strolls in the twilight, coming home to a cozy fire, a simple dinner and a glass of wine. And bed.

She'd learned so much about her body—and his—in the last four days. She was saturated with pleasure—more than pleasure. The last few days had given her a new understanding of herself. And not just in bed—though that had been glorious, and eye-opening.

When the weather had allowed, they'd gone for long walks.

And in bed or out of it, they'd talked and talked and talked—of everything: stories of their past, thoughts about the world, even favorite books, because James was a reader. Alice couldn't have imagined a more perfect time. But now it was over.

"This has been the happiest four days—and nights—of my life," she told James as they waited for the carriage to collect them.

"I'm glad." He wrapped his arms around her and kissed her, a long, passionate kiss.

"Can we do it again sometime?" The chaise arrived as she spoke.

"What? Come here, do you mean? Why not? I paid the rent for a couple of months." He grinned down at her and opened the front door. "It can be our secret getaway place."

They traveled back to London in relative silence. Alice, with James's arm wrapped around her, felt a little blue. James appeared to be lost in thought. It hardly seemed to take any time at all before they were pulling up outside Bellaire Gardens.

Too public a place for one last kiss, so James simply pulled out her valise and handed it to Tweed, then said a polite goodbye—his eyes said more—and left.

"How is your friend, m'lady?" Tweed asked.

Alice blinked and then remembered. "All better now, thank you."

She pulled herself together and walked up the stairs. James had made no attempt to speak of marriage again. Not this time, not anymore. She was his mistress now, and mistresses didn't get asked to be married.

Ironic that now she was ready to take the plunge, he'd changed his mind.

It was her own fault. Had she had more courage, she might have had it all: marriage to James and the glory of going to bed with him. But she'd chosen to become his mistress instead, and now she had to live with her choice. And she would, according to her new principle to live by: no regrets.

She'd had four glorious days and nights in James's arms. And she didn't regret them in the least.

Gerald's grandmother, Lady Stornaway, was a bit of a surprise. She'd obviously been a beauty in her day, and was still very good-looking in a plump-old-lady way. Her silver hair was swept up in a stylish arrangement, and she was simply but fashionably dressed.

She welcomed them warmly and, once they'd refreshed themselves after the journey, settled them down in a comfortable, elegantly appointed sitting room with sherry and biscuits.

"Congratulations on your betrothal, dear boy," she said to Gerald. "I suppose Almeria is delighted."

"Not exactly," he admitted.

"Not at all," Lucy said.

The old lady turned to Lucy with a faint frown. "My daughter doesn't approve of you?"

Lucy grimaced. "Your daughter despises me."

Lady Stornaway brightened. "Really?"

"Yes, really. And also, Gerald and I are not betrothed, not really," Lucy said, making a clean breast of it.

"We *are* betrothed," Gerald insisted. "And it's still official as far as society is concerned."

Lady Stornaway gave them a shrewd look. "Quarreled, have you?"

"No," Lucy said. "It was never a proper betrothal in the first place. It was a . . . a stratagem. And I didn't want to lie to you about it."

The old lady sipped her sherry. "Fascinating. Tell me more."

So Lucy explained. She didn't leave anything out, not her lack of family, her irregular upbringing, her many schools and her time as pupil/maidservant to Frau Steiner and the comtesse. From time to time, Gerald interrupted to add something, but for the most part he let her tell her own story.

She'd just reached the part about her father's blackmail

of Alice and her consequent entry into the ton, when the butler announced dinner. With the old lady's encouragement, she related that little episode over the soup.

"And you say my daughter dislikes you," Lady Stornaway said when Lucy had finished.

Lucy nodded. She didn't like to stress how much.

"Most edifying," the old lady said. She turned to her grandson, "Now, Gerald, you mentioned in your letter that you had decided to enter the diplomatic corps. How is that going?"

While Gerald explained, Lucy ate her dinner. She was rather taken aback. The old lady had barely reacted to Lucy's confession and had simply moved on to the next topic of conversation as if it were perfectly normal to hear about blackmail and deception.

Bemused, Lucy caught Gerald's eye and raised her brows in a silent question. He simply shrugged and went on telling his grandmother about his plans for his future career. And then he filled her in on the news of various acquaintances she had in London.

And at the end of the meal, the old lady rose from the table and said, "A most interesting meal, thank you. Now, I expect you're very tired after your long journey. We keep early hours here, so I'll bid you both good night."

She left. Lucy looked at Gerald, totally bewildered. "I don't understand. She didn't even react."

Gerald shrugged. "No one can ever tell what Grandmama is thinking. Just go to bed and try to sleep. I'll see you in the morning."

Which was no help at all.

The following morning after breakfast, Lady Stornaway invited Lucy to go for a drive around the estate. Just Lucy, she said. Gerald could entertain himself.

Lucy swallowed her misgivings and fetched her shawl.

They set out in a smart little tilbury. Lady Stornaway drove.

There was no groom. It was clear the old lady wanted a private conversation with Lucy. Despite breakfast, Lucy's stomach felt hollow. Lady Stornaway was, after all, Almeria's mother.

For the first twenty minutes, the old lady simply pointed out local sights. Lucy's tension mounted. What was the purpose of this drive?

Finally, they drew up outside an old cottage with a thatched roof and a crooked chimney. It was small and neat but not particularly prepossessing. They contemplated it for a few minutes. Were they going to visit someone? Children and hens ran about in the yard, and when the children saw Lady Stornaway, they ran eagerly toward the carriage, calling out greetings.

Lady Stornaway smiled and produced a bag of sweets, but apart from exhorting the recipient to share them out fairly, she made no move to get down. And no adult came out to greet her.

"I expect you're wondering what we're doing here?" Lady Stornaway said after a while. Lucy couldn't deny it.

"I was born in that cottage."

Lucy turned to her, shocked. "You were?"

The old lady nodded. "I have no connection with the tenants now, except as lady of the manor, but when I was a gel, Papa was a tenant farmer. Not a particularly good one."

"But . . ."

"How did I end up a lady?"

Lucy nodded.

"I married Gerald's grandfather." She smiled. "There was a terrible fuss at the time, but we didn't care—we were in love. Albert got a special license, and we went off and got married without anyone being the wiser. Then he took me to London, to a top modiste, and had me dressed from the skin out. That's your first lesson, my gel, and I can see you've already learned it. It's hard for people to put you down when you're better dressed than they are. And with the right clothes, you feel up to anything."

Lucy agreed. Wearing Miss Chance's dresses, she felt quite different from the girl who'd arrived in London in that horrid frilly pink dress.

"So now you know where I came from." Shc glanced at Lucy and chuckled. "That's why my daughter Almeria is so frightfully toplofty—living me down, you see. Or imagining she is. Really, nobody worth anything gives tuppence about my background. Oh, some might whisper about it behind my back, but how does that hurt me? It's who you are and what you do and say that's important, not where you come from. Are you listening to me, gel?"

"Of course I am." Lucy's brain was whirling.

"So you need not have any qualms about marrying my grandson." Lady Stornaway snapped the reins and the tilbury moved on. "If you're young and in love, you should marry."

"But Gerald and I are not in love."

The old lady gave her a sardonic glance. "Pish-tush! You told me you weren't going to lie to me."

Lucy blushed.

"You care for my grandson, don't you?"

Lucy hesitated, then nodded. "Yes, but—"

"But nothing. Now, you listen to me, my gel—you don't get many chances for happiness in this life, and when you get one, you need to seize it and hang on to it."

"But what about—"

"Seize it and make it work. Be the woman you want to be and take no nonsense from anyone." She eyed Lucy shrewdly. "You don't want people to look down on you, and I appreciate that, but you're also thinking of Gerald, aren't you?"

Lucy nodded. "I wouldn't want to embarrass him."

"Then don't. He's chosen you out of all the silly highborn widgeons who've been setting their caps at him for the last couple of years. Gerald takes after his grandfather, my Albert—he knows what he wants."

Conversation paused as they negotiated a shallow ford, then she continued, "If Gerald is the man you want, then take him and *make* it work. But be the woman you are, not the woman you imagine he ought to want. That's the quickest way to drive a wedge between you. Be honest with each other, and for God's sake, talk things over."

A flock of sheep surged down the road toward them, and the carriage stopped as the sheep flowed around it. The shepherd tugged his forelock to Lady Stornaway and nodded at Lucy.

"And forget about separate bedrooms," the old lady said when the baaing of the sheep had become sufficiently distant. "Bed is where you and your husband will do the best talking, before or after you make love." She darted a glance at Lucy. "Shocked you, have I?"

Lucy laughed. "A bit."

"Good. I like to shock people every now and then. Stops people taking me for granted. You should think about doing that, too. It's also enormous fun."

Lucy laughed again.

A few minutes later Lady Stornaway said thoughtfully, "And you know, your father—scoundrel as he undoubtedly is—didn't give you such a bad start in life."

Lucy turned to her in surprise, but the old lady continued, "He put you in good schools, even if only for a limited time, and there are worse assets a diplomat's wife can have than fluency in two major European languages. Not to mention an ability to adjust to new situations. And giving you to Alice Paton to launch was a stroke of genius, even though his methods were wicked."

Lucy frowned. She had never considered Papa's actions in that light, but now that she thought about it, there was something in what Lady Stornaway said.

They reached Stornaway Manor, and the old lady handed over the reins to a groom. "I enjoyed our little chat, Miss Bamber, and I hope you'll think about what I said."

Gerald came out to greet them and helped his grandmother down. "This gel," she said to him, "if you let her get away, you're not the man I hope you are."

He grinned. "Grandmama, I will do my best not to disappoint you."

Lucy didn't know where to look.

Gerald took Lucy straight into the small sitting room. "See, my grandmother knows everything, and she still approves of you. So can we agree that the betrothal stands? And when we get back to London, we can start to make arrangements for the wedding." He reached for her, but she pushed his hands away.

"Are you sure, Gerald, because I need you to be very sure."

"Sure of what? That I'll make you happy? All I can promise is that I'll try my very best." His eyes darkened. "Am I sure that I love you? Oh, yes, I'm very, *very* sure of that."

Lucy's heart missed a beat and then started to thump in a rapid tattoo. Stunned, she stared at Gerald. "You *love* me?"

"Of course I love you, you goose. Haven't I made it obvious?"

"Don't call me a goose!" She was breathless, shocked, poised between tears and laughter.

"But you *lovvve* geese. And so do I, ever since we were introduced by a goose called Ghislaine." He reached for her again, but she stepped away.

"Stop it. Be serious and think about how it would be. There is so much I don't know about how high society works. I'm never sure about precedence, for instance—"

"You can learn."

"Or how to address a duke or a marquess—"

"You'll pick it up. You're very clever."

"Then there's all that cutlery at those big formal dinners."

"Work from the outside in."

"See? You know all that stuff without even thinking, because you were born to it. I wasn't.

He caught her hands in his. "None of that stuff—*none* of it—matters. I love you and I want to marry you. There is only one reason I will accept that you can't marry me."

Her insides tightened. "And what's that?"

"That you don't love me."

There was a long pause. She eyed him from under lowered lashes, then made a frustrated sound. There was a limit to self-sacrifice. "Oh, very well, but if—*when*—I mess up and embarrass you, and make terrible mistakes and inadvertently insult important people, or unimportant ones, you must never reproach me or blame me or yell at me. Because I won't allow it, do you hear? If you take me, you take me warts and all."

He grinned. "That's my girl."

"Didn't you hear me?"

"I heard every word." His smile widened. "And I understood you, too. You love me."

How did he know? "I didn't say that."

"Of course you did." He drew her into his arms and kissed her, and giving up all thoughts of directing him to a better match, she kissed him back with all the pent-up love in her heart.

"Now," he murmured after a while. Somehow they'd moved to the sofa. "Where are these warts you mentioned?"

She shoved him lightly on the arm. "I don't have any warts, you fool."

"Oh well, nobody's perfect." He gave her one more long, luscious kiss, then hearing footsteps outside in the hall, he sat up with a sigh. "We'd better save things for the wedding night."

"Then we'd better make the wedding soon."

He laughed and hugged her again. "A wench after my own heart. The banns will be called for the third time this

Sunday. We can wed anytime after that—or sooner if you like, with a special license."

"As long as Alice is there, I don't mind."

"And Grandmama. She will want to attend, if only to watch my mother gnashing her teeth."

She laughed. "And I'd like a new dress." Something she hadn't worn before.

"Naturally. And a trousseau, I suppose." He sighed. "I can see the date stretching further into the future."

"No, the clothes don't matter. Only the people." She wound her arms around his neck and kissed him again. "I do love you, Gerald."

"I know."

When they arrived back in Bellaire Gardens, Alice took one look at them and hugged first Lucy, then Gerald. "I'm so pleased. You two are finally smelling of April and May. You've sorted things out, haven't you?"

Lucy's blush and Gerald's possessive grin confirmed it. They were in love.

Gerald left, and Alice and Lucy decided to go to Miss Chance's establishment after lunch, to order Lucy's wedding dress. Alice couldn't help feeling a little wistful, but she pushed those thoughts aside. No regrets.

They were in the hall, debating whether they would need umbrellas or not, when the front doorbell jangled furiously. Tweed had barely opened the door when Gerald burst in, waving a small, slender book bound in red leather. On the cover, elegantly tooled in gold, was the title, *Letters to a Mistress, by a Noble Gentleman.* "That unprincipled swine Bamber has broken his word—he's published those damned letters!"

For a moment, Alice thought she was going to faint. Or throw up.

"Alice, are you all right?" Lucy led her into the drawing room, where she sank onto the sofa.

"Are you sure they're the letters that Thaddeus wrote?" It was a foolish question; of course Gerald was sure.

"See for yourself." Gerald offered her the book, but she waved it away. She didn't want to touch the vile thing, let alone read it. "An advance copy was sent to my father," Gerald continued. "They don't use names, of course, but most of the ton will understand who Lord C. and Lady C. and Mrs. J. are, especially given the scandalous way Uncle Thaddeus died in Mrs. Jennings's bed. Papa didn't read it, but Mama did, from cover to cover. I stole her copy."

Alice groaned.

The doorbell jangled again, and this time it was James who burst into the room. "Have you heard—" He broke off, seeing the small red book in Gerald's hand. "I see you have." He crossed the room in two steps and sat down beside Alice, taking her hands in his. "Are you all right?"

She nodded. "Just a bit shaken. I'd thought we were finished with all that."

"I'm sorry," Lucy croaked. "I'm so, so sorry."

"It's not your fault," Alice assured her.

"I should have known."

"How could you possibly have known?"

Lucy's eyes were tragic. "It's not like Papa to pass up an opportunity to make money and—oh! That's what he meant by that last part in his letter—when he apologized to you, Alice, and claimed he had no choice. I thought at the time he was apologizing for the blackmail. Why didn't I realize there was more to it? No choice, indeed." She bit her lip, then glanced at Gerald. "Is there nothing we can do?"

"There certainly is," James said decisively. "I only came here to warn you. I'm off to the publisher's." He picked up *Letters to a Mistress* and pocketed it. "I'll do what I can to stop this nasty little book from being distributed."

"I'll come with you," Gerald said.

Alice rose to her feet, a little shaky but determined. "I'll go, too."

James shook his head. "It would be better if you didn't. So far, given that only initials have been used, there's nothing concrete to link you with the book. But if you're seen going into the publisher's . . ."

Alice could see his point, but she didn't like it. "But I can't just sit here and wait." That would be too feeble for words.

Lucy linked her arm through Alice's. "We planned to go shopping this morning. It's probably the last thing either of us feels like doing, but . . ."

Alice took a shaky breath, then nodded. Lucy was looking pale and shamefaced. The poor girl must be feeling dreadful about her father's betrayal. This morning, after Gerald had left, Lucy had been radiantly happy; now she looked pinched and miserable. Alice could wring Bamber's neck.

"Very well, it's not the kind of bold action I'd prefer, but I will not allow this horrid little book to get in the way of your wedding plans. So we will go out and shop. In style. Heads held high."

James squeezed her hands. "That's the spirit. Come, Gerald, let us deal with this grubby little publisher."

The publisher's premises was a narrow building in a lane off Fleet Street. It was a small operation, and as James and Gerald entered, they could see men and women at work, printing, binding and packing books. All with red linen bindings and bearing the title *Letters to a Mistress*. The leather ones that had gone out were no doubt to entice members of the ton to open them. Elegant and salacious. And vicious.

Their entry caused a stir, but there was no lull in the activity. A plump, fussily dressed little man peered out from an office and emerged smiling. "Ebenezer Greene at your service, gentlemen. How can I help you?"

James pulled the small red book from his pocket. "You are responsible for this, I believe?"

The smile vanished. "Yes," Greene said cautiously. "What do you—"

"The original letters, if you please," James said crisply.

"The orig—?" Greene glanced toward his office. "I don't know what you're talking about. What letters?"

"The letters you've printed in this grubby little book." James seized him by the collar. "Now, unless you want to see the inside of a prison cell . . ." He marched the man into his office and thrust him with a shove toward a large iron safe.

"But, but, but—"

"Those letters were obtained illegally, and I will have no hesitation in prosecuting you to the limit of the law. Now, give me the letters and I will be prepared to purchase all the copies currently printed. Otherwise . . ."

There was a crash from the room outside. Greene rushed out. "My formes! No! You can't—"

"Can't what?" Gerald said, heaving another frame full of print to the floor and smashing it up with his boots. Tiny metal letters burst from their confinement and scattered across the floor. The workers, some of whom were women, stood back watching. Nobody seemed interested in interfering.

Gerald picked up another frame and tipped it onto the ground. The wooden frame shattered. Pages of type broke into a thousand pieces, becoming meaningless. James smiled. No chance of reprinting the book now.

Greene moaned and wrung his hands.

James said, "So far we're only interested in preventing you from printing any more copies of this nasty little publication. But if I don't get those letters, my friend and I will destroy your printing press as well as the—what did you call them?—the formes. I fancy a press will be harder to replace."

Another forme crashed to the floor, another sixteen pages destroyed. Tiny metal letters were scattered everywhere.

"No, no, I beg you, stop it. I bought those letters in good faith."

"Vile letters that don't deserve to see the light of day."

Crash! It sounded as though Gerald was enjoying himself. James glanced at the printing press and said meditatively, "I've never tried to destroy a printing press before, but it can't be too difficult."

"Oh please, no." The plump little man was almost weeping. "I'll give you the cursed letters, just leave my press alone." He hurried into his office, opened the safe and pulled out a thick sheaf of letters tied with a ribbon. "Here—take them. And then leave."

James flicked through the sheaf. "They'd better all be here, because if not . . ."

"They're all there, I assure you, all that that wretched man sold me. It's him you should be punishing, not me."

"You're both despicable," James said coldly. He held up the leather-bound copy. "How many of these did you send out?"

Greene glanced at a piece of paper on his desk. "Twenty-five," he said sulkily. "They cost a fortune, too."

"That's the list, is it? Good." James picked it up, glanced at the list of names, and pocketed it, ignoring Greene's protests.

He returned to the print room and held up the book to the watching workers. "There is a large black carriage waiting in the lane outside. Sixpence for every box of these books that you load into it. My coachman is expecting you—he will keep tally and pay you."

The workers glanced at one another, then rushed to grab boxes of books and carry them downstairs. In minutes not a single box or book remained. James glanced around the room and gave a satisfied nod. He turned to Greene and held out a ten-pound note.

Greene eyed it suspiciously. "What's that for?"

"To pay for the books, of course," James said in a bland voice.

"You're paying me for them?" he said incredulously.

James arched an eyebrow. "Naturally. I'm not a thief."

Greene glanced at the shambles that was his printing works. But he didn't utter a word.

"Did you have enough money?" James asked his coachman when he went downstairs.

"Yes, m'lord. With three and six left over."

"Keep it."

James and Gerald fitted themselves in around the boxes of books. "That was fun," Gerald said as they drove off. "Filthy work, though. Ruined my gloves." He pulled his ink-stained gloves off and tossed them out of the window. "Probably wrecked my boots, too, but it was worth it." After a moment he added, "Lucky your coachman had enough change on him."

James gave him a sideways glance. "Luck never came into it. You should know from your years in the army that preparation is all."

"Of course. Clever." After a moment Gerald asked, "What will you do with all these books?"

"Burn 'em."

They drove in silence for a while. "You don't look as happy as I expected," Gerald said. "I thought it went quite well."

James shook his head. "These damned leather-bound copies are still out there."

"Oh hell, I never thought of that. How many do you think went out?"

"Twenty-four, not counting your mother's copy. I got the list from Greene while you were busy smashing things."

"You can't be sure that's what they were whispering about," Lucy insisted. She and Alice had returned from seeing Miss Chance. Alice had found the experience uncomfortable. The minute they'd arrived, two ladies in the shop had fallen silent. Then they'd started whispering, glancing at Alice from time to time as they did.

Miss Chance had taken her and Lucy into the back for a

private consultation, and when they returned, all the other ladies in the shop were covertly staring at Alice, some with expressions of sympathy, others with ill-disguised salacious glee. It was obvious to her that they knew about the letters.

"I think we can assume that it was," Alice said. "Gossip travels like wildfire."

Tweed was hovering, looking concerned. He didn't know quite what was up, but he could tell she wasn't herself. Alice ordered tea and biscuits.

Lucy frowned. "What are we going to do about the Reynolds's ball tomorrow night?"

What indeed? Alice was warmed by Lucy's use of *we*, indicating she would loyally stand by Alice. But by tomorrow night, barely a soul in the ton would be unaware of the letters. Word of mouth would happen first—whispers carried from house to house during morning calls, and details shared and discussed, details of the most humiliating moments of her past brought to life by Thaddeus's clever, vicious pen.

Scandalous stories about one of their own. Servants would be sent to the bookshops, the books would fly off the shelves and later be passed around.

James and Gerald arrived and Alice called for more biscuits and a fresh pot. James asked for a fire to be lit, which was odd because it wasn't a cold day, but she asked Tweed to light the fire anyway.

While the fire was getting started and the tea and biscuits were being handed around, Gerald enthusiastically described their adventure at the publisher's.

"And now, here's something for you," James said, passing a small bundle to Alice. A thick sheaf of letters bound with a puce ribbon.

And suddenly Alice realized why he'd wanted a fire lit. She received the letters with nerveless fingers.

"You do want to destroy them, I presume," James said when she'd sat in silence for several minutes.

"Oh yes, oh yes indeed." She knelt before the fire, pulled

the ribbon off and fed the letters one by one into the fire. She watched as each one smoked and twisted, then burst into flames. Sparks danced up the chimney, leaving a pile of gray ash behind.

With every letter burned, she felt lighter, freer. It was a cathartic experience—she was purging herself of Thaddeus, finally and forever.

The last letter curled up and crumpled into ash, and she dusted off her hands and rose. Turning, she saw the little red leather book sitting on the side table. She would like to burn it, too, but it would make a terrible stench, and she didn't want it polluting her home. The purge was not yet complete, but she felt so much better already. "Did you secure all the copies?" she asked.

"All but the leather-bound copies that were sent out in advance," James said.

"Like that one of Mama's." Gerald indicated his copy.

"Don't worry, we'll get them back," James assured her. "There are only twenty-four, and I have a list."

Yes, but if Almeria had already read it cover to cover, then others would have. Alice could tell by his somber expression that James knew that. Pandora's box was already open.

"Maybe we should send our apologies to Lady Reynolds," Lucy said. "She and Sir Alan are very kind—they'll understand."

"Lord, yes, the Reynolds's ball tomorrow night," Gerald exclaimed. "I forgot about that. Of course you won't want to go."

James nodded. "If you like, I could take you—and my girls—Lucy, too, of course—to Towers, my country estate. We could stay there as long as you want, wait until this thing blows over."

Alice sipped her tea in silence. Run from the gossip? Hide?

Thaddeus had already done his best to ruin her life. Now it was Bamber using Thaddeus's words from the grave—and what a fool she'd been to trust the promise of a blackmailer. She thought about her sister-in-law, Almeria, avidly devouring the letters that shamed her. She thought about the ladies in Miss Chance's shop and their ill-natured whispering.

She put down her cup with a snap. "I've had enough." They all looked at her cup, which was three-quarters full. "I won't run. I won't hide. I refuse to be a victim a moment longer."

They blinked at her in surprise. "I am eight-and-thirty years old, and I don't care what others think of me—especially ill-natured gossips who mouth pious words of sympathy while secretly enjoying my misfortune."

She gestured to the ash in the fireplace. "I am not the same girl whose misery those letters described so despicably. I am a different woman now—my own woman—and I refuse to hide away from awkward social encounters or cower in the country, no matter how beautiful and welcoming I'm sure Towers is."

Her glance took in all of them. "This horrid little book will reveal people for who they truly are. You, my friends, offered instant support. There will be a few others, I know. And those who don't, those who secretly revel in what they will see as my humiliation—well, who needs that sort of friend anyway? Not I." She rose to her feet. "And I *am* going to the ball."

"Brava!" James applauded, and the others joined in. "So, Cinders," he said when the excitement and congratulations had died down, "what time shall I bring the pumpkin around to collect you?"

Chapter Seventeen

In the carriage going to the ball, Lucy sat beside Gerald, and Alice and James sat opposite. Alice was obviously tense, her face pale and tight in the faint, transient light inside the carriage. But she was going to the ball, determined not to be cowed by the ugly situation she was in—the ugly situation Lucy's papa had put her in.

Lucy hoped that one day she'd have the courage Alice was showing.

Alice was an extraordinary woman. She'd taken in Lucy unwillingly, purely because of Papa's blackmail, and yet, with every reason to despise her, Alice had made Lucy feel like a friend or a beloved daughter. Even when Papa had abandoned her, Alice had insisted Lucy must stay, that she had a home with Alice for as long as she needed.

And now despite all Alice's goodness to Lucy, she was being punished.

The shame of it scorched Lucy, even though she knew it wasn't her fault. But she was determined to make it up to Alice somehow.

She nudged Gerald, leaned closer and whispered in his ear, "I have a plan."

It was obvious from the moment they arrived that Lady Reynolds knew about the book, for she stepped forward, seized Alice's hands in hers and said warmly, "I am so very glad you came tonight, my dear. One would have understood if you chose not to, of course, but I am so very proud of you for coming. If there is anything my husband or I can do to support you in this difficult time, please don't hesitate to say so." She squeezed Alice's hands. "And don't worry, you have many friends here."

Beside her, tall Sir Alan Reynolds gave a nod and added gruffly, "Your late husband deserved a flogging for writing such filthy stuff. Never liked the feller."

Alice thanked them both, blinking back incipient tears. When you were braced for spite and scandal, unexpected warmth and kindness could so easily unravel you.

Nevertheless, their greeting reminded her that most people here tonight would either have read some of the letters or heard about them. I am no longer that girl, she reminded herself. In fact, she added in her mental conversation, I don't think I ever was the girl that Thaddeus's letters described. It was a freeing thought. Thaddeus never knew her at all.

Lady Peplowe met her in the hallway and drew Alice aside. "Are you all right, my dear? I've heard some disquieting rumors about a book."

"I know all about it," Alice said. "It's a vile and hateful thing, but I'm—I'm *damned* if I let my husband ruin my life a second time." Yes, anger was better than nerves.

"Good for you." Lady Peplowe gave her a searching look. "Do I understand that you . . . ?" She glanced to where James was waiting and trailed off delicately, letting her eyebrows do the talking.

Alice felt herself blushing, but she was proud, not embarrassed. "Yes, I did. And you were right. With the right man, it's perfectly splendid."

Lady Peplowe clapped her hands. "Oh, wonderful." A martial expression came over her face. "Now, let us see what we can do to squash these vile rumors." She sailed off into the ballroom, a woman on a mission.

With her hand on James's arm and Gerald and Lucy following behind, Alice took a deep breath and entered the ballroom. The loud buzz of conversation faltered and died away. Hundreds of eyes swiveled toward her. Silence hung in the air for an instant. Someone said something and sniggered loudly, then the buzz started again, lower but more intense.

Alice stiffened her backbone. The darting glances, the nods, the whispers, the snickers and murmurs—they were nothing she hadn't expected. And she would not be cowed by them.

Head held high, she moved farther into the ballroom. Murmuring, "Good luck, Alice," Gerald and Lucy melted away to join a group of young people. Alice was a little surprised but didn't blame them. This was not their problem.

Her gaze swept the room, and for a brief panic-stricken moment, she didn't recognize a soul. Then she spied Lady Peplowe standing with Lady Jersey, one of the patronesses of Almack's, on the other side of the room. With them stood plump little Princess Esterhazy and several other ladies she recognized—acknowledged leaders of society.

Lady Peplowe smiled and gave a little nod, then to Alice's amazement, Lady Jersey lifted a white-gloved hand and graciously beckoned her over.

Alice blinked. She didn't know Lady Jersey very well, but she'd always liked her. And she took heart from Lady Peplowe's expression. Feigning indifference to the attention she was receiving, Alice strolled across the floor. Her heart was thudding. She felt hollow inside. What did Lady Jersey want with her?

"That's my brave girl," James murmured. "Show 'em you don't give a damn." She was very glad of his support and his strong arm.

To her relief, Lady Peplowe and Lady Jersey came forward with warm smiles. "Lady Charlton, my dear—what a despicable worm your late husband was," Lady Jersey said affably. "And aren't we all glad he's dead and undoubtedly roasting in the other place? Now, are we showing everyone that we don't care what he wrote, or are we pretending those letters weren't about you?"

The combination of warmth and brisk pragmatism surprised a laugh out of Alice. "I don't know—both?"

Lady Jersey laughed, then turned to James. "Good evening, Lord Tarrant. Now, I'm sure you want to stay glued to her side playing watchdog, but leave this nasty little affair to the ladies, if you please."

James hesitated. "Alice?"

Alice nodded to him. She had no idea what was going on, but she was intrigued.

Princess Esterhazy, the pretty young wife of the Austrian ambassador, imperiously waved James away. Such confidence for one so young, Alice thought. She supposed it had a lot to do with being a princess.

"Now to business," Lady Jersey said. "My friends and I were outraged by those vile letters, Lady Charlton. Oh, they might have been written about you—though you must never admit it—but we all agree, it could have been any one of us, had we been married off to that brute." She fixed Alice with a determined look and repeated, "Any one of us. The only difference was that you had no family to support you and nobody to stand up for you—and you were so young! It's unforgivable. And those letters are a slur against all womankind, not just you!"

A lump formed in Alice's throat.

Lady Jersey slipped an arm through Alice's. "I am so sorry that we didn't know how badly you needed support back then. My friends and I have realized that we allowed your husband to isolate you in those early days, when you were new to London society and we were all so young and careless. Shameful behavior, but it is all in the past, and we shall not dwell on it. We will, however, help you now." She gestured to the other ladies standing a short distance away. Alice knew all the ladies, though not particularly well. Each one of them was influential in society.

They hurried forward and surrounded her, expressing sympathy and indignation on her behalf. "Now, now, that's enough sympathy," Lady Jersey said crisply. "You'll bring Lady Charlton to tears, and we don't want that. Time to get on with our plan."

"Your plan?" Alice repeated, bemused.

"Yes, of course." She gave Alice a curious look. "Didn't you come with a plan?"

"Not really. Just to attend the ball and show everyone that I don't care what my husband wrote about me."

"Excellent spirit, but it will take more than that. Come along." At her brisk gesture, some of the ladies split off in pairs and joined other groups, leaving Alice with Lady Jersey, Lady Peplowe and Princess Esterhazy.

James had drifted away as instructed, though he was keeping a protective eye on her from a distance. Lucy and Gerald seemed happily occupied, moving from group to group of young people, chatting and smiling.

Alice turned and saw Almeria and several of her cronies approaching, their expressions smug. Her mind went blank for a second. Then she braced herself.

Stepping away from her companions—she didn't want them to be exposed to Almeria's spite—Alice greeted them politely. "Almeria, Lady Beamish, Mrs. Scorrier, how delightful to see you. Are you enjoying this charming party? Lady Reynolds has done a beautiful job with the flowers, don't you think?" The orchestra was tuning up. She seized on it. "Oh, I do believe the dancing is about to start."

Almeria's lips thinned. "I am surprised you had the audacity to show your face tonight, Alice. Are you not ashamed of yourself?"

Alice managed a brittle laugh and self-consciously smoothed down her skirts. "Oh dear, you have recognized my old ball dress. I did have it made over by my maid, but you have such an eagle eye for fashion, Almeria, do you not?" It wasn't an old ball dress at all, but Almeria wouldn't remember.

Almeria's eyes became slits of irritation. "I'm not talking about your dress, as you very well know. I'm talking about that disgraceful book—" She broke off, and her eyes widened with malicious delight. "Or don't you know about it yet?"

Alice inclined her head curiously. "What book are you talking about?"

Mrs. Scorrier smirked and pulled out a small red leather volume. "This one, of course. *Letters to a Mistress*."

"Everyone is talking about it," Almeria added. "I cannot believe you haven't seen it. Oh, you must read it." Her eyes were gleaming with relish.

Alice's hands had stopped shaking. She was furious. She hadn't expected Almeria to support her in any way, but this barely repressed glee was too much.

"May I?" She held out her hand. Mrs. Scorrier hesitated, glanced at Almeria, then with a faint shrug handed the book to Alice.

Alice glanced at it, flipped open the pages, raised her brows and said, "Good heavens." Then she smiled at Mrs. Scorrier. "Thank you for the loan. I'll read it later—a ball is no place for reading novels." Ignoring Mrs. Scorrier's dismayed exclamation, she popped it in her reticule.

"It's not a novel," Almeria said, her voice laced with spite. "It's a book of letters, written by someone very close to you."

"Oh, I doubt that," Alice said. She'd never been close to Thaddeus.

Almeria leaned forward and hissed angrily, "Those letters *are* about you Alice, and they're utterly scandalous. You're a disgrace to the family!"

Lady Jersey had come up behind Alice and overheard. "Rubbish!" she said coldly. "The only disgrace to his family is the writer of those obscene letters." She snorted. "Call himself 'a noble gentleman,' does he? He's obviously some member of the gutter press. No gentleman would write about his wife in such a manner. I'm surprised you fell for it, Almeria."

"It *is* about her!" Almeria insisted. "I *know* it is."

"How do you know?" Princess Esterhazy demanded, her dark eyes snapping. "Are you responsible, perhaps, for the publishing of this filthy material? Is this why you are so obviously happy about it?"

Almeria gasped and went white. Her two friends gave her sideways glances and moved away. "No, of course not. I knew nothing about it until someone—someone anonymous—sent it to my husband. And I'm not at all happy about it. It—it's a dreadful scandal."

Princess Esterhazy sniffed. "And yet you seem determined to spread this scandal around. And to blame your sister-in-law, who surely is an innocent in all this, no?" She shook her head, sending the plumes in her headdress waving. "Most peculiar."

Lady Jersey nodded. "Yes, extraordinary bad form, to be trying to whip up a scandal about your own family—not to mention stupid, ill-natured and pathetic." She paused to let her words sink in. "Come, Lady Charlton—no, not you, Almeria, I meant the *young* Lady Charlton."

She linked her arm with Alice's, then paused and glanced back. "I hope you don't intend to spread that vicious, wholly mistaken gossip, Almeria. We would not look on it kindly if you did." It was not quite the royal *we*, but coming from a patroness of Almack's, it carried much the same weight.

* * *

Alice circled the room with Lady Jersey, Princess Esterhazy and Lady Peplowe, greeting people, stopping to chat—nothing of consequence, and with no mention of a little red book—but it was a clear demonstration of support.

The music started and young people filled the dance floor. The first dance was an energetic country dance, the second a cotillion.

As the sets for the second dance were forming, Lady Peplowe nudged Alice and glanced over her shoulder. Alice turned and her heart sank. Her brother-in-law, Thaddeus's brother, was marching toward her, his expression grim. She had no doubt she was the reason for his attendance tonight. Edmund almost never attended balls or parties.

She swallowed and turned to face him. "Edmund."

He bowed stiffly. "Dance with me, Alice?"

She tried to hide her surprise. The number of times she'd seen Edmund dance could be counted on one hand, but she gave him her hand and allowed him to lead her onto the floor.

"Owe you an apology, Alice, on behalf of my brother. His behavior toward you was unconscionable. Indefensible. Realize that now."

Alice blinked. It was the last thing she would have expected from him. "Thank you, Edmund," she said as they took their places in the set. "I appreciate it."

He gave a brisk nod, then the dance began. They danced, Edmund stiff but correct. He never said another word, and at the end he escorted her off the dance floor, bowed to her and left the ball.

"Are you all right?" James came up to her. "He wasn't rude to you, was he?"

"No." Alice was still a little bemused. "In fact, he apologized for my husband's behavior." She glanced at the door Edmund had disappeared through. "I think the only reason he came tonight was to dance with me in a demonstration of family solidarity."

"Good. So he should."

Another gentleman, the husband of one of Lady Peplowe's friends, appeared and asked Alice for the next dance. Then she danced with Gerald, then Lord Peplowe, who apologized for being out of practice.

Alice danced every dance. The whispers and spiteful looks continued, but they'd lessened, and the kindness she was receiving, much of it from people she barely knew, outweighed the nastiness. It was wonderful, touching and a bit overwhelming.

The next dance was the waltz before supper, and Alice was engaged to dance it with James.

The orchestra played a single loud chord, and she looked up and saw Sir Alan and Lady Reynolds standing on the orchestra dais. Sir Alan's deep voice rang out. "Ladies and gentlemen, your attention please. A very important announcement is about to be made by one of our guests."

"A very exciting announcement," Lady Reynolds added with a smile. The crowd fell silent.

To Alice's amazement, James stepped onto the platform and said, "I am delighted to share with you all the news that Alice, Lady Charlton, has done me the honor of agreeing to become my wife. Please join us in celebrating." He held out his hand to Alice.

There was a short, surprised silence, then people began murmuring.

"Go on, up you go." Lady Peplowe gave Alice a little push, and Alice started walking, dazed and a little confused. He'd made no mention of this. He hadn't even asked her to marry him. Not since . . .

As she crossed the floor alone, running the gauntlet of the crowd for the second time, someone started clapping, and in seconds everyone was clapping and calling congratulations.

James stepped down from the dais and took her hand just as the orchestra began the waltz. "What . . . I . . ." she began.

"I can't kiss you in front of all these people," he said, "but I can dance with you." And he swept her out onto the floor. They circled the floor once, the only couple dancing, then Lady Jersey and a partner joined them, followed by Lord and Lady Peplowe, Gerald and Lucy, Princess Esterhazy and the ambassador, and their hosts, Sir Alan and Lady Reynolds. One by one, other couples joined them, and soon the dance floor was crowded with waltzing couples, many of whom expressed their congratulations to Alice and James as they twirled past.

Alice danced blind, blinking back tears.

"Good tears, I hope," James murmured. She gave him a misty smile.

By the time they went in to supper, the atmosphere at the ball had changed. It had been impressed upon the spiteful ones who had been enjoying Alice's misfortune—for as Lady Peplowe had said to Alice, there would always be people who took pleasure in the misery of others, whether they knew them or not—that it would now be in very bad taste to refer to the things revealed in the little red book. Not only did Alice, Lady Charlton, have the support of some of the ton's most influential ladies; she was newly betrothed and it must therefore be treated as an occasion for celebration.

Supper, and indeed the rest of the night, passed in a blur for Alice. There wasn't a moment that she could talk to James alone and ask him about his surprise—his astounding announcement of their betrothal.

Had he had a change of heart about marrying his mistress, or was it simply another public gesture of support? He was, after all, that sort of man: protective, gallant, kind. But oh, the hope building inside her was an ache of yearning.

By the time the ball was winding down and people were

starting to leave, Alice was exhausted, but in a good way. She'd come half expecting to be excoriated by society, but instead she'd found friends she hadn't realized she had.

And James had announced their betrothal.

As they prepared for the carriage to arrive—guests' carriages were lined up along the street—Lucy said something to a footman, who produced a covered basket along with their other possessions from the cloakroom.

"A basket, Lucy?" Alice asked. "You didn't bring that with you." What would she want with a basket? Alice had several she could have lent her.

Lucy grinned, her eyes dancing with mischief. "I know. Lady Reynolds lent it to me." She handed the basket to Gerald. The carriage arrived and they climbed in.

"It's quite heavy," Gerald said, grinning. "What's the total?"

Lucy bounced on her seat. "Sixteen!"

"What are you two talking about?" James asked.

"While you two were dancing and chatting and getting betrothed—congratulations again, by the way, it's wonderful news and I'm so excited for you"—Lucy leaned across and kissed Alice on the cheek—"we were busy."

"Busy doing what?"

In answer, Gerald passed the basket to James. "Look inside."

James lifted the cover and made a surprised exclamation. He pulled out a little red-leather-bound book. "There are sixteen copies in here? How on earth did you manage that?"

"It was Lucy's idea," Gerald said.

"I just—well, we, because Gerald was very good—spoke to all the young people we knew. Most of them had heard about the letters, and some had sneaked a look at them and thought they were horridly mean, so we asked them if they could get hold of their mothers'—"

"—or aunts' or grandmothers'—" Gerald interjected.

"—copies of the book." Lucy grinned triumphantly. "And sixteen people—"

"—that we know of—"

"—had brought the book with them to the ball."

"Seventeen," Alice said, pulling Mrs. Scorrier's copy out of her reticule and tossing it into the basket.

"Seventeen copies," James said. "With the one we already had from Gerald's mother, that means we only need to track down the last seven copies, and that'll be the end of that vile little book."

The carriage arrived at Alice's house, and James handed both the ladies down. He glanced at Lucy, then said to Alice in a low voice, "I'll call on you tomorrow morning, and we can talk then."

Thus ensuring she would get no sleep at all. As he turned to climb back into the carriage, Alice's hand shot out to grab him. "I would rather we talked now."

He eyed her a moment, glanced at Lucy again, then said to Gerald, "I'll walk home. See you tomorrow."

The carriage drove off. Lucy eyed them with speculative excitement. "I'm sure you two won't want to be disturbed. You have so much to talk about." And with a mischievous wink, she skipped up the stairs to bed.

Alice had told the servants not to wait up. They entered the sitting room, and James lit the fire, which had been laid. He rose, dusting off his hands, and Alice came straight to the point. "Why did you announce our betrothal tonight?"

"Because I was angry at all the whispers. Because I wanted to slay dragons for you, but the only dragons I could see were wearing ball gowns. So I made the announcement to change the focus of the evening, and it did. You didn't mind, did you—my assumption of your assent?"

"I was just surprised, that's all. I thought you'd changed your mind about wanting to marry me."

"Changed my mind? Why ever would I do that?"

"Because, well, you hadn't asked me again, and once I became your mistress . . ."

"You thought I wouldn't want you?" He stared at her and rumpled his hair, perplexed. "I thought our time at the cottage would have convinced you how passionately I do want you. I must be losing my touch."

"No, of course you haven't. But mistresses don't get proposals of marriage, do they? Not that I know what your touch was before—" She broke off, embarrassed.

A slow smile grew on his face. "Before we anticipated our wedding vows with a spot of 'um'? Several spots, in fact. And now that I come to think of it, *spot* is not at all accurate. A lavishness of 'um,' a feast of 'um,' a—"

"I mean, even though I'd proved to you that I could enjoy the marriage bed—"

He held up a hand. "Hold it right there, my sweet. It wasn't *I* who needed anything to be proved—I was already wholly and completely committed. You were the one with the doubts. Now, stop all this shilly-shallying. Will you marry me or not?"

Her heart filled and she threw herself into his arms. "Oh, James, of course I'll marry you. You won't regret it. I promise I'll make you a good wife."

She thought he'd kiss her then, but he held her back with a quizzical expression. "A good wife? Like you pick out a good apple at the market, or a good pair of shoes?"

"Of course I'll do my best to be a good mother to your daughters as well," she added hastily. "I know I could never compare with Selina, but—"

"But nothing." He cut her off gently. "Selina was the love of my youth. Yes, I loved her, and I will always love her memory. But you, my dearest Alice, are the love of my maturity, my beloved companion in this life."

He drew her toward him. His voice deepened. "My darling Alice, I didn't ask you to marry me because I thought you'd make a good wife and be a good mother to my daughters—though it goes without saying that you will. I want to marry you for only one reason—I'm madly, deeply, irrevocably in love with you. More than I ever knew was possible."

Her hand flew to her mouth and she took a shaky inward breath. "Truly, James?"

He cupped her face in his hand. "Truly, Alice. I want to live the rest of my life with you in my life, in my bed and in my heart." Her eyes sheened with tears, and he added, "Is it so hard for you to believe?"

It was, a little. In thirty-eight years, no one had ever told Alice they loved her. And now, here was this big, beautiful man, the embodiment of all her dreams, telling her he loved her. And oh, how she'd ached to hear it.

"Oh, James, I love you, too, so very, very much."

They kissed then, and for a while, time disappeared. A coal fell out of the fireplace, startling them, and they separated. James scooped it back into the fireplace, and set a screen across it. Then, to Alice's surprise, he locked the door.

"James?" He surely didn't mean to . . .

He winked. "We don't want the servants coming to investigate any strange sounds, do we?"

Strange sounds? Oh my. "No. Or Lucy."

"I have a feeling that nothing much will ever shock that young minx," he said as he swept her into his arms, laid her on the settee and followed her down.

"Well, in that case . . ." Alice pulled James's head down to hers and proceeded to show him how much she loved him.

The fire was burning low. James and Alice lay on the settee, twined together in the dreamy aftermath of making love. She stirred sleepily and woke. James smoothed the hair back from her face. Lord, she had the softest skin.

He didn't want to leave her, didn't want to have to get dressed and go home.

She was a miracle. His very precious miracle.

He gazed into the glowing coals. "I came back to England in something of a gray fog. I thought that the special love a man has for a woman was all in my past. I felt lucky enough just to have my daughters to love and care for. I never expected anything more.

"And then I went to a party, and I was bored and about to leave when I saw this gorgeous woman arriving. You smiled—not even at me. In fact, you were quite cruelly cold toward me." She started to explain, but he pressed his finger over her lips and went on, "But it was such a sweet smile, and my closed-off, battered heart opened up and whispered, *This one.*"

She sighed.

"And in the following days and weeks in which I came to know you, my heart kept insisting, *This one.*

"And all the wild, tumultuous feelings I thought were dead and in the past boiled up again, stronger than ever." He stroked her cheek with the back of his hand, and she leaned into it. "It's not the same as my first love, but it's just as strong, and it's only going to get stronger. So, my dearest love, you are already in my heart. I just need you in my life." He leaned back so he could see her face properly. "Really, the only question left is, when are you going to make an honest man of me?"

Chapter Eighteen

Alice and James decided to marry at Towers, James's house in Warwickshire. They traveled down in a cavalcade of carriages. The three little girls—and cat—theoretically traveled with Nanny McCubbin, but hopped from one carriage to another every time they stopped to change horses. Gerald and Lucy followed in a separate carriage—without a chaperone—and Mary and James's valet and a pile of luggage traveled last.

Towers was delightful. Nestled in a green wooded valley, it was a sprawling, asymmetrical pile, begun in the fifteenth century and added to by various ancestors every few centuries.

"It's a bit of a monstrosity," James said diffidently when the carriage turned a corner and the house first came into sight. But he clearly loved it.

"It's wonderful," Alice said, and she meant it. The oldest part of the building was in the half-timbered black-and-white Tudor style, other parts were stone, and one wing was brick. And there were battlements and several towers, including one round brick turret with a pointy roof.

The girls, too, were enchanted. "It's a fairy place," Judy exclaimed. "Can we sleep in the turret, Papa, can we?"

The church on the estate was small and beautiful, built of bluestone with a steep slate roof and a slightly crooked spire. Arched stained glass windows glinted in the late afternoon sun. The moment Alice saw the little church, she knew that this was where she wanted to be married, rather than the impressive, much larger church in Kenilworth that they'd seen earlier.

James paced back and forth at the front of the altar. It was ridiculous to be so nervous, he knew. But waiting for his bride in a church was almost as nerve-racking as waiting to go into battle. He just wanted it over and done with, and to be left alone with his family.

"Don't worry, she'll be here," Gerald said heartily.

James gave him a baleful look. "Wait 'til it's your turn." He knew she'd be here. He didn't know why he was nervous; he just was.

The church smelled of beeswax and flowers—the village ladies had descended and given it a good scrub and polish. Guests had been arriving over the last few days. The pews were filling up, county gentlefolk and villagers. He'd been stunned by the welcome he'd received from the local people. Apparently they remembered him with fondness, and had warmly welcomed Alice and the three little girls.

There was no organ, but the vicar had brought in a small choir to sing the bride down the aisle. They started to hum, then broke into a soft hymn. James turned and a small figure dressed in blue began marching importantly down the aisle, a small figure wearing a very strange black-and-white fur collar.

The collar yowled, stretched and leapt to the floor. Luckily it wore a smart blue velvet harness, which restrained it. The congregation chuckled, and some of James's tension dissolved.

Next came Lina, elfin and dainty, looking more like her mother every day. Then Judy, serious and responsible, his firstborn. After that came Lucy, part of his family now, and he wouldn't have it any other way. And finally there she was, the love of his life, serene and lovely in shades of sea green and blue to match her glorious eyes, shining now as they met his. She was radiant, smiling; he had the biggest lump in his throat.

He held out his hand to her and she took it.

"Dearly beloved, we are gathered here today . . ."

Epilogue

The biggest, splashiest wedding of the season was over—and nobody had been strangled. The large and lavish wedding breakfast was coming to an end, and Lucy was upstairs with Alice and Mary, changing from her wedding dress into a traveling outfit. She and Gerald were going to Paris for their honeymoon.

"Are you sure you like the murals?" Lucy asked Alice, while Mary removed dozens of tiny pink rosebuds from her hair. "If you don't like them, you can always paper over them."

"Never!" Alice said, shocked. "The girls adore them. I don't know how you came up with such charming designs, each one so different but so perfect for each child. Lina is in love with her fairy dell, Judy adores her horses, and Debo—well, we could hardly get Debo to leave her room once she saw it. She's named every single cat—all thirty-five of them!"

Lucy laughed. "I'm so glad."

The door opened, and Gerald poked his head around it. "Ready?"

Lucy looked a query at Mary. Mary stepped back, beaming. "All done, miss—I mean, Lady Thornton. You look beautiful."

"Thank you, Mary." Lucy wrinkled her nose. "So strange to be Lady Thornton. It doesn't feel like me at all."

"You'll get used to it," Alice assured her. Gerald entered, followed by James, who had been his best man. Alice had given away the bride, an action that raised more than a few eyebrows.

"The baggage is all packed," Gerald said. "We're driving to Dover and will spend the night there, then catch the packet to France in the morning." He glanced at Lucy. "Or the next day."

Alice looked at Lucy. Something in Gerald's expression suggested that she and James hadn't been the only ones who had anticipated their wedding vows. The house at Bellaire Gardens had been empty, after all . . .

But there was a faint crease between Lucy's brow, and she was looking at Alice in a very particular way. At a very particular part of Alice's anatomy. "Alice . . ." she began on a query and stopped.

Alice raised a brow at James, who nodded.

"Yes, Lucy, what you're wondering about—it's true," Alice said softly.

"Really?" Lucy gasped. "Oh, Alice, that's wonderful." She embraced Alice.

Alice placed a hand on her swelling midriff and leaned back against James. "I know. It's our little miracle. After all those years of being barren."

"You must have been mistaken."

Alice smiled mistily. "I don't understand it. Thaddeus had a son, after all. But who cares about the whys or wherefores. All I know is that I'm expecting a child, and I'm over the moon." She glanced up at James and said softly, "We're over the moon."

"Congratulations," Gerald said. "But this son of Uncle Thaddeus's—when was this?"

"He was born shortly after Thaddeus and I were married. His mistress, Mrs. Jennings, went to the country, where she gave birth to a son in secret. The baby was raised by one of his tenants in the country. Thaddeus made no secret of it to me—far from it, he was furious."

Gerald frowned. "So this son would now be nineteen or twenty then?"

Alice nodded. "I suppose so. Thaddeus never let me forget it. If old Lord Charlton had allowed him to marry Mrs. Jennings instead of forcing him to marry me, that son would have been his legitimate heir."

Gerald snorted. "I doubt it."

"What do you mean?"

"I've seen Mrs. Jennings's son, and he is definitely not related to Uncle Thaddeus."

"What are you saying? How could you have seen him?"

"It was when we were sorting out Uncle Thaddeus's will." He gave Alice an embarrassed look. "He'd made a number of bequests to her, you see. Papa got me to deal with it—dealing with a mistress being beneath his dignity. So I went to her home, and her butler answered the door. I also met a young man there, nineteen or twenty, who called her *Mother*." He paused for dramatic effect. "That young man was the spitting image of her butler."

There was a short, shocked silence.

"That would explain why she never brought the boy to the city," Alice said after a moment. "Thaddeus claimed it was too painful to meet the son who should have been his heir."

"I wonder if he knew," Gerald mused.

Alice thought about it, then shook her head. "No, he would never forgive infidelity, let alone being cuckolded by a butler. And if he'd known, he would never have left Mrs. Jennings a penny in his will."

She thought about all the years of guilt and shame she'd endured for her apparent failure as a wife. And then dismissed them forever. She was no longer that woman. James's arm slipped around her waist, and she smiled and leaned into him.

She had a new life now—a husband who told her daily he adored her, and demonstrated it in the most blissful ways. Three little girls who filled her days with joy and laughter—and cats—and a goddaughter who'd begun as an unwelcome imposition and became a beloved daughter and a friend. And soon—Alice laid a hand on her burgeoning belly—a baby.

Life was wonderful.

"Well, are you ready to go now?" Gerald asked Lucy. "The carriage is waiting, and everyone's gathered downstairs to see us off."

Lucy glanced around the room, checking that she'd left nothing behind, then kissed Alice and James goodbye, as well as Mary the maid. Then she turned to her brand-new husband. "I'm ready."

Gerald bowed and gestured gracefully toward the door. "After you, Lady Thornbottle."

ABOUT THE AUTHOR

Anne Gracie is the award-winning author of the Chance Sisters Romances, which include *The Summer Bride*, *The Spring Bride*, *The Winter Bride* and *The Autumn Bride*, and the Marriage of Convenience Romance series, including *Marry in Scandal*, *Marry in Haste*, *Marry in Secret* and *Marry in Scarlet.* She spent her childhood and youth on the move. The roving life taught her that humor and love are universal languages and that favorite books can take you home, wherever you are. Anne started her first novel while backpacking solo around the world, writing by hand in notebooks. Since then, her books have been translated into more than eighteen languages and include Japanese manga editions (which she thinks is very cool) and audio editions. In addition to writing, Anne promotes adult literacy, flings balls for her dog, enjoys her tangled garden and keeps bees. Visit her online at annegracie.com. You can also subscribe to her newsletter.